SHOULD SHE LOATHE THIS MAN—
OR **LOVE** HIM?

There were times when Lord Cormac showed a side of himself to Kate that the world never suspected—a gentleness, a goodness, a generosity, a vulnerability that won Kate's heart despite all she had undergone at his hands.

Then there were the other times. When Cormac possessed her at his whim and dismissed her without ado. When he reveled the night through with his infamous circle of friends and openly paraded his latest mistress before Kate's eyes.

Which of these two so different men was the true Cormac? What unholy agony festered deep within him? What strange secret lay behind the curtain of silence he let descend whenever Kate queried him too closely?

Until Kate learned the answer, she would be the helpless prisoner of this man's uncontrollable passions—and of her own. . . .

THE CORMAC LEGEND

Big Bestsellers from SIGNET

- [ ] **EVIE'S ROMAN FORTUNE** by Joanna Bristol.
  (#W8616—$1.50)*
- [ ] **FORGOTTEN LOVE** by Lynna Cooper.   (#E8569—$1.75)*
- [ ] **BAYOU BRIDE** by Maxine Patrick.   (#E8527—$1.75)*
- [ ] **VALENTINA** by Evelyn Anthony.   (#E8598—$2.25)†
- [ ] **LORD OF RAVENSLEY** by Constance Heaven.
  (#E8460—$2.25)†
- [ ] **LOVE ME TOMORROW** by Robert Rimmer.
  (#E8385—$2.50)*
- [ ] **GLYNDA** by Susannah Leigh.   (#E8548—$2.50)*
- [ ] **WINTER FIRE** by Susannah Leigh.   (#E8011—$2.50)
- [ ] **WATCH FOR THE MORNING** by Elisabeth Macdonald.
  (#E8550—$2.25)*
- [ ] **DECEMBER PASSION** by Mark Logan.   (#J8551—$1.95)*
- [ ] **THE MARRIAGE MERGER** by Glenna Finley.
  (#E8391—$1.75)*
- [ ] **ELIZABETH IN LOVE** by Vivian Donald. (#E8671—$1.75)*
- [ ] **HARVEST OF DESIRE** by Rochelle Larkin.
  (#E8183—$2.25)
- [ ] **MISTRESS OF DESIRE** by Rochelle Larkin.
  (#E7964—$2.25)
- [ ] **TORCHES OF DESIRE** by Rochelle Larkin.
  (#E8511—$2.25)*

    * Price slightly higher in Canada
    † Not available in Canada

The
CORMAC
LEGEND

by
Dorothy Daniels

Ⓞ
A SIGNET BOOK
NEW AMERICAN LIBRARY
TIMES MIRROR

COPYRIGHT © 1979 BY DOROTHY DANIELS

 SIGNET TRADEMARK REG. U.S. PAT. OFF. AND FOREIGN COUNTRIES
REGISTERED TRADEMARK—MARCA REGISTRADA
HECHO EN CHICAGO, U.S.A.

SIGNET, SIGNET CLASSICS, MENTOR, PLUME AND MERIDIAN BOOKS
are published by The New American Library, Inc.,
1301 Avenue of the Americas, New York, New York 10019

FIRST PRINTING, MAY, 1979

1 2 3 4 5 6 7 8 9

PRINTED IN THE UNITED STATES OF AMERICA

ONE

——◆◈◆——

I took both withered hands in mine and I spoke as gently as possible. "He'll be gone this day, Mrs. Horan, and may God have mercy on his soul. The Sullivan boy next door died this morning. Old Mike Hanharan won't last the day. They're dying like a plague has come to Kilgort, and all I can do is say I'm sorry for those who live."

"It's like that over all of Ireland," the old woman said. "My prayin' for Padraic took away the pain, and he sleeps now right into the arms of God. He is old and has no complaint, nor have I, but when they die so young, that's when it hurts."

"Aye, no question," I said. "It's a terrible year, terrible times we face."

"How many went this week, Kate?" she asked.

"It's getting to where I lose track, there are so many. I'd say eleven this week, and it's only Thursday."

"They do say some corn came from America."

"That may be so, but we here in County Connaught are clear across the country from Dublin where it arrives. So there's little left before it's halfway here."

"They do say our own corn crop has not been so bad, yet we get none of it. How can that be?"

"Because if our own Irish corn is eaten by Irishmen, that disturbs the trade, and the British will have none of that for sure."

"It's ways I don't understand, Kate. But then I'm old, and maybe my brains are addled."

"There's no need to be saying that," I told her firmly. "I have to go on now. My father's none too good, and it keeps me busy taking care of those he can't do for any longer."

"He is no better then, poor man?"

"Worse, I would say. I'll be back later to see if there's a

thing I can do. Keep the poor man warm and send up all your prayers for him. He's in no pain."

I left as quickly as I could and still maintain a dignified manner, for I wanted to flee from the cottage. From all the cottages. On the hard-packed dirt street running through the village, I paused to breathe some air not tainted with the smell of death. In seven months now, almost a hundred had died. The old and sick ones first, then those of middle years with their backs bent from work—they had not shown much more resistance than the old ones. It was striking the very young and the strong ones now. If it kept on, this would be an uninhabited village in a year, and there was no sign the terrible tragedy would stop then.

All, I thought, for the want of a few potatoes. In 1846, the crop had failed because of rot. In 1847, the next crop failed as well. Now, in 1848, the third crop had also gone to rot because of this disease that killed the potatoes before they were ready to harvest, leaving nothing in the ground but a soggy black mass that could be eaten only by those who would risk a sickness worse than the starvation of those who could not stomach it. From what I'd heard, already a million people all over Ireland had died for lack of food because they had lived on a diet of potatoes for so many years. For Ireland was a poverty-stricken country at best, and when the potato crop failed, the dying began.

Our own wheat and corn crops were exported. Those who farmed these crops had to sell every morsel of them to get enough money to pay the landlord. Those who did not were given an hour or two so they could clear the farmhouse of the few things they owned. Then the authorities moved in to raze the cottage to the ground so the cleared area could be added to the pastureland for the cattle, which made more money for the landlords than humans could have provided.

There was no rebellion because there wasn't an Irishman left with the strength to stand up to a landlord, much less the British who made the laws that governed Ireland.

I noticed the bailiff and his men were getting ready to knock down the cottage of old man Moryson. They had set up the three-legged frame from which the heavy battering ram would be drawn back and sent crashing against the whitewashed wall of the cottage. Policemen stood by, for sometimes there was a little trouble, but any resistance was weak and ineffectual at best.

I was tempted to give the bailiff a piece of my mind, but

instead, like all the villagers—like all Irishmen, for the love of God—I shrugged my shoulders and moved on because there wasn't a thing that could be done. Not by the likes of me. Besides, I had more than the destruction of the cottage to worry about. My father was terribly sick, and no wonder, for he'd spent nearly two years now ministering to the ill. At first, as the village pharmacist, he had enough medicine to help the sick, but after two years there was scant medicine left and Father no longer had the strength to go about administering what there was. I'd told him a hundred times he was killing himself for the sake of others, but he was not a man to let his friends die without at least trying his best to save them.

Now I feared for him. He'd been sleeping when I left, and his sleeping had increased day by day, which was not a good sign. I was no doctor, and neither was he, but we were all the village had ever been able to afford, and if I say so myself, we'd done a reasonably good job of caring for the ailing.

I'd long since toughened myself to face the endless series of deaths that swept over the village. Old and good friends died, and I could do nothing, not even attend the funerals. In some larger villages, even in the cities, there were no coffins, but still there had to be some form of funeral for those who died. So one coffin did for many. It was simply furnished with a bottom that could be made to swing out after everyone had left the open grave. So the coffin would then be extracted from the grave, empty, and be used for another poor soul a few hours later.

These were sorry times, deadly times, and often I wondered when my turn would come. I was eighteen, not frail by any means, but not a strong country girl either. My mother, bless her soul, died before the famine began. I remembered her as being no more than five-feet-two or -three, and Father used to say she weighed no more than a wolfhound pup. She'd been fair too, as I was fair, and with eyes as blue as the sky above me and a fine head of light brown hair.

Father was a powerfully built man, strong as country life demanded. Educated too, for he'd studied in Dublin, and from the big school there he'd received a diploma which entitled him to dispense drugs and to administer to the sick so long as there was no doctor available. There hadn't been a real doctor in Kilgort in twenty years.

The village itself was now changed, for I remembered it as being a lively place for its size, with children noisily offending the ears of their elders and running away when they were chased from one part of town to another. There'd been people on the street from early morn until night, always with something to talk about. The blacksmith plied his trade from a crude shelter covering his furnace and his anvil. The cobbler used to sit astride his stool to fashion and repair shoes and move the location at whim. There wasn't a cottage where the women didn't spin their wool and hand-weave the thread into heavy tweed.

Now there was nothing. The smithy and the cobbler were both dead, the streets were empty, and where the tread of countless feet had kept the dirt down, now it arose in the form of fine dust whenever a boot heel hit the ground. To me, it was a picture of desolation and misery, rivaled only by the fast-expanding cemetery located just off a peat field. A location where no decent being should be buried. But buried they were because all the village dead were buried there and nobody thought of creating a new burying ground where the earth was harder and less moist, and where the peat diggers didn't come closer and closer to the edge of the graveyard itself.

It was a black time for me, Kate Moran, because I loved this village. Sometimes I hated it too, and I wanted to get away. For I'd had a fine taste of what it was like in the big cities like Dublin, Galway, and Belfast. Father had seen to it I got an education, and for that I was grateful. Resentful too, of the day when I had to come home a year ago, because Father could no longer cope with the situation in the village.

I'd been in Galway then, and people were starving as fast in the city as in the country. I'd seen ships so full of emigrants for passage to Canada and America that I thought the ship would founder before it weighed anchor. I'd seen small ships go out, never to be heard of again. Some said as many died during the voyages as died from the sickness, because those who left were so weak from lack of food that they couldn't withstand the long journey in filthy, crammed vessels sailing an everlastingly stormy sea.

I was passing the destruction of the Moryson cottage when one of the helmeted policemen rattled the sword hanging at his side and told me to move on.

"You mean to say," I said, "that I'm not to walk upon the streets of my own village while you and those blathering artists of destruction go about murdering a cottage that's stood there for sixty and more years?"

"I'll have no lip from you," he told me. "You're a pretty colleen, to be sure, with your auburn curls and green eyes, but you've got a sassy tongue in your head and I'm ordering you to keep walking before you get into trouble."

"I'll be walking," I said, "if only to get away from the sight of you."

He growled a curse and turned away. I went on by until I came to Conan Hayer, leaning lazily against the door of his mother's cottage. A strapping young man with reddish hair, a wide face on a thick neck. *His* cottage now, I remembered, for his mother had died four months ago. I'd known Conan all my life, and we were good friends. He was a slow-thinking man but he was kind and loyal. I liked Conan without loving him in any way, though I suspected he kept hoping I'd look his way favorably now and then.

Which I did, as now. I stopped to talk to him. "And why's a fine lad like you standing here while the law breaks down that cottage because the poor widow couldn't pay the rent? As if any of us can when the man of the family dies."

"What'll you have me do, Kate?" he asked. "Tell them to go away and punch the ones who don't? So I get run through with their swords? You know there's not one bloody thing I can do. How's your father?"

"I don't think he's going to live, Conan. That's a fine thing for a daughter to say as casually as that, but I've seen so many die, I've cried so many times, there's nothing left inside me to sorrow with. And I hate that."

"It comes to all of us, I guess, in times like these. Have you considered emigrating?"

"Not me. Not doing a thing to bring food here is bad enough, but leaving is worse. Besides, things have to get better."

"If there's anything left by that time. I saw that policeman stopping you. If he got fresh, I'll have a word with him. They can't draw and quarter me for that."

"He wasn't fresh, except in the way he cursed me, and that was under his breath, and also my fault, for I teased him some by defying his order to move on. Don't get yourself into any fights for a small reason like that. It's one of your faults, Conan, in fighting everybody who stands up to you."

"I know, but it's my nature. Besides, I'm big enough and strong enough to handle all them policemen and the bailiff as well. Ah, there goes another big hole in the cottage. They'll have it down in half an hour."

"Are they trying to demolish the whole village, do you think, Conan?"

"Wouldn't surprise me if that's what's on their minds. We stand right in the middle of pastureland that'll graze a big herd of their cattle."

"They'll have their way too, if this famine doesn't stop soon so we can go to work and get the money for the rent. One thing about it, Conan, most of us are in the same boat. Still, it's no way to exist."

"And no way to break the backs of those who own everything. What'll you be doing if your father dies?"

"I don't know. I don't want to think about it. Maybe he won't die. We've been mighty hungry at times, but there was something left in our pantry when this started, and Father was wise enough to go easy on it. I'm surprised he's so sick."

"Kate, he's been giving you some of his share. He said so himself."

"What are you talking about, Conan? Father's not been giving me his share."

"Not entirely, to be sure, but some of it. He told me so when he began to feel himself getting sick. He asked me to take care of you if anything happened to him."

"Conan, you're not making this up to get on the good side of me?"

"I swear it's only the truth, Kate. I know I'm not in a class with you, your being educated and all, and much smarter'n me. But I'm still strong and can see no harm comes to you. That I'm willing to do, and you can't object to it, for I'll ask nothing of you in return."

"You should have told me," I said, half in anger. "What kind of man are you to keep a secret like that?"

"Not a smart one, to be sure," Conan admitted. "I can see that now."

"I'll talk of this later." I moved away from him. "Father must be worse than I thought him to be."

I ran the length of the street to the apothecary at the end of the village street where Father and I lived in a slightly bigger house than the thatch-roofed, whitewashed cottages of everyone else. What's more, it was on land we owned. Father had managed to arrange that because of his position as pharmacist, that being an important profession.

It had two floors and was the only house in the village that did. Like the others, it was whitewashed, but it was built of brick and sturdy enough to last two hundred years. It had a

yard with a fence around it too, which was a symbol of afflu-
ence, though we weren't very rich, I must say.

Within, the apothecary took up much of the first floor. Behind it was a parlor where we were accustomed to sit before
the fireplace until fairly late in case someone was sick. We
handled not only the village, but the entire countryside,
which gave us plenty to do.

Upstairs were two large rooms, one for me and one for Father. His was not being used these days, for he'd been too
weak to climb the short flight of stairs. However, I'd managed to get his bed down to the parlor, which was now a
sickroom.

Father had been propped up when I left, but he'd slid
down, and the position of his head wasn't helping his shallow
breathing any. I quickly made him more comfortable, but he
didn't know it. From sleep he'd slipped into unconsciousness,
and I knew what that meant. It was the way so many of
them went.

All I could do was cry. I bent my head and wept while his
breathing grew weaker. I thought that one big bowl of stew,
thick and hearty, would have saved him. But for a hundred
miles around, there wasn't a scrap of meat. The cattle had
gone the first year of the famine. During the second, the
horses had gone too. Without them, no fields could be
worked, but there was nothing to plant anyway, and if there
was, it was taken away. During this third year, even the
sound of barking dogs had ceased, and I knew what that
meant. I wondered how much longer this could go on, and
while I wondered, just before dawn, my father's breathing
stopped.

I didn't realize it at first, but a look at his face told me the
story. I put the stethoscope to his scrawny chest and my ear
to the other end of the instrument, but there was no sound,
no heartbeat. I closed his dear eyes and pulled up the sheet. I
left him there for the time being, as if to give the poor man
some rest after what he'd been through. He'd not spoken in
two days, he'd been so weak, and I didn't know he was giving
me more than my share of what meager food we could find.

It was strange how I could weep for him inwardly, but out-
wardly I acted as he would have wanted me to, as I'd seen
him act. Death was too familiar to us to spend our time
openly grieving, even for such as he, who was closer to me
than anyone alive.

I gave no thought to the fact that I was now alone in the

world, that I would have to fend for myself and decide whether to leave Kilgort or not.

For the present, there were things to be done which could not be delayed. I needed Conan's help, so I went in search of him, to find him asleep in his cottage. Not surprising, because there was nothing for him to do anyway.

I told him Father was gone and I needed him to help me. Conan washed quickly, dressed, and walked back to my cottage with me. He'd not taken the time to shave but it didn't matter.

We passed the site of the cottage that had been battered down the day before. It was a dreadful sight. In my cottage, Conan did what needed to be done. He washed Father's body and dressed it in his best suit and boots. He then left me to prepare a coffin from wood he had left over from the making of the coffin for his mother.

It was a simple box, quickly made in the hands of one as expert with tools as Conan. There was no one else who might help us, for what men were left had long since gone into the fields, scrounging for any particle of food, however small and unappetizing.

So it became my duty to sit alone with Father while Conan prepared the coffin. When he returned with this, I had a suggestion.

"Father always said to be buried in the village graveyard is not what he wished. He prefers a dry place, under trees where tall grass can grow above him. There is such a place he once admired. It is half a mile north of the town on that small knoll that overlooks the village. That is where he would like to rest, and I ask you now to try to manage a place there."

"Kate, that is private ground. Whoever owns it will not tolerate a grave."

"Whoever owns it does not have to know there is a grave. We will cover it well, but mark the spot with a few stones so we'll know where it is. Please, Conan, for this is what he wished, and it's bad enough there isn't even a priest to speak over him, let alone to be buried in a place he hated."

"Aye, then we must not deny him that. I'll see what's to be done at once. I have already arranged for the Monahans' farm wagon. It may not be much, but . . ."

"He would be proud to go on any farm wagon," I said. "Even such as the one the Monahans own."

"And there is a point to it, for he has the only horse left.

Scrawny as Monahan himself, or the poor beast would have gone into a stew pot long since. I'll be back."

It came about then that one of Kilgort's frequent funerals took place as almost all of them did. On a creaky, ancient wagon drawn by a horse barely able to manage it, preceded by only the most immediate of kin, in this case me, arm in arm with Conan, who carried a shovel over his shoulder and led the horse.

He had found the knoll and had dug the grave, deeply too, so there'd be no dampness to quickly destroy the coffin. I had taken my last look at my father, grieved for him, prayed, and reproved myself for not at least trying to find a priest, even though the attempt would have failed, because there was none. Most priests sent into these poor parts were ancient when they arrived, and they had been among the first to die.

I stood aside while Conan, with his mighty muscles, pulled the coffin off the wagon and dragged it to the grave. I helped him then so Father might decently be lowered in his grave. We got the coffin down, recited a brief prayer, and Conan set about filling it in. The worst part of the whole business was the sound of the earth hitting the box. I turned away. I also closed my eyes, and my ears, and my consciousness, I suppose, because I'd not heard the horseman ride up.

It was his voice that brought me back to earth. He was astride a huge black stallion, and he looked almost as big as the horse. A tall, heavy man, tapping his polished boot impatiently with a quirt. He looked as if he feared no one, including the devil himself.

He had a wide rugged face and was clean-shaven, though his sideburns came well down toward his neck. His eyes were blue and somewhat deep-set. At this moment his eyes were the eyes of a lusting man. Nonetheless, I stepped closer and looked up at him.

"This is my father we're burying, your lordship. He was a good man. A well-read and learned pharmacist."

"What do I care about that?" he said. "Your father is nothing to me, but you are a very attractive colleen. And you speak well, not like the girls who grow up with the cows and the sheep and the pigs until they are fifteen and then marry and beget more girls to grow up in the same way. Get that coffin out of my ground and take it to the village cemetery where it belongs."

"The village cemetery is filled to overflowing, sir," I said. "Besides, my father often told me he admired this small piece of ground and would like to be buried here. It is a last wish, sir. And if you give me permission, I swear I will arrange it so you will not even know he is buried here."

"You are well-spoken." He repeated the compliment. "Now, do as I say. Remove the coffin."

My anger had been growing, held in check only by the fact that I needed this man's permission that Father might rest in the place he had chosen. Now that this man gave an express order which would deny Father that privilege, my anger exploded.

"You're a fine man on a fine horse, and you look as well fed as the royal family, while we starve to death. And you have the black tongue that would order a dead man to be removed from a spot he has honored by choosing it for his last resting place. Aye, it's a black tongue you have, your lordship, and may it get blacker as the days go by until it withers and dies in your head."

The man threw back his head and roared in glee. "You've a sassy nature as well, and I admire that, but as for the rest of it, you cannot browbeat me into allowing your father to be buried here." He leaned down from the saddle and his face grew dark with rage. "Do as I say, or so help me, I'll do it for you. Get the bloody coffin out of that hole and fill it in now!"

Conan had so far kept a civil tongue, but now he rubbed his nose and threw down the shovel he was holding. "If the gentleman will step down off that thing he sits on, I'll push that black tongue down his throat for him. And that's a promise."

The man on the horse laughed again and promptly dismounted. He was taller and bigger than I'd believed—and than Conan had believed, because I saw the look of dismay on Conan's face. Still, Conan was a fighting man, and without hesitation he lunged at the stranger and hammered a bone-breaking punch that landed squarely on the stranger's breastbone. It was such a hard blow, it made a loud noise when it landed.

The stranger seemed no more affected by this than a light tap on the back of his hand. Conan's hand was so sore he rubbed it and then applied it to his lips in pain. But he tried again. This time he aimed for the man's jaw. I never saw a man move so fast. Conan's punch whistled through the air, while the stranger's fist connected with the side of Conan's head. Conan was flung sideways, to stumble and fall and lie there unconscious.

"Tell your man," the stranger said, "that he's not a bad fighter and he has a hard blow. I admire that in a man. Especially that he had the nerve to challenge me."

"It is a blessed shame he didn't take your head off," I said. "Were I as big and as strong, I'd have a go at it, and you can mark that well."

"I have no doubt but that you would. What's your name?"

"It is no business of yours. I'll have Conan—the man you licked—"

"Fairly. Mind you that."

"Aye, fairly then. I'll have him remove my father from your holy ground. If he knew what was going on, he wouldn't let himself be buried here anyway."

Without a word, the stranger picked up the shovel Conan had dropped and set about filling in the grave. He worked so diligently that it was almost entirely filled in before Conan recovered his wits sufficiently to sit up and openly marvel at what was going on.

The stranger mounded the earth and then trod upon it to make it hard so no beast could dig it up. He then looked about to find a large rock that I would have sworn no one man could have wrested from the ground, let alone carried it and set it down at the head of the grave. He then dusted his hands on his riding breeches, reached a hand down for Conan's to help him up. This done, he bowed to me, mounted his horse, and rode off.

Conan said, "Glory be! Do you know who that is?"

"I know he's a strange man who would be hard to predict. He cursed me on one hand and fulfilled my request with the other. I expected he might use that quirt on me for my insolence, but he filled in the grave instead."

"That is Cormac of Fion. He lives alone at Lucane Castle over the hill toward which he rides."

"Why have I not heard of such a man, Conan?"

"He came here when you were away at school, and he remains but a short time before he goes off to the city or somewhere. Aye, to think I stood up and dared this man. Fought him, no less."

"And were knocked cold by one of his punches, no less," I reminded him.

"Kate, it's an honor to have been knocked out by Cormac of Fion. He is the fightingest man in Ireland. A warrior who

goes about looking for trouble so he may fight. He has never
been vanquished, and most bow to his bidding and his will.
There are mighty few who would challenge him. Yet I did, in
my ignorance. Aye, I'm a happy man to have been knocked
out by the likes of him."

"Well, now that your honor was not sullied by being
knocked out, I would like it if you would kneel with me and
pray at the grave of my father."

"Oh, that I will do, and I'm a sad man that he could not
have seen me strike Cormac of Fion and be struck by him."

Conan knelt with me, and we offered up our prayers for
the soul of a fine man who had been buried here under circumstances more strange than he could have imagined. But
he was buried; this was the place he had loved, and I was satisfied with that. But not with everything.

"There is no reason why you should feel so proud of yourself, Conan Hayer, for the man you fought may be a great
fighter, but he is a man with little or no compassion."

"He agreed your father should remain in this grave. He
filled it in, did he not?"

"Oh, he did that. No question about it. But did you have a
good look at him? He has been eating well, wouldn't you say?
Living well, having what he likes to drink, and having placed
on his table all the food he wishes. And what he does not eat,
he throws away. Do you call that a compassionate man? For
he knows well we are starving to death slowly. Knows, as
well, what killed my father. To me he is a selfish, overfed villain I would not care to let my eyes rest upon again as long
as I live. He is the nobility, Conan, my ignorant man. And
nobility eats while we starve, and to the devil with him."

TWO

For a month after Father died, I visited his grave daily to kneel and pray for him. My life seemed empty and of little value anymore. By now there wasn't a pill or drop of medicine left. I wrote to the authorities in Belfast and Dublin, begging for something to help the sick. I never received an answer. Since Father died, another dozen had gone, and there were so many sick and near death that I was sometimes unable to keep track of who was who and in whose cottage I happened to be, doing what little I could.

My visits to the grave were brief, for I dared not remain away too long. At first I kept looking for that monster of a man, Cormac of Fion, to ride up, in fear that he would have changed his mind and would order me to have Father's coffin moved.

I'd heard more about this man too. There were those in the village who knew he came from a family that went all the way back to the kings of Tara, and through all these centuries every male of this family had been a renowned fighting man. There were legendary stories of their great strength and skill in battle. I had no doubt of it, if this man was an example of the family.

I hated him for the abusive way he had first greeted me, but there had been a softness to him which I could not help but admire. He had, finally, not only given his permission for the burial, but actually filled in the grave himself. So I suspected there was a mildness to this man which he would no doubt stoutly deny—with physical force for emphasis. It didn't matter anyway, for I'd probably never see him again.

I did know that conditions in the village were desperate. No food was coming in, every rotten tuber had been dug out of the ground to be eaten, whether it seemed poisonous or not. Meanwhile, there was no money, and as rents came due, so did the bailiff, his battering ram, his policemen, who now

earned their pay, for, weak or not, some of the villagers had
to be restrained while their homes were broken into rubble.

Conan was at hand whenever possible. Because of his in-
born strength, he was still able to dig a grave and keep the
village in some semblance of order. More and more, people
stopped leaving their cottages except on vital errands. I did
what I could, with Conan at my side most of the time. The
cottage I'd shared with my father was now a silent, lonely
place. I hated going home. I knew very well that if I'd mentioned it, Conan would have married me in a minute. Like
me, all his people were gone, and no doubt he was as lonely
as I.

I didn't love Conan. That was it! He was a fine man, and I
liked him, but no matter how I tried to convince myself,
I knew I would never grow to love him, even if we were married. Yet, in my desperate state of mind, there were times
when I felt that being married to a man I didn't love was
preferable to sitting alone beside a cold fireplace, rocking
away hours I should have utilized for more good. Not for the
villagers, what was left of them. I'd done everything I could
possibly do, and now I only waited until there was some
special circumstance, such as consoling families while one
they loved slowly passed away.

It was a dismal time for me. I'd grown up here, happy and
carefree. Raised by the loving hands of a father I loved and
admired to his last day. The plans we'd made. I was to receive my education in private schools and then go on to col-
lege. Father wanted me to breach the unwritten law that no
woman could be a doctor. He'd investigated and discovered
there were no laws that said a woman could not enter medical school. In fact, he'd discovered that a few women had,
though not in Ireland. I had anticipated the fight to get me
in. And when I began to doubt I would succeed, I made up
my mind that, failing medical school, I would become a
nurse. Like Father, and inspired by him, my ambition in life
had been to help others.

Certainly I'd not failed in that, though I cared little for the
circumstances. The beginning of the famine had changed our
plans. Postponed them, Father had assured me, until the famine was over by next harvest. But that harvest had been even
worse than the last and the third season a devastating failure.
Everything had grown worse and worse until there wasn't
time for Father and me even to discuss my future. There
were times when I didn't think there'd be any and I'd soon be

carried to that graveyard now encroaching on the peat diggers' area. Not that there were diggers. They'd died off long ago. Each family dug its own fuel these days.

Conan often came to visit and sometimes to bring a morsel of meat he'd somehow managed to acquire from a farm where the last pig or sheep had been slaughtered. I suspected, as Father had sacrificed for me, that Conan was depriving himself of food that I could have more than my share. I cautioned him about this, but he stoutly declared that his belly was full and he was not the kind to give up his strength for the likes of me, when I knew he'd have given up his life.

I kept wondering why I didn't marry him and damn the fact that I would never love him. Under the conditions such as we now lived, what was love anyway but a circumstance that meant little? Not that I didn't have my own secret desires. I was still healthy and quite young, and the desire to be loved was strong within me. Still, if I made the offer to Conan and he accepted, I'd find neither pleasure nor satisfaction in bedding with him. Those were the shameful thoughts that came to my mind during the endless hours I sat alone, missing Father so terribly I was beyond the ability to weep for him anymore.

On the morning that Meg Donnel came to see me, I thought the lowest ebb of the village's existence had finally come. Meg was a year older than I, married to James Donnel for two weeks when he sickened and died. A strong and healthy man brought down in a matter of days by the lack of nourishing food. Meg had grieved for him, but briefly, for her anger was so great that she devoted every waking moment of her time to trying to save others.

"It's blessed I am," she said, "and cursed as well, for I am to have Jimmy's baby, him dead but a month. If you say you are happy for me, I will disown you and maybe shut you up with a blow. How can I bring a baby into this country? To die in a week or so after birth. If it is not born dead, poor thing, because I won't have enough to eat to give it life."

"Oh, Meg," I said, "what is this world coming to? This country of ours. There will be none left if something is not done, and not a soul to see that it is."

"I am not going to have the baby," Meg said. "I cannot, even if there is mortal sin in what I am going to do. And that's not the half of it. Three died last night. I heard that a ship arrived in Canada with a third of the passengers from Ireland already dead. Are we going to be an extinct race?"

"I have been thinking," I said, "that no plea we make to the authorities, especially in London, has any meaning whatsoever. Those men are interested only in turning a profit, and if we die to help create that profit, they regard it as only something that cannot be helped."

"They have been appealed to more often than we've offered up prayers. Neither one seems to do any good. Don't try that again, Kate, because they'll not listen now, nor will they ever listen."

"I was thinking of something else," I said. "Authorities are like walls of brick. They have no minds and make rules that cannot be broken. But individuals, Meg. Now, there's something we've not tried."

"Individuals? Who'd give up something to help such as us when the government refuses to do so?"

"There must be people who have sympathy as well as riches."

Meg gave a derisive laugh. "You name one. You'll be a miracle worker if you do."

"I have met Cormac of Fion, who lives in the great castle called Lucane."

"Cormac of Fion! Are you mad, Kate? He's the greatest welcher in Ireland. If you met him and escaped with your virginity intact, you would be one of the lucky ones. The man lives for two reasons—to deflower girls like you and to fight. I don't know which he does best, but I can well imagine he does both well."

"Meg, he came to me while Conan Hayer and I were burying my father on property belonging to the castle. He got down off his horse and fought with Conan because Conan struck the first blow. Cormac needed to strike but one, and Conan lay unconscious."

"And that," Meg declared, "is the full measure of the man."

"No, Meg. He picked up the shovel, filled in the grave, and bowed to me as he rode off. I consider that he is a man of compassion."

"You are nearly right, but the word is 'passion,' my dear Kate. He must have been tired from filling the grave, or he'd likely have taken you on the spot."

"But the point is, he did not."

"Now, Kate, I don't think there's an Irishman alive who'd take the virginity of a girl who stands beside the grave of her father, just dead. This Cormac of Fion may have been possessed of some decency that kept him from doing what he really wanted to do. But if you went to him and he did not have you, then his friends would, for they are all like him. I have talked to girls who served in the castle. They told me of the orgies that went on, the crazy drinking, the riding of horses over the marble floor of the big hall in the castle. Aye, and they told of how these men treated them."

"Ah, Meg, I find it hard to believe," I said.

"Do you? Tell me, then, how many girls work in the castle now? How many men, for that matter? There's not a decent soul who'd set foot in there. Except for an old man who came here from Belfast, there is no one to care for the castle, and likely it is a pigpen by now. And who cares? Certainly not Cormac."

"I am still willing to ask him if he has the influence to see that some scraps of food are brought to our village."

"You will do so at your own risk, Kate. I would have none of it."

"Would you starve, then, and deprive your child of life just because you're afraid of a man who has a reputation for evil? Meg, I am eighteen, almost nineteen. I want to live to see twenty. All we do is sit here and wait to die. Surely we all will if we do nothing to try to overcome our troubles. I am going to ask Cormac of Fion for his help. I think I may get it—at no price from me personally—because of the softness he betrayed at Father's grave."

"Go, then," Meg said, "but before you do, I would ask for a bit of tea. You keep it for those who are sick, but at the moment I do not feel very well."

I patted her hand and arose to make the tea. It was weak, because I'd learned to brew a fairly decent pot with only enough to fill the end of a spoon. Then, out of consideration for Meg's unborn child, I added twice as much to make it stronger and brought out the last tin of biscuits Father had managed to store away long ago and to use so sparingly that the supply lasted ten times longer than it ordinarily would have. It was the last tin, and there'd be no more.

I even decided to indulge myself, and when I brought out the plate on which the biscuits rested, Meg had trouble keeping back the tears, and even more difficulty in not wolfing down her share.

I was glad to have sacrificed for her. Meg was my dearest friend, one to be trusted. She was once a buxom, radiantly healthy girl with raven-black hair worn loose in the wind.

Her complexion had been one to envy for its fairness and color. She'd changed, as we all had, but she still retained all that Irish beauty which had attracted many men, especially the lad she'd married. Now she was having his child—if something could be done for her to lend the strength to endure motherhood. And sustenance now, which would ensure the health and the live birth of her child.

"I will see Cormac this day," I said. "It may be for naught, and perhaps I will place myself in some danger, but see him I will, for there is nothing else can be done, Meg. And something must be done without delay."

"Kate, why don't you marry Conan? The man is mad in love with you. Have him take you away—to the city, where there may be a little better chance of getting food than here."

"I do not love Conan. I like him. He is a dear friend, as you are, but I will not tell the man I love him so I can get married. Nor will I tell him I will marry him though I never will love him. These are dark times, Meg, and they may grow darker, but this I cannot do. Sometimes I wish I could."

"Then there's no more for me to say. I have to go now. Mrs. Garrity's son is dying, and she is so beside herself she cannot even hold his hand as he dies. I feel better, though, because of the tea and biscuits. I will not talk of it in the village. It would not be decent of me to boast."

"Nor good for me, because there would be a line at the door asking for more," I said. "And there is no more. We had almost the last of it, Meg."

"Well, then, I'll be on my way. Please, Kate. If you value your wits, do not go to see Cormac."

"Is he married, Meg?"

"He is not, nor has he any need to be, with all the women throwing themselves at him. For he is a handsome man, it is said."

"He is handsome, aye. As big and strong as any I have seen. More so than Conan, and he is no weakling."

"If you go, tell me at once when you return," Meg said. "And if you go, take a pistol with you. And maybe a club or two."

With Meg on her way, I decided not to hesitate a moment longer, fearful I might already have absorbed too much of Meg's fear, which would turn me into a coward. I felt that Cormac of Fion was a last resort, and if the encounter was dangerous, then I would leave quickly. Though I then would have lost the last chance to benefit the village.

I would wear the only good dress in my possession. Father had insisted I buy it the last time we were in Dublin. That was two years ago, and the styles might have changed, but not in this village. Cormac may have seen better dresses, yet this one did become me. I kept it in a trunk with sprigs of lavender, and the pleasant fragrance surrounded me when I took it out and tried to shake out the wrinkles. It was fruitless, so I went downstairs to put the iron on the lid of the stove, then returned to put up my hair. I wished to present a demure, ladylike appearance and knew better than to let it hang in loose curls about my shoulders, especially since I would be wearing a bonnet. My bonnet was white, and sat halfway back on my head to leave the front of my hair uncovered. The ribbons that tied beneath my chin were also white. Besides which, they were short, which meant I could only make a knot. I'd not liked that part of the bonnet at first, but now I realized it was best. A bow was meant for coquetry, and I wasn't going to the castle with that in mind.

I center-parted my hair, brushed it back over my ears, and drew it back to form a coil at the base of my neck.

The dress was a checkered muslin, printed in pink and gray in a pattern of roses. The bodice was high-necked and the sleeves were a wide version of the fashionable pagoda style.

I ironed it carefully and returned upstairs. I had only a bureau mirror in my bedroom, though it served well enough. Despite my thinness, the bodice fit beautifully. I was of medium height, with a full figure which, with the years, would become matronly—if I lived long enough for it to happen. Which wouldn't be, if I didn't get food.

I thought of a fringed silk parasol Father had given me, and actually reached for the knobs on the drawer to get it. As quickly, I stepped back. That would indeed be frivolous, and this was not a social visit. Nor was I in a frivolous mood, but it had been so long since I had dressed up, I forgot the desperate position I found myself in. I was going on a begging mission. At the mercy of the lord of the manor. I prayed my plea for help in the form of food for the villagers would reveal him to be a man of the same compassion he had revealed by allowing Father to be buried on his property.

The dress was not exactly suited for the long walk to the castle over dusty earth or forest paths, yet it would have to do. I put on the bonnet, tied it under my chin, and gave myself a final appraisal in the mirror. I was pleased with my appearance, perhaps too much so, for it suddenly dawned on me that the better I looked, the more Cormac would be enticed. It was a time for chances, and I had no more time to lose. It was already midafternoon, and I must be back in the village by dark, for travel from the castle would be difficult in my white slippers and heavy, wide-skirted dress.

I hoped no one would see me leave, but then, it was none of their business. What I was doing was for their benefit as much as mine, and no one should complain if I was about to demean myself—and the whole village, as the villagers would see it—to beg for food. I thought I shouldn't have eaten the biscuits or drunk all that lovely tea, for a beggar can make a better point of his poverty and plea by being half-starved.

It was a long walk, one I had not relished, and there was no enjoyment in it. I tiptoed over rocks in the shallow stream that crossed the path. I bundled the excess material of the dress around my legs to make it through the forest without tearing my dress to shreds. Finally I reached the opening before the great castle. I came to a dead stop, in full admiration of what I saw, and in terror of even thinking about going there.

It was a three-story building of rough granite blocks, with one-story wings on either side of the main structure. The main building had battlements, gunwindows, and arrow-slit windows at the battlements. The castle was built on a knoll, a large one of course. There was a formal Doric entrance composed of nine huge marble pillars, but there was another peculiar entranceway as well. It was a flight of at least a hundred steps that led to the top of the highest battlement.

The castle was set amid lush trees and rhododendrons, some of them twenty feet or more tall. Azaleas were also in full bloom, and from where I stood I could smell their deep perfume.

It occurred to me that since I'd lived in Kilgort all my life the castle should not have been such a surprise to me. I must have seen it before, but only from the road some distance away, where only the rear and a portion of the side were visible. From where I stood now, the full splendor of the place was apparent.

There was a long road leading straight to the front door, one side of this approach lined with tall oaks in full leaf. I thought that I had never seen anything more lovely. I would give a great deal to see the inside, for it must be a glorious sight to behold. How, I asked myself, could a man who lived in such splendor be evil?

I resumed my walk, briskly now, for I wanted to get my errand over with, though I longed to have a look inside the castle. The steep flight of steps to the battlements also intrigued me, and I couldn't figure out the purpose of it. The castle was ancient, and when it was built, raids on such fiefdoms were common. So why on earth had the original owner constructed a stairway the enemy might use to enter the castle park behind the structure?

I climbed the four wide marble steps to the columned entrance, and without hesitation—but a great deal of fear—pulled the massive iron ring to announce my arrival.

Nothing happened, so I pulled the ring again. Suddenly the massive, brass-studded door swung back slowly. Before me stood Cormac of Fion, bare to the waist, a hairy chest as massive as I had imagined it must be. He wore riding breeches but no boots, his feet encased in heavy woolen socks. His hair was disheveled, and he looked as if he'd just awakened.

"What the hell do you want?" he demanded roughly. Then he leaned forward and peered at my face. "Well, now, if it's not the lass whose father I helped bury. Come in, lass. Enter Castle Lucane and gaze upon its splendor."

I didn't move, nor did I speak. I was tongue-tied and filled with fear. If that great door closed on me, I'd be at the mercy of this huge man. The very sight of him made me lose the courage that had brought me here. I quickly substituted determination for courage. Desperation would have been more appropriate.

Suddenly he seized my hand and literally yanked me into the castle. Behind me the door closed ponderously until it slammed shut and I was trapped.

"Come into the great hall," he invited. "Excuse my appearance, but I live practically alone and I sleep when I wish. It happens I wished to sleep on this afternoon when a pretty colleen awakened me. I frightened you, didn't I?"

His hand still held mine, and he tugged hard, so I was compelled to follow him. I'd had time only to glimpse that big vestibule that I'd entered. There was certainly nothing splendid here. The walls looked as if the plaster was peeling away, and the chandelier above me was so filthy it showed no gleam of light when the door stood open.

The great hall may once have been that, great with splendor. Now it was shabby, though the heavy furniture looked somewhat newer than the walls, which, here too, were peeling. The windows—and there were many of them—were so dirty as to almost shut out the light. The draperies were sorry things, faded from a rich burgundy to shades of pink and rose.

Cormac laughed out loud. "A shiny and wondrous place, is it not? Well, once it was. I remember those days."

"Please, sir," I said in a quiet voice, "I have come on an important errand, and I wish to state it without further ado."

He laughed again. "Without further ado! Such language! You want something of me. Tell me what it is so I can reject your request, whatever it may be."

"If you please, sir, I come on behalf of the village of which this castle is a part." I paused.

"Go on with whatever you're about to say."

"In this village, fully half of the people have died from the famine. Many more are about to die. We have petitioned the authorities in London . . ."

"London will do nothing but take away whatever little you still have left. Don't waste your time trying to get them to help you."

"Aye, that we know, to our sorrow. So there is no one but you to help us. We have been thinking it might be possible for you, with your influence, to get someone to send us enough food to live on until the next harvest. We are sure that it will be a good one, and from then on we'll require no more help. For now, we either get it or most of us will die. I ask your compassion, my lord. I beg you to help us."

He sat down, half-slouched in the great high-backed chair. I stood before him and I felt as small and insignificant as the mound of dust I saw in one of the corners of the great hall.

"Now, whatever made you think I'd help the village people?"

"Because you were so angry you knocked out Conan Hayer. No mean feat, I will say. Then, even in your anger, you saw fit to help bury my poor father."

"So you think I'm a soft one."

"That I do not, my lord. But I think you are a man with a heart."

"What exactly are you in need of?"

"In need of? Food! Plain, simple food! Anything that will fill a stomach. There are a hundred or more of us, and we are that desperate."

"You expect me to provide food for a hundred or more people? Woman, you're mad."

"Aye, that I am, for coming here," I said disconsolately. "I will take no more of your time."

"Just a minute now," he said harshly. "I'm not finished with you. Suppose I agree to send food. What do I get in return?"

He pulled himself up in the chair and spread his legs wide as he looked at me, and in his eyes I saw what he wanted.

"We have nothing, your lordship," I managed to say while I looked to my left to be sure nothing stood in my way should I have to make a rush for the door.

"Maybe the village hasn't, but you have," he said.

"I do not understand your meaning, my lord." That was a lie.

"You can give me what I want. You're a pretty lass with a fine figure. How old are you? Sixteen, seventeen?"

"Good day, sir," I said.

He was out of the chair faster than I could turn and start to run. He seized me about the waist, pulled me to him roughly. With a free hand he slipped the ribbon from under my chin, removed my bonnet, threw it aside, and ran his fingers through my hair. The few pins that held it clattered to the floor.

"You're a delightful girl, and your flesh is warm and your body is a desirable one. Bed down with me this very moment, and I'll see that your village is fed."

"Go to hell, my lord." I struggled furiously to get away.

"Sassy too, eh? Well you came to me at exactly the right time. I've had enough to drink to make me want a woman, and I've not had one in some weeks now, curse the luck. But you'll do very well indeed. Will you give me your body in return for food? Eh? Speak up! I'm not a patient man."

"Let go of me," I said. "I would rather die than let you touch me."

"I'm touching you now," he said, and he pulled up my dress and slipped his hand beneath it. "Indeed, you are desirable. Skin as smooth as silk. Buttocks well-rounded. Submit willingly and beautifully, and you'll get food. Fight me, and I'll have you anyway and there'll not be a morsel."

"I will fight . . ." I reached up and dug my nails into his face. I saw the blood flow out of one deep gouge. He lifted me off the floor and slipped an arm beneath me so I was cradled in his arms. He stalked out of the room, carrying me

as if I were no more than a child's doll. My struggles were
futile. He climbed the grand staircase to the second floor,
marched down the corridor and into one of the bedrooms.

There he dumped me unceremoniously on the bed. Then,
to my horror, he unbuttoned his riding breeches and pulled
them off. He stood there in his nakedness, letting me observe
how great his passion was.

He approached the bed. "You have a choice, my lovely.
You can remove your clothes or I'll tear them off you. No
matter what you do, there is but one end to this. I am already so impatient I cannot control myself."

I said nothing, but I clawed my fingers to try to fight him
off. Then he was on the bed and his hands ripped at my
dress. He succeeded in pulling it up over my head. His hands
were now stroking my flesh. He raked his nails along my
thighs. I cried out in pain. I felt him surge upward and come
down on top of me. Something flooded my brain, and I fell
into a deep faint.

I had no idea how long I lay there, unaware of what had
happened. Upon awakening, though, I knew very well. My
body ached, and in me was a combination of terror and anger. A small object landed on the bed beside me. It was a
bottle of smelling salts.

Seated in a chair at the foot of the bed was Cormac of
Fion, his riding breeches back on. He was grinning at me,
this ape of a man without heart or soul.

"I have noticed, by the usual signs, that you were virgin,"
he said. "Should I be sick with regret, my dear? Should I be
on my knees begging you now to marry me? Eh? Is that what
you're thinking?"

I sat up, pulling at my dress to get it down. "I'm thinking
that at the first opportunity I'll kill you."

"I admire that much spunk. What's your name?"

"It is not for you ever to know," I said. "I'm getting out of
here, unless you wish to murder me, as I expect you might."

"I'm not sorry. I was impetuous, but that is my way. I take
what I want. However, I'm not ashamed. It was high time
someone had you."

I closed my eyes in rage. "May I leave now, or do you
wish to impress me as some sort of slave to your ugly passion?"

"It's an idea," he granted. "A very good one, but no . . .
the next thing I'd hear would be your request that I marry
you, and I will never in my life marry anyone. There is no

reason to hurry. My passion is sated for now. I would not mind your company. It's a dull place living here alone."

"I will not stay a minute more than it takes me to run from this accursed place. And you. What you have done to me is unforgivable. It is done by men who are no more than beasts of the farmyard."

I slipped off the bed, almost crying aloud at the damage done to my dress. I pulled it down and tried to arrange the torn parts.

"You may go," he said, and waved a hand in grand style. "Let me see you walk out as proudly as you greeted me. Spirit you have, colleen."

"Should I now say thank you, m'lord?" I asked.

"Aren't you going to ask me if I'll supply food to your village in return for your favors, given under duress?"

"I will only say that any food you might supply would poison all of us. I'm sure we'd rather starve to death."

I left the room, stood confused for a moment, not knowing in what direction to go. Then I saw the entrance to the stairway and tried to flee, but I moved awkwardly. I was followed by his laughter, which rang through the great entranceway. It was audible until I escaped and made my way along the road.

"You there!" His voice bellowed at me. I paused and turned around. He stood in the doorway, then advanced to the end of the portico. "There was no bargain, remember. You pleased me, but not by your consent, so there will be no food."

I turned away, and now I walked, rather slowly I fear, not because of pain, but the knowledge that I'd gained nothing and lost everything. Meg had been right. I had been a fool to go to this man. From the moment he opened the door, I'd sensed he would want me, but my wits had been overshadowed by the desperation of the village and my purpose in going to see him.

I was a sorry sight. Besides having had my only good dress ruined beyond hope of repair, I ached from head to foot, for he'd been rough and without mercy. My bonnet was still in the castle, but I didn't intend to go back after it. It was a wonder I'd even escaped alive, and perhaps I should be grateful for that. I hated the man. I prayed only for a chance to get back at him, destroy him, if possible. All kinds of foolish thoughts ran through my mind; the best, I thought, was to go back, entice him to the battlements at the head of that strange stairway, and throw him down it.

Then I gasped and brought a hand to my throat as I stopped dead in my tracks. What if I bore the seed of his child? The very idea was enough to weaken my legs so I barely was able to walk. Such a thing would surely be the end of me. I could never stand up to the shame the villagers would bring down. I would have to ask Meg to tell me what the signs were so I'd know in plenty of time. But then, I couldn't tell Meg. She'd warned me about Cormac, and I'd not heeded her, so I could never confide in her. I could only hope that nothing would come of this encounter. And pray.

I reached home and went on inside, feeling as if I should tell my father about what had happened. I almost spoke aloud to him, I was in that bad a quandary. I went into the kitchen instead, set the kettle on the stove, and brewed myself a large pot of tea, using all I wished. I drank this while I finished what was left of the box of biscuits I'd served to Meg. I didn't care if it was the last food in the village and there would be no more. Nothing mattered to me anymore. I was not the same. Cormac of Fion had seen to that, and how I despised even thinking about him.

After a time, and four cups of tea, I came to my senses. I could not deny I had gone to see Cormac, for Meg knew I had gone. But I would never tell what had happened there. I would only say that he refused to respond to my plea and that I regarded him as a blackguard. A man whose food, if donated, would have been tainted by the devil himself.

I sat alone in the house that night, and my thoughts were not pleasant. If there was to be a child, I would marry Conan as quickly as possible. That would be cheating the poor man, lying to him, but it would protect me. Then again, if we did marry and there was Cormac's child, certainly the child would look like him, so how could I explain that? No, I would go away forever. Perhaps the child would not be born alive anyway. If conditions didn't change and there was no food, there'd surely be no living child to come from my body.

Then I fell to wondering what was going to happen in the village. Our last hope was now gone. It would be months before a potato crop came in, if there was to be one. By then it would be too late. I could, perhaps, make a try for Canada or America. Father had left enough money to buy passage, but I'd heard so many tales of what happened during the long voyage that I lost my heart for that too.

I thought about England. If the food didn't come to me, I could go to where it was, but I disdained that idea quickly enough. Under no circumstances could I ever abide England. I would far rather die here.

I was sure there'd be no sleep in me this night, but I did sleep, and well, too. Waking in the morning, I recalled instantly what had happened and if I'd needed reminding, my torn dress over the back of a chair would have informed me clearly enough. More than that, when I removed my nightgown I saw the bruises and scratches up and down my thighs. I washed in cold water. I would have washed in acid that morning, to get the smell of him off me, even though I'd promptly bathed when I came home from the encounter with the beast.

I examined my dress and finally threw it aside to be used from the ragbag downstairs. I still had some tea, but nothing else, and when I drank my two cups, I grew famished for want of something solid. It was then that I broke down, rested my face on the kitchen table, and wept. I had reached the bottom of my life. There was nothing left now. I could not decently marry a man without telling him what had happened. If I did this, if there was a man who'd ask me, then that man would call upon Cormac and be promptly killed by him. I knew of no one who could stand up to the oversized and depraved beast.

The rage within me made me leave the cottage and walk down the deserted street. Before I was halfway along it, I saw them carry a body from one of the cottages and place it aboard the only wagon left—the same one that had carried my father to his grave. And it was a young man who had died this time. I remembered him as a gay lad full of life and hope. Now he was dead, as all of us would be one of these soon-to-come days.

Meg was among the mourners, and as she emerged from the cottage, she saw me and promptly left the small procession that marched behind the wagon.

"I've been looking for you," she said, breathless from her haste to reach me. "Did you see Cormac?"

"Aye, I saw him, but he could not see any sense to my plea for food. He turned me away, Meg, without as much as to say he was sorry for us."

"I was afraid he might have bargained with you and you'd be a big enough fool to give in to him."

I wondered if she was possessed of the power to read

minds. "He is one of those who see no need to help the poor. Money and power he no doubt has, but not to be used in doing good. And the inside of that great castle is little better than the poorest cottage we have."

"Is that so? It was in my mind that a castle always stays grand, inside and out."

"Only if it is cared for and loved by those who live in it. This man cares for nothing save a bottle and his drinking friends. I am sorry he would not grant my plea, but then again, I'm glad I will have no dealing with him."

"We are in a bad state, Kate. There's nothing left. All the fields have been dug up by bare hands to find even a small root, and they have all been found. I've been thinking to move on. Somewhere else. Anywhere but here. What are we going to do, Kate? You are the wise one. What are we going to do?"

"I don't know. I wish I did. Going somewhere else will not help, for there is nowhere to go where we can find food." I paused a moment, thinking back. "Meg, when I walked to the castle, I crossed a stream. I forget its name, and it runs through the castle estate. It was wide and looked fairly deep in some places, though forded easily by the rocks placed across it."

"So there is a stream."

"Meg, if it is the right kind, there will be fish."

"Perhaps, and men sent out by Cormac to guard it. You know what the law is. He who poaches on castle land will be shot on the spot, and if we were caught, we would become great sport for those with the guns."

"Would you rather risk it, and perhaps be shot, or sit here and surely starve to death doing nothing?"

"Come to think of it," Meg said, "there's not that much difference, is there? Do you have fishing gear?"

"Father was a great fisherman, and it was in that very stream where he did some of his fishing, now that I think back. How is it the men never went to fish?"

"Because it has been bred into them that a poacher is only fit to be hung or shot to death on the spot. Besides, I'm sure they never thought of it."

"They hunted the forest clear of animals down to pack rats," I said. "Come on, I'll go home and fetch the fishing things and we'll be off to a day of it."

"Be sure to pack a lunch." Meg laughed.

I embraced her, touched my cheek to hers. "If we can still

laugh at it, we're not licked yet. And if there are fish, we'll send the whole village there. I happen to know that Cormac lives alone and there will be no one to see us."

"There is the old man from Belfast. . . ."

"I saw no sight of him, and it was Cormac himself who said he lived alone. He looked it, if I say so, and the castle as well. Wear boots and meet me at my house."

I found Father's fish poles, his sinkers, corks, lines, and hooks. I knew little about fishing, but I didn't think there was much to learn. By the time Meg came, I was ready, and we set off at once. We avoided any approach to the castle itself, but upon locating the stream, followed it away from the cleared estate to deep water and began to fish.

All morning and into the afternoon we sat vainly waiting for the cork to bob. We walked up and down the stream, fishing at likely-looking places, and never once did we get so much as a nibble. It was no use. As far as we were concerned, there were no fish in the stream, a fact we soon confirmed when we went back to the village. Conan Hayer told us the bad news.

"We fished the stream dry long ago. Poached it, to be truthful. There are no fish left, or, if so, they will be too small to take the hook. I myself would relish a nice portion of trout. It's been years, as I recall. And what have you been doing, Kate?"

"She's been to see Cormac of Fion." Meg spoke up before I could silence her. "She asked him for food, and he turned her away. What do you think of that, Conan?"

"Not favorably, I would say. But then, who'd expect the gentry to know of our problem, or do anything about it if they did?"

"I'm sorry," I said. "I thought from the way he behaved at Father's grave, he might listen to me."

"I don't recall exactly what he did except nearly bust my jaw and put me away like I was a four-year-old."

"He changed his mind and let Father be buried there, and he filled in the grave."

"Aye, that he did, and you mentioned you thought there was a softness to him."

"There is none," I said. "I found that out."

"Tomorrow," Conan said, "four of us men are taking the horse and wagon to ride to Ballyfief twelve miles north, and there we will see if there is any food to steal. If not, we will go on and keep going until we find enough to bring back."

"You'd best not be too slow about it," Meg said. "There is great need at this moment."

"Aye, we're aware of that. It's why we are going to steal if we can. Others may be as bad off, but if we are stronger than they, or slyer, then we shall have the food. Kate, could I be calling on you this evening?"

"I'd rather you didn't," I said. "Not that I'm against it, mind you, but with nothing to eat, I would rather go to bed and try to sleep on this empty stomach of mine."

"Well, that's not the best reason," Conan said, "but I do have to be up very early so we can get started. I'll say good day to you, Kate . . . Meg."

Meg and I resumed walking toward her cottage. "You're making a mistake not marrying that man, Kate. He is all for it, but too shy to say so."

"Perhaps I will, Meg. Perhaps . . . I don't know. He's a fine man. I don't deserve him, but . . . maybe . . ."

I left her and returned home. I searched every nook and cranny for something to eat, but I found no scrap of anything. I still had wood, so I started the fireplace. To kill time and keep me from thinking about my hunger, I began going through Father's desk and his papers. I stacked up enough unpaid bills to have kept me in food for a year, and then I threw them all into the fireplace. Certainly his affairs were not sufficient to take up any time, yet I stayed with cleaning out the desk until my eyes smarted from this work under lamplight. When I was barely able to keep from dropping in my tracks from fatigue, I made certain the fireplace was safe and then went upstairs to bed. I fell asleep instantly.

In the morning I opened my eyes to the hopelessness of another day. I would go downstairs to tea made from last evening's dregs. With the hot tea would be . . . nothing. And no hope of finding anything to eat. I'd never been so desperate, and I could readily understand why families poorer than Father's and mine had so quickly succumbed to the famine.

I picked up the torn dress and carried it downstairs to push it into the ragbag. I washed my teacup and saucer and the pot, making a ritual of it, as if there were dinner plates and sauce dishes and pots and pans to follow. This completed, there was nothing else to do, and I was beginning to realize that in a short time now I'd not have the strength to do anything.

I stepped outside into the warm sunlight. Conan was walking slowly up the street, his head down, shoulders sagging like those of an old, old man.

"Now, I thought you and the others were off scrounging for food this fine morning," I said when he was close by me.

He raised his head. "Last night the horse died."

In all my life I never thought I'd answer that bad news the way I did. "Then, by heaven, what's left of the poor animal must be divided so all get at least some meat."

Conan nodded. "It's being done, and you'll get your share. There won't be more than half a pound, if that, for there wasn't much left on the animal. We're lost, Kate. The horse was our last hope. We're all so weak we can't walk the ten miles to the next village."

"Hush, now," I said sharply. "Listen, Conan. If the horse died last night, what's pulling a wagon—more than one—coming this way from the bend?"

The sound was strange enough to bring others into the street in time to see two big drays each drawn by two fat horses trundle down the road, to pull up where Conan and I stood transfixed, for we knew what was on those wagons. Like everyone else, we could smell it and taste it before we even saw the food.

The man on the seat of the first wagon held up a large burlap sack. "Which of you is Kate Moran?" he asked.

"I am Kate," I said.

"Then I am to hand you this personally, Kate Moran, with the compliments of Cormac of Fion."

I accepted the sack and held it before me. I cast quick glances to either side of me to see if anyone watched with eyes filled with suspicion, for I knew my cheeks were flaming with embarrassment.

I had no need to worry. Not one soul had anything in mind but the food still on the wagons, as they all waited politely for the word to unload the boxes, barrels, and sacks.

The driver said, "My orders are you shall all share and share alike. Come get it!"

They needed no further invitation. I stood there, not moving, holding the sack against me and trying to compose myself. I watched as two men brought down a barrel heaped with red apples. I'd not seen one in so long I actually wondered what they were. One of the men picked up an apple, held it to his nose. He looked across the road to where a boy of about ten stood in fascination at the sight of food. The man tossed him the apple, and he caught it deftly. He also brought it to his nose to be smelled and savored. With both hands he polished the apple until he could, perhaps, see himself in the gleaming surface. Then he bit into it, and in my life I never saw a face so ecstatic. I almost burst into tears, but there was no time for that.

The men had the wagons unloaded quickly, and the drays promptly turned about to go back to wherever they came from. Now the entire population stood around the heap of containers. Very meticulously and without undue haste they separated the food. There was the barrel of apples, counted out and checked. There were loaves of fresh bread and crates of carrots and turnips, more of cabbages, and four barrels of—heaven be blessed—potatoes. It required two hours to sort out and divide the food. There was difficulty with the meat, for it came in great chunks, but flashing knives did the best they could in making the division reasonably equal.

I had gone back into my house. No one followed me. There was too much to do out on the street. In the privacy of my house I untied the cord around the mouth of the sack and began removing its contents.

First, there was a whole ham, the smell of which set my salivary glands drooling. There was beef too, a fine cut of it. And more bread then I could use, and potatoes and fruit.

The first item I'd taken out was wrapped in heavy paper and obviously not food, so I set it aside until the sack was all unpacked. Then I remembered the package and untied the string and opened the paper, to find a dress the likes of which I had not seen since my long-ago visits to Dublin. It was a shade of light green, and its softness made me cry. It was of fine silk, and at the bottom of the package was my bonnet, left in the castle when I so hastily fled from it.

That was what caused me not to give thanks. Perhaps this man was soft, after all, but he had displayed none of it to me. He'd said plainly that he would not send food, for I'd not given him the satisfaction of having me without a struggle. If he had changed his mind, there was a reason for it. And I knew what that reason must be.

THREE

——◦◉◦——

They were carrying home their share of the food outside. I gathered up the dress and the bonnet and hastened upstairs. I tossed the garment and hat on the floor of the bedroom closet. Losing no time, I went downstairs again to put away the food, though not before I'd cut a slice from the ham and had it frying on the stove. A thick slice, for I went outside to call Conan to come and eat with me.

There was tea, quite a lot of it, and for once I brewed it as strong as I liked. I cut bread, then served Conan enough ham to sate his appetite and sufficient to satisfy mine. We sat down at the table and bowed our heads in thanksgiving, though the words I spoke seemed like sheer hypocrisy.

"Glory be," Conan said. "The man came through after all. You must have been persuasive, Kate, to get all this."

"Just how much was there, all told?" I asked.

"Oh, enough for a week if we stretch it. This means those who have been starving will not die, and those who were not yet sick will have no need to take to their beds. Ah, it's manna from heaven, Kate. That such a man could see to this. Why did he do it, I wonder?"

"For him, it was no great thing," I said. I chewed carefully on the bit of ham to savor it completely. At that moment I had no hatred for Cormac of Fion.

"To have friends in high places means life or death these days," Conan observed.

"You say the food will last a week only?"

"If that, for I know everyone will feast until they realize there is not enough for forever. By then much of the food will be eaten, but glory be, that's what it's for."

"And where will food come from after this is gone?" I asked.

"Perhaps Cormac would soften his heart again."

"There is no rule that he should, or would," I said.

"No, that's true. But while the food is here, we shall all enjoy it, and leave the future to be faced later on. That's the way it's done, Kate."

"I will not beg again," I warned him.

"Then let someone else do it. I would not be too proud to ask him."

I gave way to a laugh, mostly of self-derision. What was I saying? That someone else could talk Cormac into providing another shipment of food? Cormac has a price, and no one else here could provide it. Only me!

"At least," Conan said, "you can laugh again. It's been some time, Kate."

"We will wait and see what is to be done," I said. "It seems his generosity is in stages. He could have sent enough on those two wagons to last a month."

"Be grateful for what we got. It saved our lives."

That it had, I thought. But at what expense. He would demand more of the same, and I was determined that this was the end of it. I would not again present myself to him and seek food in return for his use of my body. It was bad enough now. The villagers were too busy feeding their stomachs to do much thinking about the circumstances that provided this food. But once they had the time for it, they'd wonder. Such a man as Cormac of Fion, providing for more than a hundred starving people, when petitions to every known agency had brought nothing, must have something behind it. There'd not be another day gone by before they'd begin wondering and guessing. A young woman like me, begging from a man like Cormac, and getting results such as this, could mean but one thing, and they'd soon concentrate on that.

It was on my mind, while still at the table, to ask Conan to marry me in the morning. It was a bold thought, though that wasn't what stopped me. The times were too perilous—so I convinced myself. Actually I was thinking that if I had to go back, Cormac would be less inclined perhaps to listen to the plea of a newly married woman. There was a slim chance he might have morals enough to restrain himself under those circumstances. I doubted it, but there was that chance. I kept my lips sealed and sent Conan away, happily stuffed and with no thought of marriage on his sleepy mind.

Meg came to see me that evening. "It was the wonder of God that made him do it, Kate." She sat down as she spoke. "I had a mind that he'd throw you out."

"Or rape me," I said in a flat voice.

Meg nearly jumped out of the chair. "Kate, he didn't!"

"I asked him to send food," I said. "He refused, but he must have later thought better of it."

"Will there be more, do you think?"

"How can I answer that? It's best the food be hoarded and eaten only in small amounts to make it last. There is no guarantee he will be so generous again. It's even possible he will go back to Dublin, or London, or wherever he lives most of the time. Then there will be no more, I assure you."

"At least we have this much, thanks to you. Now, tell me, what kind of man is he? Oh, I know he's big and brutally strong, but under all that size, what's he like?"

"I had but few words with him," I said.

"You had more than that to make him loosen up with this much food."

"There is not that much food. It is only because you've not had anything for so long this looks like half the food in the world. It won't last a week, perhaps two if everyone is careful, which they will not be."

"Surely a man kind enough to supply this much will not allow us to go back to starving to death."

"There is no predicting what he will do, and stop asking me what I think about the man."

Meg pursed her lips for a moment and eyed me shrewdly. "Now, what makes you so touchy when I ask questions about him? I mean nothing by it, except to try to understand the man."

I reached over and grasped her hand. "Forgive me, Meg. I'm tired and I've eaten too much, and I'm so surprised he sent the food that I don't know what I'm saying half the time. Just be glad the food is here and all our bellies are full for once. Maybe now our luck will change for the better."

Meg was not to be mollified that easily. "Tell me, since the food will last but a week, will you go back to him?"

"I went once. I stood before the man, and without bending my knees I asked him in a civil way if he would give us food. Give us life. He replied in such a way that I had no hope he would send the food. But he did, and that's all there is to it. Would you like to have me tell you that I lay on my back to him so he would be generous?"

"Oh, Kate," she said in a shocked voice, "I thought no such thing."

"Well, you were asking in a tone that was hinting, if I know you correctly."

"Kate, I did not. If you surmised that, then you were wrong."

"Will you stop talking about it? I'm sick of the whole thing. And I know what you've been thinking. So will every last one in the village as soon as they get around to it. I half wish I'd not gone at all. If you're a friend of mine, Meg, you will stop any such talk that rises up, especially among the women. Consider the food as manna from heaven and forget the whole damn thing."

"You're mighty touchy. . . ."

"Meg, if you say one more word in that vein, I'll throw you out and never let you darken my door again. That's a warning, so heed it."

"I meant no harm. It was merely the curiosity we women must cater to. I'll go now, and no offense, Kate. You're the best friend I ever had, and I should like to keep it that way if you please."

"That's better," I said. "Spread the word, if you can, to go easy on the food. And if you see Conan, tell him I'd like him to come to supper."

"I'll do that," Meg said. She left, with her shoulders square now, and hope in her heart that her baby would not yet have suffered from her lack of food.

I went upstairs and took the gift dress from the closet, also the bonnet, which was none the worse for having been ripped off my head. I smoothed the ribbons and put it away. I held the dress against me. It was beautiful. How could a man like him have the patience or the taste to buy something like this? Then I had a thought, and I examined the garment thoroughly to assure myself it was not a castoff from one of his women.

This decided upon, I felt better. I slipped out of my dress and put it on. When I stepped before the mirror, with the light of the afternoon sun behind me coming softly through the window, I thought I had never in my life seen such a wonderful dress. It was in two shades of pale green silk. The bodice was light green with pagoda sleeves. They were trimmed with lace, the undersleeves ribbon-threaded. The skirt had a horizontally striped pattern in two shades of green, and its scalloped flounces were pinked. Beautiful as it was, it would be more so with a few petticoats beneath it to fill out the full skirt. The green complimented my auburn hair, which fell softly on my shoulders. I preened, pirouetted, smiled at my reflection over my shoulders, first one, then the other. I even laughed aloud in delight. I felt young. My eyes held a sparkle I'd never seen in them before. I was pleased and happy and delighted at being a woman.

However, I quickly got my foolishness under control, disgusted I could get even a momentary pleasure out of something I had paid so dearly for. I quickly corrected myself. I'd not offered myself. My body had been violated by a man who had shown no mercy. He was bestial in his cruelty, born without a soul.

Despite my loathing for him, I took care in hanging up the dress. It would be stupid to take out my hatred on a piece of fabric put together by some poor soul who had been paid a pittance, no doubt, for creating something so lovely.

A shame, too, for I'd never be able to wear it. To appear in it would make the tongues clack like a henyard. They'd know then what I'd done so that their bellies might be full. The dress was a waste. Also a distasteful reminder of what I'd been subjected to when I went on my begging mission.

The next days were glorious ones for the village. For a week there were people on the street, women gossiping with all their old abandon. There were few children left, but those who had survived engaged in strenuous, loud games. Men visited the pub, though there was not a drop to drink, but the atmosphere of the place lent itself to sociability and conversation.

I was the heroine for all of them to praise. I had somehow softened the heart of Cormac and from him obtained the life-giving food. I also believed that not one person gave thought to saving food, only to the fact that where this had come from, there'd be more. It would only require that Kate Moran go to the kind man and again ask his generosity.

Kate Moran didn't go to him. Not right after the food was gone and the village restored to its drab existence. Even the dying began again after a month of the old kind of scrounging about for something to eat.

Then it was that Meg came to me as a representative of the village. "I'm here to ask that you see Cormac again, Kate. For the sake of all of us, and especially the baby who is beginning now to swell and prove that it likely is alive in me. Will you go to see him?"

I said, "I will not. I warned you that the food must be made to last, but few heeded my advice, if any."

"Kate, there was not enough for that."

"There was sufficient that I have some left. Not much, but I can live on it another few days perhaps. Soon, now, we'll know about the new crop. The best guess is that we will have potatoes before long, and the famine and the dying will be over."

"We can't wait that long, Kate. For the love of God, try to remember how it was only these few days ago before that kind and understanding man gave us food."

"That's just it, Meg. I do remember, and because I do, I saved some of my food."

"Then you refuse to give us the means to go on living?"

"Oh, Meg, you know better than that. But if I go now, they'll devour whatever I can get out of the man and then just sit around and wait for more. I tell you we're almost out of this trouble now. I've heard the crops are going to be good. In three months' time there will be no more famine in Ireland."

"Three months! How many will die in three months, Kate?"

"Why don't *you* go ask him?"

She drew back in the chair as if I'd rendered the greatest insult possible. "Kate, I am with child. I would no more go near that man . . ."

I shook my head. "No matter what I say or do, every time Cormac comes into the conversation you imply that I surrendered to him so I might buy the food that way. I'm tired of it. I got the food, and I'm blamed and damned because I did. Let someone else go."

"No one would have the nerve, Kate. But I'll see if anyone will agree. They all said the same thing before you did see him. That it would take a pretty girl to make the old bastard listen."

"So I was nominated," I said bitterly.

"No, you can't say that. You went of your own accord. No one asked you to."

"Pass the word about that someone else will have to do it this time. I have demeaned myself enough asking his charity."

"Then I will ask others and tell them you refused," Meg said. "It's been some time now since I had a decent thing to eat . . . and maybe some tea . . . if you are also of a charitable nature."

I gave her the last of Cormac's ham and slices of bread

gone stale, but nevertheless it was good food and Meg didn't turn from it. I made tea also, for I still had a good supply of that, thanks to the burlap sack Cormac had sent me. Meg looked at me as if she'd have enjoyed more, but I made no effort to supply her with anything else. I was a little put out with her lately.

I knew, even if she asked, that no one in the village would go to see Cormac. They were much too proud, but not so proud they wouldn't eat the fare someone else would beg for them. I also knew that if things became as serious as before, I would go to Cormac. I also knew the price I would have to pay.

Conan came to supper most nights, but not because he would be fed. More often than not he brought along the little food he had managed to save. But conditions in the village were just as bad as before. I waited until the time I was called to the Kilgore cottage, where the youngest girl lay prostrate with the sickness that comes of not having enough to eat.

There was nothing I could do for her. Nothing anyone could do, except provide her with food—and quickly. All over Ireland, things were even worse these days, though the planting had been successful and there would be enough for all soon. That was too long. That was the irony of it. People were still dying, and more would die. I decided that among these must not be Maureen Kilgore.

So that night, well after dark, when the village had withdrawn to the cottages and there was no one about, I put on the pale green silk dress that Cormac had sent. I knew very well that he had deliberately sent only enough food to tide us for a short time, and that if I wished more, I would have to come to him. And with me, would come his price.

On my way out of the village, feeling like a thief, I walked rapidly toward the forest path, but on the way I did stop at the chapel. There'd been no priest these many months, but it was still a chapel, so I entered the darkened building and prayed for a few moments. I sat quietly after that, telling myself that what I was about to do was not to be considered as anything except a sacrifice on my part so that people would be fed and kept from dying. Circumstances had placed me in this difficult position, and what happened was not of my will and therefore forgivable. I recalled Maureen Kilgore's pinched face. She'd been such a pretty girl. I knew the older

people were again in grave circumstances and needed immediate help.

The thoughts and the prayers fortified me with the courage
to go on. Soon I found myself approaching the great castle
with its columned entrance and big brass-studded door. I
stood there, suddenly in a quandary. What if Cormac was not
at home? What if he'd gone off, as he frequently did, to stay
away for weeks and months? I should have come before now,
but my hatred of the man had kept me from even consider-
ing it.

I took a deep breath and pulled on the heavy ring that
sounded a bell somewhere within the castle. There'd been no
light showing anywhere, but that was no real indication the
castle was not occupied, because it was lit only by candlelight
and maybe oil lamps, but even so, the light would scarcely be
enough to fill one of those enormous rooms and also escape
through the windows.

I was about to turn away, not quite sure if I was pleased
with the idea or frightened to death that my mission had
failed. The great door swung back. Cormac, fully dressed this
time, stood there with a lamp in his hand. He raised it,
leaned forward for a better look, and then exploded in loud
laughter.

"So, you've come back, have you? Why? Because you liked
the treatment you received in Lucane Castle? Or are you here
to beg for more food?"

"You know why I came, my lord," I said as politely and
meekly as I could manage. My blood was boiling at his attitude, but I kept myself under control. Getting the food was
more important than telling him what I thought of him. I
would keep a civil tongue in my head until he either refused
my plea or made his demands of payment for the food.

"Come in," he said. I hesitated out of plain fear of the
man. "I said come in! What's the matter with you? Must I
slam the door in your face and deny myself an evening of
fine pleasure?"

I walked into the castle. The only light was from the lamp
he held. Now that he'd made very plain that he expected me
to spend the evening, my fear of him was changing to righteous anger.

"If you are implying that I came here to bed with you in
return for more food, you're wrong, my lord. If you deny us
the food, I will leave at once."

"Just like that, you'll up and leave! The last time, you were fighting mad and it was not the pleasure it should have been. For either of us. Tonight it should be different."

"I will never in my life—"

"Be quiet and let me finish. It should be different if you are more amenable. If not, then it will be as it was the first time. That is your decision to make, but this night I will have you again, and this time you will not escape so easily, for the night is long and I am a lonely man."

"Then I will go," I said. "You will prevent me, I'm sure, and do whatever you will with me, but you will never gain my consent. I shall regard you tonight as I did the other time—a beast without heart or the power of reasoning and mercy."

"Oh, damn," he said. "It's better without a fight."

"No doubt for you it may be, but I will fight again as hard as I can."

He set the lamp down. "Well, now, you'd best begin, because I'm as impatient as I ever was. It'll be worth the clawing you'll give me with your nails."

He seized me as I reached the door, swung me around, bent me back, and brought his face down to mine. His lips pressed hard, his free hand pulled the dress off my shoulder to reach my breast, and then his passion made his kisses more determined than ever. Suddenly I knew there was no use in fighting him, because I didn't have the strength. If I kept resisting, the end would be the same. Yet, I couldn't allow this monster to even remotely think I'd given consent. I let myself go limp in his grasp and began sliding toward the floor.

Completely unfazed by this, he promptly picked me up, and as he had that first time, carried me upstairs, though the staircase was dark and pitch black at the top. He knew every inch of the way. I found myself gently deposited on the same bed, and I lay there, just as he'd placed me.

I could hear him moving about, and I knew he was taking off his clothes. I made no move, gave him no inkling that I was not still in a dead faint. I hoped he might be gentleman enough not to take advantage of someone unable to resist, but that hope was quickly gone. He breathed hoarsely as he climbed on the bed.

"I don't know if you're playing a game or not. No matter. I'd prefer you awake, but I cannot wait."

Then he quickly unbuttoned my dress, and in a moment he bent to kiss me, and my rage got the better of me. I bit his lip until I tasted the blood that came from it.

He laughed loudly. "Now, that's better. I like life in my women."

I was so utterly helpless beneath him that I ceased any resistance, so that it might be over with. He turned to lie beside me then, still holding me to him. For all the cooperation he got from me, he might as well have been fondling a rag doll.

It upset him to the point that he cursed me aloud and rolled off the bed.

"I'll send your damned food," he said. "Get up and put on your dress. If I damaged it, I'll send you another."

"If you do, I'll burn it," I said. "And no matter if this one is damaged. I will burn that too. I want nothing of yours, Cormac of Fion, except the privilege of going to your funeral."

"That could be too," he said with a laugh. "You're a spirited lass, I will say. Tell me, did you know what I'd demand of you in return for some food?"

"You sent only enough to last a brief time, and you knew I'd have to come back. You're a devil, Cormac. You may even be old Beelzebub himself. At best, you must be his brother."

"Why do you fuss so?" he asked. "What's happened between us is just pleasure."

"For you, perhaps, though I hope it was not. For me, it was hell. And this, what you call pleasure—you gentry can claim it when you like, and it means nothing. But let a plain Irishman rape a girl of the gentry and he will swing from the nearest tree. Deny that now and make of yourself a liar among all the other evil things you are."

"What's your name again? Oh—aye, Kate. Well, now, Kate, if you'll be reasonable and not try to tear my eyes out, I will give you my word that for this night I will bother you no more. In return, I ask that you sit and talk with me, for, as I said before, I am a lonely man."

"I would rather die," I said promptly.

"Oh, come now. What's the harm done?"

"You—" I shouted, but his voice was stronger than mine and interrupted me.

"The first time, perhaps you had reason to complain, but that's when the damage was done. From then on . . . You're old enough to know what I'm talking about."

"Sometimes, after what's happened to me, I feel a hundred

years old," I said. "If you've finished with me now, I'll be on my way."

"Will you not sit with me for a time? This is likely the last time you'll call upon me for help, and there is no reason why we should not end this as . . . can I say . . . friends?"

I winced at the word being associated with him. "I have no desire to be in your presence a minute longer. But I will ask what you meant by this being the last time."

The room was in total darkness, and that is how we held this rare conversation. I couldn't see his face and I could judge him only by the quality of his voice as he parried my question.

"Ah, then you must be interested in a next time."

I was as flustered with the man as I'd ever been with anyone, in addition to hating him. I arose and fumbled about for my dress, grateful for the darkness that he couldn't see me. I found the garment and tried to get it on, but I couldn't determine which was the front or the back in the dark.

A match was struck and applied to a candle wick. The weak light seemed dazzling after all that intense darkness. I pulled the dress down over my head.

He had the decency to have put his trousers back on, but his hairy chest was still bare.

"I made a statement, Kate. Did you hear me?"

"I don't want to hear you," I retorted. "If you've done with me . . ."

"You said that before. Go, if you like, but I do have a bit of news that might encourage you and the village."

I stopped trying to button the dress. "And what would that be?"

"Let's go downstairs where there'll be more light and maybe a bit of sherry or port, whatever you wish. Brandy, if that suits your palate."

I was again intent on trying to button the dress with hands that shook so badly I was unable to complete this simple task. He arose and came to me. He smiled, gently for a change, and it lit up his face. He grasped my hands.

"You are a scared little lass. Let me help you."

And the man who had all but torn the dress off me now buttoned it slowly, and without touching me. At first I'd tried to draw back, but I sensed there was no longer any harm in him.

"I will sit with you," I said.

"Ah, good." He picked up the candleholder, took my arm,

and led me downstairs to the great hall. There he went about lighting one lamp or candle after another. The room was supplied with both. In a short time the great hall was well-flooded with light, at least around the portion where he indicated we would sit. He disappeared for a moment or two and came back with glasses and two bottles, one of brandy, the other of a fine sherry. He poured the drinks and handed me the wine as casually as if we were old friends and this was an aftermath of a tea or a supper.

"I should have put on my shirt," he apologized. "Forgive me."

"What does it matter to me?" I asked, still on the offensive and none too sure but that he would not once again carry me upstairs.

"Well, no, I think it does, because, for a villager, you're a lady. Yes . . . quite a lady. I suspect you have had something of an education."

"I do not care to talk about myself to you, sir," I said. "You were to tell me something of importance that applies also to the village people."

"Oh, yes. Well, I thought we might end this on a pleasanter note, but have it your way. The famine is about over. It may last another two months, but the agriculture commissioner says all over Ireland the potatoes are doing well and the harvest will be a good one."

"That we already knew," I said.

"Possibly, but in England they have become frightened and worried at world opinion of how they handled this famine."

"They handled it not at all," I said tartly.

"Kate, I have a mind that you forget I'm an Irishman too."

"In my mind I find it hard to believe there could be an Irishman like you."

"Oh, Kate, there are others who say I'm typical."

"Whatever you are, get on with it, man. I want to get out of here. This castle and you hold no dear attachment for me."

"The British are sending shiploads of food. After three years, while a million or more starved to death, they are sending food. It will take a month to get here, the famine would last but another month after that, so don't expect much. I will send drays loaded down with enough food to keep the village until the British food arrives, and by the time that is gone, the potato crop will be ready to harvest and this will be over with. That is why I said tonight would be the last time you would come here."

"For such things I am eternally grateful," I said.

"Of course, if you wished to come . . ."

"Your lordship is a vain and impossible man. I would not come here again if I were dragged."

"Am I as bad as that? Really?"

"You ask that of me whom you have twice raped? You think I would come here again to this pigsty? A castle that falls to ruin and is covered with dirt and dust. It's for the likes of you to live here, sir, but not the likes of me."

I sipped some of the sherry, set the glass down, and arose. He didn't stand up.

"If you change your mind, I'll probably be here, though when the whim takes me, I go elsewhere. However, if I thought you might return of your own free will, I would stay."

"My own free will would keep me from going within a hundred miles of you," I said. "May I go now?"

"You've been free to go anytime. Good night to you, Kate Moran."

I didn't answer him, but gathered up my skirt and fled to the door. As it had the first time, his taunting laugh followed me. I ran down the drive from the castle, but slowed up to walk the rest of the way back. I felt as dirty and foul as I had after my first visit. Truly, not as physically abused, however, for resisting him would have been a foolish gesture. It only got me aches and pains that lasted for days that first time.

But when I was safely in my own cottage, I heated water and washed myself thoroughly. After that I got ready for bed and inspected the green silk dress. It had not been ripped or damaged beyond the wrinkling of it. I hung it up. I knew I'd told him I would burn it, but that too would be only spiting myself. I went to bed, but I didn't sleep.

There was a certain satisfaction in knowing that Cormac would send food and that the British were taking care to see no one else starved before the potato crop came in. So the great famine was now over and once again we could resume our normal lives.

It would not be normal for me. My father was gone and I was alone. I loved no man, not even Conan, and I hated one to the point that I could have cheerfully destroyed him. I wondered what I'd stay in the village for. There'd be little I could do and no way to make a decent living.

I hoped I'd not been seen either going to or coming from the castle. Once the second delivery of food was made, everyone would look to me to see if I was responsible for the lord of the castle sending more. And if I was, what had been the price?

Late the following afternoon the drays arrived, this time well-laden with twice the amount of food as before. Once again the villagers cheered the man who sent it. Division was fairly made. I brought my share home, thankful that Cormac had not sent me a personal package this time.

I had everything stored away when Meg arrived, already well-fed and bursting with curiosity.

"Did you go to see him again, Kate? What was he like this time?"

By nature I was not a liar, but this situation called for at least an omission of the truth. "He sent me word it was coming and that this was the last time, for help is also on its way from London."

"Aye, we have heard such rumors. If Cormac says it is so, then it must be correct. He did not come to see you?"

"He did not," I said, wanting the matter to end there.

"Kate, I have told no one, but last night I saw you leave your cottage, and you did not return until late. You also wore a dress I never saw before. Where did you get it, dear Kate?"

"Meg Donnel, you have been spying on me. What a disgraceful thing to do."

"It was not spying, Kate. I only wished to know if you went to Lucane Castle so that if you did not return, someone would know what happened to you."

"What a liar you are, Meg."

"Speaking of lies, only this moment you told me you had not gone to the castle, and yet you did. Can you explain that?"

"Of course I can explain it. Yes, I went to Cormac of Fion to beg him again to be generous, and, as you see, he was."

"You must have talked for a long time. You were gone more than two hours. Do you and the lord of the castle have much to talk about?"

"We talked of food for the village, and he told me the news from England. I lied about going there because I know what the village women are going to think as soon as they eat enough food to enable them to resume their gossiping. I wished to give them nothing to talk about, because of small things they make mountains. You are not above it yourself."

"I do not care for your insinuations, Kate Moran, and I will take my leave if you do not mind."

"I welcome it," I said with a sigh. "I'm tired of the whole business."

She left in a high state of anger, and I shook my head at the shallowness of the woman who had pleaded with me to do what she now refused to condone. I knew very well what was going to happen, for I'd been born in this village and brought up among these people. The word would spread that no man such as Cormac of Fion would give away so much as a scrap off his little fingernail without being paid in return. They would eagerly assume that a girl like me had but one asset to grant him.

Nothing happened, which surprised me, but about a week later I began to notice that some of the women greeted me with a civil but cold nod, not taking the time to speak further. Meg had not returned for a visit since I'd asked her to leave, something I was sorry for. One could not exist in a small town like this without at least one close friend.

Oh, I had that friend, all right. Conan came as often as I asked, and sometimes oftener than that. He made no comment, but spoke only of the renewal of his farm and the prospects of his crop. How he one day hoped to own his land and not pay rent out of his harvest.

"It's a hard life, Kate," he granted. "Sometimes I have not the heart for it, but I know nothing else. Still, after what we've been through these three years, I suppose I should be grateful and give praise to God that I have what I have."

"Aye, Conan, that you should. We have all learned that there were those even worse off than we, if that is possible. There is pride in being a farmer."

So our conversations continued in that innocuous vein for almost a month. Then the food from London began to trickle in, and there was a sigh of relief from the whole nation that must have been heard around the world. Also, the potato crop was now guaranteed to be a success. The worries were over, and normalcy returned at once.

For me it meant cold side glances from people who knew they no longer had to depend on anyone for food, including me. They were no longer under obligations and therefore free to think what they liked.

Conan warned me there was talk. "They say you sold yourself to the lord of the castle so that you would be fed."

"Ah, yes," I said, "but do they also include themselves? Do they say that I alone would be fed, or also the village?"

"They speak only of you, as you very well know."

"Tell me, Conan, why don't you ask me the question everyone else asks in silence whenever we pass?"

"I have no reason to ask anything, Kate."

"Thank you, Conan. You are a dear friend. An only friend, I fear. I'm not sure how long I can remain in this village."

"You saved it from being wiped out, Kate. Not ten miles from here are three villages such as ours that no longer exist, for almost everyone died there. Those who did not left long ago. It could have happened here in Kilgort, but for you."

"Aye, Conan, I know. But you and I seem to be the only ones who do."

"You know, Kate, what I think of you. In all this time, I have never gathered the courage to ask—"

"Please, Conan, don't."

"I see."

"No, you don't see. If I loved you, I would marry you this moment, but I do not love you, Conan. Not to live with you, bed with you, bear your children. I would be miserable, and so would you. We are friends. Warm and good friends, nothing more."

"Aye," he said.

"I'm sorry, Conan."

"So am I, but there it stands, as you have said it. I will always be your friend, Kate, and if such happens that you are . . . in some kind of trouble, I will marry you then too, and be proud of it."

I kissed him as he left, and I felt warm in the knowledge of his friendship. I knew what he meant by telling me indirectly that there was going to be trouble. Each day made me more and more aware of what the women thought of me. With renewed success of the village itself, a priest had been obtained to say Mass each Sunday, and on Saturday for confessions. He called upon every household in the village, but remained away from mine as if it were the home of lepers.

I was growing angry, and I hoped I'd not betray this by exploding in the face of someone. It was Meg who finally made me explode. She informed me that when she had her baby, I was not to be in attendance. While I had never practiced midwifery, it had been customary for me to be there to lend what assistance I could. Meg sent word I would not be allowed in her house, and that sent me there as fast as I could walk.

She was in bed, though her time was still many weeks away. She'd been glorying in pity for her pains and her worries, but she sat up when I came in unannounced.

"You will have your baby," I said, "but you will owe its life to me, and that is an obligation you can never repay. Were it not for me, the child would have been born dead by now. Whenever you gossip about me, keep that in mind or you will be the most ungrateful person on the face of this earth. That is what I have to say, and nothing more. You are no longer welcome in my house, but I wish you well for the sake of your baby."

I walked out before she could make any response, though she'd been bursting to do so. I went home and sat alone. It seemed that was how I would spend the rest of my life.

FOUR

Mrs. Harnell, her arms akimbo, blocked the doorway to her cottage, from which I could hear the moans of her daughter who was in childbirth.

"You'll not be coming in here, Kate Moran. My grandchild is being born and I will not have the child near such as you for fear it will be blackened with your sins before it takes its first breath."

I said, "I was sent for. I have medicine now, fresh and good, which I know how to prescribe, thanks to the teaching of my father."

"The midwife sent for you, not me. She is not from this village and knows nothing of what happened here."

"Just what did happen here?" I asked. It was time to face up to this situation before it really got out of hand.

"You're asking me what happened? You know very well, Kate Moran, and you should be ashamed of yourself, bringing this blackness to us who live by the rules of heaven."

"I went to Cormac and begged him for food so you and others might live. Is that a sin, may I ask?"

"Begging is no sin, but paying as you did is the most dreadful kind."

"What did I pay, Mrs. Harnell? Tell me that. And while you're at it, tell me why you didn't go to Cormac begging for help. You or anyone else in this village."

"I do not have to answer your questions. You are not welcome in my house, and I bid you good morning."

"You are ignorant and stupid," I said.

"You are a whore," she screamed. "Whore . . . whore!"

I fled with my hands against my ears. Her shouting had attracted the attention of others, and doorways were filled with housewives who didn't need more than a glance at me running from that madwoman to know what was going on.

In my cottage I sat down and wept. They wouldn't understand. They'd gratefully accepted the food that had saved their lives, but now with full stomachs and no worries about future food supplies, they turned on me because, in their small minds, I had thrown myself at Cormac in order to gain the food. Even if it was true, I should have been the last person to be condemned.

That night, just before I went to bed, someone hurled a rock through my window. When I rushed downstairs and onto the street, there was no one about, and if I asked questions later, none would answer them.

Conan came next morning with tools and a pane of glass to fix the window, without my asking for his help. He set about the job and had it done in no time. Then he put the tools in the heavy wooden box he carried and sat down at the kitchen table for a cup of coffee, the only reward I could give him.

"Things are bad," he said. "There's too much gossip going about, and none of it good."

"Conan, I don't want you to come by again," I said.

He looked up, startled by the command. "What are you saying, Kate?"

"If you keep coming here to see me, they'll put you in the same boat as me. I suppose you heard I was called a whore yesterday, at the top of Mrs. Harnell's voice, which is no louder than a lion's roar."

"I heard, and I have gone about reminding people they are alive because of you."

"Oh, Conan, that they know, but while the food was fine and life-sustaining, they cannot abide the way they think I got it. The way they carry on, you'd well believe they were all guests in Castle Lucane while Cormac and I went about our sinning."

"It's their narrow minds," Conan said.

"I'm going to have to leave," I said. "There'll be no living here for me after this. In their minds I'm a wanton woman, and nothing I can do will change them—because they don't want a change. It gives them pleasure to think of me in that light. Then they do not have to be grateful to me for providing the food."

"Ah, Kate, darling, you're letting this destroy you. Pay them no need."

"After being called a whore? Conan, I couldn't stand that. I have some money. Not a fortune, but some, to see me through until I find a job. I'll be going to Galway first, because that's close. If I find nothing there, I'll travel all the way to Dublin or Belfast. But I will no longer live in Kilgort, where I was born and raised, and where my dear father and mother lie buried."

"You can't mean that, Kate."

"As soon as I can get packed and make some kind of an arrangement to be rid of this house, I'll be on my way, and don't try to change my mind."

"I will," he said. "Until you are on your way, I'll do my best to stop you. I might even follow."

I placed my hand on the back of his on the table. "Oh, Conan, please don't make it any more difficult for me. You'd die away from this village. You must remember that I am no longer a child, a little girl who needs guidance and a strong arm to help her. I'm a woman now. I have been for some time."

"Aye, a man half blind can see that. Oh, the thick-headed people of Kilgort. I could break their backs."

"They are surely breaking mine," I said, "and I have a feeling they won't stop until they're rid of me, which won't take long, I promise. I would rather you did not come back, but I know you will, so I won't ask again. Without you, Conan, surely I'd be lost."

"Something must be done," he said. "Something will."

And something was done, but not by Conan. That night I awakened from a troubled sleep to hear sounds downstairs. At first I paid no heed to them until they grew too persistent to disregard. I lit the lamp beside my bed, got into a flannel robe and slippers, and hurried down to the parlor.

The first thing I noticed was that the front door was not tightly closed. I stepped out into the night. No one was about—who would be at two in the morning? Someone had been here, though nothing seemed to be disturbed. I gave up trying to guess what had happened and began to climb the stairs. Halfway up, I turned back and went directly to the kitchen, where I opened the cabinet and looked in the wooden box in which were my father's gold watch and the money he'd left me. The box was empty.

I sat down, checked the tears that first threatened to flow, and instead swore a mighty oath that never again would I help anyone, nor would I remain in this town of narrow minds and thieves.

Then I worried. My money was gone. I'd never get it back. If I complained, it was likely they'd say the money must have come from the castle and that I was paid in more than food. None would ever admit to robbing me of everything I owned except this cottage. It had been no secret that I kept money in the house.

I went back to bed, for there was nothing I could do except weep, and I was far beyond that. I had but one escape left—Conan Hayer. I shook my head. I couldn't take advantage of the only friend I had in this world. But what would I do?

Things had changed now. I would have to beg for the sustenance that would keep me alive. As if anyone would grant me a morsel. This was a situation I'd never foreseen. So long as I had the money Father had left, I was fairly secure. With that gone, I was destitute.

In the morning, after about an hour's restless sleep, I made my breakfast, wondering with a wry laugh where my future breakfasts would come from.

Because I'd done it most of my life, I began to put the cottage in order. Everything I did was mechanical and mindless. I moved about as if asleep. No one came by, not even Conan, and this day I would have loved his company, if only to listen to his condolences and his renewed offer to marry me. Perhaps I would. There seemed to be no alternative now.

Right after noontime, the black stallion trotted down the village street with Cormac of Fion in the saddle. He was wearing a leather weskit over a heavy shirt, and a checked cap covered his head. With his polished boots and leather gloves, he was a fine specimen of manhood.

The sound of hoofbeats was still strange enough to bring me to the window, and when I saw Cormac dismount, tie his horse, and head for my door, I wanted to crawl beneath the carpet and never again come out.

He banged on the door loud enough to attract those who were not already glued to their windows and doorways to watch. Now all of their accusations would become true in their minds. This was the final proof of my infidelity. I opened the door and stepped back.

Cormac came in, his bulk seeming to fill the small parlor. He glanced about before he sat down.

"I've come for you," he said.

"You have, m'lord? That is grand of you, I will say. Most grand, and will you now get out of here? It's bad enough you came at all."

"I hear they're calling you a whore," he said with a grin.

"I don't know who told you that . . ."

"Conan. Conan Hayer came to me."

"Damn him," I exploded. "For a friend, he hasn't shown much wisdom."

"You were robbed of your last farthing last night. He told me that too."

"And how could he know? I've not stirred out of here to tell anyone."

"The man who robbed you has been treating everyone to drinks at the pub."

"And there'd be none to call him a thief," I said resignedly.

"I have come with a proposition."

"The answer is, never would I submit to you again."

"You're not being wise, Kate. There's nowhere you can go. No one you can turn to except possibly Conan, and he can do little for you."

"Do you intend to pay me in money now? Instead of food for the village?"

He looked at me with narrowing eyes. "Out of the softness of my heart I came here, but it is a softness I can dispense with quickly enough. Will you come to live at the castle and take care of the place you saw fit to call a pigsty?"

"And what else would I be expected to do, sir?" I asked as sarcastically as possible.

"Sleep with me on occasion."

"Aye, I thought that would be part of the bargain."

"Do you know where you can find a better one, Kate?"

"I do. With Conan."

"No! He is a fine man, a good man, but he would stifle you. He himself has told me you are not in love with him."

"You will please me by taking your leave now," I said.

"You're a fool. Look here, in a few weeks' time I'll be going away for perhaps a year or even more. You will have the castle to yourself, and plenty of money to do with what you wish."

"No!" I said in anger I did not try to suppress.

"Conan said you would be difficult."

"Conan can go to hell, along with you, sir."

"Kate, I happen to need a woman to take care of the castle. I know what it's become, out of neglect. I'll make you this offer now. Come there and take over the place, and I will not climb into your bed."

"The word of a gentleman, I suppose, m'lord?"

"I've been told I'm not a gentleman, but I do keep my word."

"I went to you once and asked you in a civil way to help the people of this village. You seized me and you raped me. The second time, when the village starved again, I begged once more because there was no one else to beg from, and I would have pleaded with the devil if that was possible, rather than return to you. So again I was raped. The ugly business of my first visit was repeated, and if I'd gone back a third time it would have happened again. I've had quite enough of gentlemen like you."

"Kate, if you will not come with me, I'll leave here in the next minute, and as I do, I'll toss a bag of coins through your door and tell you I got a bargain from you. Then I'll come back again and let it be known you came to me . . ."

As he spoke his threats, I listened, but barely. It came to mind that I had to accept. Otherwise there'd be little for me to do except turn into the whore I was accused of being. These were the thoughts of one so enmeshed in hopelessness as to think neither clearly nor well.

"I will be at the castle before nightfall," I said suddenly. I made that decision abruptly and on purpose, so that I'd not weaken and change my mind.

"Ah, that's being wise. Very well. In the late afternoon, I'll send a carriage for you. Wear the green dress and the bonnet. Take what you will with you. Leave the rest, for it will be safe enough once I let it be known you are now employed by me. I wonder if it ever occurred to these people that I own this village, every stick of it."

"Are you then responsible for sending a bailiff and the police to batter down cottages of those who cannot pay your rent?"

"It has been done, I suppose. I left that to my lawyers, though I did instruct them to demolish no more cottages until after the famine was over and the men had time to harvest their fields."

"I wouldn't care a whit if you razed the entire village," I said.

He arose, lifted me from my chair, and set his great hands on my shoulders. "I mean you no harm, Kate. I want you to believe that. You will come and live at the castle and be safe there. For as long as you like. And I swear I will never stand in the way of your leaving."

"I go, without the will to do so, because there is nothing

else for me," I said. "Your kind words do not influence or comfort me."

"As you wish." His fingers tightened on my shoulders and he thrust his face closer to mine. "I want one thing understood now and forever. I will not marry you."

It was my turn to throw back my head and laugh, uproariously, and in the silly fashion of near-hysteria.

"I would not marry the likes of you if it would save the world from coming to an end."

"Listen well," he said in a hard voice. "I meant that. Women are changeable creatures, but I do not change. I shall never marry. I shall never fall in love. The women I have must know that, as you know it now. Do you understand me, Kate Moran?"

"Aye, and have no fears, m'lord. It is more likely I will kill you than marry you."

He pulled me close and hugged me. "Ah, that's what I like to hear. This afternoon—a carriage. Ride out in style as befits the lady of the castle. And if there are those who are cruel enough to make you weep, tell them they are in arrears in their rents, as every man jack here is. Tell them their cottages will be given to the bailiff and his ram if you say so."

He tilted my head back and kissed me. Gently, for the first time. He slammed the door loudly as he left my cottage, and outside he spoke in a loud voice to his horse, mainly to draw attention to himself. Then he rode down the street all the way to the end, turned the stallion, and galloped back, yelling and waving as he passed my cottage.

I sat down limply. It came to me that I'd made a foolish promise that I could not possibly keep. I damned Conan for interfering with my life, though I knew he did it only for my own good. I feared Cormac enough not to continue challenging him, because he might even have picked me up and set me behind him astride the animal while he carried me off to the delight of all in the village. That would have been the absolute proof of my fallen virtue.

I sat there for perhaps an hour in the midst of the greatest quandary of my life. Of anyone's life, I would have guessed. I could sit here until doomsday and there'd be none to give a damn. I could face up to the village people and defy them to do anything. There was no gain in that, for they'd do absolutely nothing save shun me and let me know by glances, if not words, what they thought of a girl with a loose character.

I still could go Conan's way, but I simply would not let myself consider it.

So I had but one alternative. With no money, not even for the morning's pitcher of milk—if it would even be delivered—I could plan nothing, go nowhere. Just stay here and starve. I sighed at that idea, for starvation was what brought about the entire dilemma that now beset me.

Without really having made up my mind what to do, I automatically went through the house, wondering what I could manage to take if I left on my own. I was upstairs when I heard the laughter. I stepped toward a window overlooking the street just in time to see them drawing back the battering ram, which was aimed straight at the wall below my window.

It crashed against the wall, breaking it down and making the house shake. The ram was drawn back and delivered another blow that crashed right through the wall. The man who directed those operating the ram was Boyle Harnell, whose wife had called me a whore.

No doubt the dozen men gathered about were drunk, or close to it—on my stolen money—but it was no joke to me. I ran downstairs and out the door. They stood their ground, laughing at me, and I lost hold of my wits and my temper.

"Boys will have their fun," I said. "Ah, indeed, to knock a hole in the house where once a good and great man lived. Who broke his heart and his health doing for the village. And you, Boyle Harnell, with your boastful laughter. Are you having a fine time, may I ask?"

"You may," he roared aloud, and slapped his fat thigh. "If you wish, we shall take down the whole house and so be rid of you, which is not a bad idea."

"Boyle Harnell—and the rest of you—have you paid your rent yet? Now due for more than a year? Have you? Or would it be more to your pleasure—and your great laughter—to stand and watch your own houses cut to the ground so only a heap of stone is left?"

"The woman's gone mad," one of them shouted in fresh glee. "She talks to us as if she's a landlord."

I said, "Cormac of Fion is the landlord. He owns everything in this village, having bought it some time ago. Now, if you think I have slept with Cormac, do you not think I have some influence on the man? If I but say the word, he will have his bailiffs begin at one end of the street and not stop until there is no longer a village here."

"Kate . . ." Harnell approached me, bowing and scraping

like an idiot. "Oh, now, Kate, you wouldn't do that to an old friend."

He knelt before me, raising his hands in supplication. "Oh, Kate, I would be destitute. I've my own house for years, though not the land it stands upon, and I cannot pay the land rent. I beg of you, go to Cormac and ask him please not to destroy the village. If he stands aloof and refuses, go down on your back before him and he will do whatever you say."

The howling laughter did what my common sense had warned me not to do. It drove me straight into Cormac's castle. Into his arms, if that need be. I'd been taunted and laughed at enough. I'd been defiled so these ignorant people might live, and they reviled me for it. The famine and the dying were forgotten. Something new had arisen to grasp their attention and nourish their humor. The new subject was named Kate Moran. And now they'd not have to be grateful to her for saving their lives.

I turned my back, walked to my house, and closed the door. There was a gaping hole this side of the kitchen, but the men outside had given up trying to enlarge it, having had their fun with me. Upstairs, I packed the few belongings I owned, put things not easily carried into drawers and closets. I closed father's bedroom door for the last time. I'd touched nothing there. Now I dressed very carefully in the green dress. I put on my white bonnet, gathered up the two carpet-bags, and carried them downstairs, where I placed them near the door.

Next, I found a large piece of paper, and on it, in big letters, I printed a warning: "WHO ENTERS OR DEFACES THESE PREMISES WILL ANSWER TO CORMAC OF FION." I found suitable nails and fastened the notice to the outside of the door. Then I sat down to wait. Not for long. Cormac's carriage arrived with a coachman in a bright red uniform. He pulled up with a flourish, came into my house, and picked up my luggage, which he placed in front. Then he escorted me to the coach, removed his hat, and bowed as he handed me onto the back seat of the carriage.

This done, he returned to close the cottage door and to make sure the warning notice would not blow away. Then he climbed onto his seat and drove the carriage all the way down the street, just as Cormac had ridden his horse before he turned it around and drove all the way back. I sat in the middle of the back seat with my head high and my spirits low enough to be run over by the carriage wheels. I half-expected some shouted ribald humor, for the street was lined with people. No one uttered a sound.

"I was looking for trouble." The coachman turned his head and smiled my way. "And I'm sorry there wasn't any, because my orders were to use the whip on any who might try to stop us."

"It's well that you didn't," I said. "I am in enough trouble now."

"That you are, but they'll forget the whole thing soon enough, miss."

"You work for Cormac at the castle?"

"I've worked for him many years, aye. He has told me I am to take orders from you after this, miss."

"I assure you I won't be issuing many. What is your name?"

"Gavan Temple, miss."

"Thank you, Gavan Temple. I won't make any trouble or work for you."

"No matter if you do, miss. It will be my pleasure."

"At least you're a polite man, which is more than I can say for your master."

"Oh, he can be the fine gentleman when he chooses to be, and mean as snakes when that suits his fancy. Mostly he stays somewhere in between, I would say. It does not pay to rile him, nor does he submit to compliments and flattery. I will say that if you treat him fairly, that is how you will be treated."

"No doubt," I said. "I suppose he is at the castle waiting for my arrival?"

"Perhaps. I'm not sure. He was to ride close to the village and watch as you left. I think he believed there might have been a bit more trouble than I could handle. I'm near seventy, with more strength in my head than in my arms and legs."

I settled back for the brief ride, but within another minute I heard the sound of Cormac's stallion as he gained on the carriage and then rode alongside it.

"I heard you tell them off, Kate, and it was worth the listening. The one who acted like a clown in asking your pardon, or whatever he was doing—his cottage will be knocked down in the morning."

"Cormac, no," I exclaimed. "His daughter just had a baby."

"You told him what would happen, and happen it will. I'm glad you decided to come to me."

"It was that clown who made me decide," I said. "The one whose cottage you will destroy."

"Oh? Then I will not have it down, for I owe him something after all. Are you a good cook?"

"I have had no complaints, sir."

"Fine . . . everything you need is in the kitchen. I'll want my supper in about an hour."

"If it is possible to prepare it in that time."

"See that it is possible. Kate, you will dine with me. From now on you will eat all your meals with me, with the exception of breakfast, for there are times when I am still foggy with drink in the morning, and I will sleep then."

He rode on, spurring his horse to more speed. I leaned back once more and wondered what I'd gotten into. He was not on hand to greet me formally when I was helped down from the carriage. The castle door was open, so I went on in. Gavan carried my luggage upstairs, so I assumed there was a room assigned to me there.

I didn't take the time to look for it. Cormac wished his supper in an hour, and I would have it ready. So I went straight to the kitchen, by way of two or three other rooms I blundered into, until I was finally drawn to the kitchen by the smell of the stove, which was too well-stoked and looked as if it might melt if another piece of wood was placed in the firebox.

There was a room off the kitchen in which great cakes of ice were stored, making it cold as the dead of winter. Here was where sides of beef, lamb and pig carcasses, and about two dozen game birds were hung. I'd not seen the like of this before, and it appealed to me for its practical value.

I was by no means a butcher. My meat came already cut from the carcasses, but here I was on my own. I found knives, and I thought I did a creditable job in slicing off two steaks, one of double or maybe triple size for Cormac. There were potatoes too, and turnips, which I had not seen these three years.

There was no time to make either pudding or cake or bread of any sort. But in an hour's time I had the long table in one of the once-fancy rooms set with linen, somewhat yellowed by age, and silver sorely in need of polish. Two tasks I set for myself in the morning. Things were ready, and I went looking for the master. I found him in the great hall, practically obscured by the semidarkness in one of the far corners.

"M'lord, you wished supper in one hour. It is ready."

"Oh, good." He set aside his empty brandy glass. He grasped my arm tightly and propelled me into the small dining room, which, by some fortunate chance, I'd guessed was where he was accustomed to dine.

He sat down, waved a hand at the chair I was to occupy, and at once began to eat. He was no glutton, but it wasn't hard to tell that he was fairly starved to death in his castle of plenty.

"I'll have more of the same tomorrow," he said, as he arose. I'd not half-finished.

He was off, but I sat there eating because I was hungry and the food was better than anything I'd enjoyed in many a month. Afterward I washed the dishes. Handily, too, for the cookstove had, of all things, a sort of tank built into it so the fire that cooked the food heated water piped into his tank, from which it was drawn by a faucet over the sink.

One thing, I told myself, this kitchen had likely never had a scullery maid working there in a green silk dress.

I would have dearly liked to inspect this great pile of granite, but by night it was not an easy thing to do. Perhaps I was lucky, for it might be so far gone under layers of filth and dirt as to be impossible to clean.

Besides, I was bone-tired after the strangest and most frustrating day of my life. I found the great hall dark except for a single lamp burning at the foot of the grand staircase. I made certain all other lamps were dark before I picked up this one, climbed the stairs, and discovered to my great surprise and satisfaction that my carpetbags had been placed in a room where the bed was unoccupied. I had no idea where Cormac slept, but apparently he didn't intend to sleep here. I lit two more lamps, pulled down the bedcovers, to find them clean and fresh. I washed in the side room, where there was a sink and water that apparently came all the way from the stove in the kitchen.

I unpacked one bag to find my nightgown. I drew this over my head, blew out all but one lamp, which I placed on a little table beside the bed. I found the bed comfortable, and I lay back to begin wondering what all this would lead to.

So far it was quite satisfactory, and I was astonished not to find Cormac naked in the bed, demanding of me to hurry. Finally I blew out the last lamp, and my exhaustion claimed my desire to stay awake and think. I fell asleep at once.

The bed sagged as he clambered into it. I gasped and tried to sit up. His big hand pushed me down again.

"You didn't think I'd let this chance go by, did you? I want to talk. I'll stand for no fighting, and if you bite or scratch, I'll throw you out of this bed."

"I was a fool to think you wouldn't expect this," I said. "I should have known better."

"They were calling you a whore in the village, so you might as well start acting like one."

"Oh, you terrible man," I said. "Go to hell, Cormac of Fion. You belong there, for you have not one human instinct in your body."

"So I've been told more than once," he said pleasantly. "You're an armful, Kate. A delight when you don't struggle. Behave yourself now."

At least tonight he was gentle and not impelled to great haste by his carnal desires. There was no use in fighting him. I let him have his way.

FIVE

It was strange awakening next morning in a room I'd never seen by daylight. Lying there, trying to forget what had happened last night, I stared at the ceiling, because I thought, under the layer of soot from the large, well-blackened fireplace, I could see color, as if something had been painted there. I was so intrigued that I dragged a small table over to stand on. I could barely reach the ceiling with my fingers. I scratched experimentally, and it was true. There was something actually painted on the ceiling.

Now, in the spirit of this discovery and the fact that I was going to live in this castle for some time—if I could stand the master and his nocturnal attentions—I should learn all I could about it.

The bedroom floor, bare of carpet, and even more soiled than the ceiling, was of hard, durable, and well-grained wood. That much came through the layer of dirt. I began to wonder what the rest of the castle was like.

I washed, again with the luxury of warm water, so I supposed Gavan Temple, the man of all work, had started a fire early in the morning.

I wasn't about to wear out my green silk doing housework, or even an inspection of the castle. From my bags I produced a simple dark brown linen dress to work in. I put up my hair, held it in place with a ribbon. I drew on soft shoes, applied a little rouge, and then went grandly down the corridor between all those rooms, and even more grandly from the balcony down the staircase, which now I could really see.

I went down to the entrance hall, itself four times as big as my cottage back in the village. A few portraits hung on the walls, some aslant, none giving the appearance of having been touched by a dust rag in years. Here, too, a study of the ceiling, vaulted in this room, showed there was a painting to look down upon whatever visitors passed beneath it.

In the kitchen I set about making breakfast. For one who so recently had been on a diet induced by actual starvation, this kitchen and pantry contained a glut of food. I settled for eggs, wondering where they came from and how old they were. They proved to be quite fresh and excellent. There was no bread, but I found a tin of biscuits, which were a fine substitute. There was tea—perhaps fifty pounds in all, and of several varieties. Knowing little about them, I selected one at random, which turned out to be a deep orange in color, with traces of the fruit in its flavor and aroma.

I ate slowly and with relish. I was here, and I might as well enjoy it. So I drank three cups of the tea while I wondered if Cormac was awake yet, and if I was supposed to prepare his breakfast as well.

I thought about last night. He'd asked no permission to engage in his pleasure, and I could only consider the way he got into my bed after I'd gone to sleep as a demand upon my body. And afterward I'd gone to sleep in his arms.

I should have kicked him out of bed, I thought.

And so, with my morning spoiled by the memory of last night, I washed the dishes, cleaned up what little mess I'd made in preparing my food. Then, being of a practical if angry mind, I began investigating the kitchen and the pantry to see what was on hand. I thought that if the men in the village had ever known this much food existed not a mile from where they were slowly starving to death, they'd have come here to storm the castle instead of sending a girl to soften the master and obtain something to eat.

While I was engaged in this task, unhappily discovering how badly everything in both rooms needed a thorough cleaning, I jumped at the sound of what sounded like a church bell ringing two feet from me.

It was the door pull, but the bell, wherever it was, must be a huge one. I dried my hands on the apron I'd put over my dress and hurried to answer the door.

Conan stood there looking somewhat sheepish because he was calling on what could rightfully be called a house of assignation, where a girl he had known all his life and with whom he was in love was the principal performer.

"Conan, darling," I exclaimed in sheer joy. I hugged him and kissed his cheek, and taking his hand, I brought him into the reception hall. I'd no time to ask him any questions, especially what could have brought him here, for Cormac came marching down the grand staircase. He was fully dressed, which was a wonder to me, for I'd believed him still in bed.

"What do you want?" he demanded roughly.

Conan, who had removed his cap, almost brought himself to bow, but thought better of it at the last moment. So he faced this big man, eye to eye, and he spoke his mind as Conan was so wont to do.

"I came to see that Kate was all right."

"And what if she wasn't? What if you now saw her with bruises and lash marks and perhaps indecently dressed after the kind of orgy your village likes to dream about?"

"I would have struck a blow," Conan said frankly. "I would likely be flattened as quickly as I once was from your own fist, but you would have known I was here, I swear."

"Well, now, you did deliver a blow that near tore my jaw off, and I remember it well, because it was sore for a week after."

"I am willing to try again," Conan said.

"No doubt, but I'm not willing to risk having my jaw busted this time. Come in, man, and have a spot of brandy with me."

"Aye," Conan said in wonder. "That I will."

I walked behind these two veritable giants as they made their way into the great hall. They sat down facing each other, Cormac sprawled lazily in his chair, Conan sitting on the edge of his stiffly and uncomfortably.

"What are they saying in the village this morning?" Cormac asked with a laugh. "We gave them something to talk about, now, didn't we?"

"Aye, that you did."

Cormac glanced my way. "Fetch the brandy, woman. What are you standing there for, doing nothing?"

I fled to the dining room, where the sideboard was decorated with a row of decanters and bottles. I seized two glasses and one bottle, placed them on a tarnished silver tray and carried the drinks to the great hall and served them. By now the two men were talking as if they were old friends, and my heart warmed to this, for Cormac could have been a bitter and dangerous enemy, and Conan was too fine a man to have such enmity to deal with.

"Sit down," Cormac said to me.

I sat on a chair just to one side of them. I wanted to know if anything had happened in the village, but Cormac gave me no chance to enter the conversation at that time.

"So you're a builder, are you, Conan? Look about and tell me what you think of this place."

"It is in need of embellishment, my lord."

"Embellishment! Do you think you can do this place over and make it as it once was?"

I said, "Conan, darling, look straight up at the ceiling. In this room, the painting is quite clear. In other rooms, the ceilings are too dirty to see what lies beneath the layer of muck, but there's something, and I think it must be beautiful."

"Are you implying, woman, that the castle is dirty?" Cormac asked with a laugh.

"When one cannot clearly see a ceiling, or even the floor one's feet step upon, aye, the castle is dirty."

"She speaks her mind," Cormac observed dryly.

"That, Kate Moran has always done, sir," Conan said.

Cormac leaned back, slid a little farther out of the chair. "Once," he said dreamily, "this was one of the finest castles in all Ireland. It was here that those who came before me gave such fine dinners and dances as to rival those in the palace in London. It's true the beauty is hidden under soil and soot, but the beauty is still there."

"My lord," Conan said, "it is shameful that such wonders be wasted."

"That is no more than the truth," Cormac admitted. "Tell me, if I order Kate to redo this entire castle and its surroundings, do you think you could help, Conan?"

"I could not do it alone, sir. A dozen men couldn't. And I have seen but two or three of the rooms."

"Let me think of this," Cormac said. "A day or two, no more, so hold yourself in readiness, Conan, in case I say to go ahead with it."

Conan came to his feet, sensing the interview was over. Cormac arose too and extended his hand. "You're a man I can respect, Conan, and I have a feeling you're a fine artisan. Perhaps I'll find out. Kate, cork that damn bottle and give it to Conan."

"Thank you," Conan said. "I'll await your orders, sir. Good day to you. And to you, Kate."

I accompanied him to the door. Cormac remained in the great hall. I hugged Conan again.

"He's an evil man, but there is some good in him as well. I shall be fine here."

"It's best," Conan said. "They have read the notice on your door, and I was afraid they would tear it down and steal everything inside. I guess they're not quite up to that yet, fearing Cormac. It will be safe until they come to believe it is your warning and not his."

"Whatever they do, I shall not go back," I said. "I don't know what I'll do. Not stay here, for sure. Only until I find my own mind as to what I should look for."

"Kate, do you think he means it? About doing this castle over?"

"The man's mad," I said. "The whole thing has gone to pot so many years, it can't be done over. He's talking, that's all, and he's used to the dirt."

"Well, he told me to hold myself in readiness, and that I'll do. Just in case. He hasn't harmed you, Kate? Laid a hand on you?"

"Oh, Conan, I'm here for his pleasure—there's no doubt of that. I won't deny it. However, it's better than living in the village and being insulted. One thing, he is not a dangerous man to me. So far as others are concerned, I think he is a man who could easily kill an enemy. And he is no doubt the strongest man I have ever known, you included, and that's saying something."

"Well, now, maybe it'll all turn out well," he said.

I shook my head and spoke softly so Cormac wouldn't hear me. "It may at that, but not with me here. I can put up with so much and no more. We'll talk of this later."

Conan went off. If my problems worried him, he didn't show it, for before he was well along the road, I could hear him whistling, and when he did that, he was a happy man without a care in the world.

Cormac shouted for me to join him as I turned in the direction of the kitchen. Without being asked, I stopped to bring another bottle of brandy, which I set down before him.

"You're learning," he said with a grin. "Kate, what's that man to you? Have you ever bedded with him?"

"You ask that?" I exclaimed in high anger.

He nodded, and his smile grew broader. "I did forget, Kate. Forgive me. But since then, perhaps . . ."

"Just because they shouted whore at me in the village does not mean I am one. Not as far as you are concerned."

"Don't be angry. I only wanted to know."

"Would it make any difference?" I asked.

"I . . . don't know. You fascinate me, Kate. You're so outspoken, you drive me close to anger sometimes. Yet I like

it, coming from you. I think I would not like it if you forni-
cated with anyone else."

"And that," I said tightly, "is also the art of being outspoken."

"Let's say no more," he said. "You're right about the ceilings. All of them down here are covered with murals. Two or
three of the rooms upstairs are too. If I want this place done
over, will you have a go at it?"

"I'd not live long enough to finish the job," I said.

"No, it's not as bad as that. Conan knows his business, and
when I mentioned embellishment, his eyes lit up. He thinks
he can do it, given all the help he needs and sufficient
money."

"Is there that much money?" I asked.

"Kate, I'm a rich man. In some ways too rich, and in other
ways too poor. I can't explain that now. However, I can easily spare the fortune it would take to put this castle in order.
Will you take charge of it?"

"No, m'lord. To be honest, I care little for remaining
here."

"Would you leave me, Kate?"

"Aye, that I would."

"Suppose I left you? Would that change your mind?"

"I don't understand that, sir."

"I'm going away. Perhaps for six months, even a year. I'll
be back, you can be sure of that, and when I come, I'd like
to walk into a castle to which I can invite my friends."

I looked about. As Conan had been, I too was intrigued.
My father had taught me to love beauty and I had a feeling
that this castle could be extraordinarily beautiful.

"Will you stay away from me and not molest me again if I
agree?"

"No," he said curtly.

"Then my position here can only be as the whore they say
I am. Under those conditions, I do not think I am one to admire the beauty that lies under the dirt."

"Kate, will you try to understand me? I am not a man ever
to marry anyone, and yet I am in need of a woman. There is
no shame in that. Not for me."

"And for me?" I asked.

"I am not in a mood to discuss this, Kate."

"Nor I, so you will be kind enough to excuse me. I have
work to do. Even such as I must earn my keep by day as well
as by night."

"Go to the devil," he mumbled, and poured half a glass of brandy as I left the great hall.

There was nothing to do in the kitchen, a world of work to be done all through the rest of the place. The kind of work I doted upon, for it would likely be up to me to do all the planning and the giving of orders as to how things should be done. Just thinking of how his castle would look, properly restored, was a challenge. But I would not accept it. I would stay here until I had plans made as to my own future, until I could beg enough from Cormac to keep me, and then off I'd go. To where?

I sat down at the table and tried to figure that out. I was trained in the ways of a small village, to do what I could for the people there. To dispense medicine, attend those not ill enough to need a doctor, if there ever was one. But for me to attempt to live by this kind of work somewhere else, where I wasn't known, would be a disaster. In a big city, what I had to offer was worth little. I could not go back to Kilgort, even if Cormac's threats made the villagers accept me. I had too much pride for that.

I heard Cormac barging through the rooms on his way to the kitchen, and I braced myself for the angry tirade to be directed at me because I'd refused him. But he showed no anger, only a humility I never expected of him. He sat down at the other side of the table.

"It has come to me, Kate, that I must put this castle back to its ancient glory. It is now an obsession with me, and only you can direct the work."

"You already have my answer."

"Aye, but you can change your mind. I will promise you this. In four days' time I shall go off for months. I have urgent business elsewhere. During those four nights I will not come to your bed."

"Cormac," I said, "why the obsession when for years you paid no heed to the castle?"

"Because," he said softly, "I wish something of mine to endure beyond my lifetime." He raised his bowed head and his voice at the same time. "More than that, when the work is done, I will pay you what you ask. Be it two farthings or ten thousand pounds. And I swear I will hold you here no longer."

Suddenly, in this strange, sometimes brutal man, appeared that sensitivity again that I'd noticed before. He was like two different people.

"No expense spared, no questions asked?" I put it to him, for I was weakening fast.

"Agreed. I will arrange with a bank in Galway to honor any draft you may draw upon it. There is no limit. You may hire whom you will, buy whatever you wish. All I ask is that when I return, this castle shall be gleaming with gold and color, as it once was."

I was suddenly exhilarated to the point where I almost hugged him. Instead, I sat impassively, not letting him know how I felt. My future was indeed cared for now. For months I'd be busy here, and then I'd be paid respectably and sufficiently. Not for being the mistress of this man, but paid in gold for services rendered in the business of bringing beauty back to Castle Lucane.

"There is one room . . ." he said in a brooding kind of voice.

"Yes?" I asked, wondering what he meant.

"Have you seen it? At the very end of the east wing upstairs?"

"I have seen little, especially upstairs, sir."

"There is a room . . ." He jumped up, grasped my hand, pulled me out of the chair, out of the room, and clear to the second floor. He marched me to the end of the corridor and there threw open a door that led into a room totally dark, for it had no windows. I judged it was in one of the towers.

"Wait here," he said brusquely, and he entered and found a lamp.

It wasn't a large room, it was all but empty, containing only one piece of furniture—a small reading table on which rested a book so large and heavy-looking that I doubted I could have lifted it. A book done in faded red leather and big brass hinges. I paid scant heed to that, for at the other side of the room, just above the book, were five niches set into the wall. They were lined with what seemed to be gold leaf, for it shone with the richness of that metal, even in lamplight. In each niche was a bust. Four of the busts, all of men, were of white marble. The fifth, in the center, was black as a raven's wing.

"Look at it," Cormac invited. "The black one. Look!"

I stepped closer. "It's of you, sir. It's a grand statue of you."

"Kate, it is a thousand years old."

"But . . . the likeness is so perfect, the lines so delicate and clear."

"No question of that. These gentlemen, Kate, are my fore-bears, who lived over a period of hundreds of years."

"The room," I said, "is in fine order. Like the castle will be when you return."

"I have kept this room because it is sacred. To me, at least. Have you noticed the great book?"

"Of course," I said. I placed a hand on it, and he quickly and roughly brushed it aside.

"Do you read Gaelic?" he demanded.

"No. I haven't the least education in Gaelic."

"Good. If you ever study it, and you read this book, I'll have your head, and I mean that literally. This is a private book, open only to me. Is that understood?"

"I have no wish to pry into your family history," I said. "The book is safe with me."

"See that it is. No one else must enter this room. Before I go, I will lock it securely and take the only key with me. When I come back, I expect to find nothing changed in here."

"Except that it will be nearly as dirty as the other rooms are now."

He thought about that. "True, Kate. Aye, that's how it would be. I will trust you with the key, but the door must be locked except when you go in to dust."

"As workmen go about doing what must be done," I said, "there will be great gobs of dust in here. I will allow no one but myself to enter. Does that satisfy you, sir?"

"It does. You're a wonder, Kate. You are no doubt my salvation, though I will say you could be better in bed."

"Sir, we'll have none of that. You promised."

"So I did. I'll try not to break the promise, but remember, I am a man, and we are alone in this castle."

"You promised," I objected with fresh worry.

"The hell with you," he said, and walked out of the room. I closed the door and decided I might as well begin my planning up here. From the second floor there was an archway that led to the very thick walls, wide enough to walk on. The walls were almost up to my shoulders, spaced with arrow slits and occasionally larger windows to accommodate guns, I supposed. To have stormed and taken this castle would have been a genuine feat, even in these days, for it seemed to me it could be defended against almost any army.

All the way around to the west end of the battlements, I came to the top of that unique stairway leading down to the ground. In the face of all that had been expended on these walls, battlements, windows, to make the castle assault-proof, this stairway seemed to defeat every other defense the castle could offer.

But there it was, a mystery along with that room of the five busts and the Gaelic book, and not for me to solve. My task was to restore the castle.

The next morning I set about it with an honest vigor. I had my meals with Cormac, though he seemed exceptionally silent. I saw little of him during the day, but as time went by and he kept his promise not to come to my bed, I mellowed toward him to a degree that I came quite close to liking the man.

"You are called Cormac of Fion," I said one evening. "Do you not have a first name, for I know that Cormac is your family name."

"I am called Mack," he said. "Mack Cormac. It's well you asked, for my friends call me Mack, and you'd not know whom they were talking about when I invite them here after you have finished your work."

"I suppose there will be many great ladies among them," I said.

"Kate, could it be you're showing a twinge of jealousy? I hope you are."

"Never," I said. "I cannot be jealous of a man I care little for, after what you did to me. I ask only because I must know how to decorate some of the bedrooms to suit the taste of your ladies. Or do you entertain them only in your room, as they go there to satisfy your hunger?"

"They come to me," he said. "You are the first who has compelled me to go to her."

"They are ladies and gentlemen of the court, no doubt."

"Most of them are not even ladies and gentlemen," he said with a laugh. "Kate, when I come back, stay awhile. Go to Galway and order all the dresses and dinner gowns you wish. Have them sent from Paris. It is on my mind that, of all the ladies who may come, you will be the most beautiful. And the best dressed. That is how I wish it."

"Thank you, m'lord," I said. "From what you just told me, I will also be of the same moral character. And I'm not sorry I said that."

"How many times must I say to hell with you? You're a sharp-tongued woman, Kate. I do not care for a tongue that drips with acid."

"Then I beg your lordship's pardon," I said. "I forgot that I am in your employ."

"That you are, so remember it," he told me brusquely before he left me alone.

I didn't mind. I was too engaged in planning what must be done. Before the day was over, I asked Gavan to bring in a tall ladder. I climbed to the top of it with a pail of soapsuds hanging off my arm and a stiff brush and rags tucked into the band of my apron. I applied soap, water, and brush to the ceiling in a long, rather narrow room that Gavan had pointed out as the formal dining room. The one where Cormac and I had dined was the family room.

This was a room for affairs of state. The table of oak had thirty-two leather-covered chairs around it. By pushing these chairs closer, I estimated forty people could dine here at the same time and with sufficient elbow room.

I cleared away a fair section of the ceiling and let the colors of the beautiful mural painted there come through. With Gavan's help I moved the ladder and climbed it to wipe off some of the chandelier crystals so I could see how well they sparkled. Next I washed down part of a wall to reveal the pale red paint beneath the cracking plaster.

There was elaborate plasterwork around the ceiling mural, and more of it on the walls. Behind the head and foot of the table were roundels in plaster decorations.

This was but one of the rooms. I'd counted seven on the first floor, excluding the entrance hall, which was practically the size of a house by itself. Upstairs were sixteen bedrooms, and that was only in the main building. The two wings contained suites of rooms for guests—five in each wing. Three rooms to a suite, all large. All could be most attractive when the work was finished.

I'd never been faced with a task as huge and compelling as this, yet I welcomed it. Partly because it would keep me occupied so I might not think about the circumstances that brought me here. Nor what I had really been in this castle up to now. It was a challenge I welcomed, for from this I might emerge as a competent decorator.

On the fourth night, I awoke suddenly, aware that I was not alone in my room. I sat up. The darkness was too intense to see anything, but when I listened, I could hear breathing.

"Who is it?" I asked. "Speak up!"

"I want to get into your bed," Cormac said tensely. "I have

been sitting here for an hour. I could not sleep knowing you were so close."

"You gave me your word . . ."

"Aye, and the word of a Cormac is kept. But you could invite me."

"I will not," I said.

I heard his chair scrape, and I braced myself, for in a moment he would literally throw himself upon me. Nothing happened. I called his name in a whisper. There was no reply. I lit the bedside lamp. I was alone in the room, and for a little while I thought I'd dreamed the whole thing. It had been real enough. Probably he would be back before dawn. I couldn't stop him. I could only damn him for breaking his word. I fell asleep finally, and I was not disturbed during the rest of the night.

I dressed and went downstairs to really begin my work. Gavan was in the kitchen dumping firewood in the box near the stove.

"Good morning," I said. "If you've not had breakfast, I'll be glad to make it for you."

"Thank you, miss, but I eat mine in my own little cottage."

"You live within the castle walls, then?"

"Aye, down near the stables. To see that the horses are all right during the night. It's a fine place for the likes of me."

"Then I will get breakfast ready so that when Cormac—"

"He is gone, miss. He left before daylight."

"Gone? On that long journey of his? He won't be back?"

"Not for many weeks, miss. He left orders with me. I'll tell you of them if you wish."

"Gavan, where has he gone? For what purpose?"

"To somewhere not far from Dublin. To kill a man."

"Kill . . . ? He is going to fight someone? To the death?"

"Aye. It happens often that he is required to do this."

"Gavan, what if he is killed?"

"He cannot die, miss. He cannot be defeated—until the last time and it is ordained. . . . I will say no more, for he would not wish me to. But you will not worry, miss, for he'll be back. He always comes back, and this time I'm surer than ever that he will."

"I'm glad you are," I said. "I can't be that sure, if it is a fight to the death."

"He will be back because of you, miss. Because of you."

SIX

I began my planning next day by having Gavan drive me to Galway, where I visited the bank Cormac had designated. I was received with the same attention that would be given a queen, and catered to by every employee from tellers and bookkeepers to the president of the bank. There I learned that Mack Cormac had not exaggerated. At my disposal was an unlimited amount of funds. I was issued a book of checks for my use, and I requested a nominal sum for everyday purposes. When I left the bank, I felt like a millionairess.

"I can't have you driving me about," I told Gavan. "I'm going to buy a sidecar and a new horse."

"Aye, and it would be best if you also saw that you were properly outfitted with riding clothes, miss. For it is easier to ride a horse to the village and about the grounds than to use the carriage or a sidecar."

"I'll do that," I said with an emphatic nod. "I shall visit a dressmaker at once. Now, there must be many things needful to your part of this task, so I will give you cash enough to buy whatever you wish."

I turned over a substantial sum, had him drive me to the most fashionable seamstress shop in Galway, and there he left me, to be picked up in two hours. The poor man had to wait two additional hours, for I didn't stop with a riding habit in black, with a white shirtwaist, a red weskit, and a derby. I also decided to obey Cormac's order that I be ready to dress for his company, so I ordered four new gowns, plus day dresses, selecting patterns just in from Paris. Along with shoes and complete accessories.

How suddenly my life had changed, I thought on the way back. I had been a despised girl without a sovereign to her name, but I now controlled what to me was a fortune, and I was spending some of it on myself, which I deemed quite proper under the circumstances.

Then the real work began. I left it to Conan to find the artisans, and he had my permission to hire men from the village who had driven me away under conditions I deeply resented, but we needed hard larborers, many of them, so while I forgave the village in no respect, I was not about to spite myself by refusing to hire these men.

The artisans came from Galway, some from Belfast, and others from cities and towns where they had worked on some of the great Irish castles. Within a week's time the castle grounds were alive with workers, and the customary calm was broken by the sounds of hammers and saws and shouting of men. I conferred with the experts in fretwork, in the installation and repair of mantels, in restoring murals. I came to know all about plasterers and masons, carpenters and their helpers.

Following their advice and using my own judgment and Conan's, I had them begin with the great hall. In my opinion, it was the most important room in the castle. I had it completely done over. Its arched ceiling was repaired and painted white. I had the old fireplace torn out and a new one, even larger, with the mantel supported by two carved nudes, installed. With Gavan's help I discovered treasures in the attic and basement, which saved a great deal of money in furnishings. From this treasure trove came the huge mirrors I placed in the great hall. I found furniture in a French motif, high-backed with red plush seats and backs. The room's four beautiful chandeliers were taken down, thoroughly cleaned, and equipped with fresh candles. The attic yielded some extremely fine and no doubt very valuable tapestries that had somehow escaped the usual decay so prevalent in the castle. On the walls of this large room they were shown splendidly.

The small drawing room I had done in red with a white ceiling; a bright red carpet now covered the now-gleaming floor. I had an ample supply of paintings of all types, and I utilized many of them in this room.

The main drawing room, four times as large, presented a different problem, but it was surmounted after careful planning and much work. Here the oak floor was restored and left uncarpeted. The walls in this room were paneled, with each square an individually carved scene. I purchased chairs covered in pale lavender to contrast with the dark wood paneling. I used various side tables from other rooms and the attic, but in the center of the room I had placed an enormous round marble table.

The bedrooms were done in various color schemes. Three-quarters of them were intended for women. The others were in a heavier style, more suited to male visitors who came alone.

The halls were freshly and expensively carpeted and the grand staircase was made to shine as brightly as the chandeliers lighting it.

Some seven months later I was able to walk through the castle, no small feat in itself, to inspect the rooms and give to each my approval. I had also seen to it that the gardens within the castle walls, which almost entirely filled the castle park, were restored with brightly colored flowers and green shrubs. All the trees were pruned, those adjudged sick were cut down, and new, nearly full-grown ones were brought in.

Sometimes the amount of money I was spending frightened me, but the Galway bank cheerfully informed me there was still no limit. By mid-spring of the following year, the castle was ready. And none too soon, for my first letter from Cormac arrived. It was brief, a few lines only, informing me of the date of his arrival and saying that he would be bringing friends. He didn't say how many, what sex, or how long they'd stay. I would have to get used to this irresponsibility on his part.

But then, I didn't intend to remain much longer. He had promised to pay me for my work. I had established what I deemed a fair and reasonable sum, which, a year ago, would have seemed an impossible amount to be presented anyone, no matter how much work had been done. Dealing in Cormac's money had made me forget what it was like to consider a pound sterling as a respectable sum.

With the knowledge of his return, along with guests, I proceeded to hire maids for scullery and upstairs work. I had already retained men to care for the stables and the grounds and to do the heavy work around the castle.

Three days before he was due to arrive, I began thinking about Cormac of Fion again. There'd not been time to devote to this before, but now that the work was done, the castle fully restored, the memory of him returned. I'd been extremely careful to keep up that strange tower room with the large book and the busts. Beyond applying a dust cloth, I had made no attempt to examine the great leather-covered book. It was none of my business. Besides, he'd warned me it was written in Gaelic, which I could not read.

The night before his return, I lay in bed dreaming, as I'd

grown accustomed to do in these days of luxury and now lei-
sure. I decided I'd really missed Cormac. Despite his vile
temper, his seemingly insatiable desire for a woman, I came
to remember best those rare moments when he was a soft
man, an endearing man.

I prayed he would approve of what I'd done, and the afternoon of his designated arrival I had one of the maids help me
into the best of the several gowns I'd purchased. This one
was dark green in color. I remembered he'd chosen a pale
green gown for me, and if I stayed within the range of that
particular hue, it might please him. Besides, it complimented
my hair and my eyes.

As when I just went to see him, I center-parted my hair,
but this time I drew it up on the sides, allowing it to cascade
down my back in curls. I was lucky to have hair with a na-
tural curl, so it took little time to arrange. Earlier I had found
a metal-bound cask of old jewelry in my room. From it I
chose a diamond-and-emerald brooch shaped in the form of a
peacock. I suppose it was an indication of vanity, for I felt as
proud as one. Though I'd been supplied with an endless sum
of money to accomplish it, I'd transformed the castle from a
filthy dungeon to a structure of magnificent beauty. Cormac
could not help but be proud of it. Over my shoulders I
draped a shawl of fine silk. Yes, I had accumulated quite a
wardrobe, adding to my original purchases from time to time
when I was in Dublin and Galway. As the castle improved in
appearance, so, I hoped, did I. It wasn't all vanity. It would
have been sacrilege to be less than elegantly dressed in what
was now a splendid castle owned by a fiercely proud man.

Prior to getting dressed for the occasion, I went first to the
village to purchase supplies. I anticipated four or, at most, six
guests for whom I must provide food. Nowadays in the village I was treated with a coldness that I believed came
mainly from jealousy, but also with considerable respect.
With Cormac no longer in residence at the castle, there was
no more talk of my submitting to his lovemaking, though
memories were long here, especially about such scandalous
subjects, so I did not try to deceive myself that all was forgiven. These people would never forget, nor stop speculating
on my ultimate finish. Nor refuse Cormac's money—from my
hands.

Late in the day a man from a stable in Galway arrived,
herding twenty new saddle horses, and I began to suspect that

there would likely be more than six or eight guests. It was too late to do anything about that, though I did have the maids prepare every bedroom in the castle, upstairs and in the wings.

I had the table in the main dining hall set with silver and china, and I was prepared to set the table in the family dining room as well, at a moment's notice.

I was eager to see Cormac again. I felt this eagerness was due to the fact that I'd worked hard for eight months and I wanted his approval of what I'd accomplished. I wanted to hear his great shout of joy. I wasn't worried that he would again force his attentions on me, for he'd have too many guests in the castle to risk that. Not long after meeting Cormac's guests, I realized this was only the assumption of a country-bred girl.

They arrived earlier than I had anticipated. However, I was already dressed when two coach-and-fours pulled up in midafternoon, and I stood by the open door to welcome them.

The gentlemen lifted the ladies down from the heavy vehicles, to their cries of delight. The men were as loud, and there was much laughter and cavorting about, which made me suspect they must have been drinking rather heavily during their journey from the railroad station. Or perhaps even before, judging from the way the drivers turned about and departed hastily, as if relieved to be rid of their mad throng of noisy passengers.

The guests were young, older than my nineteen years, but still under thirty. They were very well dressed, and with them came so much baggage that it was piled up in a sizable heap. No one paid any attention to it. That would be my province, to somehow sort it out and have it placed in the proper rooms.

I saw Cormac then, for the first time. He had an arm around a lanky, giggling girl with straw-colored hair who had so much of it piled on top of her head, she must have been wearing a hairpiece. She was attractive, and from the way she clung to Cormac it was quite obvious she was willing to oblige him in any way he might suggest.

I had no more time to speculate on the guests, for as they entered the castle, some handed me wraps and hats, others flung them at me, and two merely hung them on my shoulders as if I were a clothes tree. No one spoke to me.

Cormac was the last to enter, still encumbered by the blond. He glanced at me and nodded. That was all. Eight months this man had been away, and upon his return he greeted me with a nod, not even a spoken word. I felt as if I'd been slapped in the face. Ridiculous as I felt and certainly looked, encumbered by garments, I managed a dignified nod.

Inside the castle, the guests ogled the decorations and the restoration I'd accomplished with so much work, my back still feeling broken from my efforts. Cormac was barely inside the great hall when he drew the blond girl to him and kissed her with outrageous abandon, at which spectacle the guests howled and cheered.

I was too startled and overcome by the attitude of these people to know what I was doing. I managed to hang up their things, and then went to the kitchen to warn the serving maids and the cook that they were going to have to earn their pay serving this crew Cormac had brought with him. Moments later I heard shouts for brandy and wine. I dispatched the girls to provide the refreshments. I eased myself wearily into one of the kitchen chairs.

Gavan Temple came in, sweating some from having had to contend with all the luggage and the horses brought in the day before. He too sat down as if he were bone-weary.

"What manner of man is he?" I asked. "To return after such an absence without even greeting me. To have provided all that money to restore the castle, and he never even looked about at what we've done. Is the man mad, Gavan? Or an ungrateful boor?"

"Aye, that you will think many times, to be sure. Yet he is not mad. Strange, perhaps, and promiscuous, but he has not taken leave of his senses. He will know what you have done, and in his heart he will appreciate it, though he may never give voice to his thanks."

"These people he brought with him—where in the world did he find them?"

"They are of the society in which he is popular in the cities. They are young, many are rich, and all they live for is to get as much pleasure from life as they can wring out of it. You will find them cruel, inconsiderate, and impolite at times. You will have to put up with it, Kate."

"Oh, no, I will not," I said. "Cormac and I have an understanding. It was that when he returned, I would be paid for my services whenever I made the demand on him. And I would be free to leave whenever I wished. I think I will go tomorrow."

"You will be doing yourself a disservice, miss," Gavan said quietly. "Cormac often grows tired of these people quickly and sends them away."

"Doesn't the man have a single ambition in life?" I asked.

"I'm afraid . . . he does not."

"But everyone alive must have some kind of ambition, make some plans," I argued.

"Aye, but not Cormac. He is different."

"In what way, Gavan? And why?"

"I cannot answer that, miss. It's a fool I am, for I have said too much now. I do not care to talk about him more, only to say that it is easily possible to misjudge the man."

"Have you spoken to him since he returned?"

"No. He will have to settle down some before we talk."

"I shall give him one more chance," I said. "Only one, Gavan, and if he does not respond, I shall pack up and leave as soon as possible."

"That is your right," Gavan said. "I will have my supper now if you will tell the cook I may. Later I'll be too busy handling these people."

"Handling them?" I asked, puzzled by the word.

"Put them to bed. Usually they are too drunk to climb the stairs."

"Tomorrow," I said, "I leave or they do. I will instruct the cook. And then I will put Cormac to the test. The final one."

I gave the word to the cook, and then I went upstairs by way of the stairway used by the servants. I didn't care to pass through the reception hall or the great hall. I knew well Cormac's guests regarded me as a servant, and that's how they'd treat me. I was in no mood to be pinched or lewdly kissed. I wondered if Cormac regarded me as a servant too.

In my room, with the door closed, I prepared to put Cormac to the test, as I'd warned Gavan I would. I took down my hair and put it up again in a far more attractive fashion, this time arranging a few ringlets across my brow. Then I put on one of the Paris-designed gowns. It was of fine silk, a pale lavender in color and off the shoulder, with a pronounced dip in the middle allowing more than the usual cleavage to show, according to the newest vogue. My gown was likely more *à la mode* than anything Cormac's guests had seen, for I'd been assured this was the fashion for next season, not the current one. It was supposed to be worn over several petticoats. I used but two, so the gown remained soft enough to flatter my figure. I applied rouge, but more expertly than the ladies downstairs seemed to have used it. My slippers were soft, matching the gown in color. I'd tried this outfit on before, in the process of selecting the one I had meant to wear at Cormac's return. This one, I had judged, did the most for me. Looking at my reflection in the bureau mirror, I smiled bitterly. Why would he notice this gown, when he ignored me in the lovely tea gown I'd selected for his arrival?

Still hopeful, I went to the head of the grand staircase and waited until several of the guests were assembled below, everyone drinking and talking in loud voices. Then I began to descend the staircase. I knew it was a perfect descent, for I'd practiced it secretly. The laughing and roistering stopped, and all eyes were upon me. The other guests—and Cormac, happily—came to see the cause for the reduction in noise, and they too watched me descend.

As I reached the floor, one of the men sprang forward and pulled me into his arms. I struggled, but he held on, laughing and turning me about in a fashion that was making me dizzy.

Suddenly this man was torn from me and hurled to one side. Cormac stood before me, his eyes glittering in anger.

"What are you made up for?" he demanded angrily. "How dare you interfere . . ."

My eyes blazed in anger, and I gave free rein to my tongue, for I'd never been angrier in my life.

"I am made up, as you call it, to greet you, Cormac. I made myself as attractive as I could so I might meet with your approval. For months I have worked to make this castle livable and beautiful, and you have paid no more heed to it than you have to me. So the devil with you. And your castle." I turned away toward the stairs. Then I looked back. "And your friends as well," I added.

I went up the staircase with what dignity I had left, which wasn't much. And if my anger knew few bounds a moment ago, it went even beyond that point when I heard Cormac speak.

"She is a village girl with more gall than brains. I'll attend to her later."

"Cormac . . ." The man who'd grabbed me spoke up with

a loud laugh. "I will pay you ten pounds to let me take care of the wench, for she is most attractive."

"Mind your own damned business," Cormac growled.

That was the last I heard, for I returned to my room and almost ripped the gown off, refraining from that by my decision to take it with me when I left, along with everything else I'd bought for myself. I would demand payment for my services in the morning, and then I'd be on my way. I had no idea where to go, but so long as it was away from Cormac, I'd be satisfied.

I was in no mood to give vent to tears. I was too angry for that. Instead, I began packing. Downstairs, the roistering grew louder, and it kept on until very late. By the time they finally quieted down, after the guests with rooms upstairs had shouted their way along the corridor, I was already in bed. With the final silence my anger dissipated, to give way to the tears I should have shed long before.

I was accustomed to disappointment and frustration. My life had been full of both since the famine began. I'd grown tough enough to cope with almost anything, but this was too awful an experience to pass over.

For all those months I'd worked from sunrise to well after dark, arguing with the artisans and the tradesmen, demanding perfection of merchants. I had an easy time of it only when I needed more money, for the bank never once questioned an expenditure.

Now the work was done and Cormac had returned. So far as I knew, without any conception of what had been done to the castle, and, by his attitude, probably caring even less. I told myself, as coldly as possible, that I should have expected it. This man cared for nothing. Ordering me to do the castle over at any expense had been no more than a whim. Probably meant to calm any anger and resentment at what he had done to me. I wondered if he'd regaled his friends with the whole story of the country girl who had come begging for food for her village, and being taken by him forcibly, only returned to ask for more food. He could, quite likely, have made quite a big joke of this.

I went to bed feeling sorry for myself, drained of all anger and filled only with doubt as to what my future would be when I left the castle.

Finally I blew out the bedside lamp, prayed that none of these wild ones would decide more roistering was preferable to sleep and keep me awake all night. I was tired to the point of sheer exhaustion, augmented by my disappointment over Cormac's attitude.

I fell asleep immediately, perhaps as an escape from my troubled mind. The last thing I thought of was to wonder if Cormac would come to my bed this night. Perhaps to lavish his passion upon me, more happily, to tell me he was sorry. At that moment I think I would have preferred the man's passion, rather than no attention at all.

Therefore, when the bed sagged under an additional weight, I came half awake, and when an arm went about me and a hand explored beneath my nightgown, I didn't fight.

"Oh, Cormac," I whispered, "how could you have treated me so abominably? Never a look or a compliment."

He didn't say anything, but he employed his hands more busily than ever. He lifted himself, braced with one hand, and he used the other to part my legs, and then he was upon me—and at that moment I felt whiskers brushing my face. Cormac was clean-shaven.

I pushed at the man, I screamed as loudly as I could, and I fought him with all the strength I could summon. He wasn't as strong or as heavy as Cormac, but I was no match for him. He was breathing hoarsely, and there'd be no stopping him.

Then the door was flung open, and someone with a lamp came in. Suddenly the weight pressing upon my body was relieved and the man pulled off the bed. I sat up in time to see this man hurled against the far wall by Cormac.

The man slumped to the floor, stunned by the force of his collision with the wall. Cormac stood over the bed. Others were in the room by now. Cormac glared at me. I was seated with the bedsheet pulled around me, and I was too confused to utter a word.

"Did you invite him in?" Cormac demanded.

"I was asleep," I said. "I did not invite him, as you should very well know."

"I believe you, because I know him. But since when does a young lady not secure her bedroom door by night?"

"I mistakenly trusted in you and your friends to behave like ladies and gentlemen."

It was the skinny, straw-haired one who came to Cormac's side. "If you believe this strumpet in the face of Jack's denial, you're a fool."

"I haven't heard Jack deny anything," Cormac said.

"Give him a chance."

"You will oblige me by keeping your damned mouth shut, Ellen," Cormac said.

One of the men came forward. "Mack Cormac, do you realize what you've done?"

"I'm not quite sure," Cormac admitted. "But I don't think Jack asked anybody's permission to get into bed with this girl."

"A little fun," the woman called Ellen said. "That's what we're all here for. A little fun."

"If," I said with the small amount of dignity left to me, "you have all had your little fun, you would oblige me by getting out of this room so I may dress and leave this accursed place."

"Shut up!" Cormac snapped. "I'll talk to you later."

"There may not be any later for you," one man warned Cormac. "Jack isn't going to let you get away with this. He's possessed of a violent temper."

"Who cares?" Cormac thundered, still in a rage.

"You will, when he challenges you, as he very well will."

"Let him."

"Mack, have you forgotten he's one of the best swordsmen in England?"

"Whatever he chooses to do suits me, so we'll find out what the gentleman desires."

Cormac lifted the still-groggy man to his feet and shoved him roughly up against the wall. "You're a bastard, Jack. This girl works for me, and my employees are to be respected, even by the likes of you."

"I'll kill you," Jack said. "I'll gut you, Mack. Let me get my wind back, give me a rapier, and I'll attend to you. No man hits me and gets away with it."

"I did," Cormac reminded him. "Now you're talking about a duel. Fine! That suits me."

"My seconds will call—"

"The hell with your seconds. I've got dueling rapiers. We can settle it right now."

"While I'm still weakened by your blow? You'd like that, but it won't work. In the morning, after I'm rested, then we'll see."

He raised a hand and slapped Cormac across the face. I had heard this was a customary preliminary gesture to a duel, but perhaps Cormac hadn't heard of it, for in return for the slap he struck this man a blow that rapped his head against the wall and caused him to slide down on the floor again. Cormac picked him up, carried him to the door, and threw him into the corridor. Then he herded everyone out of the room, stood at the door a moment looking back at me before he slammed the door shut. Silence took over the castle moments later.

I got up and put on a day dress. There was no sleep in me. I didn't know what to do. I sensed that the man Cormac had struck was regarded as an expert with a sword and Cormac was not. That I gathered from the talk of his friends. Cormac had actually risked his life to protect me, and I felt grateful for that.

I wanted to go to him and ask him to apologize to this man they called Jack. I'd even go to Jack and plead with him, but I realized neither would do the least good. Jack was a hothead, now doubly insulted by being hauled out of my bed and assaulted twice in front of his friends. He would be determined to rectify that insult, and the only way, under his code, was to kill Cormac.

I needed both help and advice. This was a matter I was unable to handle alone. There was one person I could turn to. If Gavan Temple was not awake, I would arouse him. Something had to be done, and quickly.

I drew a shawl over my head and shoulders, opened the bedroom door quietly, and listened there for a few moments to make certain no one was still abroad. When the silence assured me it was safe to go, I tiptoed down the corridor, down the grand staircase, and let myself out the front door without making a sound.

I walked along the front of the castle to an entrance through the high wall which led me into the castle grounds proper. It was a dark night, but I knew the paths here as well as I knew my own bedroom. I began to run now, in my haste and growing fear for Cormac. When I reached the little gardenhouse not far from the stables, I saw a weak light in the window. It made me think Gavan was probably awake. I tapped on the door and whispered my name.

Gavan, fully dressed, with a lighted pipe between his teeth, let me in and closed the door behind me. His cottage was ample and pleasant, made so by leftovers from the castle small enough to fit in this little dwelling. It was tidy and clean.

"What's happened?" he asked. "You're all in a dither."

"Cormac is going to be forced to fight a duel, Gavan. He'll be killed."

"A duel, is it? With one of them monsters he brought home?"

"Aye, one called Jack."

"And what brought this on? As if I couldn't guess, you're so worried about him."

"A man named Jack . . . a very terrible man, came to my bed and tried to rape me. Somehow, Cormac heard me scream and came to help me."

"This happened but a short time ago?"

"Aye—not a half hour."

"Cormac was on his way back after visiting me. He must have been right outside the door when you screamed."

"So that's it. He came to see you, Gavan? He didn't give me more than the bat of his eye and a word or two not spoken in a friendly way."

"He was upset, Kate. About you. He said you were not decent in dress."

"Oh, that man," I exclaimed. "His friends wore gowns lower than mine, and the way they were cavorting about, I wouldn't try to guess who slept with whom this night."

"That's the way of it, lass."

"Still, Cormac struck this man twice, and he was slapped back as a challenge to a duel. Do you know of this man called Jack? Is he a fine swordsman?"

"Aye, the best. He has fought many duels and is considered unbeatable."

"What can we do to stop this, then? Cormac will surely be killed."

"And would you grieve over his coffin, Kate?"

I was stunned by that statement to the point that I couldn't reply.

"You're not a shameless hussy who would give herself to a man no matter what the conditions were," he went on. "I know that if you bedded with him you were raped. Perhaps more than once. I know of your anger and hatred for him. So why do you worry if he is killed?"

"Because I wore myself out fixing up this damn castle," I said in loud exasperation. "I want the man to at least look about and tell me I did a good job—before he is run through."

"And that is the only reason, Kate?"

"I don't know, Gavan. I don't know. But the duel will be fought over me, and I will not have it. I will not stand by and let Cormac be killed."

"He will not be," Gavan said quietly.

"You say that, but Jack is a master of the sword. You said so yourself. Cormac fights with his fists. What good are fists against a sword?"

"Kate, Cormac will not be killed. Not a month ago he fought a man in Belfast and killed him. This man was supposed to be the strongest and best fighter alive. He challenged Cormac openly many times until Cormac was finally forced to oblige him. They fought for three hours without letup, and in the end the other man died. Cormac finally broke his neck. If Cormac had been badly beaten in that fight you would still see signs of it on him. Scars and stitches. Have you seen a one? He wasn't even scratched, though the fight took three hours."

"Fighting with fists is one thing. But against a swordsman who is so skilled, it is a plain fact that Cormac will die."

"Would you care, Kate? Tell me now, would you really care? After what he did to you?"

I said, "Yes, I would care."

"I had that feeling, lass. Are you in love with him?"

"No. I hate him. But I would not wish to see him dead, for there is some good in the man when he lets it come through."

"That is how we will let it stand, then. But, Kate, if you ever come to believe you are falling in love with him, come to me. It is important that you do."

"You speak in riddles."

Gavan laughed curtly, without mirth. "The man himself is a riddle. Mind you, now, come to me before you fall in love."

"You're making it seem such a mystery," I said. "Is there something about the man I should know?"

"There is something about him you should *not* know at this time," Gavan said. "Now, go back and get to sleep. There'll be excitement enough in the morning."

I left him, more sorely puzzled than ever. Here was a man Gavan admired, almost worshiped, and yet he displayed no concern about the fact that Cormac was to fight a skilled swordsman with little chance of defeating him. I walked slowly back to the castle and let myself in. All the excitement had died away, and the castle was quiet in this dead of night. I lit a lamp kept just inside the door and carried it up the stairs. At the landing, looking down the length of the corridor, I saw weak light coming from the room at the far end. The tower room, which contained that strange book and the five ancient busts. No one had any business there, for Cormac had declared it private. I began walking rapidly toward it, just as Cormac himself emerged.

He closed the door to the room, after extinguishing the light, and walked slowly in my direction. Without a word he took my elbow and piloted me into my own room, where he seized my shoulders and looked straight into my eyes.

"If you lied before, say so now, Kate."

"If I lied about what, may I ask?"

"Did you invite that popinjay into your bed?"

"Would I have been screaming for help if I had?"

He let go of me. "No. I should have known. What are you doing up at this hour?"

"I went to see Gavan Temple," I said.

"Ah, yes, and what about?"

"You, of course."

"And what did Gavan have to say about all this?"

"I don't know, because I don't understand the man."

"Why did you go to him in the first place?"

"You are to fight to the death tomorrow."

"Why should that concern you?"

"Because the fight is over me. And . . . and . . . you owe me a lot of money."

Cormac sank slowly to the edge of the bed, where he practically held onto his sides in his laughter.

"It is true," I said, irritated by him now. "You do owe me a great deal of money. For doing over the castle."

"Oh, Kate, I'm aware of that. It was your answer that gave me the first real laugh I've had in months. And a fine bit of work you did with the castle."

"I didn't think you'd even noticed."

"Ah, but I did. I'm dazzled by it, if you want the truth, and I've not yet even seen the whole place."

"It has cost you a fortune," I reminded him.

"I'm satisfied with it, no matter the cost."

"The castle is another reason why I want you to arrange with this terrible man that the duel be called off."

He shook his head. "I can't do that, Kate. In the first place, he wouldn't listen. He's been aching to fight me for years. But I had to be sure that he deserves this duel. That he was entirely to blame for what happened."

"He was," I assured him. "I told you that before."

"I had to be certain," he said slowly. "I would not like to kill him without sufficient reason."

SEVEN

I arose early and in time to supervise the preparation of breakfast for the party. Not that I cared for any of them, but Cormac would demand this service for his guests, and I could not reasonably deny him that right.

They straggled down, all of them now well-acquainted with what had happened during the night. Conspicuously absent was Jack, the man who had come to my bed with the intent of violating me. The women looked at me with amused smiles, though not one addressed me. The men were singularly intent on not even looking my way if they could help it. I concluded that Cormac's reputation as a fighting man with a short temper was well known to each guest and they wanted no part of what the despicable Jack would suffer for his indiscretions.

Cormac was the last man to arrive, and he looked the worse for wear, like a man who had indulged once too often. His rugged features looked haggard and his hands trembled as he ate. He never favored me with so much as a glance.

He did, however, enter the conversation at the table, and although I withdrew quietly after seeing they had all been served, I remained well within hearing distance as the talk turned to the duel Cormac and Jack would fight before the morning was over.

"He might listen to you if you're willing to apologize," one guest suggested.

"I'm not in the habit of apologizing," Cormac said blandly.

"But you must know of his record with a blade."

"I've heard he's supposed to be skilled," Cormac admitted.

"He is more than that," the spokesman warned. "When he was fourteen, his uncle disapproved of something he did and went out to fetch a switch to beat the boy. Jack was waiting when he returned. His uncle had the switch, Jack had a saber. He ran his uncle through."

"My dear Peter, that does not make him a hero. Though I do like the saber aspect," he added thoughtfully.

"More a villain, I'd say. But he went to France and studied swordsmanship under the best teachers, until he was good enough to teach the art of dueling himself. And he was good enough, Cormac, to become a *maître d'armes*."

"He's a bloody Englishman, and I don't like him."

"Mack, listen to us! He likes to kill people. He glories in it."

"All the more reason to be rid of the man," Cormac said cheerfully.

I stood transfixed in terror. Cormac wasn't listening to them. He regarded the upcoming duel as lightly as if it were no more than a horse race. I wanted desperately to go to him now, even if the others heard me, and beg him to reconsider. I even thought, wildly, that I might tell Cormac I had lied and that Jack had come into my bed by invitation. As quickly, I rejected the idea. He wouldn't believe me. It would serve no purpose other than to increase his anger toward his opponent, and that would make him more vulnerable.

I ran back to the kitchen and on outside, so no one would see my tears. I remained there for five or six minutes to recover my wits, and then I went back to listen again, drawn there because I had to know what was going to happen.

Jack had apparently come down to breakfast. I didn't let anyone see me, and a maid served breakfast to the latecomers.

Cormac's voice was calm and steady. "Have you changed your mind?" he asked.

"Never! Don't bother to apologize. I will not accept it."

"I've no intention of apologizing," Cormac said. "I thought you might consider it."

"And why should I apologize? I was struck, not once, but several times. You are the one to apologize, but it is too late for that."

"May I ask you something?" Cormac said.

"If it is a civil question."

"Do you always have breakfast before you fight a duel?"

"I fight well under any conditions. In a few moments I will run you through, Cormac of Fion."

"Will you, now? I was thinking more of another way to duel."

"You cannot talk me out of this," Jack warned, "except by admitting you're a rank coward."

"You challenged me," Cormac said. "I was the one who was slapped. So, under the rules of gentlemanly conflict, I may name the weapons and the conditions."

"You spoke of rapiers . . ." Jack said indifferently.

"Oh, come now, that's no way for strong men to fight. I suggest sabers. I understand you are proficient in the use of such weapons, especially against a man armed only with a switch he should have used on you."

Jack must have been stunned by that suggestion, for I heard him draw in a sharp breath, but he wasn't to be put off.

"Sabers, if that is what you wish. I'm as handy with a saber as a sword."

"On horseback," Cormac said quietly.

"What do you mean?" Jack asked. His anger was rising now, along with his voice.

"You're good at everything concerned with killing a man. Why not try it from the back of a horse? I'll furnish you any mount in my stable."

"We ride at one another and fight?" Jack asked.

"Something like that. We'll bring the horses to the top of the castle walls. They are five or six feet thick. Plenty of room to ride each other down, and neither of us will be able to avoid direct combat. Now, that's a fine idea. Original and intriguing. What do you say, Jack?"

"It's insane."

"Oh, then you reject the idea? Maybe I'll let you." Cormac's voice suddenly abandoned its bantering tone and grew deadly serious. "If you go down on your knees and admit you tried to rape a girl in my house. An employee of mine. No doubt you're an expert at rape, that likely being the only way you'd get a girl in your bed. No—even if you beg, I won't agree the fight is off. It's on, as soon as I get a man to lead the horses to the castle walls. Be ready in half an hour. I'll turn over the sabers to anyone you suggest. I have them. That's all there is to it. We've no need to talk any more. Someone pour me another cup of coffee."

"Mack, you're out of your mind," one of the men said.

"He's a perfectionist with any kind of weapon," someone else warned.

Cormac laughed aloud. "But did you see him turn pale when I suggested horses on the castle walls? That disturbs you, doesn't it, Jack?"

"I'll cut you in two with the first slash," Jack shouted in a rage that I think Cormac deliberately led him into. He stormed out of the dining room and went upstairs.

I waited where I was, hoping for a chance to see Cormac alone. If I barged in now, it would only enrage him. Finally he arose and left the room along with all the others, to allow me to sit down at the table they had just vacated.

I told myself that I'd brought this on with my low-cut gown, leaving my shoulders bare, moving proudly among the guests. Cormac was going to be killed, surely. I had to talk to someone. Once again I left the house through the kitchen door into the castle grounds, surrounded so grandly by the thick walls Cormac had chosen as the dueling place.

I was in time to hear the sound of a reluctant horse being urged up those stairs, and presently the animal was outlined against the sky. Gavan had led the horse up the stairs, and it was Cormac's mighty jet-black stallion.

I returned to the house, made my way upstairs in haste and continued out onto the walls. By the time I reached Gavan, another employee had managed to coax a second horse up those outside stairs.

"Gavan," I said, "it's a terrible thing they're about to do. Fight with sabers, on these horses . . . on the walls."

"Aye." Gavan wagged his head. "It's one I never heard of before."

"How can you be so unconcerned?" I demanded. "Cormac won't have a chance with this man."

"Now, I wouldn't say that, miss. He's got a better chance, if you ask me. I'd best get things ready. They'll be here any minute."

I retreated to the wall on the opposite side. There was a great distance between me and the scene of the battle, but I didn't want to be close. Though it seemed everyone else did. The guests emerged onto the wall, the men well-dressed, the women in their afternoon finery. Then Jack appeared, soon followed by Cormac, who hadn't changed his attire and wore the same black trousers and white ruffled shirt, open at the neck. Behind him came one of the guests, bearing two sabers covered with a white cloth.

There was some sort of preamble, accompanied by gestures, but finally it was Cormac who marched off down along the wall toward his black stallion. Gavan, with the horse meant for Jack, passed Cormac without a glance his way, and I'm sure no word was spoken. These two were indeed madmen, for neither seemed in the least worried about the out-come.

The man with the sabers took a post between the two horses, beside which stood the contestants. At a signal, the men advanced until they were prepared to accept the sabers, which were ceremoniously revealed by the whisking off of the white cloth. I damned them for making such a formal specta-cle of this.

Now the pair again retreated to where their horses waited. They mounted, made passes through the air with the sabers to test their weight. The man who held the white cloth de-cided he was in a risky position when the fighting began, so he beat a hasty retreat until he was behind Cormac. Then he gave a shout, and the duel began with both riders holding the sabers' points forward to try for a first blow. I held my breath and stood motionless. It seemed as if even my heart held its beat. The horses were understandably skittish, being driven hard on a six-foot-wide walk with a considerable drop off either side.

Cormac lifted his saber high to give it a mighty swing, but Jack was so skilled in all manner of fighting to the death that he flung himself to one side, and his saber, instead of slashing at Cormac, slit the throat of the black stallion with a single deep cut.

The horse gave a brief, nerve-jarring shriek of agony and then toppled toward the edge, falling off it as Cormac leaped from the saddle to the safety of the castle walk. He still held the saber, but he was no longer interested in the duel. He was looking down at the final struggles of that magnificent ani-mal he'd sacrificed to this insane idea.

I screamed. So loudly my throat became raw, but he'd not heard me. Not only because of the distance, but mainly be-cause the other women were screaming also. Some, out of horror; others, to warn him.

Cormac straightened up, to see Jack bearing down on him astride his horse. His saber was poised for a quick and fatal pass. Cormac did what no sane man would ever have done. He stood in the middle of the castle wall and deliberately threw away the saber he held.

Jack howled in joy and aimed for his helpless target. The saber came down, but Cormac wasn't there. He'd nimbly sidestepped at the last possible instant, and before the horse passed by, Cormac reached up and hauled Jack out of the saddle. It took Cormac two seconds to tear the weapon from

Jack's grip. Then he picked the man up, so easily it seemed a miracle. He raised the struggling victim over his head and marched down the walk to the point where it was breached by that strange flight of stairs. He stopped there, turned, and with one heave threw the screaming victim down the steps with such force that he bounced halfway down and performed two somersaults before he reached the bottom, where he lay still in a crumpled heap of broken bones and torn clothing.

A second after Cormac had hurled the man down the steps, I was running as fast as my legs would carry me. I made it all the way around the castle wall, risking my own neck on some of the turns when I came too close to the edge in my haste.

Cormac had walked back to where his stallion had gone over. Gavan appeared, to lead the other horse away. Cormac bent over the edge of the wall and peered down at the silent hulk of the stallion. The guests had also grown silent when Cormac hauled Jack off his saddle, and they were still silent, awed by either the strength and dexterity Cormac had displayed or by the horrible, bloody deed performed before their astonished eyes.

I was at Cormac's side, and I seized his arm. "Oh, Cormac, I'm sorry about the horse. . . ."

He gave me a push that almost sent me off the edge of the walk. He looked at me with a glance so baleful that I trembled. He did nothing more. He walked along the crowd, pushed his way through his friends, now clustered close to the entrance of the castle. He disappeared inside. His guests followed slowly. I was stunned, frightened, puzzled, and remorseful all at the same time.

It was as if Cormac blamed me for the whole affair and for the death of his stallion. No matter. In all my life I'd never seen a braver man in battle, nor a stronger one. I was sure Cormac had never believed for an instant that he would not win. Gavan was of an identical opinion, I knew. Cormac was a great fighting man, and they both knew it.

I was actually afraid to go into the castle because of Cormac's rage. He wouldn't listen to my words of happiness over his victory. He had pushed me aside with the same contempt he'd have used if I had invited Jack and all of his male friends into my bed.

So I decided it was wise and healthy to stay out of his way for the time being until that monumental rage subsided. I walked quickly to the head of the outside stairs and went on down them. Gavan or someone had dragged the body to one side. Gavan saw me descending the steps and met me at the bottom.

"That man—is he dead?" I asked.

"Busted his fool neck. As who wouldn't have, being thrown down the steps like a sack of potatoes. I'll get him buried soon as I can. And believe me, miss, when I say Cormac saved many lives by killing this man. There'll be many who won't have to face his swordsmanship that was so good he made entertainment out of his challenges."

"You were so sure Cormac would win," I said. "Why were you certain, Gavan?"

"You saw him!" Gavan's eyebrows rose sharply. "You know the kind of man he is. How could he lose?"

I nodded slowly and walked away. I studiously avoided looking in the direction of the dead horse, and I returned to the castle by the front door.

It was the one called Ellen who saw me and shouted for me to stop, which I did, not knowing what she wanted with me.

"You," she said, "fetch brandy and glasses for all of us, and be quick about it."

Before I could think of a suitable reply, she was back in the great hall. I went into that room, to find all of the guests assembled, none of them looking very happy. Cormac wasn't with them.

I didn't care to make any further trouble for him. He certainly had had more than his share. I brought the brandy and glasses on a tray and set them down on the big marble table.

"You're not bad." The man who made the statement eyed me with the same lust that was in his voice. "I wouldn't mind having you curled around my legs any night of the week."

He laughed, and the others joined him. For a moment I wondered if they were going to share me among them, for the men were closing in slowly, while the women watched with hooded eyes, finding some kind of weird pleasure in listening to the men tantalize me. I'm not sure what would have happened, had not my Irish tongue and nature come to my rescue. I put my hands on my hips and managed an amused smile.

"Well, now," I said, "I might be willing to oblige the gentleman if that's what he wants."

"I think she means it." The man who had addressed me stepped closer.

"Because Cormac would then kill you, which you would rightly deserve. And your friends would enjoy watching."

He stopped short, then backed away. I turned around to leave.

It was the one named Ellen who, as before, gave me orders as if I were a scullery maid.

"See to getting all the luggage down here, save mine," she said. "At once, do you hear me? And if you touch a thread of my clothing, I'll have your head."

My first wave of joy over the departure of these people was sadly tempered with the knowledge Ellen had not been summarily sent away. It was difficult to conceal my dislike for her, though I managed. I sent one of the maids to fetch Gavan. When he came, I instructed him to bring down the bags and to harness whatever vehicles were needed to transport the guests.

Then I went up to my own room, and I felt safe, for I knew I was under the protection of Cormac of Fion. It was a good and wonderful feeling.

I sat down, uncertain what to do, and what my future here might be. Our agreement was that when he returned and the castle was in satisfactory order, I would be paid and be free to leave. But that had been months ago. He might have changed his mind, and, strangely enough, I found myself hoping he had.

Until I remembered Ellen, with the thin face and the flat figure, who gloated over the fact that Cormac had not sent her packing along with the others. If he kept her on, it was for one purpose, and I tried to convince myself that I didn't care. We had made an agreement before he left, and now it was time to fulfill it. If only I knew where I was going and for what purpose when I left Castle Lucane.

My house still stood in the village. Conan had repaired the hole battered through the wall, and no one attempted to go near the place for fear of incurring Cormac's wrath. Whenever I visited town, it was like going to a strange place where I wasn't known and I knew no one. Not a soul offered to speak to me. Many averted their eyes as I passed by. Families for whom I'd struggled, sometimes successfully, to save someone from the ravages of the famine, now refused to acknowledge that I existed. It gave me cause for great anger, but I held back, on the theory these poor people didn't know what they were doing.

In the midst of these none-too-cheerful reflections, I heard Cormac storming down the corridor, and I held my breath. He opened the door without so much as a tap on it, let it slam behind him, and sat down on the edge of the bed facing my chair.

"It's time we had a talk," he said.

"Indeed it is," I agreed.

"I want to know one thing. When I was fighting that *shpalpeen* of a braggard, you were so worried I saw tears in your eyes, and when I was to be warned that he meant to ride me down and cut off my head, you yelled the loudest. Now, it was in my mind that you hated me for what I did to you during the time of the famine. So why were you carrying on that way, may I ask? I would have supposed you'd enjoy seeing me killed."

"You . . . owe me money for my services in restoring the castle. If you were dead, where would I get it?"

"So you're sticking to that answer."

I wanted to tell him I was afraid for him because I didn't hate him any longer, but the words refused to come. I remembered all too well the first time I came to the castle, and the second time, when the same thing occurred. Granted, those two events happened months ago, during times that were anything but normal, but I didn't believe that excused Cormac.

He was eyeing me sharply. If he felt disappointment at my answer, he gave no indication of it. I'd spoken my foolish words, and I could do nothing but complete the picture I gave him, of wishing only to be paid off so I might leave. It was time to finish the final break with this man, and my heart was shattered to even think of it. I asked myself, in those few seconds, if I was in love with him, and I rejected that idea promptly. I could not love a man who had enticed me into the castle and raped me twice.

"So," I said, "I'll begin packing. We shall have to come to terms about how much my services were worth."

"They were priceless," he said. "I can't let you go, Kate. Stay on, make your own terms, but don't abandon me now."

"You need me?" I asked, and the unhappiness that had fogged my brain lifted as if by a miracle.

"More than you could know. If I must apologize for whatever I once did to you, then I do so now. I want you to stay."

"For what purpose?" I asked bluntly.

"Not to grace my bed. There are plenty of women for that. I've placed you above them. I swear you'll be as safe in this castle as if you were in a cathedral."

"And what of her?" I gestured in the general direction of the door to my room. There was no need for names.

"She stays this night."

"After that?" I asked. I disliked being so candid with this man, but it was needful for my own peace of mind.

"Why don't you wait and see? And why the hell are you so interested in my personal life?"

"I have to live with you, Cormac. I have to know what to expect."

He arose abruptly, his features stormy. "Do what you wish, then."

He was at the door when I spoke again. "I'll stay."

"Good," he said, and went on out, letting the heavy door slam. It opened again after a second or two, and he stuck his head into the room. "The devil take you, Kate Moran, but don't change your mind."

I promptly unpacked the little I'd made ready for my departure, and I was content, in a way, though not wholly so. Now I was installed in this castle, probably in full charge of it, so that Cormac, after his many and lengthy trips elsewhere, would have a fine place to bring his friends back to.

That was all right with me, but down the corridor from my room was the one called Ellen, and Cormac had urged her to remain after the others left. I hated her intensely. She wasn't a person one could take to under any circumstances, so while she was in this castle I would avoid her as much as possible. Only in that way could I conceal my dislike of her. I didn't ask myself why. There was no need. I knew very well why I resented her presence.

I had committed myself. I resolved not to change my mind. At least I was secure here and no longer under the threat of being again violated, for Cormac had given me his word, and I respected it.

I changed into a heavier dress, more suited for my work, and I went downstairs to see that the kitchen was in order. Two carriages were just leaving, taking to their respective homes the servants who did not sleep in. Cormac had stipulated he wanted none of them living in the castle, for, he claimed, they'd adopt it as their home. In reality, he wanted them gone so they'd not be able to carry any tales about what went on, and I had a fine idea there was a great deal, when Cormac was in the mood for days and nights of roistering. I told myself quite firmly that what Cormac did was his own business. Mine was to keep the castle in order and see that meals were served on time and that they were never less than perfect.

Cormac had given no instructions as to when his supper was to be served, and the help had left because of the lateness of the hour, so it was up to me now. I decided Cormac liked thick, red-centered steaks. Certainly not the kind of food that skinny female upstairs would have chosen. So, thick steak it was, with potatoes baked in the oven and a gravy made from the drippings of the steak. If there was a green salad, she'd be likely to concentrate on that, so there was no salad, and I selected a wine that was none too good. Cormac drank whiskey with his meals, so he'd not mind the inferior wine.

I waited patiently for some sign they'd be hungry. What they were doing upstairs I knew well, and it bothered me, and I wouldn't listen to myself telling me it was not my business.

I began moving about the first floor, admiring the results of those weeks of hard work. Truly the castle was a thing of splendor, and I was proud of it.

Cormac came storming down the grand staircase quite late. I waited in the hall for him, and he cast a baleful eye my way.

"There will be supper, I hope?" he asked.

"Aye, it will be ready when the great lady comes down, and not before, for she is a guest."

"She's an idiot," he said with a sly grin. "But quite satisfactory, Kate. She may be bordering on stupidity in some ways, but in other ways she fills a man's need."

"Indeed," I said, gravely insulted by his frankness, which I knew was deliberate and meant to rile me.

"She'll be down in five minutes. Go about getting us something to eat, woman."

Ellen didn't like the steak. It was too rare, but Cormac said it was just right. She hated baked potatoes, and I stood mute, not offering a substitute. If she expected me to wait on her like some serving maid from the village, she was mistaken. She drank her wine and, to my disappointment, seemed to like it. When she glanced significantly at me as she set down her empty glass, I refrained from taking the hint, and let her pour her own wine.

For me it was a satisfactory supper; for Ellen, an impossible one. Cormac never knew the difference, though it did please me to see him reach over and spear the steak Ellen had barely touched, to devour this with a gusto that appealed to me.

Cormac brought the meal to a close by scooping up the brandy decanter and his glass and marching off to the great hall. Ellen arose slowly and threw her napkin onto her plate. She looked at me with a scowl.

"I'll have your head sooner or later, you country bumpkin. You'll not take him away from me."

"I'm pleased your highness enjoyed her supper," I said quite casually as I began clearing the table. She marched off to join Cormac.

By the time I had the kitchen in order, it was quite late. I took time to trim the wicks of several lamps in need of it. Tomorrow the maid in charge of that chore was going to hear about it. When I completed the task, I carried one of them to the hall. From the great hall I heard the sounds of Cormac's half-drunken laughter and several squeals from Ellen. I walked up the staircase as grandly as I could, though there was none to see me.

I had not yet gone to bed when I heard them coming upstairs and on down the corridor past my room. The way Ellen was carrying on, and from the heaviness of Cormac's footsteps, I gathered he was carrying her, and she was protesting like a virgin on her wedding night. A door closed with the authority of Cormac's foot behind it, and peace settled down over the castle. With the exception of two rooms: in one, Cormac was enjoying Ellen's favors, and if I knew him, rather noisily, for I suspected they were both somewhat drunk when they went to bed; in the other, I was trying to restrain the tears and not submit to loud crying, which was what I felt like doing.

By the time Ellen was ready to come down next morning, I had everything ready and the servant staff standing by. I supposed Ellen slept late, especially after a night of such activity, but I finally went up to see what was delaying her. At Cormac's door I could hear him snoring lustily. From Ellen's room came the sounds of someone moving about. I decided not to cater to her. Breakfast was ready, and it was time she was told.

She opened the door in answer to my knocking and glared at me through eyes that were red from lack of sleep and, possibly, from a rage possessing her to the extent that she began throwing things about the room after she let me in.

"Have the best carriage ready in an hour," she said. "I want it clean, not a speck of dust. Do you understand?"

"Aye, that I do, your highness. May I ask where you are going? So I may tell the hostler what to expect."

"I'm going to that filthy little town the railroad runs through."

"Aye, you're leaving us, then?"

"If I asked for the use of the carriage, would I be doing anything else? Now, you get a move on. I want breakfast in ten minutes, and don't serve any of that slop you deliberately served last night."

"It will be as madam desires. Did Cormac make known any wish to breakfast with you?"

"Cormac probably won't wake up until tomorrow, the drunken fool."

"Then I'll let him rest," I said as I turned away.

"Just a minute," she said. "I haven't dismissed you yet."

"I beg your ladyship's pardon," I said, maintaining a calm that infuriated her.

"I've seen the way you look at him."

"May I ask whom I'm supposed to have looked at?"

"Don't bandy words with me. You're in love with him."

I smiled graciously. "I'm the housekeeper of Lucane Castle, madam. I look to Cormac's comfort, and that is all."

"I know well the way you comfort him. Understand me now. I'm going to marry Cormac."

"When he gives me the order, I will prepare the castle for the wedding," I said. I didn't believe a word she said, but I continued to humor her.

"The first thing I'll do after we're married is fire you."

"Madam will not find the need, for the day you and Cormac marry is the day I leave the castle. Breakfast and the carriage will be at your ladyship's disposal whenever you are ready."

I left the door open and walked calmly down the corridor. I didn't believe her. I said so mentally a hundred times. I did not believe Cormac would ever marry the likes of her. In a week's time she'd drive him insane with her stupidity and her dominating nature. Before that week was out, there wouldn't be a servant left in the castle. None would put up with the likes of her.

And yet, I argued on my way down the stairs, it was possible Cormac, in a softness brought on by his passion and her guile, had asked her to marry him. If he had, he'd go through with it. I could only hope and pray she was making it all up. Or, by some chance, if it was true, Cormac would have retained no memory of it when he awakened.

"What," I asked cook as I passed through the kitchen, "are you serving her excellency?"

"A slab of ham, miss."

"Burn it," I said, and went on out the door into the castle grounds. I crossed them to the opposite wall, and still I felt the need for more exercise to cool the wrath that threatened to consume me. It hadn't been easy to control my temper. Through one of the smaller exits in the wall, I went outside the castle proper, to find Gavan driving by in the carriage I'd ordered for Ellen. He pulled up.

"You're looking like the face of Beelzebub when he's unknowingly stepped on sacred ground. It's too fine a day for that, miss."

"I'm mad," I admitted. "The way he carries on."

"You mean Cormac and his women? Aye, I'll be the first to admit he's often in need of a woman and cares little for who it might be."

I wasn't flattered by that remark, but I could make nothing of it, naturally. "She says he's about to marry her, Gavan. Do you think he'd marry the likes of her?"

Gavan was suddenly very serious. "I don't know. One day he'll plan to marry. Of that I'm sure. But it won't be for some time, and if she says he's about to marry her now, she's lying, and I can testify to that."

"You're talking in riddles again, Gavan."

"Aye, I suppose I am. I'd best get the carriage there. The driver is putting on a fresh uniform. Her ladyship, may the devil take her, complained that he was not fit to be driving a carriage. That was when the crew of them were returning and leaving her behind."

"Be sure to tell the driver he must get her to the railroad depot in plenty of time. If she misses the train, Cormac will have the driver's head, and if he doesn't, I will."

"Aye. It's a fine morning for a walk, miss. By the time you get back, she'll be gone."

"For how long?" I asked. "I'm getting scared, Gavan."

"It'll be some time, if ever, to my way of thinking, miss."

"I wish I was sure of that," I said.

"More than likely she'll never be back. He cares naught for her. Not in his heart."

"Has he one, Gavan?" I asked bitterly.

"Aye, he has that, miss. He hates to show it, being the kind of fighting man he is."

"Why does he have to fight? What's there in it for him? Tell me that."

"He fights because that is his nature. What's in it for him? His life, miss, that's what's in it. There are those who defy him because they think they are better than he. As yet, there is no one who can beat him."

"You say that as if you expect one day there will be," I said.

"Aye, it happens. Without fail it does happen, but before it does, Cormac will lead the kind of life he enjoys. And the devil take those who do not agree with him."

"I'm still not well able to understand the man. Will I ever, Gavan?"

"I cannot say. Except this. If you do not, no one ever will."

"And that, too, is one of your riddles. What's the meaning of that strange bare room with the big book and the busts?"

"So you've seen that, have you? With Cormac's permission, I trust."

"He took me there."

"It's for him to tell you if he wishes. And you're very inquisitive this day, if I may say so."

"It's the only way I can find out anything about him or the castle. Gavan, was he really well-pleased with what we did?"

"Aye, many times pleased and grateful. He will not forget what you did for him."

I felt content with that statement. "Why can't he tell me that? Oh, he said he was pleased, but a person likes to hear it said in a gracious manner."

"He has his way, miss, and that's how it is with him. I'd best get the carriage in place, or she might decide not to go."

"Whip the horses," I said lightly, "make sure she goes. I'll be taking a walk. It's come to me that I haven't visited the grave of my father in weeks, and it's high time I did."

He brought up his hand in an informal salute and drove off. I strolled leisurely through the afternoon sunlight, so gentle and warm on the grassy fields. The castle began to disappear behind the knoll as I kept going. In some ways, I was content. I could stay on as I wished. In other ways I was dismayed about Cormac and the way he carried on. It was a shame how he wasted his life in the way he did, with his carousing and his women. But one had to admire the big ox, for he was such a compelling man, as sure of himself as anyone alive, and contemptuous of the ordinary things that fill the existence of ordinary people. Like me. I sighed and came to a stop, because I thought for a moment I'd lost my way.

It was the site of Father's grave, but it had changed. The great stone Cormac had placed at its head was still there, but all around the grave was a metal fence painted white. A low fence, no higher than my waist, and equipped with a little gate that opened quietly and easily to admit me to what was now a private cemetery meant for one man.

After some time Gavan joined me where I knelt in prayer for a man I'd loved. Gavan knelt as well, at my side, and then helped me to my feet.

"He did this?" I asked, indicating the fence.

"Aye, he gave me orders to see it was done."

"There is a softness to him," I said. "I have always suspected there was, but he manages to hide it well. If only I knew just what manner of man he is. One moment, carousing. The next, being kind and gentle and then turning into a demon of strength and shouts. I cannot understand him."

"Perhaps," Gavan said, in one of his riddles, "it's just as well, miss."

EIGHT

It was going to be an exciting morning. Cormac had asked me to go riding with him. Looking forward to this happy possibility months ago, I was pleased I had purchased, along with my wardrobe of fashionable dresses, a riding habit in the English style. I'd been aching for an excuse to wear it, and the time had now come.

It was modern, perhaps a bit too much so, because while there was a skirt, under it were trousers long enough to strap under my riding boots. The bodice was plain, with a full row of buttons extending clear up to the high, tight neckline. Completing the outfit was a silk top hat, which I placed squarely on my head and arranged the black ribbon into a large bow at the back. It was, in my opinion, an elegant outfit, and Cormac complimented me on it.

"You'd be a hit at the races in England," he said. "I've seen princesses and baronesses in riding habits more elegant than yours, yet they didn't look like you. But then, they weren't Kate Moran."

"I do thank you, Cormac," I said graciously. I knew my cheeks flamed with color at the compliment.

"Pity we're not going riding in some big city park so you could be seen." He smiled warmly, adding to my pleasure.

"So long as you see me and approve, I'm satisfied," I said, returning the smile.

"That you can be sure of, Kate. I've had a gentle mare saddled for you. I myself prefer a stallion. They have more vigor."

"Aye," I agreed archly, "that I have noticed. In humans as well as horses."

He grinned and slapped me lightly on the buttocks. It was a friendly pat. I took no offense. To have done so would have been hypocritical. We made our way to the stables, and Gavan gave me a boot up. I was more accustomed to sit astride

107

a horse, but fashion called for women to use a sidesaddle, so I made no protest. Cormac and I rode hard, away from the castle and along a winding path through the forest. When we came to open, rolling country, we slowed the horses and rode side by side in order to converse.

"You're a wonder, Kate," he said. "I've learned how you and your father cared for the sick and the dying all through the famine. And then you took over the castle and changed it into something to be proud of. A remarkable woman, I would say."

"I'm grateful, Cormac, for the little fence you had Gavan build around the grave of my father. It was a thoughtful thing to do."

"That was after I discovered what kind of man he was. You take after him, Kate. I'd have a hard time doing without you now. I hope you have no intention of leaving."

"Not at the moment," I said. "Not when you're kind and gentle, as you are now."

His face clouded. "I'm a fighting man because it is ordained I must be. Were you shocked, or offended, when I killed that popinjay by throwing him down the steps?"

"I was neither shocked nor offended, because he would have gladly killed you. But it was a violent thing, Cormac."

"Perhaps I wouldn't have killed him if he had not murdered my horse. That was deliberate. He knew how I prized that animal."

"Could it also have been his aim to unhorse you so you'd be easier to slash with his saber?"

"Oh, aye, that too of course. But still . . . I loved that horse, and my rage was such that I was unable to control it."

"I have heard you also killed a man some time back."

"To be sure," he said casually. "It was one who deserved killing. Besides which, he thought he could beat me, and that would have been a fine feather in his cap. It was a fair fight."

"I have no doubt of it. Tell me, do you go looking for these fights?"

"No chance of that. As a young lad I gained a reputation as a fighter, and the word spread that I could not be beaten. In Ireland that becomes a challenge to one and all to come and beat me. Either I stand up to them or I'll be branded a coward, so I have to fight."

"But to the death, Cormac. Why is that?"

"Some consider any fight *not* to the death as the fighting of weak men. Those who believe that way are almost always men who are cruel and domineering, gifted with a passion for hurting people. Especially those weaker than themselves. We're a fighting race anyway, Kate."

"Aye, that I have learned from the history books. In the old days, they went at one another with every weapon imaginable. It seems that was all they lived for."

"You're wrong there, Kate. It was not a reason for living, but one of plain survival. Either you killed the other man who swung his sword at your head, or you died. To show you what I mean, I'd like to guide you to another castle, eight miles from here. Are you fit enough for the ride?"

"Twenty miles if you say so, Cormac," I replied.

"Then we will stop this chatter and get on with it." He kicked his mount into full speed. I trailed well behind him, but he never got out of my sight, which I thought was commendable riding for me. It was mostly level, open country, the day was fine, and my horse was not given to antics, which ensured a good ride.

Cormac would slow down now and then, wave me closer, and then take off again in a little game I always lost, for I never did quite catch up with him until we reached a long, rather high and grassy knoll. Here he pulled up and waited for me.

"You'll this day meet a man I'll one day have to fight. He lives in a castle just behind this hill, and he'll come to meet us, for he has sworn never to allow me under his roof, nor will he come to my castle until he is the owner of it and all the lands that go with it."

"Cormac, you have no intention of selling the castle after all the work . . . ?"

"He will gain the castle only when I am dead. He came to me to buy it, and I threw him out. He came again and said he would challenge me when he was good and ready, and the terms of the battle would be that the victor owned whatever the loser possessed. Before he was killed, that is."

"What do you want with two castles, that you would risk your life for?" I asked, puzzled at this male desire for material things.

"It will not be a question of my owning two castles, but to save the one I have. Flynn claims that many years ago my ancestors took Castle Lucane away from his forebears. Whether that's true or not, Kerry Flynn believes it and has vowed to take the castle back."

"Will you have to kill him, then?" I asked in a hushed, shocked voice.

"Unless he kills me."

"Is that likely?" I asked. "I've not laid eyes on this man, so I don't know if he is bigger and stronger. . . ."

"It would be an equal fight. We are both proficient in the use of all kinds of weapons, and besides that, we hate each other enough to welcome the fight."

"Is there not some way to settle this without a killing?" I asked. "Each of you has an ancestral castle. What will you do with two of them?"

"I've no desire to take his property. I told you that. It is he who covets mine. Come, now, ride beside me, and right after we top the knoll, he will come to meet us."

"Does he know we're coming? Have you intended all along to call on him?"

"He will know we're coming when his servants warn him and he sees us through his glass. He is a great man for a telescope. No one reaches his castle that he doesn't know about beforehand. He has many enemies, and he takes no chances."

We did top the knoll, and I had my first look at the castle of Kerry Flynn. It was half as large as Castle Lucane and looked like one easily stormed in the old days of sword and catapult. It was also sorely in need of repairs, especially about the roof and the battlements, which seemed ready to fall down.

"I can see why he wants Castle Lucane," I observed. "His is surely not worth fighting for."

"He's a lazy lout, and that's the cause of the way it looks."

"Oh, aye," I said with a light laugh. "I once knew another suffering from the same malediction."

"You're a clever lass." He grinned. "Yes, I admit I didn't much care what happened to Castle Lucane until you made me realize what a prize it really was."

"I'm glad I had something to do with it," I said. "You owed it to those who came before you and built that castle in pride and fine taste."

"Mmmm," he grunted. "And what did I tell you? Here he comes, the laird of Castle Rundown. I'll have to tell him that one day. It'll rile him some. And don't be offended by the way he looks at you. He's a man who fancies any woman with two legs and a bosom. I have leered at you, to be sure, but Kerry Flynn can give lessons in the way he studies a woman. Especially one as beautiful and spirited as you."

"Should he get familiar, I'll use my quirt on him," I warned.

"You have my permission. Look at him now! Big as a house with an attached barn. Not bad to look at in the face, for he comes of a family of handsome men. I think he is an inch or two taller than I, and he has about twenty pounds on me. He will not be an easy man to take."

"You two will not fight now?" I asked, and I was really worried they might.

"No chance of it, Kate. When we fight, it will be on my terms and when I say so. At this moment, while we close the distance between us, he has seen enough of you that he thinks only of getting you on your back in his bed. No woman would have him for a husband. No woman would last under his treatment, for he is a man of all passion and no tenderness. I have known women who slept with him, and they say he is a beast. That I had known before anyone told me about him."

We pulled up and let Kerry Flynn ride to us. As Cormac had said, he was a huge, muscular man, apparently in as fit condition as a man could be. He had a large head and a big face, but not an unattractive one. He would have gained a second glance from me if I hadn't known who he was and what he was. His attire was somewhat garish. A motley collection of riding clothes, some of which fit and others that did not. His boots were the most disreputable pair I'd seen on a gentleman.

Cormac raised his quirt in a salute. "God save you, Kerry Flynn, so the devil can have you at his will."

"You'll fry off his pitchfork before I do, Cormac of Fion. Is this the village whore you have placed under your protection?"

"Because all of your women are whores, you should be well enough trained that you do not mistake a lady for one," I said sharply. "You will watch your tongue, Kerry Flynn, or I'll take my quirt to you, I swear."

"She has gumption." Flynn laughed. "And a lot more. I would pay handsomely for a night with her. Are you interested, Cormac?"

"Enough to place that statement with fifty others you have made concerning me and mine, so when it comes time to kill you, I'll feel no remorse."

"When will you fight me, Cormac? If you wait too long,

we'll be old men and laughed at by every man jack in Ireland."

"The time is mine to choose, Kerry Flynn."

"But you will fight, and the winner takes all?"

"That we agreed to long ago, and all of Dublin, Belfast, and Galway know it."

"I'm more anxious than ever, now you've let me lay my eyes on your newest possession." He looked squarely at me, and I almost gave way to a shudder of fear. I could actually sense what this man was, and a woman would be lucky to be alive after he finished with her.

"I am not the property of Cormac or of Castle Lucane," I said. "If I were, I'd kill you before I'd let you touch me."

"No doubt. We can discuss that later, when Cormac is dead. I have been given to understand you have made over the castle so it shines like a pot of gold. Which is to my liking, I will say, for I will appreciate it all the more when it becomes mine."

I glanced at Cormac. "Is this man as brainless as he talks? Or is he so stupid he believes what he says?"

"Both," Cormac said laconically.

Kerry Flynn smiled. He was not a smiling man, and this parting of lips to show bad teeth was more of a snarl, though he meant it to be a gesture of mirth.

"I'm thinking now, Cormac, that you will never fight me, out of plain cowardice, and if that is so, I'll kill you anyway. You see, I know enough about you to make a certain story come true. I am the man whose will you will bow to, and when you do, I'll cut your head off. And after that, my fair one, I'll have you."

He wheeled his horse, dug spurs deep enough to make the animal cry out, and then lashed the horse's flanks unmercifully with his whip as he rode back to his castle.

"Cormac," I said, "he is already possessed by the devil himself. He must be, or he is a madman."

"Neither." Cormac sighed. "He has a mission to fulfill, like all of us. I will not talk about him."

"Only answer me this," I implored. "What did he mean by saying you were bound to bow before him and present your neck to his ax?"

"He only boasts, Kate. Pay no heed to his rashness and his wild talk. We will ride back now. It's a considerable distance, so don't ride too hard."

"I'll ride with you," I said.

"Will you always do that, Kate? Ride with me?"

I didn't answer. Instead, I turned my horse and let him catch up with me. I was afraid he might press the question, and I knew what the answer would be, but I was too confused and worried about the man to give him any encouragement now. And I couldn't forget Ellen, in his bed only a few hours ago. I had to remember his carrying her to his room and her boasting she would marry him. I wondered if he had given her any reason to brag, especially for my benefit. The warmth I'd felt for him gradually turned to coldness. At the moment, forgiveness was not in my heart.

We were in time for supper, which I'd ordered prepared and served in the small dining room. Here the table was of a dark, rich wood polished to a shine that reflected our faces if we looked down. I'd arranged for fresh flowers to be placed in the center of the long table and for two gold candelabra, each supporting a dozen fresh candles, to be placed so each end of the table was individually lighted. I'd discovered the priceless silver thrown into a wooden crate and stored in one of the closets. This now graced the table, along with the ancient thin, beautiful china not in use for years.

Oddly, Cormac enjoyed this gracious living and commented on it several times. It was my opinion he had grown up in luxury but had carelessly allowed this old castle to become no more than a roof over his head. He'd never spoken of his family. I didn't know if his father and mother were alive, if he had sisters or brothers or both. He was so reticent concerning his personal life, and it came to me gradually that he must have a reason for this secretiveness, because he was so open about everything else.

I was sorely tempted to extract what information I could from Gavan, until I discovered he could be as reticent as Cormac himself. Gavan was a master at evading any question he did not elect to answer. Perhaps, I thought, these two men shared the same secret that made Cormac's life so strange.

I was content, however. Watching him across the long table, I knew I respected this man, and what he had once done to me was now forgiven. I loved the hours after supper when we sat in the great hall while he sipped brandy and smoked his cigars as I had my glass of wine, which I had come to enjoy. He was a well-read man. I suspected he had been college-educated, as my father had been, and in some ways the two were alike. Not physically, heaven forbid. Father had been slight in stature, a quiet man who would avoid

physical combat at any cost. Cormac, on the other hand, was
rough. A tough adversary, a kindly, helpful man in everyday
life, and a terror of unmerciful wrath when fighting for his
life.

I still didn't know what made him that way. His answers to
my questions were not enlightening, though they were intriguing. He'd given his word not to lay a hand on me, and
he continued to abide by that promise. When we went upstairs, to my pleasure, just the two of us, alone in this great
fortress, we said good night before the door of my room, and
that was that.

Tonight, getting ready for bed, I found myself nervous and
unstrung. I thought this might be due to our meeting with
Kerry Flynn and his vague promises of death. Not that I believed even Flynn could overpower Cormac, but the trend of
the talk, the threats, both veiled and outspoken, all served to
bother me. I washed, took down my hair and brushed it,
sometimes so violently as to make me wince. Something was
wrong with me, and I knew it. But I didn't know what it was.

In bed I pulled up the covers and tried to sleep. After half
an hour of this, I raised myself to a sitting position and tried
to figure out why I could not sleep. It had been a long day,
an exciting one, and a tiring one. We'd ridden for hours. Yet
here I was, wide-awake, trying to figure out the puzzle of
why.

I thought about Cormac again. I tried to go back to the
time of the famine and his coarse raping, but my mind
tended more to dwell upon the man I'd come to know since
he'd returned after a considerable absence.

I thought about Ellen and the others too, but they were not
of any importance. No matter what vein of thought I had
about Cormac, I always came back to him as kind and
gentle. If I'd ever followed my threat to leave the castle, even
with all the money he might have paid me, I'd have been in
untold agony by now. Lonely and frustrated and missing him.

That was the word! That was the reason I couldn't sleep. I
missed him because I was in love with him. Of course! All
the past events, good and bad, had served to conceal this
from me and make me believe I liked the man and had ac-
quired respect for him, but no more. When all along it had
been a deep love that I knew would endure.

I slipped out of bed, knowing very well what I had to do
now. The urge was overwhelming, and armies could not have
stopped me. I didn't bother to put on slippers or a robe.

There'd be no need for either one. The cold floor felt good to my bare feet, serving to steady me. I walked calmly down the corridor in the dark, and when I reached his room, I never hesitated for a moment. I turned the latch, pushed the door open, and went in.

He was quiet, apparently asleep, I thought. I closed the door so as not to awaken him. At least, that is what I told myself. I crossed the floor, lifted the bedcovers, and got into bed beside him.

He raised himself, turned around, and his arm went about me. "Glory be," he said in a whisper, "I've been waiting a long time."

"There will be no waiting now, Cormac," I said. "I could not find sleep, and I didn't know what was wrong."

"I couldn't sleep either, but I knew exactly what was wrong. Now you've come to me of your own sweet will. There can be no more pretense between us. We need each other far more than what an ancient relic of a castle calls for."

"Aye, Cormac," I said. "You are a gifted man with talk, but there is a time when talk is linked with torture. I didn't come to you to listen to your bloody jabbering."

He laughed aloud and drew me to him in a tight, yet tender embrace, and I learned what kind of man he really was. I discovered that his kisses could combine passion with a gentle warmth. His hands caressed and further aroused me. Tonight there was no fighting, no passive submission as before, but a genuine fire of love and passion the likes of which I never knew could be. Our moans of pleasure and desire mingled.

And when it was over, we lay there, our arms about each other, quiet in our newfound bliss, and wordless because it would have been a shame to break this bond of love between us.

Finally he kissed my lips and raised himself on one elbow. "I loved you from the first, Kate. Did you know that?"

"I did not," I replied promptly.

"I couldn't let you know. It happened after . . . that first time. I was ashamed of myself. That had never happened to me before. I didn't need a hammer on my thick skull to make me realize why. You were the kind of woman I'd always dreamed of. Shy, pretty, with strength of character that matched my will. When you came back the second time . . ."

"You made sure there was only food for a brief time so I'd have to come back," I accused him. "I was so angry I felt

like coming with a gun. But maybe it wasn't that bad. I di<
come. Oh, yes, Cormac, I was in love with you then, but my
anger rose above it so I was not aware of it."

"God help me," he said in a voice that cracked with emotion, "I do love you, Kate. What will come of it, only heaven
knows, but we've at least had this, even if there is so littl<
more."

"Riddles again," I said. "What's the meaning of all those
strange, half-suggested prophecies, Cormac? We are young
we're of healthy Irish stock, we're strong, and we're in love."

"Listen only to the words I spoke, Kate. Let that suffice fo<
now. Let nothing interfere with it, and we shall believe only
that we'll live forever and be this much in love when the nex<
two centuries turn."

"Cormac," I asked daringly, "will you marry me?"

"There's not a man or a creature in this world who coul<
stop me."

"I'm not of the nobility," I said. "I've no importance o<
family behind me and am not a lady of society."

"You're no lady," he said with a laugh. "You're th<
woman I'm in love with, and there's not a duchess o<
baroness who could compete with you in any possible way."

I snuggled closer to his nakedness and sighed with content-
ment. "Oh, Cormac, it's all so unreal. I can't believe it. Unti<
I'm in your arms as I am now. Only then will I know this i<
not a dream. When shall we marry?"

I felt his body grow rigid, and his breath came in one grea<
gust as he exhaled. He didn't reply for a few moments. Ther<
he relaxed, and his arms held me tight once again. He spok<
softly, and as he did, his hands once again moved gently, stir-
ring the fires of passion within me.

"It's not a thing to talk about when we are in bed. Marriage is a serious business, and tomorrow we'll discuss i<
calmly, and not in the heat of the desire I now feel."

"But we will talk of it tomorrow?" I asked.

"Aye, tomorrow," he said. "But this is tonight."

"Filled with moonlight and leprechauns and fairies an<
legends," I said softly. I felt his body give way to anothe<
shudder so strong as to be almost a violent spasm. It was ove<
in a flash.

"Never has a man needed a woman as I need you," h<
said. "You'll be the life of me, Kate. For however long <
last."

"That will be for our lifetime, which will be forever. Els<

how can you govern our children, Cormac? You would not
have them run wild, would you? Even when they are sixty
years old."

It was foolish, reckless talk. The talk of all lovers since the
beginning of time.

"No, Kate," he said. "Never will I allow that. And will you
stop jabbering, as you ordered me to do not so long ago?"

"With pleasure," I said. And for a third time that night we
made love. This time with more restraint, for we knew the
joy and ecstasy of fulfillment.

NINE

Cormac was not in bed when I awoke. It required a moment or two for me to realize that I was in his bed, not my own, and instead of getting up, I lay there luxuriating in the memory of the night.

We were in love, Cormac and I. We had been for a long time, though I hadn't known it. Cormac, on the other hand, had realized it, according to what he'd told me, but he'd been afraid I'd back away if he ever told me so. Or even worse, scorn him. That knowledge had come as quite a shock to me. A pleasant one, I might add.

I had duties to perform, a castle to supervise. I finally got up and prepared myself for the day, taking extra pains with my appearance for the sake of the man I loved. I expected he'd be either at the breakfast table or in the great hall, but he was neither. I learned he'd come down early and gone for a ride.

I was so disappointed that I lost my previous hunger for breakfast and ate little. I wondered why he had not been waiting for me this particular morning after he had professed his love for me. I had to grant that, in some ways, he was a strange man, but I adored him, and for us there would be a future rivaled by none.

I gave orders to the cook and sent the upstairs maids about their duties. I ate my noonday dinner alone, more concerned than ever about Cormac's absence. It was midafternoon when he returned, sweaty and tired. He must have ridden hard and far, but if there was a purpose to it, he didn't confide in me. I hurried up to him as he entered the castle, but he held out a warning hand.

"I'm so filthy I must have a bath at once," he said.

I moved out of his way, and he hurried up the staircase to his room. Surely he didn't think I cared if he was sweaty and perhaps dirty from the ride. I'd not thought of him as a man as sensitive as that. All I could do was wait until he came down, but that didn't happen, and after an hour I went looking for him.

His door was closed, and I knocked on it hard, just in case he had fallen asleep. He opened the door, and I looked upon the face of a man so changed I believed him to be seriously ill.

"Cormac," I exclaimed, "what's wrong with you? What's happened?"

"Listen to me, Kate, and listen well. Forget whatever happened last night. So far as I am concerned, it didn't even happen at all. What I said was a man talking in the heat of passion, and it has no meaning the morning after."

I moved back a step to better make certain this was Cormac and not a stranger who looked something like him.

"What is that you're saying?" I asked. "Tell me again."

"We're not in love, you and I. What happened was because we've been thrown together. We have seen too much of each other. What we did is what any two normal people would do who live under the same roof."

I was too stunned to formulate any kind of reply. I kept thinking this was not true. Not after last night.

"I want you to stay, Kate," he went on. "I do need you, but the other—all of it—was a fancy of the night which you too will recognize when you think about it calmly."

That was when I found my voice. "Last night my emotions may not have been calm, but my thinking was, and when I went to your bed it was because I wanted to, and because I was in love with you."

"Don't say that, Kate!" he exclaimed.

"I will say it because it's true. For I feel the same as I did last night. Perhaps more so, and your dismissal of it as nothing at all, I refuse to accept. I love you. I always will, and neither you nor anyone else can change that."

He bowed his head so I might not see his face. "I've told you how I feel. If you cannot believe what I say, then it's best you leave me and the castle. I will provide handsomely—"

"Cormac!" I said sharply. "What's wrong? Tell me! I've a right to know."

"The answer is simple. This morning I came to my senses."

"Look at me!" I said. "Raise your head and look me in the eye. Then repeat that and make me believe it, for in heaven's name I do not believe it now, and I don't think I ever will. Do you have the courage to say it again?"

He raised his head. "Kate, we're of different walks of life. Not that yours is any less worthy than mine, but there are social values. There is noble blood in my veins. You are a village girl, low-born, if I must use that term."

I said, "Cormac, will you now tell me something of yourself? Of your family? Tell me these matters and make me believe what you are saying. For now, at this moment, I do not think you're lying to me, and you are not, by nature, a deceitful man."

"Why should I lie about such a matter?" he protested.

"Because you're hiding something from me. You have been all along. That strange room of the five statues is one secret you all but flaunt at me. So is that great book in Gaelic."

"You've not laid a hand . . . ?" His voice rose in quick anger.

"I gave you my word. Besides, I cannot read Gaelic. Will you sit down with me at this moment and convince me you are right?"

"If I must. We'll talk here in my room, where the servants can't disturb us. First, I must have your word in this matter too. Will you accept my decision with understanding and remain at the castle if I persuade you that I'm right?"

"No," I said candidly, "I will not. But what you will say to me may soften the pain."

"Then it's worthwhile." He opened the door to his room and stepped aside that I might enter. He pulled a chair closer to the large, leather-covered one he used, and I sat down. Cormac didn't. He began pacing the floor in a nervous manner. I sat primly, my hands folded on my lap, in my mind a prayer that Cormac would relent and admit that he was in love with me.

"My family's roots belong to the glorious days of Tara's Halls when men fought for the sake of fighting, but when the land was threatened, enemies clasped hands and fought side by side against a common threat. Those days made Ireland great. You know what has happened since. Still, I was born to a father and mother who loved me as I loved them. I was raised in this castle in the days when it was as fine as you have made it now. I was the firstborn, and the title and estate were mine."

"You say firstborn. Do you have brothers and sisters?" I asked.

"My father died when I was but four. My mother, rest her soul, married again and bore another son. She then died in childbirth, and my stepfather moved out of the castle, taking his son with him. I was brought up by an uncle and aunt, and the castle was abandoned. My stepfather had no claim on it. That's how it came to be so run-down when you first saw it."

"Is your stepfather still alive?" I asked.

"No, he died a few years ago. My half-brother is named Nial Dermot. He lives in London and is a barrister of some note."

"Now tell me why you cannot admit you are truly in love with me, as I know you are."

"Ireland is no different than anywhere else. The blacksmith's daughter does not marry the earl's son. In any event, should I die, the castle would not be yours if we did marry. It would go to my stepbrother and, in the past, he has coveted it. Not aggressively, but he would glory in being the master here."

"Do you like him?"

"Yes. He's a decent-enough fellow. I did not care for his father. After Mother died, he left the castle under protest, resenting the fact that his son had no claim on the estate while I lived."

"Last night," I said softly, "you told me over and over again that you loved me, and you proved it in a grand way. Now, by day, you say you didn't mean it. Do you take me for an idiot, Cormac? Do you believe I am a woman who cannot know for certain that the man who says he's in love with her is telling the truth? If it wasn't love that inspired you to such gentleness and ardor, then what was it?"

"Infatuation. Desire! No different than how I felt the first time you came to my door begging for food. You were desirable then, and I satisfied that desire. Last night was the same."

"You're a liar," I said calmly.

He turned about abruptly, mouthing an oath. "Regard me in any way you choose. Stay here if you like, or go away when you wish. It matters none to me anymore. Perhaps you should go."

"Why? To avoid any more of these confrontations? I'll stay to confront you whenever possible, and make you finally admit you really are a liar. There's more reason than the one of noble birth that makes you reject the love you feel for me right now."

"Stay, then," he shouted. "The hell with you, Kate Moran."

He walked out of the room, leaving the door wide open. I heard him moving down the corridor in a direction opposite the location of the staircase, and when I hurried out of the room too, I was in time to see him unlock the door of the bare room of the five statues and go inside, closing the door behind him.

I found it impossible to remain in the castle itself, so I left by a door leading into the castle grounds. I made my way to the little house where Gavan made his home. He was not there, for Gavan was no man to waste time by not tending his duties. He was at the stables, but he saw me and recognized the fact that I was looking for him. He approached me, removed his cap, and then sighed.

"Come inside," he invited me. "It is better to speak of trouble sitting down in comfort, and there is trouble written on your face, miss."

"Thank you, Gavan. I do have need for talking to someone who makes sense and speaks as if he is not both liar and madman."

I entered his cottage and discovered it was tidy and clean and very comfortable. There were but two rooms and a small kitchen, but it was easy to see that it sufficed. Gavan indicated a plush-covered chair adorned with doilies on the arms and back, immaculately white.

"Cormac has informed me that I may stay or leave as I wish."

"You would be sorely missed. What else did he say?"

"Gavan, what is his secret? What tears at the heart and soul of this man?"

"Only Cormac can know that."

"You're as good at evading my questions as Cormac. Now, understand this so you'll know why it's important to me that I know the truth. Last night Cormac swore he would marry me. This morning he says it was no more than the desire of a man for a woman that made him say that. He also said he was born of nobility and it is impossible for him to marry such as me."

"And what are you asking of me?" Gavan said.

"What makes him change his mind? The nobility excuse is just that—an excuse. He loves me as dearly as I love him.

Yet he will not admit it, and he gives me a choice of going away to forget it all or staying to be reminded of my love for him day by day, hour by hour. I don't know what to do."

"Leave. This day, pack up and leave. He will provide generously, I know. Go far away. Dublin, perhaps, or even London, if you can stand the British. Get away from him. For as long as you remain, it will be torture for both of you."

"I would rather accept the torture than the loneliness," I said.

"If you stay, you will be sorry, miss."

"Why? Won't someone let me know what is going on? I think I've a right to know. And what's the meaning of that strange room and the big book in Gaelic, and the statues? When he told me this morning that it was impossible for us to be in love, he went directly there as if it were a chapel. I don't understand, Gavan, and somehow I must."

"You asked my advice, miss. I told you to pack up and go. I'll drive you to Galway if you like, or to the railroad, which will take you to Dublin or Belfast or, as I said, London."

"That's what you'd like, isn't it? That's what he'd like. Get rid of me, and the trouble is over. Perhaps bribe me with a great deal of money. Convince me it's better this way. Well, Gavan, I'm not going. I will refuse to leave this castle until someone tells me why I cannot marry Cormac and why he must tell me he is not in love with me when I know he is. That's final."

"He may not think so," Gavan reminded me.

"He wants me to stay. First he begged me not to leave. Tell me, Gavan, is that the way a man talks when he is not in love with a girl? By asking me to stay, he admits he is in love with me. Saying he needs me is of little meaning. He could find someone else as good as or better than I. He wants me. He loves me, but for some strange reason he feels he cannot afford to. It makes little sense."

"Aye, miss, not much does these days."

"You're as bad as he," I said angrily. "An explanation is due me, but neither Cormac nor you will grant me even a glimmer of what lies behind the way he's acting."

"Yes, miss," Gavan said. "It will be as you wish it. To leave or stay."

"You would have me leave. Why?"

"Because it would settle things. Ease the dear man's mind, relieve the cares that have weighed on him for years."

"I still refuse to go."

"As you wish."

I walked out in a state of high anger and frustration. For the rest of the day I devoted myself to improving the castle by the completion of small details and by the planning of major ones. I had to keep mind and body busy.

During the days that followed, Cormac was stiffly polite at the supper table. His other meals were eaten at random times and alone. Our conversations were stilted and dull, concerning the weather, the crops, and the village.

At night he stayed away from me. I was impelled by curiosity and by my love for him to listen outside his closed bedroom door at times. I tried to open it more than once, but learned it was kept locked, but he slept little—and not at all well when he did. This indicated itself in his drawn face and the great hollows beneath his eyes. I grew accustomed to hearing him pace up and down in what he thought was the privacy of his room. There were moments when he would swear great oaths and hurl something about.

I found some strange comfort in his agony, for it was plain proof that he loved me but could not allow himself to confess it to me. I suffered with him and for him too. He was a man beside himself, and there was little I could do to comfort him.

His restlessness grew too. He would take himself off for a ride in early morning and not return until dark, tired and disheveled, riding a horse that foamed at the mouth from sheer exhaustion. Even Gavan quietly criticized him for this, and Cormac answered him with an oath.

Apparently he was unable to quell the inner anger raging inside him by long rides or by pacing the floor in his bedroom. Finally, one evening, he joined me at the supper table and began taking the British to task over their treatment of Ireland during the famine. That catastrophe was still painfully fresh in the mind of every Irishman, though I doubted the British gave it a single thought.

"In their stupidity," Cormac raged, "they almost destroyed a fair and good country. Out of their greed . . . no, by damnation, it was not greed alone. It was their damned idea that nothing, not even the death of millions, must interfere with the smooth flow of trade. I've been thinking hard on this for a long time."

"It's well someone has," I agreed. I was happy to be taking part, once more, in his life. Even if it was no more than talk of British government and trade.

"It may be I was as damned stupid as they, for I did nothing about it, and I'm an Irishman," he commented.

"What could you have done?" I asked.

"Something, by God. I could have brought in food. Perhaps only enough to keep a few souls alive, but I had the influence to get food."

"You did provide," I reminded him. "If it had not been for you, there'd be no village."

"For me? Have you forgotten why I provided the food? To get you in bed. And I'm as ashamed of that as my lack of understanding of what was going on. Well . . . almost as ashamed. At least, there was pleasure in my bribe."

"If you're trying to make me angry," I said, "you're not doing very well."

"I'm trying to make myself angry. I'm late about this, but I'm going to London and take advantage of my birthright to address Parliament, and I'm going to give them a fine piece of my mind."

I was suddenly afraid. "Cormac, you must not . . ."

"Especially the one called Edmund, who was in charge of all trade. Oh, I know what he and the others did, how they felt. And even now, with the million and more graves in Ireland, they still think they were right. I'm going to show them they were not."

"They'll not only throw you out, they'll likely jail you as well," I warned. "They've put many a man behind bars for talking too much and too loudly."

"If they lock me up, I'll shout louder than ever. I'm going to make that speech. In a week's time. It will take me that long to think of what to say without blistering their ears with cursing, which is no way to convince a man he's wrong."

"Cormac," I begged, "will you speak to our own leaders first? What you intend may do more harm than good. The famine is over now. God willing, it won't return, and for the time being, things are quiet. Let them remain that way for the present, at least. There will be enough fire-eaters to take up the fight after we've recovered from the ordeal of starving to death."

"It will not wait. The longer we do nothing, remain quiet, the more they'll treat us like some Oriental colony where they rule by mandate and cannon. I will make my speech."

There was no way to discourage or dissuade him. He went into what was practically solitary confinement so he might write and polish the speech to the perfection he required. I did consult with a few others who lived close by, but they were as hotheaded as he, and were all for it, especially since it was not their heads that would roll.

On the day before he was to leave for London, I asserted myself for the first time since he'd made his decision.

"I'm going with you," I announced.

"The hell you are! I'll have no woman on my coattails, not even you. If you follow me, I'll have the bloody English lock you up as a spy. They'll do it, too. Anyone who speaks with even a tinge of brogue is suspected these days."

"Aye." I nodded complacently.

He eyed me with an angry gleam. "You're not one to give in so fast, Kate. Don't try anything behind my back. I won't have it."

"I will not go to England," I said. "I could not stand the scene."

"What scene? What are you talking about?"

"I would not enjoy seeing them swing you from the end of a rope."

He laughed aloud. "That'll be a day in history. They'll not swing me, Kate. If they did, there'd be an uprising the like of which they've never seen. And well they know it, too. I'll be safe enough."

"You care little or naught what I think," I said as I arose from the table. "So I care little for what you do. Go, then, and be damned to you, Cormac."

I fled from the dining room for the seclusion of my own bedroom. I knew my defiance had not made the least impression on his plans. I remained wide-awake until the small hours, lying there hoping against hope he would come to me in the night. With an apology at least, with love at most. He did not come.

Gavan drove him to the railroad for the trip to Dublin and from there by boat to England. The castle was as lonely without him as it had been during his first long absence. I let three-quarters of the servants off on a holiday to last until he returned. I kept mostly to myself, being busy for hours at some delicate task of restoration, for the reclaiming of Castle Lucane was not only still incomplete, but would never be finished.

We heard no word, and I lived in deep anxiety. Gavan, too, was a silent man these days. Conan, who came to help with some of the difficult renovations, did his best to cheer me up.

"Cormac," he said, "has noble blood. Aye, that's the truth for none to deny, not even a blockhead of an Englishman. They may call him names, they may even arrest him, but they will not otherwise harm him, for he is one of their own. If they respect nothing else, they do respect titles."

"He has a stepbrother," I said. "A barrister, no less. If we reached him, perhaps he would help."

"Kate, if Cormac intended to make his speech, it is already done. He's spoken by now, and no British army has appeared in Ireland yet."

"Do you think so?" I asked. "That he has spoken?"

"It is possible the newspapers will come this afternoon, and I expect his speech will be printed."

"Unless all the newspapers seeking to print it have not caught fire. I read his speech, Conan, and it blistered the hides of those who deserved it. There was no unfairness in any of the words, but they will sting, and they will make him enemies."

"Aye, he's not one to mince words, Kate. It'll be a wonder to me if he doesn't begin fistfights with all of them. It's in him, mark that well."

"You will see that the papers are brought promptly?" I asked.

"Aye, that I will. Now I'd best get on with the fireplace mantel in the small dining room, for it has pulled away a bit from the wall. Because of old age, nothing else."

I made my own way to the room of the five statues, as if being alone in there might provide me with some answers. I looked closely at the statue in black marble, or whatever it was, the one that resembled Cormac to such an astonishing degree. What it meant was far beyond me. I opened the big book, finding the cover remarkably heavy. On the pages, in the hand of an accomplished penman from a century or more in the past, were the strangely spelled words of the old Gaelic language. It was not, like Latin or French, or even German, a language one might study at random and see a similarity with some English words. I knew that I could get some meaning out of French, for instance, though it was not more than superficial. But Gaelic was something else again. For me it was no more than a jumble of letters forming meaningless unpronounceable words.

I left the room, locking the door as usual. Downstairs, Conan was wholly involved with putting the mantel back in place. He looked over his shoulder and smiled.

"Conan," I said, "can you read Gaelic?"

"Aye. Is there something for me to read? I am not skilled, but I can manage."

"No," I said slowly. "I was only wondering how difficult a language it is."

"You will not learn it in a day, to be sure, but it can be learned."

"I don't think I'll try," I said lightly. "Not now, anyway."

"I'll be taking one of the horses for a ride to the village if you don't mind. The papers from Dublin and London should have arrived by now."

"Hurry back," I implored him. "We don't even know if Cormac is dead or alive."

"I'd bet my hat he's not dead." Conan laughed. "Not that one."

I resented the time it took Conan to get back, but finally he did, waving the newspapers as he rode in. I hurried out to meet him and take the papers from his hand. I began reading them on my way back to the castle door.

The Dublin paper bore a sketch of Cormac, a remarkably good one. The article appeared to have been published before the full story arrived in Ireland. It was easy to understand why the Irish paper was far behind the London newspaper, for the news from England had to come by messenger and boat.

But the British newspaper had it all, a long article printed under the headline "TRAITOR'S SPEECH BEFORE PARLIAMENT." There were comments on Cormac's words, branding him as a rebel who must be watched. But they did print much of the speech, and it was the most outspoken condemnation of the British Empire ever made, with reference to Ireland and the famine:

As Ireland lay sick and dying at the feet of British trade, it was deemed to be a serious mistake to give charity to the Irish, for that would upset the usual balance of trade. Nothing must interfere with that. Dan O'Connell tried to reach this distinguished body, but he was not heard as he spoke, and the effort killed him. In view of the existing circumstances in Ireland, the word came that there must be no interference with normal trade, and that is likely what caused the end of this great man.

There was no cause for alarm, Lord Dervor said, and a million and a half people died. Lord Dervor was, and is, not only a liar, but a man who profited by the deaths of that multitude, for he bought corn, raised on Irish farms, for half the customary price, because the farmer had to take his terms or not have the money to pay the rent on his cottage and the land. No doubt, in many cases, Lord Dervor was also the landlord.

We asked for help and we got the Labor Rate Act, allowing the Irish to tax themselves while they died. After that came the grant of a million pounds for relief. A fine gesture from the good Queen—but did she ever find out that three-quarters of it was spent for the salaries of the commissioners and clerks assigned to distribute the money? Which was used to hire labor at half pay. Not to rebuild Ireland or supply seed potatoes or improve the fields. Ah, no, nothing as simple as that. The labor was used to build bridges where there were no streams or rivers. To cut roads over which no one traveled, to chop down mountains and destroy beauty without purpose.

And again, let me bring in the activity of the great and generous Lord Dervor. While this august body I now address did little and heard none of the grim stories that came out of Ireland, along with pleas for help, Lord Dervor was at hand to receive corn paid for by generous people all over the world and shipped to our Irish ports.

In the name of your government, he ordered this charitable shipment of food for the starving to be sold. And while he managed this enterprise, ten times as much corn grown in Ireland and bought at half price was being shipped to England. The ships passed one another.

A member has just shouted me down to announce that I have said nothing about all the additional money sent for relief. But it was used for public works, not agriculture. A farmer might be granted some of this money, but in return he had to give up all of his farmland with the exception of a quarter of an acre. A high price. Then they were generously paid sixpence a day, not to farm, but to perform the nonproductive work I spoke of previously. A Vagrancy Act was made law, and starving people without money—and how could they have had any?—were imprisoned at hard labor.

These events—which are crimes—comprise the manner in which Ireland was treated. I have related facts, every last one of which can be proven. What I can't prove, to my sorrow, is how such individuals as Lord Dervor managed to grow rich while millions of my people died.

I expect nothing from this speech. I have made it only to let the entire world know what happened here. If I have outraged this august body, I am not sorry. The truth is painful to hear sometimes, but truth it is, and all of you well know it.

I refolded the newspaper and exhaled slowly. Conan stood by. Gavan came into the room, and I handed him the paper to read. While he did so, Conan told me he had read the paper in the village, and so had everyone else there.

"Will there be trouble for Cormac because of this?" I asked.

"There may be, though there was only truth in what he said. If they call him a liar, there are a million to testify it was truthful."

Gavan laid the paper down. "They may not take this lightly, miss. Their ears are not accustomed to hearing about their own omissions in Parliament. And Cormac saw to it that his speech was made known to newsmen from all over the world. It's a black mark against those who were responsible. They are powerful men. I pray to heaven Cormac gets out of England before they decide to take action against him."

"Oh, Gavan, you should not have said that. I have enough worries without fresh ones. Is he really in great trouble?"

"It's hard to tell up to now," Gavan said.

"Would they dare harm him?" Conan asked.

"Men who are harmed by the truth become dangerous to the one who tells the truth about them. But I wouldn't worry. Cormac is one to take care of himself."

"Aye," Conan agreed.

"Besides," Gavan went on "it is a well-known fact that Cormac is one of the greatest fighters on earth. Those who would try to overpower him would not find it an easy job. They will surely think more than twice before they tackle him."

"I wish I was sure of that," I said. "Cormac can't live a charmed life forever."

"If he gets away, he'll be home in four days," Gavan estimated. "I'm so sure he will come that I'll be waiting at the railroad with the carriage."

"You and I will be waiting," I said, amending his statement. "I'll have your head if you go without me."

"Then for the sake of my head, which I love dearly, I'll make sure you're with me," Gavan said.

"We have to have everything in perfect order for Cormac's return," I said. "That means we work hard, for there is much to be done."

So the next three days were busy ones. I kept everybody at work until the castle shone with polish and fresh paint. I was up at dawn the morning we were to go for Cormac, and I wasn't the only one. Gavan had the carriage waiting before I finished my breakfast. I dressed carefully, in a traveling dress of tan wool, for the weather was growing colder day by day. Gavan provided me with a blanket for my knees, and I rode quite comfortably during the ride to the railroad depot.

The steam train came in with its usual hissing and squealing of metal. There was a crowd waiting, and I wondered if so many people were about to take this train. It turned out that they were there to greet Cormac, and they did so with loud cheers and shouts.

Before we could reach him, he was surrounded, his shoulders whacked, a score of voices asking him questions or heaping praise upon him. When he finally broke through and saw me standing at the end of the depot platform, I saw his face light up with pleasure, and he began to hurry in my direction, then abruptly reduced his steps to a normal, unhurried walk. The light on his face died away. He reached out a hand to take mine in a formal handshake.

"It was nice of you to meet me, Kate. I do appreciate it. Gavan, you imp, I'm glad to see you too."

That was the greeting from the man I was in love with. I may have shown my anger, I'm not sure, but Cormac took pains to walk ahead of me to the carriage so I'd have time to cool off.

He handed me into the carriage, but he didn't sit beside me, being content to occupy the front seat beside Gavan. He looked over his shoulder as the ride began.

"Has everything been going well at the castle?" he asked.

"Yes," I said.

"It will be good to get back. I cannot say I like the excitement in London."

"I would not care for it," I said curtly.

"Have you been using Conan for some of the work?"

"Aye," I replied.

"Why are you so angry, Kate? I'm not accustomed to being greeted in this manner."

"I'm angry, and if the manner of my greeting shows it, I'm not sorry."

"But what have I done? When I got off the train, I was met with cheers."

"If they knew the sort of man you are, they'd not have cheered. They'd have shivered from the coldness of you."

"I see. I'm sorry, Kate. I didn't mean to offend you, but I'm not in the habit of greeting women with hugs and kisses."

"The devil you're not," I said tartly. "I've not only heard you're good at it, I've also had the experience."

Gavan was striving hard not to break into laughter, and when I saw a side view of his twisted features, I could no longer restrain my own desire to laugh, and I did.

"Now, that's more like it," Cormac said.

"It won't last," I warned him. "I am proud enough of the speech you made that I can forgive much. It was strong as a widow's black tea, and just as acid, and it may have made those sleepy, rusty-boned lawmakers wake up enough to open at least one eye."

"They woke up." Cormac chuckled. "They damned me to the extent of their lung power, and Lord Dervor, the dear man, was purple. I thought he was about to bust a blood vessel. He shook his fist at me."

"One of the few men who ever did without being given a blow." Gavan joined the fun.

"The man would not stand up under a tap on the cheek," Cormac said. "He's that frail-looking. I did give him something to live for. He'll want my liver."

"You're not in trouble?" I asked, suddenly worried.

"Not after I got out of England. I traveled very fast, I'll tell you. They wouldn't be above charging me with something that would get me in jail."

When we reached the village on our way back, everyone was waiting to cheer him, and even I was included in some of the praise. It made me feel as if this was my home once again, and I was surprised to see that my cottage had been freshly painted white, to gleam like a jewel in the sun.

We broke away finally, and when the carriage stopped outside the castle, Cormac jumped down and strode with long, rapid steps to the door, not waiting for me.

"For your own knowledge, Gavan, the man's afraid of me," I said. "He's scared stiff of being too near me, because, damn his soul, he wants to take me in his arms as much as I want him to."

"Aye, I will agree to that. Do nothing to upset him. Bide your time, miss."

"I thought you wanted me to go away."

"That I did, but the look on Cormac's face when he stepped off the train and saw you there made me change my mind. There'll be nothing but pain and trouble from this, mind you, but I can see now there is no way to stop it, and he is going to need you."

"We're back, and one minute after, there are riddles again," I complained. "When will you tell me why Cormac is afraid to be in love?"

"That's not for me to tell, miss. It will be he who does it, in his own good time, and let it rest your heart that he has his reasons."

"One day, Gavan, I shall provide myself with a very exciting book, and I'll sit you down in the great hall and read it. Halfway through, that's when I'll throw it in the fireplace to burn while you wonder what would have happened if I'd finished reading it. That's how I feel with these mysteries you and Cormac face me with."

"Aye." Gavan nodded. "Sometimes the books do not end well, as I have discovered."

"Will this one about Cormac and me? At least tell me that."

His eyes clouded, and he began to turn away. I called him back and seized his elbow, gripping it hard. He turned his head and looked directly into my eyes.

"No, miss, it will not end well."

"Gavan, how will it end? Will he throw me out or cause me to leave of my own accord? Is that how it will end?"

"No, miss."

"Then how, Gavan? Someone has to tell me."

"It will end in death," he said, and pulled himself free of me to walk back to the carriage, which he drove at a fast clip down to the stables. I could only stand there in sheer horror and surprise. I wondered whose death he meant. And why he was so sure.

TEN

before.

For two full days Cormac kept away from me. He must
have watched every move I made and managed to go riding
and have his meals when I was elsewhere. The fact that he
kept out of my way so meticulously didn't sadden me, for I
knew the only reason could be that he loved me so much he
couldn't risk being close. If I was beside myself with worry
over him, he must be concerned about me too. There was a
bit of satisfaction in believing in that.

On the morning of the third day, I was ready for him. I'd
gone boldly and noisily downstairs, but I slipped back to my
room without making a sound. I managed to hear his door
open soon afterward, and I looked out to see him unlock and
enter the statue room, leaving the door open behind him.

I reached the doorway without alarming him. He was
standing before that black bust of himself flanked by the
other statues. Just standing there, saying nothing, doing nothing. He turned slowly about, and I blocked the door.

"To get out, you'll have to pick me up and toss me to one
side . . . or agree to have a sensible conversation right now.
Those are my terms, Cormac."

"What do you want with me, Kate? Haven't I insulted you
enough that you've grown to hate me?"

"I'm angry with you. Hate you? That will never be. I want
to help. I want to know what's eating the insides of you. I
want to know what this room means in your life. What's in
the book you prize so dearly. But more than anything else, I
want to know why you won't come to my bed by night, or invite me to your own. Mind you, I'm not speaking of marriage. Not right now."

"This room and the book are a private matter you are not
to be concerned with. I will not come to you, or have you
come to me, for I am a changed man these days. If I bedded

with you now, I would have to marry you, and I am not a marrying man."

"You're also a bad liar, and it seems I've called you that before."

"I will not marry—"

"I don't refer to that. You are not a man who would feel bound to marry a woman because you slept with her. If your motive was noble, you would have been married many times. There is some reason you are afraid of me."

"Move aside," he ordered.

"I will not. Only the force of you will make me move until you answer my questions."

"What else is there for me to answer? I told you I will not marry you or anyone else."

"You would let the castle fall into the ruin it was, after you die without wife or children?"

"It will go to my half-brother. That is the law. He is a man who will care for it."

"There is one more thing."

"Oh, God! You are a persistent woman."

"Why will all this end in death?"

"Whose death? Whom have you been talking to? Wait! Gavan, no doubt. I'll have the hide of him!"

"I wore him down to where he didn't know what he was saying," I said. Not exactly the truth, though Gavan had been under the pressure of my persistent questions.

"The man's a loose-tongued idiot. You want me to answer that. I can't, because I don't know what the man was talking about. Does that satisfy you? Let me by, Kate. I'm growing impatient."

I stepped back. "Cormac, will you listen to me for one minute without opening your mouth to browbeat me?"

"Kate, you do wear a man down."

"Thank you. This is all I have to say. When I left this castle for the first time, you had violated me and I hated you. By the end of my second visit I had fallen in love with you. I didn't know it then, but it's true. Then you admitted that you love me as dearly as I do you. From that moment on, my life really began, and now I am beset with worries and problems because you will not—or cannot—tell me what is troubling you. I want to share in that because I love you. So there is nothing you can do—or anyone else can do—to change me. I will love you until my dying day—or yours. One or the other will be the same to me, for without you I would care little to go on living. That's what I wanted to say. You do not have to answer me. Do what you like, but those things I have spoken of will never change."

"Ah, Kate," he said softly. "If only I could let you understand." He took me in his arms and kissed me long and tenderly before he thrust me from him and stalked down the corridor with angry strides.

"I'm grateful, Cormac," I called after him, and I didn't care who heard me. "Now I do know the truth."

"And damned to you," he shouted as he turned to go down the stairs. I went contentedly to my room.

His frank statement that he would never marry did worry me, but I knew he was in love with me and it would be up to me to change his mind. It wouldn't be the first time a woman had succeeded in doing that. I was consoled by the fact that, so far as I knew, Cormac had given up his other women and, especially, the thin one named Ellen. Her boast that she would marry Cormac had been just that—an attempt to convince me I had no chance with him.

So I was reasonably satisfied with the outcome of all the things that had happened lately. There was time enough for me to convince Cormac to marry me.

Then the two men arrived, and everything changed. They came in a rented carriage, and even Cormac was puzzled as to their identities. That they were men of substance and importance was evident in their dress. Their formal tailcoats, gray weskits, and somber neckcloths were further enhanced by tall silk hats, which they doffed at my appearance.

"Welcome to Lucane Castle," Cormac said. "To what do I owe the honor of this visit?"

The instant they spoke I knew they were British, and I began to worry all over again. There were too many Englishmen in Ireland these days, but those who were, made certain to be discreet about it.

The taller, who was also morose-faced, became the spokesman. "I am honored to present my colleague." He indicated the shorter man. "He is the Honorable Paul Jeffry, and I am George Madden. You, of course, are Mack Cormac. We must be sure of that."

"I am Cormac, at your service."

"We represent the interests of Lord Dervor, and we are here to issue a formal challenge."

"A challenge?" Cormac frowned. "Certainly you do not refer to a duel?"

"That is precisely what we refer to, sir." The shorter man added his part in the proceedings.

"But I couldn't fight that pipsqueak," Cormac said reasonably.

"You are once again malicious," the tall one warned. "We will tell you that Lord Dervor is a fine marksman."

"But look here, gentlemen," Cormac said, "this is 1848. Dueling is against the law except in some of the colonies and in America, where I understand it's practiced in some of the southern states."

"We wish to acquaint you with the details," the tall man said. "It will be fought in secret, with only necessary witnesses. It will be at dawn, one week and two days from this day. When you arrive, you will be met and informed of the location. It will not be in London or any great city, but in some remote country spot."

"I have nothing to say about this nonsense?" Cormac asked.

"Not unless you wish to apologize to Lord Dervor, and that will have to be done before Parliament."

"You may inform Lord Dervor that I will be on hand," Cormac said curtly.

They bowed quite formally and backed away. Cormac watched them in silent amusement. I held open the door, and they stalked out to climb into the carriage and drive off.

I turned to Cormac in alarm. "They meant it! Cormac, you can't fight a duel. Didn't you hear what they said? This Lord Somebody-or-other is a marksman and has no doubt fought other duels."

"Granted. I think I heard at one time or another that he was quite quick to issue a challenge and to fight."

"If he has fought several duels, he must be good or he wouldn't be alive to challenge you. It will be with pistols, apparently. What do you know of dueling pistols, Cormac?"

He chuckled. "Well, now, as I understand it, they load the pistol with powder and add a ball. At a signal, the guns are raised, the duelists walk a prescribed distance, turn, and fire."

"Yes, yes, I know. But what do you know about guns?"

"You pull back a little thing called a hammer, you aim it at the spot you want to hit, and you squeeze the trigger. The gun makes a noise, there is a little smoke, and the man you fired at falls. It's quite simple."

"Yes, it would be, if he didn't fire back. Or first, or was more accurate."

"He will get no chance to fire back."

"You are impossible!" I cried out. "Your life is at stake, and you joke about it. Wouldn't it be best to try to come to better terms? I'm sure they won't insist you appear before Parliament to make an apology."

"You're a traitor to Ireland," Cormac said with a grin. "What you have just suggested is a treasonable offense."

I fled from the castle because I couldn't help it. Talking to this big stubborn baboon, faced with a good chance of being killed because of his obstinacy and pride, made it needful for me to get away from him. I went down to the castle grounds to find Gavan. He seemed to be looking for me. I told him what had happened.

"I saw the pair come and go, like two undertakers," he said. "So Lord Dervor wants to fight a duel with Cormac. Lord Dervor is a bloody fool."

"Do you know anything about him, Gavan? Especially about his skill with dueling pistols?"

"I've heard he is undefeatable. His handling of a gun is quick and his aim is true."

"Then Cormac will be killed, Gavan!"

"I'm more worried about the duel taking place in England."

"How can you be more worried about anything more important than his being killed? There is nothing more important."

"It depends," he said thoughtfully. "I will have a talk with him about this. No doubt it never occurred to him that there could be danger fighting a duel in England, especially for him."

"I am talking about getting himself killed," I insisted doggedly.

"Oh, aye, that too, but a man takes his chances."

I doubled my fists and beat at his chest in rage. "How can you speak so lightly of him being killed?"

Gavan stepped back out of range of my fists. "I will go to him now, so he will have time to think about this."

"I don't know what you're talking about, Gavan, but I'm going with you, and don't try to stop me."

We found Cormac in the great hall, reading again the newspaper copy of his speech. He was so proud of it he'd read it a dozen times already, and one of the newspapers had been carefully put away in a dark place to preserve it.

"You two have been discussing the duel, no doubt," Cormac said.

"Aye, that we have," Gavan replied. "It has come to me that the duel could be very dangerous to you, sir."

"Don't you think I can win?"

"I would not argue that point, sir. It's not the duel itself that worries me. It's what happens afterward. If you are killed . . ."

"Gavan, don't say those words again," I said.

"Pay no attention to that female," Cormac said. "What about after the duel?"

"If you kill him, they'll arrest you for murder. Dueling is against the law in England. If, by some chance, the duel is called off or it fails, you will be arrested for conspiracy, sir. They can find all kinds of charges to levy against you."

"Good," Cormac said. He set aside the newspaper. "It's fine thinking. I myself gave it no thought because I didn't believe it was needful to give any consideration to the fight. But you're right."

"As you fire your shot, sir, you'd best turn and run for it."

"I'll have to think about that." He picked up the newspaper again. "Have you seen the letters to the editor, Gavan? In the papers after my speech? Half say I ought to be hanged and half say I should be sainted. It's hard to please everyone these days."

I sat down slowly, my anger gone, my frustration cooled, only curiosity remaining.

"How can you two be so calm in the face of what is to happen next week? You can't avoid the duel, and you are outclassed, Cormac. Unless you know more about pistols than I've been led to expect."

"I don't like guns, my dear Kate," he admitted. "I'm for a fight with swords, sabers, rapiers, knives, or fists. I favor the fists, though it's not as easy to break a man's neck as to shoot him."

"Then why don't you suggest something other than pistols? You are the challenged one. You have the pick of weapons, as you did with the man you threw down the outside stairs."

"I would only show cowardice in the face of his reputation with a gun. I doubt he can use a sword, or even a dagger, so I'd be accused of taking advantage. I'll fight him the way he wishes, and damned to the man for causing all this trouble. It's a long, dusty way to London, and I'm not in a mood for it."

"Is there no way I can stop you?" I asked.

He glanced at me in surprise. "Now, why should anyone wish to stop me? I've killed men before."

"Aye," I said wearily, "but until now you've not been killed yourself, and one day there has to be the time when you will. There is no need for this duel. Apologize if there is no other way. What's the difference? You spoke your mind, and the words have been sent over the world. No apology will change them."

"I've my own pride," Cormac said curtly. "I'll fight him and anyone else who comes to me with a challenge. I'll be leaving in two days."

"You don't even know where the fight is to be held," I said.

"It won't be far out of London. One place is as good as another."

"Where will you be staying in London while you wait word from them?"

He studied my face a moment. "Why do you ask, Kate?"

"No reason, except if there is some change in their plans and they send word here, we can see you learn of it."

"Let them find me if there is a change."

"How can they?" I asked reasonably. "Besides, if you are hurt—or worse—we can come to you with what help we can offer."

"You're the most morbid female I've met in my life, Kate. But if you must know, it's called the Shamrock. I chose it for the name, and I stay there whenever I'm in London. You have but to ask anybody who looks Irish and they'll tell you where it is—well on the outskirts. Now, have done with all this. I don't want to hear any more about the silly business."

"Silly, is it?" I said angrily. "You may be killed, and you call it silly. Well, then, get yourself killed if that's what you look for. As you said, we'll have no more talk of it. Either you'll kill the daft man who challenged you, or you'll be killed and we'll come to bear your body home. There is nothing else we can do."

I walked away to the accompaniment of Cormac's loud laughter, but I was too chagrined to turn back and give him the edge of my tongue.

This time I stayed out of Cormac's way, for fear that I would dissolve into tears. It broke my heart to begin preparations for his journey. Only one thing happened to grant me at least a small measure of relief. Cormac decided to take Gavan with him.

"I don't know why he changed his mind," Gavan told me. "I offered to act as his second, but he refused that. He wouldn't need one, he said. But the English will make it formal, no doubt."

"He will leave in the morning, then?" I asked.

"Aye, first to the railroad, as always. Then the train to Dublin and a boat to England."

"This inn, the Shamrock, do you know of it?"

"Aye, I've been there with him twice."

"Would you put into writing exactly where this place is located?" I asked. "Without telling a bit of it to Cormac?"

"You are going there? Miss, he'll be angry."

"He won't even know about it unless he's hurt. You know anything can happen in a duel, and I want to be there to help if that becomes necessary."

"He'll hide me for it, but I will write the directions. Mind you, miss, he won't be killed."

"How many times have you told me that? He won't be killed—and he is not killed. How do you know this? Is Cormac blessed by the Little People or some kind fairy that he can fight without the danger of himself being killed?"

"He is skilled, and he is brave. A steady, thoughtful man when it comes to fighting. That's why he wins, miss. That's how it will keep on being."

"He is also human," I said, "and can be hurt. But I will take your word for the fact that he is a fine fighting man."

"Then why would you wish to follow to London, miss?"

"You have said, and we have all agreed, that if Cormac kills this man, he is likely to be arrested for murder. The way he is now regarded because of his speech could get him slapped into prison for life. If he does not kill his opponent, perhaps only wounds him, or maybe doesn't harm him at all, then he will still be arrested for dueling. They will swear he caused the duel, he issued the challenge. They can lie themselves green in the face, Gavan, and make it sound like the truth. If Cormac gets into such trouble, perhaps there is something I can do to help him escape from England. Once he's back here, they won't dare come for him."

Gavan nodded. "You're a sensible woman, miss. What you say is true, and we have agreed on it before. I don't know how it could be managed, but it is possible Cormac will need help in escaping."

"Then I'll take Conan with me. He's a fine man when there's trouble about. Will you meet us near the Shamrock, Gavan? So we will know what to expect."

"Aye. We will arrive early the day before the duel. That night I will go for a walk, as I have done before when we were in England. If you watch the inn about eight, you'll see me, and it will be safe, for Cormac has friends at the inn, and about that time he will be drinking with them."

"Drinking the night before he's going to fight a duel?" I asked in astonishment. "Is he completely daft, Gavan?"

"There are times . . ." Gavan said, and then he relented. "It makes no difference. Drunk or sober, he'll win. Even if he has a head on him like a balloon, he won't get himself killed. Because he's better than the other, and he knows it."

Before Gavan could change his mind, I took the sidecar and drove to the village. I wanted to find Conan, and that was no problem, for he was at home and happy to see me. I even got the idea he was more worried about the duel than he pretended to be.

In his cottage, I gave him the details. "I want you to come with me. We'll take the next train and the Dublin boat after it returns from bringing Cormac to English soil. Gavan is going with him and will meet us that night and tell us what to expect."

"Aye, it is a good idea to follow him," Conan agreed, "but what can we do when we get there? If Cormac finds we've followed him, he'll be so angry he might lose the duel."

"We'll see to it he does not see us. So be ready, Conan. We'll drive him to the station, but we won't come back here. We'll put up the horse and take the next train."

"I'll be ready," he said. "We won't be able to take any baggage without giving ourselves away."

"We'll not be there long enough to need baggage. Only what I can get into my handbag and what you can get into your pockets without making them bulge."

That night, before he left, I had the cook prepare a special meal to be served the two of us, and I made sure Cormac would be there by telling him about it first.

"I'll not talk of duels, or marriage, or even bedding with you, Cormac. I will speak only of such things as more improvements on the castle, what I will wear when I greet you as you return, and how long I should stay in mourning if you do not."

At the table I talked on any subject that came to mind,

foolish or important. I asked him about his half-brother and learned a little more concerning the man. It seemed Cormac didn't hate him, but he had no real affection for him either.

"I will admit it's my pleasure to see you across the table again, Kate, but if you're up to something, I'll take a club to you."

"Now, what could I be up to? You'll not even be here. I will go to the railroad with you in case it's to be the last time I'll ever see you."

He chuckled at that statement. "You can be there to see me return as well, and that would be to my liking."

"Then I will be there. Have you had any practice in the firing of a pistol since the challenge?"

"No! Why should I waste my time? I'll go to England, I'll shoot the daft man who asked for the fight, and then I'll come back. That's all there'll be to it."

I leaned an elbow on the table after the last of the dishes were cleared away. I rested my chin in my hand and I studied him closely.

"Tell me, Cormac, can anyone kill you?"

I expected a roar of laughter, but there was no mirth in him when he got to his feet. "Who told you to ask me that?"

"Nobody. It was only a foolish question. But you are so cocksure, it seems you have made yourself believe you cannot be harmed."

"That had better be true," he warned.

"How daft do you think I can be to believe you live a charmed life? There is no mortal who does, not even you."

He quelled his anger and nodded. "Aye, that's true enough. I didn't want you to get grand ideas about me not being human."

"Oh, of course, Cormac," I said as sweetly as possible. "And if there was ever one to testify that you are human, it is me."

That was the right comment, for he smiled again.

That evening we spent in the great hall, he with his cigar and brandy and I with my wine. It was as it had been during the best days at the castle. Yet he was also edgy, and I took good care that I not speak on subjects that would make him more nervous.

His easygoing manner hadn't changed the following morning when the four of us drove to the railroad. It was more like the beginning of a journey for pleasure than one concerned with dueling and death.

I kissed him good-bye at the trainside, and Conan and I stood watching the train pull away in a torrent of steam and enough noise to wake the countryside.

Now Conan and I had time, for there would not be another train for six hours. We ate our noonday meal at the inn, ordering too much so we might kill time in comfort. Then we took a ride into the country and came back in time to put up the horse and carriage, to fill our stomachs again, for there'd be no food on the train.

I slept during most of the ride, for it was mainly done in darkness. Conan also slept, so when we reached Dublin we were so rested we toured the city on foot until the boat to England was ready to cast off.

I enjoyed the journey and the boat because I'd not been this far from the village in years. We reached London that evening and went at once to keep our rendezvous with Gavan. I prayed he'd been able to get away from Cormac without arousing his suspicions. The inn was some distance from London proper, in the green countryside.

Shortly after eight, Gavan emerged from the inn and walked slowly along the street, giving us the opportunity of meeting him where we saw fit.

As he passed us, I stepped out and walked beside him. "Is everything as it should be?" I asked.

"Aye, nothing much has come about that we didn't expect."

"Then tell me," I said. "But first, did he wonder if I would follow?"

"It occurred to him more than once," Gavan admitted. "But not anymore. There is, half a mile behind the inn, a field that is partly clear, as if for a park. There is one stand of trees, not too close. A grove, I would say. There, hidden by the trees, the duel will be held in the morning, just as there will be enough light that they may be able to sight the guns by. Each man will be allowed one shot at twenty paces."

"Have you learned more about the skill of this Englishman with a pistol?"

"He has no equal, but from what I have heard said by the few who know about the duel, Lord Dervor is respectful of Cormac's reputation as a fighting man, even without pistols, and he is more nervous than he has ever been before one of his duels."

"There is no chance of preventing it from happening?"

"None, miss. Cormac won't have it, for one thing."

"And what about the danger of Cormac being arrested no matter what the outcome of the duel may be? Except in case Cormac . . ." I couldn't bring myself to say the rest of it.

"There have been no signs of the police," Gavan said. "I have been watchful. Of course, they may be ready to arrest Cormac. They don't have to appear until after the duel."

"Does it come to your mind that they plan to arrest him?"

"Too often, miss. This is the kind of chance the English are famous for taking advantage of. They'll have him as a rebel and they'll put an end to his shenanigans by locking him up until he's an old man."

"I've been thinking. . . . If there was a carriage hidden close by, could Cormac make it in a fast run?"

"Perhaps, if he knew the carriage was there."

"Can you tell him that you arranged for one to be there? Or will you have to be on this so-called field of honor?"

"I am not permitted to be there."

"Well, then, I would say you should hire a carriage and take him off to some safe place."

"There isn't time—" he began.

"Leave it to Conan and me. We'll be on hand in the morning, though none will see us if we're lucky. You will tell Cormac that the carriage will be waiting. Have you been able to go to the place of the duel yet?"

"Cormac and I went there this afternoon. It is well-wooded, this small area. If I could have a carriage waiting as close to where Cormac will stand as possible, and he knew it was there . . . aye, he might make it."

"Then be sure to tell him your plan tonight. And be at the spot before dawn. We're trying to save his life, Gavan, or at best his liberty, so don't fail him."

"And what will you and Conan be doing? I've seen him following us at a distance."

"We didn't think it wise for him to be with me, in case Cormac happened to step outside."

"And what if he did, miss, and saw you?"

"It would only be from the back and at a good distance. You could tell him an English fancy woman was trying to lure you into her den of shame. Cormac will surely understand that."

"Oh, aye," he said with a resigned nod of his head.

"In the morning, then," I said. "Be watchful there are no police."

I dropped back, let him continue on, and at the next corner I waited for Conan to catch up. As we continued to walk, I laid out the plan I'd been scheming all day and night.

"Gavan will have a carriage ready, but we will supply the carriage. We must now find a place where we can rent this carriage and two more just like it."

"Three carriages?" he asked.

"Three, all the same. All waiting, and when Cormac comes running with the police at his heels, they'll be hard put to know which of the three carriages to follow."

"Ah, yes," Conan said with a big smile. "It's a clever lass you are. Three carriages, all the same."

"Each with two horses for speed, and all six horses much the same, if that is possible. We'll find out now."

Renting six horses and three carriages, all of them plum-colored broughams, was not difficult, but very expensive. I concocted a likely story to satisfy the owner of the stable, something about a large wedding party where all the attendants would dress exactly the same and we wanted the vehicles they would ride in to also look the same. I wasn't sure the stableman understood exactly what I meant, but he understood the money well enough.

It was a busy night, for Conan had to drive one of the carriages to a safe place close by the site for the duel. Then he returned to drive the second, while I had already taken the third one to the place where Conan had left the first brougham.

An hour before dawn we drove two carriages to the inn where Cormac was staying, and we turned one of them over to a hostler working for the inn. I instructed him to leave the carriage in front of the inn, and when Gavan came out with Cormac, to lead them to this carriage and see that they used it. I gave him money enough to make sure my orders would be faithfully carried out.

Now Conan and I drove the second carriage back to the dueling grounds, where he got aboard the third brougham, which we had left there while we completed our plans.

It was a mad scheme, but I could think of nothing else. I was convinced, as I knew Cormac must be, that the British would never let him escape England if they could manage it, no matter what the outcome of the duel.

It was almost dawn. By now Cormac would be on his way to the dueling grounds. I sat inside the brougham, curled up for warmth, while my anxiety grew greater and greater until I felt I couldn't stand it any longer. I left the warmth of the vehicle to mount the seat and wake up the dozing horses.

Conan also woke up and walked over to join me. "We'll hide ourselves and the carriages now," I said. "Gavan told me he would not be allowed on the field. He will be on the third carriage. Once everyone has arrived, we must be ready to pull out as soon as the duel is over."

It was all carefully thought-out, but in the dead of night when I was both tired and sleepy, I forgot that if we were compelled to flee with Cormac, it would be due to the fact that police were at hand. Not once did I let myself think that Cormac might never live to leave the field.

When I left the carriage at a safe distance to approach on foot, I saw them. They were on the far side of the grove. They were waiting in light carriages and buggies able to travel very fast, but positioned out of sight, well beyond the dueling place. They'd not seen us yet, and I prayed they'd be so busy watching the duel they'd not look for friends Cormac might have sent for.

There was nothing for me to do now except wait until Gavan drove up with Cormac. Then I would have to move quickly, and I prayed it would not yet be daylight when they arrived. If I knew Gavan, he'd see to it they arrived first so I might put my plan into operation with enough time to ensure its success.

I remained concealed in the shrubbery of the grove. When I heard a carriage driving up, I held my breath, hoping it would be Cormac so I'd have time to put my plan into action. But this was not the plum-colored brougham I'd left for Cormac to use.

From the carriage two men stepped down, both wearing black cloaks and high hats. I could barely see in the gray light of dawn. One carried a flat box, no doubt containing the pistols. The other held a small black valise, and I guessed he would be a doctor. Both men dismissed their carriage, and the coachman drove it off the rough road leading to the grove, to wait there for them.

It was barely light by now, and I began to worry. Then Gavan drove up in the brougham and Cormac alighted. He was not given to dressing for formal occasions, and unlike the somber dress of the two men who had arrived ahead of him, Cormac wore a lightweight leather jacket and a frilled shirt open at the throat. He wore trousers tucked into brown boots, and his dark hair was as unruly as ever. The two men bowed after tipping their hats politely. Cormac strode past them toward the entrance to the grove. Gavan remained on the seat of the brougham, though he did drive it a few yards away, turning it about to be ready for a swift dash from this spot.

It was full dawn when Lord Dervor's carriage arrived. He was unaccompanied, and I was surprised to see how slight of build he was, though that was all I could really see of the man in this false light. Once he entered the grove, I came from my hiding place. Gavan came down from his brougham, and Conan drove up in the third one. I hurried to where I'd hidden my vehicle and quickly brought this around too, so that three identical carriages now waited for Cormac.

The coachmen who had driven the seconds and Lord Dervor were not to be seen, but Gavan and Conan were just closing the door of one coach. I got down and joined them.

Gavan said, "We put the two coachmen to sleep."

"After reminding them it's early in the day and no sensible man should be awake at this hour," Conan added. "They'll wake up with a sore head, but that's all."

"I wondered what we would do with them," I admitted. "I'm going to try to watch the duel. When I dash out, be ready."

"Aye, we'll be waiting," Gavan said.

I ran toward the grove, pressed my way through the thickets at the foot of the trees, and was in time to drop to my knees behind a bush at a point where I could see the whole field of honor. The ground was level, covered with short grass. The sound of the pistols would never be heard, and a duel with rapiers could be conducted without detection even by anyone passing on the road that led across the cleared area outside the grove, where I'd left the brougham unattended, praying the horses would not stray.

There was little ceremony to this secretly held duel. The two men in high hats were apparently Dervor's seconds. Of course Cormac had none. The flat case was opened, presented to Cormac, who removed one of the long dueling pistols without even looking at it. Dervor examined his most carefully.

They stood facing each other. There was no signal given, they merely backed up the required and agreed-upon number of paces. I held my breath, wondering for the first time if I'd leave here alone, or urge Cormac to escape as fast as he could.

The police were well hidden opposite the spot I'd picked, and I was careful not to show myself. The two men waited, standing firm, until the light was better, I supposed. One of the pair in high hats stepped forward and raised a white handkerchief.

Dervor was a sight to behold. He wore a morning coat, an immaculate weskit, striped trousers, gray gloves, and a high silk hat.

The handkerchief fluttered to the ground. Dervor raised his pistol, and apparently without aiming, fired. Cormac jerked about to his right. He'd been hit, but he had not fired.

I almost cried out, expecting him to fall slowly to the ground, but he steadied himself and now raised his pistol. He used both hands in holding it, and he aimed very carefully. Dervor, I admitted to myself, took it bravely enough. Cormac had given him the first shot, and Dervor's bullet had failed to hit a vital spot. At least Cormac was on his feet. I heard the sound of the gun. My eyes flicked over to watch Dervor fall, but the bullet ripped through his high hat, knocking it off. Cormac advanced toward the man. He picked up the high hat, placed it carefully on Dervor's head, and then, with one mighty fist, smashed the hat down so it covered the poor man's eyes.

Cormac then threw the pistol as high in the air as he could. He turned and began walking steadily across the field. Suddenly he raised a hand to grasp his right shoulder, and he seemed to lose strength as his gait became the wobbly one of an injured man. Yet he kept going.

In this manner he reached the opening in the stand of trees. I went racing to where the brougham waited, and as I cleared the brush, I saw Cormac running like the wind. He'd pretended weakness from a serious wound in order to delay the police from closing in too soon. As they must have seen it, their man was unable to move fast and certainly could not run from them.

They were after him as he broke into this fast run. I was on the brougham and had it moving, with the door open. Cormac dived inside headfirst and pulled the door shut. Ahead of me, Conan was driving one brougham at top speed, and Gavan, in the third plum-colored brougham, pulled in behind me. All three of us whipped the horses and got all the speed we could from them.

It was about a mile and a half to the outskirts of London,

and we headed there by prearrangement on the theory that Cormac could hide best where there were many people.

The police, who had tied their horses well behind the grove, were delayed in getting after us. When we came to a fork in the road, Conan took it while I continued straight ahead, with Gavan behind me. The police had taken up the chase now. There were three vehicles. One veered off at the fork to follow Conan, but with little chance of catching him. The horses pulling my brougham were almost on the verge of bolting, and it required all of my strength to hold them back and yet demand the utmost in stamina from them.

Looking back, I saw the two police buggies beginning to catch up, their lighter vehicles being somewhat faster. But we were nearing the outskirts of the city now, and there were people and other vehicles on the streets.

Suddenly I heard Gavan give a strident yell as he turned off onto one of the other streets. I instantly pulled up, turned a corner, and came to a stop. The police couldn't possibly have seen me do that, but they'd watched Gavan turn down the other street.

I felt the brougham rock as Cormac stepped down and then clambered onto the seat beside me. He pulled the reins from my hands.

"Get into the carriage," he said. "Hurry!"

I asked no questions but jumped to the ground and got into the carriage as Cormac brought the team to a trot and proceeded somewhat unconcernedly down the street. No police buggy came into sight, so far as I could see. Apparently we'd confused them so well they'd both taken off after Gavan. Cormac kept the horses at a steady pace and drove straight into the busy area of London proper, teeming with tradesmen and lumbering wagons at this early hour of the day. I had no idea what he was up to, but it was impossible to carry on any sort of conversation with him on the high seat.

It was full daylight by now, and I began to relax a bit, settling back on the padded seat to rest. Something brushed my hand as I touched the seat, and when I looked, my fingers were smeared with blood. Cormac had really been hurt!

I leaned forward and rapped on the glass, but he waved a hand to indicate he couldn't stop now. Apparently he had some destination in mind. When he did pull up, it was before a large and opulent house set on a small estate behind iron gates.

Cormac got down, opened the gates, drove through, and

stopped again to close the gates. This time he pulled open the brougham door and reached out to help me down, with an arm soaked in blood that dripped off his hand.

"You're hurt!" I exclaimed. "Cormac, we have to find a doctor."

"What do you think I drove here for?"

I looked about. "Where are we?"

"My half-brother lives here. The house and estate are mine. I lent them to him. Go around to the back and wake up the stableman. Tell him to unhitch the team, take care of the horses, and hide the carriage in the barn at once. We don't want it seen by any constable who might come by. Then go into the house."

I didn't question those orders, because it was apparent they had to be carried out promptly. I summoned the hostler, told him what to do, and then hurried to the front door, which had been left ajar. I went in, to find Cormac seated in a chair, holding onto his wounded arm. I looked about, saw a dining room to my left with the table set for one. The linen was immaculately white. I removed the dishes and silver, pulled the cloth free, and ripped off one end. With it I formed a crude but efficient-enough bandage and brought it to the hall where Cormac sat. He already had a pocketknife ready. I used it to slit his sleeve the entire length, exposed the wound, and wiped away most of the blood gently so it wouldn't begin bleeding again.

"You're a damned fool," I told him as I worked. "I saw the duel. You gave him the first shot, and that could have been like committing suicide."

"I am surprised I got pinked," he admitted.

"You're lucky, with the Irish luck granted only to the brainless. The ball went clean through your arm, and there's nothing to dig for. Which is a disappointment to me. I'd like to go after it with a dinner fork or a meat knife. Cormac . . . Cormac, why do you do these things? You'll be the death of me yet."

"It's I who should be angry with you. I told you not to interfere, but you always do, womanlike, I suppose. You will learn to mind your own business or you can walk out on me for all I care."

I pulled the bandage tight enough for him to squirm a bit. "You need me like a small child needs a mother. You're about the most insane man I ever met."

"You saw the duel?" he asked mildly.

"Why didn't you kill him?"

"He's too small and fussy. . . ."

"He meant to kill you, didn't he?"

"Oh, aye, that he did, but it was enough to let the man know the contempt I had for him. Sometimes that hurts worse than a bullet."

"You're still a wild-eyed Irishman, Cormac," I said before I lowered my voice. "But I'm glad you're safe. Thank God it was no more than the wound you have. But even that must be cared for. Where is this half-brother of yours, that he's impolite enough not to be here to greet us."

"Woman, it's still so early the hour's not fit for a man to be awake yet." He stood up and grasped my hand with his sound one. "I'm grateful, you know. I may not act as if I am sometimes, but that's only my pride not letting me give way to my real feelings. If it had not been for you—and Gavan and Conan—I'd likely be in a cell by now, with little chance of getting out in the next few years."

For a moment I thought he was about to take me in his arms, for I could see the warmth of his love gleaming in his eyes. But that was the moment his half-brother chose to come down the stairs and, with a great shout of joy, greet Cormac.

"Be easy with him," I called out. "He's been hurt."

"It's nothing," Cormac said. "Pay no attention to the woman. She's a bit woozy when it comes to seeing blood."

"Now, that's a lie," I said hotly. "Being with the likes of you, Cormac, one has to live with the sight of blood, because you're forever spilling it before my eyes."

"She's a spunky lass," Cormac's brother observed.

"Her name is Kate Moran, and I will say she got me away from the constables who were waiting to put me in jail, especially if I killed Lord Dervor."

"You didn't?" his half-brother asked. "I'm surprised."

"He gave Dervor the first shot and then put a bullet through his high hat," I explained, "before he jammed the same hat down over the man's eyes. Which won't make him liked, any more than if he'd killed the man."

Cormac said, "Kate, this is my half-brother, Nial. It's a fine Irish name, and he gets away with it in this city where the Irish do not usually settle."

"But those who have are clients of mine. Many more since your speech," Nial said. "They've flocked to me, and that's a profitable business, I must say."

"Well, in return, Nial," I said, "you might do his honor

here the favor of calling a doctor you can trust. Before he dies from loss of blood, though I must say he likely has gallons of it to spill."

"At once," Nial agreed.

As he moved away to call a servant, I had a good look at him. He was as tall as Cormac, but not nearly so heavy. He might be a fighting man too, but I judged he would fight more with words than weapons. Though their mothers were the same, Nial bore no facial resemblance to Cormac. Instead of possessing a wide face and head set on a muscular neck, Nial was thin of face, with the same blue eyes, which was about the only thing the two had in common.

Cormac turned to me. "Go home," he said. "You can't stay here or in London. You were no doubt seen on the carriage seat, and the police will be hunting you too. What of Conan and Gavan?"

"They will make their own way," I said confidently. "If they don't, your brother can act like a barrister and get them out of their trouble."

"Will you go back to the castle, as I have just asked you to?"

"If I am not wanted here," I began indignantly.

"Kate, listen to reason. Every bloody constable in London is trying to find me. They'll come here sooner or later, for they know Nial is my brother. But I won't be here. I'll be on the move, and I can't travel fast enough with you hanging onto my coattails."

"I'll go," I agreed. "How soon will you come back?"

"I don't know. It depends on how long the search for me goes on."

"You have somewhere to go in London, then? Where you will be safe?"

"Aye. I've friends here. Many of them. You are not to worry about me. But I want you to leave at once."

I bent my head in surrender. "It's against my wishes that I'll leave you. After seeing how you handled that duel, I don't think you've the brains to keep away from the police."

"And you've a sharp tongue. Talking this way to a dying man like me, bleeding his life away."

I stepped closer to him and pressed my cheek against his. "Oh, Cormac, I don't mean to lecture you, but you are so bold and unthinking."

"I know, Kate. I didn't mean to say you had a sharp tongue. Though it's not a dull one, either. Go home now. I'll have one of Nial's coachmen drive you to the railway, from where you can reach the steamer. Go back to the castle and keep it for me until I return. I won't be long, I promise."

"You will be safe?" I asked again.

"I told you, I have many friends in London. I'll be fine but go now so I can arrange to see a doctor and not have you to worry about."

I reached up on tiptoe to kiss him, and there was warmth in his answering kiss.

I disliked leaving him, but I could see the wisdom of it. He'd be laid up with this wounded arm, which would take some time to heal, if it was not infected. I'd be in danger while I was here and might even accidentally lead the police to Cormac.

I was brought to a railway and had no trouble during the remainder of the long journey. Cormac had provided me with plenty of money, so I traveled in comfort, which enabled me to find a little rest after the harrowing days before the duel.

Cormac, I thought, had seen to my welfare generously and well. And I knew he loved me. No matter that he spoke of marriage in such a negative way, I had a strong feeling he didn't mean it. And I looked forward to the day when he would tell me so.

ELEVEN

It was good to be back at the castle. My return journey had been a lonely one, and not accomplished without worry, for every time I saw a policeman I left the vicinity if possible. But I wasn't questioned or even stopped. I had taken the precaution of writing to Gavan before I left London, and as my return trip was slow and the mail somewhat faster, he was at the railroad depot when the train pulled in.

"I wondered if you and Conan had managed safely," I said. "The last I saw of you was the back of the carriage you were driving to draw the police away from us."

"They never did catch up with Conan," Gavan said with a laugh. "They caught me, and I told them I whipped the horses because I was sure they were highwaymen. I don't think they believed me, but there wasn't much they could do, for they had no proof I'd broken any laws."

"I'm glad," I said. "You and Conan did save Cormac—and me. They would have had us for sure except for you two."

On the ride back, I went into more detail for Gavan's benefit. "We managed to reach the house where Cormac's half-brother lives. I didn't stay, for Cormac insisted I go home because I was slowing him down. I suppose that was as good a reason as any for getting rid of me."

"It was probably true." Gavan defended his employer and friend. "If the constables are making a strong search, a man has to run and duck. He'll make it because he knows how to do both very well indeed. You met Nial?"

"Aye. Decent-enough man, I suppose. He's not much like Cormac, I will say."

"That's true, also. Nial is quieter. He has to be, because he's nowhere near as big and powerful as Cormac. A clever man with the law, they say. Did you care for the likes of him, miss?"

"I don't know, Gavan. I saw too little of the man. When do you think Cormac will risk coming back here?"

"That depends on a number of things, headed by luck, I'd say. But he'll make it."

When we were back at the castle, I took up where I'd left off. The servants hadn't grown lazy or indifferent while I was away, and the castle was spotless and beautiful. During the empty days that followed, I tried to find ways of making the castle even better, and I kept Conan busy at renovation work.

The days turned into three weeks, and not a word did I hear from Cormac. I was beginning to worry about him. Then one of the servants called that a carriage was approaching. I untied the large apron I was wearing, tucked in the ends of my hair, prayed I would look well to him, and then went downstairs—to find Nial walking from the carriage bearing two large suitcases. I sent a servant to relieve him of them and went out to welcome him.

"It's nice to see you again. You look charming," he said. "Isn't Cormac at home?"

"He's not come back yet," I said. "Do you think he's in trouble?"

"I'm sure he's not, at least not up to the time I left London, or I'd have heard from him. I'm surprised, though. He said he'd return last week. There must have been some kind of delay."

"Just as long as he's not arrested or hurt," I said. "Do you intend to stay, Nial?"

"Yes, for a day or two. I've business with Cormac."

"I'm pleased to have you, Nial. With Cormac away, there's not much to do, but you can ride, and there's fishing in a stream not more than a mile away."

"I'll be happy to sit about and rest, if you don't mind, Kate."

"I'll be glad of your company. I wonder why Cormac didn't come back as he told you he would."

"Oh, I suppose he's mixed up with his old friends again. When that happens, there's carousing and everything that goes with it. Tell me, what is the situation between you and him?"

"I'm the keeper of the castle. No more."

"You regard him with some favor, do you not?"

"Aye, that I do. And I have reason to believe he holds some measure of affection for me as well."

"He'd be an idiot if he didn't. You're a lovely lass, Kate,

But take my advice, don't depend too much on him. He has a tendency to stray, and many's the scrape I've had to get him out of. He wouldn't make a very good husband."

"He would if I were his wife." I spoke with enough conviction to make Nial nod in agreement.

"I'd say that as well, Kate. You're a strong woman. Not strong enough to hold Cormac, I'm afraid, but if anyone can do it, I would say you'd be the one. Have you two talked of marriage?"

"I have," I said ruefully. "Cormac keeps telling me he's not a marrying man, and I'm beginning to believe it."

Nial laughed. "He's a man who doesn't know his own mind."

"You have known him all your life," I said. "Don't you think it strange, his living such a charmed life? With all his fights, the first time he was ever hurt was in that duel. I meant to ask about his wounded arm."

"It healed quickly and well. There was a great hue and cry for his hide, but that quieted down. Yes, he is a lucky man. He goes hunting trouble and never backs off when he finds it. He's a great fighting man, Cormac is."

"Has he told you of the room upstairs where there is a large, heavy book printed in Gaelic?"

"I have been there, Kate."

"Come with me," I said, and led him upstairs to the barren room. I unlocked it, and Nial looked about. He gently touched the black bust of Cormac.

"I know all about this. Cormac never was a man to talk about it, though."

"He told me it's centuries old," I explained. "And that it's the bust of one of his ancestors."

"So we were told." Nial examined it more carefully. "Yes, it looks as ancient as the castle. And have I told you what a miracle you have wrought here? Last time I visited the castle, it looked like the inside of a big shanty. Cormac told me how you had brought it back."

"It was pleasant work," I said. "Now, look at this big book. I don't think I could even heft it."

Nial opened the book at random. "This is handwritten in Gaelic," he said. "It's very old. The paper is brittle and the ink faded some. A relic, like the black statue. The white busts are not that old, but they're not modern either. I'm good at telling how old things are, and these are quite ancient."

"The white busts resemble Cormac somewhat," I judged. "Can they also be ancestors?"

"It's possible. You understand, I'm not that well-versed in the family history, because I never cared much for such things. Though I know the family goes all the way back to Tara, and that's not the day before yesterday."

"I wish I knew the meaning of this," I said. "I think whatever it does mean is responsible for the strange way Cormac acts at times. Were members of the family always fighters?"

"Always. Most of them died fighting for some cause or other. They spoiled for trouble and always found it. Then came the sword swinging, and the heads rolled. I'm of the same family, but thanks be to God, I'm not a full-blooded one."

I closed the great book and we left the room to go back downstairs. I had a maid bring glasses, wine, and brandy. It was nice to have someone to sit and talk about Cormac and his family.

"What was Cormac like when he was a boy?" I asked.

Nial sipped his brandy and thought back, pausing to assemble his thoughts on the subject. "Well, now, he was a boy who liked to fight. No doubt of that, and you know, I never did hear of a fight he lost. Not one! I remember one day after church, two big bullies said something about Cormac's family. I don't know what it was. Some foolish chatter of boys. You know how they are. Besides, they said it to pick a fight with Cormac. It seemed later that they wanted to teach him a lesson. He sailed into the pair of them, and, saint's alive, there was a battle. Both were older and bigger than Cormac. They knocked him down a dozen times and kicked him until he was more black and blue than white. Each time, Cormac got up, and in the end it was that pair of devils who lay flat on their backs yelling to high heaven for Cormac not to punch them again."

"He hasn't changed much," I said ruefully.

"Maybe the sweetness of that victory turned him into the spoiler he's been since. He regards himself as invincible. Now, that duel with Dervor. There was no reason for it. Dervor would have been glad to accept Cormac's apology. I even urged Cormac to settle Dervor's ruffled feathers. Cormac would have none of it. I warned him how proficient Dervor was with a gun and how many duels he has won in his life. Cormac just said this one he would not win. That's confidence for you."

"Do you know Kerry Flynn who has a castle ten miles west of here?" I asked.

"Aye, he's a spoiler too, but an evil man to boot. He and Cormac have feuded since they were boys."

"It comes to me that Cormac is afraid of him. Is that possible?"

"No! Cormac fears no man."

"But the big hulk worries Cormac. I can tell that."

"Maybe because he thinks he'll have to fight him one day. I don't know, of course, but it used to be said that they were bound to tear each other apart before they died."

"Everything is a mystery," I said. "Nobody knows anything, and so many unexplained things crop up. You'd think Cormac would trust me."

"He killed a man here in the castle not long ago, I heard."

"The man deserved what he got."

"It's not too easy to rile Cormac. What did this poor man do?"

"He attacked me. Had he been successful, it would have been a rape."

"And he killed the man for that! He's never been one to follow a straight path, nor one trod by any ordinary man. Maybe there is something not quite human about him. Who knows? There's many a legend in this land of ours, and most are pure fancy, but then, there might be one with substance to it."

"You have business with him?" I asked.

"Only a few papers for him to sign. I handle his legal problems. They're not many, or nearly as complicated as the man himself. If he does not return in a day or two, I'll be on my way, and he can come to me."

"You'd think a man who had barely escaped with his life would come home to lick his wounds."

"Trouble with Cormac," Nial said, "he has too many friends who will lick his wounds for him. He's generous, and his friends are so fickle they'd drop him if he went busted. But that won't happen, even if he tries to make it so."

"I think I'm about ready to give up," I confessed. "Unless he begins to act like a sane man. Where do you suppose he can be?"

"With some of those friends. He's not a sainted man, Kate."

"That I have known for some time," I admitted. "I'll see to supper now, and tomorrow we'll go riding if you like."

"I'm not much for it anymore. City life has made me soft, but you go ahead with whatever you normally do. I can take good care of myself."

Cormac didn't come back, and finally Nial decided he could wait no longer. He left documents on Cormac's desk for him to sign. He left instructions with me about each document. I saw him off and then went back to the monotony of waiting for Cormac's return.

When he finally did come home, I almost wished he hadn't. He and a dozen of his friends arrived in two hired coach-and-fours, yelling and causing all the commotion they could. The good village people must have been shocked, for the two vehicles with their screaming, shouting passengers rode up and down the little street.

I heard them coming from half a mile off. So did Gavan, who hurried to the front of the castle to stand there with me. He had opened the big gate, and we were ready for them.

Cormac, at sight of us, gave a welcoming yell and leaped from the first coach. He ran to me, picked me up, and did a wild dance. His hands were too familiar to suit me, and I fought clear of the man. Cormac was drunk, and so were his companions, except for Ellen. The flat-chested, washed-out blond had come back, as she had predicted. She walked regally into the castle and began giving orders to the startled and confused maids.

Baggage was unloaded, indicating the party meant to remain for a time, which was a discouraging idea to me. The women were as drunk as the men, and they went screaming through the castle door, pursued by the men.

Cormac seized one brown-haired woman who was old enough to know better and carried her in his arms into the castle. No doubt he didn't pause on his way to one of the bedrooms. I was suddenly filled with disgust. Gavan went about gathering the baggage to be brought inside and sorted out. He had no comment to make, and it was lucky he didn't say anything to me about being loyal to that baboon of a man who couldn't be trusted out of my sight.

In the castle the drinking, which must have lasted at least a few days, was now resumed, and the brandy bottles were running dry with a remarkable speed. I went to my room, disillusioned and angry. This was a fine homecoming.

Twice that night Cormac pounded on my door and even tried the latch, but I told him to go away. I was in no mood for the roistering that had never stopped since the party arrived.

It was on the second day that my ire finally reached a point where I could no longer contain myself. Most of them, led by Cormac, had gone for an afternoon ride. When they returned, instead of turning the horses over to the hostlers who stood by, they rode them into the castle, through the front door, and down the hallway to the great hall, where the animals knocked over tables and ground dirty hoofs into the polished floor. One of the men, too intoxicated to stay in the saddle, started to fall and grabbed a heavy drapery, pulling it down and almost smothering himself in its heavy folds, to the ribald amusement of everyone else.

I tried shouting at them to stop, but no one, including Cormac, paid the slightest attention to me. I gave up and walked out of the castle. Gavan, having finally finished his struggles with the baggage, found me wandering about as distraught as a lost child.

"Once," he said, "I warned you to go away from this place, and now I repeat that warning. He is not for you, miss."

I faced him squarely. "But he is, Gavan. Truly he is in love with me."

"He shows it in strange ways, miss."

"I feel there is a reason for it. Don't you see? One day he is gentle and tender and loving. The next, he is a beast, and this time he has made himself obnoxious. He deliberately brought these terrible friends of his to the castle so I'd be upset and finally decide to leave."

"Well, then, it seems you must," Gavan said softly.

"I'm damned if I will. Should Cormac tell me why, and if the reason is sufficient, then I'll consider it, but he can't get rid of me this way."

"Some things," Gavan said, "cannot be told."

"You know why he acts this way. He's told you his reasons. Why can't you tell me?"

"Miss, I do not have that much of his confidence. As you well know, he's not an ordinary man in his ways and his thinking. I don't understand him any more than you do."

"I understand you, Gavan. You have not answered my question."

"Perhaps," he said, as he turned away, "I don't know what you mean, miss. I will say again: it would be best if you left."

"And I will say again," I called out to his retreating back, "that I will not."

I was fond of Gavan. In fact, I liked the man as much as I did Conan, but he did exasperate me. I went back to the castle reluctantly, to see what damage had been done. It was considerable, I noticed with a sigh of resignation. Not difficult to repair, but the senselessness of it galled me.

These people played hard, and they slept long and at odd hours. At the moment they were all upstairs, sleeping it off, no doubt. I knew Cormac was deliberately keeping out of my way, and I was tempted to go to his room and knock on the door, but I decided against it. He might have Ellen in bed with him. I could, with considerable effort, tolerate the other boisterous hangers-on, but Ellen I could not and I would not. The rest of the pack took what Cormac handed out in the way of pleasure, but Ellen was conniving to land him as her husband, with the sole purpose of becoming mistress of this castle.

When the cook informed me that supper was ready and nobody had come to the table, I told her to keep the food warm even if it went dry or became charred. I went into the dining room to inspect the table setting, found it quite proper, and walked into the great hall to gather up the torn-down drapery.

I heard steps behind me as I was bent over to roll up the heavy material. I glanced up, to see one of Cormac's friends was making a dash for me, intent, I suppose, upon getting me while I was bent over. I managed to straighten up in time, but I was off balance and he clamped a bear hug around me so that we both went crashing to the floor. By the time I recovered my breath and my wits, I found myself fighting him off. I wasn't sure if he was still drunk, or just overcome by lust, but I knew what he meant to do.

I brought up my knee sharply and heard him gasp in sudden pain. I doubled my fist and struck him squarely in the face. He was more than a match for me, but my blow had rendered him temporarily helpless, and I was able to gain my feet.

By the time I did, I found Cormac and half a dozen of his companions watching the fracas, and all of them were obviously enjoying it. I strode toward Cormac with the purpose of telling him I would no longer remain under his roof, but I never got the chance, for the man who had attacked me came at me with a savage fury. His hands tore at my dress. I called on Cormac for help, but he stood there like a great oaf, enjoying the sorry spectacle.

I turned my attention to the madman who held me, and I managed to dig my nails deeply in the side of his face and inflict something a good deal more than mere scratches. That only infuriated him.

"I'll have you right here," he said harshly. "Right in front of my friends. You'll submit or I'll brain you."

"Cormac!" I shouted in desperation, for the man was beginning to carry out his threat.

Cormac finally moved. He stepped behind the man, curled an arm around his neck, and bent him backward. He kept this up until the man was compelled to let go of me. I staggered away and fell into a chair. Cormac pushed the man away from him, struck him once in the stomach and once on the side of his face. The man plunged to the floor and lay still for a few moments while Cormac stood over him rubbing the pain out of his knuckles.

When the man stirred, Cormac reached down and hauled him to his feet. "I told you and everybody else not to lay a hand on this girl. I meant it."

"Aye, I suppose you did," I called out, "but it took you one damn long time to do anything about it, Cormac."

"You keep quiet," Cormac thundered my way. He let the man go.

"Wait here," the man said.

"For what, Brian?" Cormac said. "It's time for supper."

The man called Brian disappeared. I got up, expecting Cormac to come to me with an apology for his wayward guest, but he did not. He began walking to the door, heading for the dining room. Before he reached it, Brian came flying down the staircase carrying two rapiers.

"Cormac!" he shouted. As Cormac turned to him, he threw one of the rapiers. Cormac didn't even try to catch it, and the weapon fell to the floor.

"Pick it up and defend yourself," Brian said loudly. "Pick it up, Cormac, so I can kill you fairly."

"Listen to the man," Cormac said contemptuously. "Give him enough brandy and he thinks he's a fighting man. Put away the rapier, Brian, and behave yourself."

"Pick up the weapon or I'll run you through right now," Brian warned.

Cormac drew back his right foot and kicked the weapon as hard as he could, sending it skittering across the floor, to stop only when it hit the wall. He turned his back on Brian and began walking toward the dining room.

Brian poised the rapier he held and began moving up behind Cormac.

"Cormac!" I screamed. No one else gave him a warning.

Cormac turned about in time to avoid the thrust of the blade at his back. He moved away under the threat of the rapier. Brian was red-faced with rage, and it wasn't difficult to realize he meant to kill Cormac if he could.

"One more chance," he said loudly in a high, strained voice. "Arm yourself, or you'll taste the bite of this sword."

Cormac didn't move. "Brian, I don't want to hurt you any more."

"You dishonored me in front of my friends."

"Well, now," Cormac said easily, "you're not exactly what I'd call a grateful guest. I remind you that the castle help does not go with the free brandy."

"She's a whore in residence," Brian snarled. "I know about her. We all know about her."

"Do you, now?" Cormac asked. "Has it ever occurred to you that she saved my skin in England just a few weeks ago? Has it entered your thick skull that I owe her something for that? Besides, I think she did well for herself in fending you off. Maybe I should let her pick up the rapier and have a go at you."

"Stop it!" I said sharply. "I'm telling you two, stop it! This is all nonsense. The fool did his best to rape me, and bad as that is, it's no reason for a bloody duel."

"You heard the lady," Cormac said mildly.

Brian lowered the rapier. "I'll be damned. Cormac won't fight. He's turned weak and yellow. That British lord winged him, and since then Cormac's not the man he was. I'll not have it on my conscience that I killed a coward."

Cormac went for the rapier on the floor just after I did, and I got there first. I picked it up and with all the effort I could summon drove the point of it into the wall, causing it to snap in half. Then I threw the piece I held onto the floor and walked away.

Cormac said, "Brian, you can see the lady does not want blood spilled on this carpet, so take hold of yourself, man, and stop this foolishness."

Brian shrugged and laid the rapier across the arms of a chair. "I might as well, not having anybody to fight. I say again, Cormac, that you're a coward. You had guts for ten, but Lord Dervor pinked you, and that ended your bravery."

"If it did," Cormac said, "you're a lucky man because of it. Now, you and the others pack up. Get out of this castle and don't come back."

Brian then made the mistake of his life. "Would you like to try to put me out, Cormac?"

Cormac's howl of rage brought me back to the great hall in time to see him flatten Brian with a single punch that must have torn half through the man's middle. He dropped, and Cormac picked him up.

He saw me standing there. "Open the door!" he shouted at me. "I want to be rid of this offal."

I obeyed him, because if I hadn't, I was afraid he might throw the man through one of the windows, and there was enough damage as it was. Cormac raised the struggling victim over his head, just as he'd done with the man he threw down the outside stairs. He hurled Brian, sent him crashing into the dirt before the castle. Then he dusted his hands and turned about to glare at the others.

"You heard what I said. Those of you who didn't, listen well. I'm ordering you to get out of here. Kate, find Gavan and have him bring around carriages to take this scum off my hands."

I didn't move. Ellen was among the last to come down in answer to the loud fracas.

"Cormac," she said, "does that include me?"

"No, not you," Cormac told her. "These others take all a man can offer. So do you, but at least you give a little in return. The rest of you leave before I lose my temper completely and throw you all out."

I didn't go for Gavan. I walked up the stairs, pushing the smilingly triumphant Ellen out of my way as roughly as possible and giving no heed to her cries of protest. In my own room I took a suitcase from the closet and crammed into it clothes I gathered at random. I didn't care what I took or what I left. I slammed the case shut, picked it up, and went down the corridor to the stairs.

Some of the guests were still in the act of departing reluctantly. Cormac stood by the door. Ellen was still on the stairs about five steps up. When she saw me coming, she hastily ran down the rest of the steps and cleared the way for me. Cormac stared at me as if he couldn't believe it.

I said, "I'll not wait to be thrown out."

Someone, a maid probably, had warned Gavan to bring the carriages, and he was driving one of them toward the castle entrance. It didn't take him more than a moment to figure out what was happening. One guest was still on the ground nursing his bruises. The others were gathered about, help-lessly waiting for the carriages. None dared to go back for their belongings. He saw me too, advancing with my suit-case. Gavan brought the carriage to a stop, jumped down from the seat, and opened the door. The guests who ap-proached were waved back, and I alone stepped into the car-riage. Gavan closed the door and drove away. The last I saw of Cormac, he was standing openmouthed watching my grand exit.

I rapped on the glass front. "Gavan, take me home, please."

"Aye, I will that, with pleasure," he called back.

"You were right, I should have gone long before now. Oh, Gavan, what a fool I've been. If I'm not accepted in the vil-lage, that's to the good. I want peace and quiet, if there is such a thing."

TWELVE

Returning to my own cottage was one of the most difficult things I ever had to do. I was heartbroken at leaving the castle and Cormac, but under the circumstances there'd been nothing else to do if I wanted to retain at least a shred of my pride. Then too, I had no idea how I'd be received in the village. As the erstwhile mistress of the castle, they had been compelled to receive me with some respect, or lose the ample trade the castle provided. Now, as a woman whose honor had been thoroughly soiled, I might be totally ostracized and find it impossible to continue living here.

I had taken money with me on the assumption it was earned money and I was entitled to it. At best it was a tiny fraction of what the work I'd done was worth.

For an entire day I stayed inside the cottage, which of course was barren of food, and I went without rather than venture into the street and the stores. By now, word of my departure would have reached the village by way of the servants, so everyone would know I was back.

That day I sat in solitary isolation, depressed of spirit, hoping that Cormac might come by. He did not, but on the second day, when I was going to be forced to go abroad because of sheer hunger, Meg Donnel came to see me. She was carrying her baby, a ruddy-cheeked boy sucking industriously on his thumb.

"I've come to bow my head and ask your pardon, Kate Moran. A fool I've been not to realize what you did for the village. Were it not for you, Padriac here would likely not have been born alive. As it is, you can see how healthy he is."

"Come in, Meg," I said, trying not to show how relieved I was at her change of attitude. "It's been a long time, and I'm glad to see you and have you in my house."

I took the baby from her and held him for a while as we talked, mostly of the famine days.

"Do you remember how we grubbed for food?" Meg said. "It was an awful time, with the burying ground filling day by day. I don't know how we lived through it."

"Many did not," I reminded her, "and we must remember, so it cannot happen again."

"With the English the way they are, it likely will." Meg sighed. "I hope it does not happen in my son's time."

"It will not happen again," I assured her. "Steps have been taken. There will be no more famine. Should crops fail again, nobody will starve."

"How do you know this?" Meg asked.

"Cormac of Fion has said so."

"Aye, then it cannot be but true, for he certainly spoke his mind before that Parliament. We were proud of him, Kate."

"Yes, he risked his liberty to make that speech."

"How is he these days?" Meg asked. I thought she was showing an extraordinary interest in Cormac.

"He's fine, last I saw. To be honest, he brought in a number of guests. From Dublin, I suppose. A drinking bunch they were, and noisy and unpleasant, so I left."

"For good?" Meg asked in unconcerned alarm.

"I don't know. It depends on many things."

"But, Kate, they do say Cormac is a changed man."

A surge of hope went through me until I realized there couldn't have been much of a change in two days.

"In what way, Meg?" I asked.

"They say he has lost his will to fight, perhaps out of fear because he was wounded."

"Who is saying these things?"

"Oh, seems like everyone. The word is about that he is afraid to fight."

I couldn't let that claim go unchallenged, because certainly Cormac was not deserving of it. "Now, Meg, whoever says such a thing should have been at the castle when Cormac disarmed a drunken idiot who wished to duel with him. Cormac threw down his rapier and in the end he threw the wretch out bodily. There is no lack of courage in Cormac, and you can rest on that. Neither is he a wanton killer."

"I'm glad, Kate. He is a great man and a generous one. After you left . . . ah . . . became housekeeper . . ."

"That is a good word for it," I acknowledged.

"Well, anyway, Cormac kept sending in food until all danger of the famine was gone. And there was no more battering down cottages for lack of rent. We will not forget that."

"See that you and everyone else do not," I said. "And don't place Cormac in disfavor by claiming he is a coward. Above all, he is not that."

"It may be he has need of you, Kate. We have heard what you did for the castle, and it would be a shame to let it all go back to what it once was for lack of care."

"Cormac's pride in the castle has been restored, and he will not allow it to fall to ruin."

"What of this woman from Dublin who lives there now? Has she taken your place as housekeeper?"

It was a none-too-gentle thrust into my private affairs, but all women in the village were like that. It was best to satisfy their curiosity.

"She is there as an old friend, Meg. She will not be caring for the castle."

"I see." In those two innocently spoken words Meg placed a great deal of meaning.

"No, you do not see, Meg," I said sharply. "I told you she is an old friend. She has often been at the castle, and Cormac sees her when he goes to Dublin."

"She came to the village this morning to buy supplies . . . food and the like. As you once did."

"They do have to eat," I reminded her.

"Oh, aye, that they do, but she made plain hints that she will soon live here and be Cormac's wife."

"What she says and what you hear will not come true, Meg."

"Why do you say that after she made such statements?"

"Because I know Cormac. He is no great admirer of this woman. She is but an old friend, as I have said."

"I don't know, Kate. I wouldn't be so sure."

"And why not, may I ask?"

"She is running the castle already. Two of the maids and a hostler were fired, and the woman is looking for someone to replace them."

"Poor Cormac." I sighed. "He has no liking for the care of the castle and lets whoever wishes take it over. I still say she will not stay there long and Cormac will not marry her."

"You should know, having lived there so long. And it would be well if Cormac would mend his wild ways. The time he and his friends rode through the village was not the kind of visit that makes friends. They were all very drunk, including Cormac, and they shouted curses at everyone, and there was more than one open offer to a comely girl."

"That is the way of life in Dublin," I said. "Among that kind of people. I would offer you tea, Meg, but there is nothing in the cottage. I was about to go shopping when you came."

"I came only to see how you were getting along, not to have tea. That is not necessary, because I know from the past how generous and kind you are, and that's the truth."

"Thank you, Meg. I may be here for some time. I may never go back to the castle, for, in my opinion, the work I was hired to do is now finished, and I have no desire to live in the castle as a mere servant."

I was really happy to have Meg call on me. We discussed the baby for a while, and then I accompanied her on my way to the store, where I was well-received. There was some whispering among the older women, but when I confronted them, they were pleasant. I returned to the cottage with my sacks of supplies, put them away, and prepared to dine. After that I sat down, because there was nothing else for me to do. The cottage had been kept very neat and was not even in need of dusting.

It was going to be a monotonous existence after my life at the castle and all the work required of me there. Here, there was nothing at all. When Conan came to call, I was delighted.

"Thank you for coming by," I welcomed him. "I was sitting here wondering what to do."

"I only heard a short time ago that you were back. What happened?"

"Cormac's friends, the gentle creatures. There was a fight. Someone called Cormac a coward and said he lost his nerve after being wounded in the London duel."

"I pity the man who said it," Conan observed.

"Aye, when Cormac was through with him, he was in need of pity and perhaps the attention of a doctor. Cormac is not a gentle man when he is riled."

"But was it only the fighting that caused you to leave, Kate?"

"Oh, no! I was getting used to that, I suppose. You saw what they did to that glorious wooden floor in the great hall, riding their horses through the room."

"Some of the marks will never come off," Conan said. "I

did the best I could with them, but there is only so much one can do in a case of that kind."

"Well, there you have it," I said airily.

"I don't think so, Kate. It's in my mind more than that happened, but then it's none of my business, and I should not ask."

"He is keeping that woman on."

"So that's it. It is also in my mind that he will not keep her."

"And why not? She satisfies him, or he wouldn't let her remain."

"And what will you do now?"

"Nothing for the time being. One day I'll go see Cormac and settle what he owes me for all the work I did. After that—perhaps Galway, even Dublin. I don't know, Conan. I can't stay here and rot away until I'm a crabby old maid with nothing but memories, not all of them fond."

"An old maid you'll never be," Conan said.

"Would you stay for supper?" I asked, hoping he'd consent so I'd not have to spend a lonely evening.

"Now, what did you think I came by for? Of course I'll stay."

So the evening was a pleasant one. Mostly we discussed the ways of Cormac, and we agreed he was not an ordinary person. A conclusion that would get no argument from anyone.

Next day was really lonely. I took a long walk, hoping that would tire me, but it only served to put my nerves on edge. I ate alone that night, wishing I'd asked Conan to come for another meal. On the morning of the fourth day, I wondered how much longer I could stand it here. The village people may have forgiven me my sins, but they were not yet inclined to come calling on me, and I would not go to see any of them without an invitation, which I knew I'd not get.

That afternoon Gavan came, driving the sidecar I'd been so proud of. I greeted him with a hug and a kiss on the cheek.

"Before I go back," he said, "I'll be bringing in wine and a ham and other things. How has it been, miss?"

"Oh, well enough. I had a caller from the village, and Conan came to spend an evening with me. I hope you can stay."

"Not for long. I'm taking that woman to catch the night train to Dublin."

"Ah, that does my heart good," I said fervently.

"Aye, I thought it would. By all the saints, miss, there's been a hell of a time in the castle since you left. The woman ordered the servants about, and half of them quit. She complained about everything, and she was about to throw out everything you left . . ."

"I left about all I own," I said. "Gavan, she didn't destroy all those dresses? . . ."

"Cormac caught her in time, and I haven't seen him so angry since he threw out the crazy man who wanted to fight a duel with him. He opened his mind to her and called her what she is. Then he ordered her to pack up, which she was doing when I left to come here."

"Please bring all my things next time you come," I begged. "There might be another woman who would either destroy my things or steal them for herself."

"I came mainly to see if you'd not come back, miss."

"No, Gavan. I'm finished there. Cormac as much as told me so, and I do not have to be told twice. The castle is not a place for me anymore."

Gavan shook his head sorrowfully. "I wish I could go back and tell him you will return."

"Tell him I can take so much and no more."

"He'll be . . . he is . . . as lonely a person as you, miss. He sits around all day, and he's taken to carrying a bottle of brandy with him. He only does that when his spirits are low."

"My spirits are low too, Gavan, and he caused them to be that way. I cannot go back, except to talk business so I can clear out forever."

"I will tell him that."

"If you please," I said. "I'm not very angry with the man. It's only that I can't put up with him any longer."

"I'll not tell him that," Gavan said with a smile. "He would have my head for the telling of it."

"Gavan," I said seriously, "there's a fancy tale going about that Cormac no longer has the lion's heart he so often displayed. That he has become a coward since he was wounded in the duel with Lord Dervor. Have you heard this?"

"I've not, miss. If I had, I'd be here now with bruises over me from the fights I'd have been in. The man who says that to me had better be twice as big as I am."

"It's not true, I know, but I wonder what is the purpose of spreading such an incredible story. And who is doing it."

"I can't say as to that. Cormac has his enemies, as an

great man does, but I know of none who would risk saying such a thing about him."

"The only reason for it may be the kind of jealousy big men have to worry about. We know there is no cowardice in the man, so we will not worry about it."

"Well said," Gavan agreed.

"Cormac is fortunate in having a friend like you."

"He was also fortunate in having you, miss. If I ask on my bended knee . . . ?"

"It would do no good," I said promptly. "Bend your knee to no man or woman. I'll go back when he settles down and can discuss business with me, and not before."

"Then there is no use in my begging any more. It will be as you say, miss, but I think you are making a mistake."

"If I am, I'll suffer for it, not you."

"Aye, there's truth to that, but Cormac will suffer too, you must remember."

"I'll remember the man deserves it," I said. "You can tell him that as well."

"Then I'll be bringing in the stuff I gathered. I will say you're a cold woman, miss."

"Perhaps, but I'm a wiser one too, for having lived at the castle. I will not be flung aside for those demons he brought back with him, and especially that skinny . . . that terror of a woman."

Gavan smiled. "It's jealous you are, miss. That's a good sign. You'll one day think about it and come back to the castle. It's true he has need of you, but more than that, the castle itself is in need of you."

"One thing more," I said as he arose. "You have begged me to go back, but up until I left, you begged me to leave him. Now which way do you blow, Gavan? Or do you change your mind as often as Cormac does?"

"Things have changed," he said. "It's different now, miss."

"In four days, things have changed so much you now want me back, after warning me to go away? Exactly what's changed, Gavan? Tell me in detail."

"That I cannot do, for the change is one my poor mind is not capable of explaining."

"Once you told me it would all end in death. Now, what was the meaning of that, may I ask?"

"There are times when a man says too much, miss. I'll go fetch these things now, and I thank you for letting me have my say."

I walked to the door with him and took the things he brought from the sidecar.

"You are welcome here at any time, Gavan," I said. "I regard you and Conan as my best and trusted friends."

"Thank you, miss."

"Gavan," I said hastily as he turned away, "do you think he'll come?"

I saw hope reborn in Gavan's eyes. "Aye, that he will, though it will stretch his pride as never before. Be kind to the poor man, for there will be much unkindness in store for him."

"Riddles again. Always riddles," I complained.

"Good day to you, Kate Moran," he said with a doff of his cap.

For a week I lived the most monotonous existence I could have imagined. I arose early because I couldn't sleep, and that made it a long day to begin with. I ate breakfast, fussed around the cottage, went out to buy a few supplies I really didn't need. I did some reading, but it was hard to keep my mind on a book. I retired early and lay awake for what seemed to be an eternity. I sought no company, and except for an occasional visit by Conan, I saw no one, and I didn't want to.

All this while I kept listening for Cormac's loud voice announcing his arrival. When he finally came, he seemed to be a changed man, for he arrived with no shouts, no flourishes, and he drove a carriage instead of riding one of his frisky stallions. He was serious, too. So much so that I began to wonder if the stories about him no longer possessing the courage of a dozen men were true.

I admitted Cormac, and he sat down sheepishly, fiddling with his hunter's cap and not looking up.

"I have been as foolish as a man can be," he said. "I made many a mistake in my life, but none as serious as letting you get away from me."

"Why did you do it?" I asked bluntly, while I ached to put my arms around him and let him find comfort in the warmth I could offer.

"I'm going to be frank with you, Kate. You must understand one thing first: I am in love with you."

I almost went to him then, but something kept me riveted to my chair, my features immobile. I felt there was more coming.

"No man has ever loved a woman more," he went on.

"That is why I brought those scalawags here and let them all but wreck the castle. That's why I flaunted Ellen to make you angry. And cause you to think of me as wanton and reckless with no regard for anyone. I have never cared for Ellen, and if you must know the truth, the last days she was in the castle, I locked my door against her. I could no longer accept the false love she offered me, because I had experienced the real thing with a real woman in whose arms I found what I've looked for all my life."

"Cormac . . ." I said softly.

"But wait." He held up a hand, and his voice grew stern. "There is one thing more. This girl whom I sought all my life, I must never marry. I want you back, but with no promise that we shall ever wed. Without my name, you will still be mistress of the castle, and all that I possess will be yours."

"Without your name, it would all be meaningless," I said sadly.

"But will you come back anyway? Not that I may satisfy my passion with you. I just want your company. I want to see your dear face across the table from me, and listen to the softness of your voice. Come back to me, Kate. Whatever the price, I'll willingly pay it."

"Aye, Cormac," I said. "There is a price."

"Then name it," he said earnestly.

"Why can't you marry me?"

"That is the one thing I cannot tell you, my dear Kate. Don't ask me again."

"Yet you expect me to come back?"

"Not expect. Only hope you will."

"And what would be the point?" I asked. "Shall we live together without marriage and without the marriage bed? For the rest of our lives?"

"The rest of our lives!" He heaved a great sigh. "Mine may not be long, but while I live, every waking moment will be devoted to pleasing you."

"Why can we not marry, Cormac?" I asked again.

He shook his head. "Woman, how many times must I tell you . . . ?"

"Cormac," I said, "I'm as much in love with you as you say you are with me. I left the castle because I could no longer stand watching you make a fool of yourself. Of your being taken advantage of by those so-called friends. I know now for a fact that everything you did was meant to drive me away. The more I refused to go, the worse you became. I know that this reason you keep so well hidden is behind it, and that what you did was a sacrifice on your part, for you were driving away your love without an explanation."

"Then you do understand," he said hopefully.

"I will never understand fully until you tell me the secret that blights your life and, now, mine. A man and woman in love cannot have secrets from each other. There can only be love, which must overpower anything else in life. Will you tell me this secret? If you share it, perhaps its great weight on your soul may be relieved."

"I will not tell you."

"Good-bye, Cormac, my love. There is no more to be said."

"But one thing. Will you hear me?"

I had risen, but I sat down again. "I will hear you forever if there is any chance you might tell me the truth."

"I will say only this. I wish to the depths of my soul that this marriage could be possible, but if it happened . . . No. It could not happen. The finish of this is beyond your control or mine. So . . . you have rejected my need for you. The castle is in need of you too. Those bloody idiots did much to wreck the place, and it must be brought back to all the splendor you created for it. I will go away again for many months. As before, all the money you need will be at your disposal."

"You will go away? I have your word?"

"Tonight . . . tomorrow . . ."

"If you are there, if you return, I will leave, and you'll not see me again."

"Agreed. Come tomorrow. I will not be there."

He was on his feet, backing away from me. I had difficulty not rushing into his arms, whatever the consequences might be. To the devil with them, I thought. I stood riveted to the spot, not raising a hand toward the man I loved. I was silently sending him into an oblivion from which he would never return to me.

As I stood there watching him take his leave, I knew full well that one day I'd call him back. The moment I discovered what that awful secret was, I'd go to him with all the joy in my heart.

He drove away, and I closed the door, to sit down and weep for him. Not for the love I had lost, or the riches, or the fame, or anything else. I wept for the man I loved because he was beset by a problem he was unable to solve, one so awful he couldn't even suggest to me what it was.

I found some comfort in knowing that he was not the wastrel he had pretended to be, along with his insufferable friends. I knew he cared nothing about Ellen, which served to cheer me some.

I had done the only thing possible. I'd not planned it, simply taken advantage of his promise to leave the castle in my hands while he remained away. Whatever secret held him in its tight grip, the answer must lie within the castle walls. When Cormac promised to go away, I saw my chance. If it was necessary, I would have the castle taken apart room by room to uncover the mystery that spoiled both our lives. But I doubted I'd have to go to such an extreme. If the secret was there, it lay in that room of the five statues. Four in white marble and one in jet black. And in the heavy, clumsy book that lay before the statues. I was already making plans in my mind before the beat of his horses' hoofs faded.

Once again I prepared the cottage for an emptiness rivaled only by that within my heart. I knew that if my plans failed, I'd come back to the cottage, but only long enough to plan and prepare for a journey from which I'd never return. In my mind was America, for I would need a mighty ocean to separate me from the man I loved but could not have.

I thought Gavan might come for me, and he did, late in the morning. He helped me carry out my things and then took care to lock the cottage before he joined me on the carriage.

"He is gone?" I asked.

"He left before daylight, miss."

"I am to repair the damage done to the castle by his friends."

"Aye."

"I will have Conan come to help, for he knows well how to do these things."

"That he does, miss."

"I will leave when the work is finished."

"Aye."

"Gavan, your manners are lacking and you talk like a man going to a funeral."

"That is how I feel, miss. I could not have said it better."

"Now, whose funeral would it be? Mine or Cormac's?"

He said nothing and gave all his attention to guiding the team. I gave up, for Gavan was as stubborn as his master.

Ah, but it was good to be in the castle once again. When I
stepped through the massive door, my heart lightened, for it
was like coming home.

I settled down at once and began my work by inspecting
all the damage, which would tax neither me nor Conan to any
great extent. But I did make plans to improve the great hall
by rearranging furniture and by paneling over one wall that
was of rough stone. There were changes to be made upstairs
as well, and about the only room I would not touch was the
one with the five statues.

I summoned Conan the next day and put him to work. I
missed Cormac bitterly, but otherwise everything went well. I
heard nothing from him. The bank in Galway told me the
funds I would draw upon were as unlimited as they had been
before.

Gradually my nerves settled down, and at least temporarily
I was at peace with myself. I was, however, still determined
to somehow discover the grim secret of this castle and of
Cormac's life.

It seemed the only place to begin was with that strange
room where the busts of his ancestors were so neatly placed
in their proper niches. During the next few days I thumbed
through that heavy book several times, but it still had no
meaning.

I did find, at the very last page, written in the English language, a list of names and dates. They intrigued me, for every entry was the date of birth of an even dozen Mack
Cormacs of Fion. All of Cormac's ancestors must have had
the same name as his.

Then I noticed a strange thing. Each death was exactly one
hundred years apart, with never a deviation. The only date of
death unfilled was that of the Cormac I knew and loved, but
if this strange sequence of deaths was adhered to by some
weird power, then my Cormac would die on the thirtieth of
this very month. If the sequence applied to him, he had less
than three weeks to live.

I was stunned and mystified. I intended to query Gavan on
this, for I had a strong idea he would know what it meant. If
Cormac was destined to die on the thirtieth, that explained
why he would not marry me and why he could make no
promises. It may also have explained the deep gloom of the
man, so intense that people were taking it as a manifestation
of cowardice.

Inspired now to take some action before it was too late, I

turned my attention to the five busts, which I had never examined with care. The four white ones, evidently chiseled out of granite, all bore a resemblance to Cormac; the black one was identical to him. When I lifted it, it seemed noticeably heavier than the others. In fact, I could barely raise it from its niche. I studied it intently, but it was just a heavy replica of Cormac's features—even though he himself had told me it was centuries old. On the base, faintly engraved, was a shield with the initial A centered. It had no meaning to me.

I put it back and stood before the five busts trying to determine what they really meant. Were these the busts of some of the Cormacs who were listed in the big book? It was quite likely. I thought of trying to locate Cormac and compelling him to explain the exact meaning of this room and its contents. Yet I knew in my heart he'd not explain.

But Gavan would, if I approached him properly. If I made him understand the absolute necessity for telling me the truth before the thirtieth of the month.

I drew a shawl over my head and went out onto the battlements to see if I could find him. It was fall, and there was a nip in the air. Standing here, looking down at the castle ground enclosed in these thick walls, and at the walls themselves, I realized that they enclosed the secret of the castle and of Cormac's life. Something had happened, ages ago, the shadows of which existed today and threatened the man I loved so dearly.

To what purpose the weird stairs of concrete built from the ground right up to the wall? Certainly not one of defense, for it was an open avenue for any attacker to take advantage of during the fury of a siege. I recalled how Cormac, in the blackest rage I'd ever seen him exhibit, had thrown that terrible man down those stairs. Why the stairs, when he could have far more easily thrown him off the wall?

Had this castle been standing the twelve centuries, in each of which a Cormac died, and had those steps been here all that time too? I could almost visualize the enemy storming up the stairs to be met by volleys of arrows and kettles of boiling water, pitch, or oil. Then stopped by hand-to-hand combat and finally crushed. For, so far as I knew, no enemy had ever captured Castle Lucane.

Now that I'd established the fact, in my mind at least, that the book might tell how and when Cormac was destined to die, I would summon him back and demand an explanation. For the time being, one might be forthcoming from Gavan.

It was nothing to be discussed before the servants from the village, so I waited until after I'd had my supper and all the servants were gone. Then I made my way down to the stables and the little cottage where Gavan had made his home these many years.

"Well, it's become a glorious evening now that you've come to visit," he said, but with an air of uneasiness, as if he'd guessed my visit was not entirely social. I sat down, and I didn't approach the subject directly, for I might scare him into protecting himself—and Cormac—with lies.

"I've been working in this castle now for a long time, as you have, Gavan. Tell me, how old is it?"

"I wouldn't know that. Maybe five, six hundred years, maybe a thousand. Praise heaven it will last another thousand."

"Has it always been in the Cormac family?"

"Aye, so far as I have been given to understand."

"I have been prying into Cormac's business again, Gavan. I have found, in that locked room, a page in the big book which lists twelve men named Mack Cormac of Fion. Were you aware of that?"

He nodded somberly. "Aye, and it is none of your business, miss."

"Perhaps not my business, but a woman is curiosity-bent by nature. Eleven of those Cormacs died exactly one hundred years apart, and every one on the same day. What does it mean?"

"I don't know, miss," he said, but it wasn't hard to know that he lied, for he was a man accustomed to telling only the truth, and that made him clumsy at evading a question with a falsehood.

"I think you do. If eleven of those men died on a certain date, then the date of my Cormac's death will be in accordance with the exact sequence of all the others. My Cormac will die on the thirtieth of this month. Do you realize that, Gavan?"

"Aye, too well."

"Does Cormac believe he is going to die then?"

"I cannot say, miss. I gave my word, and it shall not be broken. Not even for you, and if there was one alive who would make me do that, it would be you."

"If it is true, tell me, is there a way to save him?"

"I cannot talk of this. Do not press me."

"Very well, Gavan. Then you and I will just sit here and

wait until the thirtieth, and find out then if all Cormacs die on that certain date."

"By the saints, I will not discuss this. It is my wish that you will leave. If Cormac knew of this . . ."

"I am going to find the truth, Gavan."

"Not from me. No, not from me."

"The story and the answer are in that big book, isn't that so? Written in Gaelic, which few can read, especially in the ancient script form in which it is inscribed."

"I know nothing of the big book."

"It must be a family history of some kind. Not a Bible. There are no holy passages there, no symbols. Can you read Gaelic?"

"No! That is the truth. No one in the village can read that book. It would take a scholar of considerable consequence."

"There are many people who can read, write, and speak Gaelic, Gavan."

Gavan stood up abruptly. "Miss, I have told you, warned you, begged of you, have no more to do with this business. Only harm can come of it. Harm and sorrow, all without helping Cormac one whit."

"I'll not speak of it again, Gavan. But I must say that for a man so devoted to Cormac for so many years, you give up very easily. We are dealing with the chance of Cormac's death in such a short time. Perhaps it is of a nature we could not prevent, but we could try. And sleep better for it, no matter what the outcome."

He sat down again, slowly, like a man who had aged twenty years in as many minutes. "I have thought of it, miss, but there is nothing to be done."

"You have lived with it so long you've come to accept that," I persisted. "I will not. I will look at it with a fresh viewpoint. Gavan, how will he die? In a battle, or will he sicken? Or will he be assassinated by some enemy we're not aware of? How were the others killed? And why this steadfastness to exactly a hundred years apart?"

"I gave my word. Cormac trusts me. I would violate his confidence."

"You would stand by while he dies? That's what you'll be doing, Gavan. Think of that."

"I have! I have! Many's the time I've thought of it."

"Gavan, I will wait for you in the castle. Think well, and when you come to a decision, find me and tell me, one way or another. We have yet time, so be in no hurry. I'll wait for you. I trust you, as Cormac does, but you have to trust me too. For I am going to save him if I can. With your help, or without it, but for the love of God, don't just sit there and let this happen."

"You hound a man clear to death," Gavan said with a slow shake of his head.

"I'll keep on hounding you," I told him. "And if Cormac is killed because you refuse to give me a chance to save him, then I will hound you to the death. Your death, Gavan."

"There is nothing—"

"Hound you forever, Gavan. Giving your word to a man who is in danger of being killed does not become a matter of conscience in breaking your word. It's a matter of saving his life. Will you tell me?"

"I cannot. I have kept silent so long . . . but I will consider it, miss. Give me a little time. Let me think and make up my mind in the next hour or so. I will come to you at the castle and, once and for all, abide by Cormac's order—or do as you say. Tell it all on the chance you might be able to save his life."

"If it takes you more than ten minutes to make up your mind as to that," I said, "you're not the man of intelligence I've believed you to be."

"Yes, miss. Leave me alone now, if you please."

"That I will. First, though, should we have to reach Cormac in a hurry, how can we find him?"

"He is at that same hotel. The Shamrock. A letter will reach him in two days."

"Don't take too long," I warned. "There are not many days left."

I left him, staring at the floor, bent over like an aged man. I felt sorry for him, but he was the sole solution to the mystery, his telling of it restrained by a promise to Cormac. I must make him break that promise. I'd failed with Cormac, but Gavan was not as strong-willed.

I crossed the castle grounds and entered the castle itself. I walked into the great hall, realizing that I was alone, for all the servants had gone home, as they always did.

There was an elongated shadow on the farther wall of the great hall, and I came to an abrupt halt. I looked through the early-evening gloom, for no lamps or candles were as yet lit. A man stood before me. The bulk of him reminded me of Cormac, and I almost rushed up to him. Only the voice of the man stopped me.

"Good evening to you, Kate. I've come for you."

I peered intently, but it was the voice that did most to identify my visitor, and I felt a wave of revulsion and fear. This was Kerry Flynn, who hated Cormac with an intensity that one day would cause the two men to fight. Probably to the death.

"If you're looking for Cormac," I said, "he is not here."

"I'll settle Cormac later, when the time is proper. It's not Cormac I'm interested in tonight. It's you, Kate. I'm going to spend the night with you."

I began backing away. "If you touch me, Cormac will kill you."

"No, he will not kill me. I will kill him. Tonight, I will have you. After Cormac is dead, I shall have both you and the castle. Tonight I'll be satisfied with just you. So you might as well come to me, for you'll not escape, and the more you fight, the worse it will be for you."

"If Cormac does not kill you, I will, and that's a promise. You're a blackhearted man, Kerry Flynn, with no sense or principle. But you will not have me without a fight."

"Then that is how it will be. But have you I will. And now!"

He walked toward me, this hulk of a man who didn't know right from wrong. I backed up. I knew very well I'd never escape him. All I could do was make it as unpleasant for him as possible, and then let Cormac handle the matter. Too late to save me, but at least I'd have my revenge.

Then, as I kept backing away, with Kerry advancing and laughing at me, I had this awful thought flash through my brain. Cormac was to die on the thirtieth. If I told Cormac of this, he would instantly seek out Kerry with the purpose of killing him; but if the legend was true, it would be Cormac who died.

Everything seemed to be prearranged by invisible hands and a cunning mind that existed a thousand years ago but maintained its power over the centuries.

I'd stopped backing away, wondering if I could strike some kind of terrible bargain with this man so that Cormac would not be involved, even though I half-guessed that Kerry Flynn would never keep his word if I surrendered to him. He was to be the instrument by which Cormac would die, and nothing I could do would change that.

In those few seconds of indecision, the castle door opened, closed, and Gavan came into the great hall. The gloom was deeper than ever now, and Gavan, while he knew someone was with me, had no idea who it might be.

"Run, Gavan," I shouted. "Run! It's Kerry Flynn."

Gavan didn't run. I should have known better than to think I could have made him abandon me. Instead, he came charging toward Kerry Flynn, who was twice Gavan's size and a hundred times more bloodthirsty.

Perhaps if Kerry Flynn had not been in the midst of his overwhelming desire to get at me, he might not have been quite so filled with rage toward this insignificant-looking man who lashed out to strike him a good hard blow to the face.

Kerry simply drew a dagger from the sheath strapped to his belt. He slashed once. Gavan gave a strangled cry, staggered back a few steps, and then fell to the floor, making no further sound or movement.

I ran to his side and turned him on his back, but one look and I knew it was too late. Kerry Flynn's dagger had pierced poor Gavan's heart, and he had died instantly.

I looked up at the big man looming above me, and the same kind of rage, hopeless though it might be, filled me with foolish courage, and I sprang at Kerry Flynn, only to have him enclose me in a great bear hug that rendered me almost helpless. I did manage to reach up with one hand and try for his eyes. I failed, but I did inflict some deep scratches on his face before he hurled me to the floor and pressed down on me.

THIRTEEN

My struggles were feeble ones and hopeless, for I could never contend with this huge, abnormally strong man. His thick, rough hands pulled my petticoats off, tearing them in the process. My dress was already torn half off. His breath stank of cheap brandy, and his kisses clumsily sought my throat and then my breasts, his hands never still.

He had me so exhausted that I was unable to fight back anymore. Better, I thought, to let him have his way, else he might grow so crazed he'd kill me as he had murdered poor Gavan.

He arose to his knees, and with that much pressure off me I was able to draw a few long breaths and to make one more useless attempt to get free of him.

I was no more successful at this than I had been with my first attempts to keep him off me. He slapped my face so hard my ears rang and my wits went off into space momentarily. He took advantage of my helplessness now by tearing my dress completely off. My undergarments clung to my skin, moist with the sweat of fear. He pulled apart the shoulder straps, and then he was upon me hungrily, behaving like a savage with the instincts of a beast.

Finished for the moment, he fell over to one side, laughing gleefully. When I tried to get up, he slapped me again and threw one brawny, hairy leg over my body, pinning me down. I didn't know what he'd try next, but it turned out that he was only regaining his strength and bringing back his wild desire. Then he was on me again, unmercifully cruel, taking a fiendish, sadistic delight in causing me all possible pain.

He grasped one of my breasts and squeezed it until I screamed. Next he began pinching my thighs, perhaps twenty or thirty times, making me cry out again at first, but then, as my strength waned, I could only moan.

At last he stood up and rearranged his clothing. "It has

been a fine evening, Kate. If you were so maidenly as to not
enjoy it, that's your fault. Perhaps one day you will, for this
is not the last time. Mind me well, there will be many more
times when I am in the mood for you. I will say you're better
than the strumpets I pay for their favors, even if they do not
resist me as you do. I have been harsh, but you brought that
on yourself. Next time, perhaps, you'll not be quite so anxious to fend me off. Because, Kate Moran, I'll have you
whenever the mood takes me, and Cormac nor anyone else
cannot stop me. You will tell that to Cormac, for he is a
coward and dares not fight. Show him your bruises. I gave
you plenty of them so that Cormac might be enraged enough
to seek me out. I don't want to kill the man in cold blood,
but in a fair fight to the finish. For that is what it shall be.
Good-bye, Kate, until next time."

He paused beside Gavan's body and nudged it with his
foot. "The fool's dead, eh? Good! That will make Cormac all
the more angry."

I couldn't move. I was so filled with pain that even with
the knowledge that Gavan's body lay within reach, I could
not summon the stamina to arise for a long time, and then I
had to crawl over to him, every move I made filled with pain.
I closed Gavan's eyes and straightened his left leg, which had
curled beneath him as he fell. I crawled farther to a chair,
which I used for support.

I finally got to my feet, but I was unable to stand, and I
fell into the chair. However, in this position, some of my
strength began to return. I massaged my legs, but not above
the knee, for my thighs felt as if they were on fire. Every
inch of me ached with almost unendurable pain. Only the
sight of Gavan's body on the floor inspired me to press hard
for my strength to grow.

I made it to the door and even had it open before I realized that I was dressed only in my pink drawers, which were
torn in several places. I reached the stairs and crawled up
them, pausing every three or four steps to rest. I thought, at
the time, that I must be near death, though later I knew I
was far from that. Perhaps the agony and shame overcame
the common sense that told me I'd only been fearfully
abused.

In my room at last, I hastily washed. Scrubbing was out of
the question, though that's what I felt the circumstances
called for. The agony it would inflict was impossible to accept after what I'd been through. I slipped on a fresh pair of

drawers, stepped into petticoats, and rummaged for an old dress I could wear. I couldn't stand the slightest pressure against my breasts, which were throbbing with pain.

I stumbled down the stairs. Every few moments now I was feeling the return of more and more vitality. I hurried through the night to the stables, and there I harnessed a horse to the sidecar. Perching myself on the seat, I sent the horse at fast speed down the road to the village.

I had to pound on Conan's door to awaken him. The whole village slept at this hour, for which I was grateful. In my present state of mind and physical condition, I would have hated to meet anybody.

Conan finally opened the door a slit to peer out. When he recognized me, he threw the door wide. He lit a lamp and held it toward me, while his face lost its heavy sleepiness, to be replaced by horror.

"What happened?" he asked. "Who struck you?"

"Kerry Flynn came. He murdered poor Gavan. Never mind about me . . ."

"I'll be dressed as fast as I can," Conan said. "Sit down, Kate. You're ready to collapse."

That's how I felt, and I gratefully eased my pain-filled body into a chair. Conan didn't take long. He didn't ask me any questions then. Not until we were on the sidecar. He drove carefully, out of consideration for me. Then I told him what had happened.

"He did this for more than mere lust," I said. "He purposely inflicted so many black and blue marks—heavy bruises—that it's clear his purpose was to infuriate Cormac."

"Why would he do that, Kate?"

"It's a long story. It's hard to believe, and I don't have all the facts. I talked to Gavan earlier, and I think I persuaded him to tell the whole truth—but when Gavan came to talk to me, Kerry Flynn was there and poor Gavan never had a chance. He was brave, but foolish, for he charged that revolting ox. Kerry was in no mood to delay what he was after, so he met Gavan's attack with a dagger point. Gavan died instantly. Then . . . then Kerry Flynn did this to me."

"It'll be a matter for the police now," Conan said.

"No, Conan. Wait until you hear the full story. But first, there's Gavan."

When we reached the castle, Conan picked up Gavan's body and carried it upstairs. I hastily pulled down bedcovers, and we placed the dead man on the bed and covered him respectfully. Then Conan and I stood side by side, saying our prayers for the repose of the soul of a fine, wonderfully courageous man.

Downstairs, Conan gave me a glass of brandy while he poured himself another containing three times the amount. While we sat next to the bloodstains from Gavan's wound, I told him what I knew. It was precious little, and mostly surmise, but it did make some sense, though not enough to draw any good and fast conclusions from.

"Upstairs in that room of the five statues is a big book. You've no doubt seen it."

"But once, and then from the door, as it was closing."

"The book is written in Gaelic."

"Aye! So that's why you once asked me if I could read the language."

"Yes, Conan, that was why, but at the time I wasn't free enough—or even informed enough—to give you any details. The last page of the big book is written in English. It lists twelve Mack Cormacs of Fion. Twelve of them, Conan! Each one died young, and, exactly to the day, one hundred years apart."

"Your Cormac's name is not there, I hope?"

"Ah, but it is. For now, only the date of his birth is recorded. The day of his death is not yet filled in. But on the thirtieth of this month, exactly one hundred years will have passed since the last Cormac died. There is a connection. If eleven of his ancestors died at a certain time, a century apart, then it will be Cormac's time to die in a few days, and he knows it."

"I will do my best to read the book thoroughly," Conan said.

"It would take too long. Go over it quickly."

"With Gaelic, one does not read swiftly, Kate. It's not that kind of language. Now, looking at you, I can see you're so exhausted you're almost ready to fall down. Go to your room and try to sleep. If there is a sleeping draft handy, take it."

"There is none, and I would not have it if there was. But I'm tired, and sore from head to foot. I know I must have rest, so I'll do as you say. But if, in reading the book, you come to an answer, waken me at once."

"Aye, you have my promise to that, Kate."

We went upstairs together, with Conan holding my elbow for support. I had been growing weaker and quite limp from exhaustion and pain, so his kindness was gratefully accepted.

I walked with him to the room and unlocked it for him. I waited while he lit a stub of a candle in the room and hunted about for more of them. At last he had three candles. He placed them in a row at the top of the table on which the book rested. He began to read, leaning over the slanted table and moving the candles so as to supply the most light.

I quietly turned away and walked to my bedroom. There I undressed, put on a nightgown, and got into bed, wincing as the cold sheets touched the swollen, blackening parts of my body. Despite the pain and the terror that still remained within me, I went to sleep. Knowing Conan was in the castle helped, but I kept thinking about poor Gavan, who lay three rooms down the corridor.

With morning I awoke slowly, reluctant to bring back the memory of the horror I'd endured. Then I moved, and the pain seared through my body and memory returned with a rush. I shuddered at what had happened. I threw aside the covers and studied my body. My inner thighs were swollen and livid from bruises, so badly they didn't look like parts of legs. My breasts were equally bruised, and my stomach and sides bore vivid signs of Kerry Flynn's extreme and sadistic cruelty.

I'd been hard put to move about immediately after Kerry Flynn had departed, but this morning it was worse. It even hurt to breathe, and when I moved my legs to the side of the bed, it was with a series of gasps inspired by pain.

I got to my feet and walked to the chest for fresh clothing. I dressed slowly and moved awkwardly. But gradually I began to feel a little better. There was nothing I could do to alleviate the pain, so I made up my mind to bear it and do what had to be done.

I recalled Conan at work reading the big book when I went to bed. The door to the room was wide open, but Conan lay across a bed in the next room, sound asleep. He must have been at it all night, for the candles had burned down and he had secured fresh ones, which were now half burned.

I didn't waken him. Crisis, pain, or anything else, one had to eat, so I went down to the kitchen. It was still too early for the servants from the village to have arrived, which was a relief. I made breakfast for two, and by the time it was ready, Conan stumbled into the kitchen, rubbing his reddened eyes. He sat down at the table.

"I have read some of the book. Not all, for it is slow reading, and there were many strange things I cannot explain as yet. But it will be necessary to get Cormac back here as quickly as we can."

"To meet Kerry Flynn in combat?" I asked bitterly.

"It may come to that, but if it does, Cormac should be prepared. Somewhere in that book lies the entire solution. I have reached only a small part of it, but enough to make me realize this is a situation not for modern times such as the middle of this century, but something far back in the days of Tara, when it was easy to believe anything."

"Eat first," I said, "then we can talk. Upstairs, for the servants will soon be here, and they must learn nothing of what went on."

"Except that Gavan lies dead in one of the rooms. There is no way of keeping it from them. Certainly his absence would have to be explained."

"Of course," I said. "I don't think very well this morning. And I'm not free of pain by any means. I ache all over."

"Of that I have no doubt. He didn't mark your face, thanks be to God. It was swollen a little last night, but that's all gone."

"He struck me several times, I recall, and I'm glad it wasn't hard enough to inflict the kind of damage that he did to the rest of my body."

"Would you have need of a doctor, Kate "

"I've far more need of what you have discovered. Must we really get Cormac back to the castle?"

"Aye, but then he will come, according to the legend, whether we send for him or not. He is destined to be here."

"And to die?"

"Not if we can help it. Never mind the rest of breakfast, fine though it is. I have to tell you what I have discovered, and then we must find a way to get Cormac back."

"He stays at the Shamrock near London."

"The inn where he stayed before the duel?"

"The same, Conan. A letter will reach him in a day or so if we can get it on the next train."

"Then we'll talk during the ride. Get yourself dressed and write the letter while I see to getting the carriage ready. And I'll inform the servants of Gavan's death. Without giving any details. We will attend to his burial when we return. For now, we must get the letter to the depot."

I saw the wisdom of his suggestion. We would waste no more time and talk during the ride to the railroad depot. I wrote the letter, a brief one to be sure, but plain enough that he would not delay returning. I said only that Kerry Flynn had come to the castle without invitation and behaved like an animal. I knew that would bring him back in a hurry. I did not write anything about Conan reading the big book, nor did I mention Gavan's murder. That might lead Cormac to stop off to kill Kerry Flynn before coming home, and that might prove to be a mistake—for Cormac.

We were no sooner on our way to the railroad when Conan told me what he had learned from the book. It was a tale that horrified me, but I listened intensely, without comment.

"More than a thousand years ago," Conan related, "the first Cormac of Fion was a well-known warrior who loved fighting above all else. He was a kind and gentle man except when it came time to do battle, and then he became a demon, fighting like one possessed. And never once was he defeated. But there came a time when he decided to marry, and his bride to be was a descendant of Queen Maeve, a beautiful princess whose hand had been sought by many a suitor. The wedding was to take place at high noon in a castle owned by Cormac.

"To this wedding came royalty from far places, and it was to be a most festive affair. The bride was prepared, the ceremony to start before a huge banquet. But on his way there, Cormac met a man who had sworn to kill him and take his bride in marriage. Cormac immediately drew his sword, as did this other high-tempered man. They began to fight that morning, and when it came time for the ceremony, they were still fighting. Ireland had never seen such a battle. They were well-matched, possessed by a hatred of each other so great that it foretold that one would die. The wedding was postponed. Next morning they were still fighting, both of them wounded several times and covered with blood, but still they fought on. Cormac had forgotten he was to be married—and thought of nothing but the fight."

Conan drew a long breath in the midst of his story, and I commented briefly. "Then it seems our Cormac will fight an equally bloody battle with Kerry Flynn, and history repeats itself."

"Aye, and that is the strangest part of the story. Let me get on with it." He touched the whip to the horses for more speed and kept a tight rein on them as he spoke again.

"The fight was conducted at the bottom of stairs exactly

like those built outside this castle. The reason given was that the original Cormac's father, being a righteous man, was determined to put an end to all this bloody fighting between the kings and princes. He proclaimed that he was no longer a fighting man and that if those who sought his life or his kingdom came to claim either, they would find stairs leading into the castle at their disposal."

"I never heard of such a thing," I said, "and I read Irish history."

"Aye. This was never a well-known tale, and anyway, some foolish enemies did try to use the stairs, and Cormac's father fought like a demon and drove them away. Yet, the stairs remained, and that was where the first Cormac of Fion fought his bloody battle to the death. While his bride waited in the castle with her assemblage. They fought up and down the stairs for two full days, and then Cormac made an error and his enemy ran him through."

"Oh, Conan, how awful," I said in horror.

"That was but part of the legend," Conan went on. "When he abandoned his bride to go on fighting, only to be slain, then the fury of all those assembled brought forth a curse upon the original Cormac, who had just died. Each one hundred years he would be reborn as the undefeatable warrior the original Cormac was. He would be doomed to fight many battles, and he would always win. He would never be bloodied—until the last battle, which would recreate all of the awfulness of the one that killed the first Cormac."

It was a tale that portended nothing but death for Cormac. As the twelfth reincarnation of the original, he would live the same kind of life and be invincible until the final hour, which was foreordained to be exactly one hundred years after the last of the reincarnated Cormacs. Then he would die in a similar battle.

"Do you believe it?" I asked Conan.

"There were ten Cormacs who met the same fate after the original. It happened with no deviation from the curse brought down on the first Cormac of Fion. The book has recorded each one."

"Conan," I said, "this castle cannot be a thousand years old. It's impossible."

"Aye, I will agree to that, Kate, but the stairs to the top of the wall are there. Perhaps the curse that brought down all Cormacs was so powerful it caused a duplicate of the stairs to be built. There is nothing in the book about that. Much of the book is a description of the fight between Cormac and his enemy. It is told in detail, and no bloodier or more hard-fought battle between two men was ever recorded up to that time or since."

"Of course, our Cormac knows the full story," I said, "and he is convinced that when his time comes, there is nothing he or anyone else can do to prevent the same outcome of the battle."

"He believes it," Conan said. "And there is every reason why we should believe it too."

"I would have to be convinced by more than what is recorded in an ancient book," I said.

"There is the fact that Cormac has fought many a battle. More than any man in Ireland has ever fought before. And never was he bloodied . . ."

"You're wrong, Conan. Lord Dervor's bullet struck him. Oh, he was bloodied, all right."

Conan turned to look at me with a frown. "In the excitement of learning what the big book said, I forgot that. Aye, he was bloodied. But even so, Kate, he was not killed, and Lord Dervor had killed others in duels and was known to be a man with an unerring aim. It has been the talk of those who knew about the duel that Lord Dervor had finally failed to kill an opponent. It is possible that Cormac cannot be killed until it is his time, one hundred years to the day after the last Cormac died."

"What can we do?" I asked in shocked awe.

"Nothing, Kate."

"Nothing?" I asked while my jaws set hard and all through my aching body came a determination as savage as Kerry Flynn's attack upon me. "Conan, whatever else, I'm in love with Cormac, and I will not let this happen. I refuse to believe in the legend, for we live in modern times. We no longer live with beliefs in demons, or the Little People, or the fairies, or even the presence of Satan himself, wandering the earth looking for likely Irishmen to harass."

"There is the book, a recorded history," he reminded me.

"Aye, a history recorded by whom? Conan, when was the last time you saw a leprechaun? Or a fairy dancing beneath a toadstool? Or saw a creature with horns, cloven hoofs, and a tail? All these are the offspring of people who lived in darker ages, when any story became worthy of belief if it was told often enough. Cormac is not the reincarnation of the first stupid Cormac who preferred a fight to the death to get-

ting married. Ah, no, Conan, our Cormac is not going to die
that way."

"I can only hope you are right, Kate."

"You believe in the legend, don't you?"

"There is some measure of belief in me, aye. If something
in me goes back to the times when such belief was not only
accepted but also quite possible, then these unexplained
things have stayed with me through the generations of my ancestors before me."

"Poor Gavan must have believed too," I said. "I think
when he came into the castle to meet Kerry Flynn and death,
he was coming to tell me the whole story, as I had urged him
to do. Aye, Gavan believed."

"And if his belief was firm, then so must be Cormac's,"
Conan observed.

I could only nod agreement. There were even doubts in my
mind. When we reached the railroad, I dispatched my letter
to Cormac and begged paper and envelope from the depot
master so I might write a brief note to Nial, Cormac's half-
brother. I asked him to come at once. I felt I might have
need of him, for he was a man who thought clearly and was
versed in the law, so he might find some solution to the problem.

Conan and I discussed each aspect of the legend in detail
on the drive back to the castle, but in the end, as he pulled
up, we had only concluded that the one sure thing was the
fact that one hundred years had elapsed since the last Cormac died and soon it would be my Cormac's time.

We had other matters that required immediate attention.
Conan procured a coffin for Gavan, and late that afternoon
servants dug a grave next to my father's, and there we buried
Gavan.

"They were men alike," Conan said in his simple tribute.
"They should lie side by side. And neither would have us
grieve over them when we have important things to do."

"Thank you, Conan," I said. "Without you at my side, I
know how helpless I would be."

"I wish I could do more," Conan said. "I wish I could be
more to you, Kate. But I can't, and I accept the sad fact."

"Will you study the big book with me? Will you help me
try to prove the legend is wrong? If there ever was such a
legend."

"Aye, I have already made up my mind to this, Kate."

"Cormac will be back in less than a week's time," I said. "My letter will see to that."

Conan shook his head. "More than your letter will convince him to return, Kate. As we have agreed, he believes in the legend, and he knows when the hundred years are up. He is destined to be back here then."

"I'd forgotten again. The whole thing is so impossible it refuses to remain in my mind with all its details. I must find a way to convince Cormac that it's all a lie, a fairy tale."

"He will not be easy to convince. There is no doubt but that he has lived with this and prepared for the day he will die."

"Kerry Flynn will kill him?" I asked. "I don't think Kerry is the equal of Cormac in battle."

"Kerry is a strong man, an evil one who enjoys bloodletting. He will kill Cormac if he can, and glory in it. The facts of the legend are on his side. It's fortunate that he does not know this."

"Perhaps if he was told, he'd be overconfident," I suggested.

"Kate, if the legend is true, nothing can be done to prevent it from repeating itself. If it is not true, Cormac will fight Kerry anyway because of what he did to you and Gavan. So it does seem that Kerry's attack upon you is only part of the pattern, for something must have inspired and enraged the previous Cormacs to fight their last battles with all the fury in them."

"You believe too much," I chided him.

"When I read the book for you, then you will be more inclined to believe, for it prophesies everything that would happen to our Cormac. And much of it has already come true. I think perhaps that was a reason why Gavan did not wish to relate this legend to you, for he surely believed in it, and he knew Cormac's fate was already written and sealed."

"Cormac may fight Kerry because of what he did to me, but I believe he will fight because of Gavan's death. They were friends, and Cormac will be bound to avenge his murder."

"Then that too is part of the prophecies of the legend," Conan said. "I wish I could stop believing in it, but the evidence in the book is too powerful. Face it, Kate, some Irish legends have more truth to them than the poetry in which most were recorded."

"If it is untrue, it is a cruel thing," I said. "Cormac has

been led to fight over and over again, to risk his life because
of a thousand-year-old curse."

"Knowing he will win all but the last fight," Conan added.
"Aye, a cruel thing no doubt."

"We will now go to that room of the statues. I cannot read
Gaelic, but I ask that you read it for me, word for word, to
see if we can find anything that would give the lie to this terrible tale of tragedy."

"It will gain you nothing," Conan said, "but if that is what
you wish, we do have time for it. There are ancients in this
village, and they may have heard of this legend. It might be
that if I talked to them, I will learn more."

"Perhaps," I said. "But you have just now given the lie to
it. You say belief in the legend is only among the ancients.
We who are more modern do not believe, and therefore it
isn't true, no matter what the old men may say."

"Yet, asking their opinions may be of some help, Kate."

"That I agree with. Go see them, but not until you have
read parts of the book to me."

We spent what was left of that day standing beside the
book, while Conan translated the significant parts, none of
which were very encouraging. The lyric qualities of the language, and the apparent sincerity in which the book was written, made it sound plausible and real. The description of the
fight in which the original Cormac was slain was vivid and
detailed, and bloody enough to make me wince at some of
the passages.

The curse bestowed upon this dead Cormac, that he be reborn every hundred years, only to die again, was almost po-
etic, yet an awful thing to read or hear.

The days went by quickly. Conan read the entire book, in
sections, for it was slow going. He also talked to seven old
men and one ancient woman, all of whom knew of the
legend but had never realized that our Cormac was the man
to carry out the grim finish of the tale. That they fully believed in it was impossible to deny, but as I pointed out
again, they were ancients and lived in a time when such
things might have held credence. Conan said he agreed, but
his heart wasn't in it. More and more, Conan had come to
believe in the legend.

And then came Cormac's brief note. He would return, and
he ordered Gavan to be at the depot at a specified time. Cormac was going to be shocked when he learned of Gavan's
death.

The night before he was to arrive, I lay in bed, alone in this massive granite structure, and I'd never felt more lonely, or missed anyone so much in my life as I missed Cormac.

I would marry Cormac now. If he still wanted me, I'd marry him as quickly as the banns would permit. I found myself counting the allotted time before we could be married in the church and, to my dismay, it was well beyond the date of Cormac's death, according to the legend in the big book. No matter, I thought. I didn't believe in the legend, and I could wait. But I also found myself wondering if I should not marry him the moment he returned, banns or not. Like Conan and everyone else, I found myself doubting. Otherwise, why would I be afraid to wait? In my mind lurked the chance that Cormac would be killed.

In the sheer desperation brought on by that kind of thinking, a terrible fear for him overwhelmed me. The man I loved would die on the hundredth anniversary of the last Cormac to succumb to the terms of the legend.

I slept little, or none at all. Early in the morning I went out onto the castle walls just after dawn, when all was as silent as the two graves I could see from the farther end of the castle walls. I paused at the head of the stairs and finally sat down on the uppermost step to look down the steep incline and recall the not-long-ago when Cormac, in a frightful rage, had thrown a man down those steps. Was that symbolic of what was to happen? I asked myself.

I wasn't giving proper thought to the problem. I should be trying to find the answers, and a way to circumvent the legend. If there was no substance to the old tale, then see that Cormac would no longer live in fear of the day he was supposed to die. There had to be something to prove the lie to that age-old doomsday book in the room of the five statues.

I returned to the castle proper and gave orders to the newly arrived servants that Cormac would be home before the sun set and they were to make certain nothing was out of order. Then I dressed, devoting care to the way I looked, because I wanted to see Cormac's face light up when we met. Conan was waiting in the carriage, and we left in plenty of time.

"You've heard nothing new?" I asked him.

"Nothing," he replied.

"I will marry him tomorrow if he asks me, Conan."

"Ah, Kate, be sure of that."

"I am sure. You must have known for some time now that I will marry him. He has already asked me."

"He is a strange man, Kate. He is a wanderer, for one thing."

"Then I shall wander where he goes."

"He is not given to being faithful to one woman. You have seen enough evidence of that."

"He will be faithful to me, for he has changed."

"Perhaps. You would have a grave responsibility."

"All marriage entails responsibility. Stop speaking like the voice of doom. Wish a girl well when she says she is going to marry."

"I wish you well," Conan said softly. "And I wish that it was I you were to marry. You know that. So I pay no heed to your scoldings."

I moved closer to him and linked my hand under his arm in a small gesture of affection. "I'm sorry, Conan. A pity you never stirred me as Cormac has. I don't even know what it is. I only know that I love him with all my heart."

"Aye, that I know, but again I say, be careful. Think it over for a while. Don't agree to anything until after this . . . this day listed in the book has passed."

"I'm surprised at you," I said. "You're trying to discourage me. What have I done to you to deserve that?"

"It's blarney I'm talking, Kate. It's because I'm in love with you and I'm overcome with jealousy."

"I don't believe it, Conan," I said. "You seem to be holding something back. I had the same feeling about poor Gavan."

"Will you do me the favor to begin our conversation all over again, colleen, as if what I said had never been said?"

"I'd be delighted to," I said, somewhat stiffly, I'm afraid, and much of the remaining drive was in silence. It wasn't like Conan to speak this way. Certainly I knew that he loved me, but that was over and he knew it. We were the very best of friends, but no more than that, and he knew it well.

When the train pulled in, we were on the depot platform to greet Cormac. He stepped off the train slowly, like a man exhausted. His face was lined with care too. I knew the reason. He believed he was coming home to fight his last battle, the one in which he would die.

His movements were slow, and unlike other returns, he made no attempt to pick up the luggage, but left it for Conan to retrieve. I held my breath now, because the first thing he'd ask would be the reason for Gavan's absence.

He smiled, for my benefit alone, and embraced me, but the gesture was more like one of duty than a man hungry for love. He settled in the seat beside me while Conan loaded the bags.

"Is Gavan sick?" he asked.

"He is dead, Cormac."

The unhealthy sag to his features abruptly changed as his body tightened up first in shock, then sorrow.

"The man was in fine health when I left."

"He was murdered," I said. "Will you wait until we are back so I may tell you the whole story?"

"I will not wait. You say murdered! What happened? Who killed him?"

"It was Kerry Flynn."

"Ah," he said, as if the name was a total revelation to him, and I knew why the news had affected him that way. He had come home to learn the motive for his fight with Kerry—and his own ultimate death.

"Why did he kill Gavan? What were the circumstances, Kate? For God's sake, tell me! Gavan was the best friend I had in this world. Why would Kerry Flynn murder him?"

"Kerry Flynn came to the castle and . . . almost killed me too when I resisted him. He left me with this . . ."

I managed to raise my skirts and petticoats enough that Cormac could see the still-ugly bruises on my thighs. I heard him inhale sharply.

"My breasts were injured in the same manner," I told him.

"Damn him to the devil's worst works. Tell me the rest of it, Kate."

"He tore my clothes off. I was raped. Twice, I think. Gavan came into the great hall, unaware that Kerry was there. The servants had gone for the day. Gavan saw what was going on, and like the bravest—and most foolish—of men, he tried to attack Kerry. I suppose Kerry was in no mood for a fistfight, short though it might be, so he merely drew a knife and drove it into Gavan's heart. Gavan died at once, and then, with his body beside us, Kerry proceeded to carry out the purpose for which he'd come."

"I'll see Kerry," Cormac said tensely.

"Cormac, wait until you're stronger. It's been a long journey, and much else has happened as well. You'll be more fit to meet the man tomorrow."

"I'll attend to that business the moment I get back."

"It's what he's waiting for. To get at you when you're not at your best. A man in a blind rage like yours is never a good fighter. Don't give Kerry the chance of beating you, Cormac. It will hurt none to wait until tomorrow."

"Perhaps you're right, Kate. I don't think it will make much difference, but I'll wait. I want to hear all the details of his visit so I can decide just how close to death I'll bring the man before I let up."

"He boasts that he will kill you," I warned.

Cormac let himself smile for the first time. It was not a sunny, carefree smile, but one ardently sardonic. "He will not kill me when I see him tomorrow, and that I can promise."

"So you will go to him, but not this day," I said.

"You're a wise girl, Kate. Wiser than me most times. So I'll do as you say, but my anger will not be any less in the morning. Did you attend to Gavan's funeral?"

"Aye, and we buried him beside my father."

"Then two good men lie there, Kate."

He paused and then made a statement that proved to me how great was his belief in the legend: "I would be proud to lie there with them, if it comes to that."

"Yes, Cormac," I said. "I'll try to remember that, though the many years before you'll have need of a grave may make me forget."

"Did Gavan have anything to say about me or the castle before he was killed?"

"No, Cormac. He said no more than he would in normal times."

Cormac glanced at me suspiciously. "He did not live long enough to say anything after Kerry stabbed him?"

"I told you, he died instantly, with not so much as a moan."

"Thank you, Kate, for telling it all to me gently, so the shock of it didn't flatten me as I'll flatten Kerry Flynn's face tomorrow." He raised his voice. "Conan, can't you make these animals move a little faster?"

FOURTEEN

———◦◦◦———

It was a long day for all of us. Conan went directly to the village after putting up the horses. Cormac ate lightly of a special meal I'd ordered prepared for him, and he was very uncommunicative, mostly grunting answers to my questions. He was a worried, anxious man with but one thing on his mind. The death that awaited him on the stairs of his castle.

He retired early, merely saying good night in a perfunctory way before walking slowly up the staircase. I soon followed him. Once in bed, I lay there physically tired but mentally wide-awake. I waited for him to come to me, but it was a vain wait, for he never did. Once I thought I heard him in the corridor, and I tensed, hoping he'd join me, but the sounds died away and no one came.

I knew I would have to confess that I was fully aware of his problem. Conan could in no way help me find any more answers. Perhaps Cormac could, for I was convinced the answers existed, and I still refused to have any faith in the prophecy written into that book.

Finally I could stand it no longer. I'd stay awake all night anyway, so I got up. The moment I opened my door, I saw the candlelight from the room of the five statues. Cormac was there, probably reading the book and trying to find the answers that wouldn't come to me either.

I walked down the corridor, pulling my robe about me, for it was chilly. When I came to the door, Cormac had his back to me. He wasn't reading the book but staring at the statues, dimly illuminated by the single candle on the table.

"Cormac," I said softly.

He spun about as if he expected there would be a deadly enemy behind him. His face clouded up in what I had come to recognize as suppressed anger.

"What are you doing here?" he demanded.

"I know what is in the book," I said.

"You . . . no! You can't read Gaelic."

"Conan read it for me. I know of the original Cormac and of the curse brought down on his head by the assembled lords and kings who had come for his wedding to a princess."

"Come with me," he said. He blew out the candle, seized my hand, slammed the door behind him, and tugging at my arm, walked rapidly along the corridor to the stairs, which we descended to the great hall. He all but pushed me into one of the big chairs, while he sat down in one opposite and very close by.

"I should have known better than trust you, Kate. I asked you not to meddle."

"It is not meddling when one searches for some way to save you. Especially if that someone is in love with you. Don't be angry with me. All I'm trying to do is prove this whole prophecy is a fraud, a fake, a fairy tale."

"Do you know I am the twelfth Cormac?"

"Aye, but surely you don't think you're the same man who was killed a thousand years ago."

"I am the reincarnation of that man. I have been reincarnated ten times before, and I pray this will be the last."

"I suppose then you will go to Kerry Flynn's castle and be killed there by that horrible man."

"No. I will go there. Oh, yes, I'll go. But I will not be killed. I'll beat the man near to death. For me to fight that final battle, I have to be challenged. Kerry will challenge me when he recovers enough to hold a sword."

"Why don't you kill him tomorrow?" I asked. "Then your worries would cease."

"Someone else would come along."

"In the brief time between tomorrow and the hundred-year date?"

"You've had the book read to you, all right. It would make no difference. If I killed Kerry tomorrow, and perhaps I will only an instant of time before that last day will produce the man I will fight to my death."

"I believed you to be a brave man, a kind and wonderful man. Not once did I ever think of you as an idiot."

"Mind what you say, Kate!"

"I'm not afraid of you. But I shall lose all respect for you if you go on believing in that miserable legend. Yes, the first Cormac may have died as the book says he did. But he was not brought back to life every hundred years, for a thousand years, just to live that fight over again."

"Kate, I have enough proof to satisfy me."

"There is no such thing as a curse upon a person, and there is no such thing as reincarnation. Mind you, if you think about it seriously enough and without fear, you'll see that I'm telling you the truth."

He shook his head. I drew my robe closer around me. I knew I was making no impression on him.

"It's well we have this chance to talk," he said. "I don't know what my ancestors did just before they died in that last fight. Perhaps they were in love too, as I am in love with you. I well imagine it was so, and in those former lives of mine, perhaps I did love someone. But if that is true, never in those other lives did I love anyone as much as I love you."

"Cormac," I said softly, "your love for me is no greater than mine for you. Take strength and courage from that and refuse to surrender to this false legend."

"I cannot do that. Remember, I was once damned, and perhaps rightly so, and part of my punishment is to be madly in love knowing nothing can come of it because I'm to die too soon. I believe firmly that also happened in the past."

"I'm sorry for you," I said. "With you, I've gone through every emotion. At first, I hated you for violating me. I wanted to kill you. Slowly, my hatred turned to love. You are destroying that. I will not love a fool."

"What else did Conan, damn his soul, find in the book?"

"What I have told you. There was a Cormac, many centuries ago, who preferred to fight a battle to the death rather than marry his beloved. A fine man he was! If you ask me, Mack Cormac of Fion, his bride was lucky."

"Aye, lucky," he said heavily. "Go on."

"The book said the soul of your ancient Cormac was cursed, that he would be reborn every hundred years, live a free and easy life, and fight as often as he wished without any danger of being harmed by an enemy. But when the hundred-year anniversary came, he would then suffer the fate of the accursed original Cormac. He would go into battle knowing he would be killed on that anniversary."

"And you don't believe that?"

"I believe that the original Cormac should have been drawn and quartered and not allowed to die the easy death that took two full days to accomplish. A man who would leave his betrothed to fight is a fool. That is how I regard the original Cormac. That is the way I can regard you for believing in the legend."

"I believe it all. I have fought thirty or more times with men my equal and sometimes more than my equal. I won every time, though the fight was hard. And I have not been bloodied yet. The law of averages would not permit such a thing to happen, but it did. To me, the legend is stronger than this law of averages."

"Not quite," I said. "There was Lord Dervor's bullet. I saw the wound. I bound it up. Now, if the legend makes you infallible, how did this happen? And if the legend insists you are infallible, then the legend is a lie."

"You try a man's heart and soul, Kate. You also have made me see a different side to you, and I don't like it."

"Cormac . . . I'm only doing my best to make you see reason."

"You're doing more than that. You're ridiculing me and my ancestors, and what I believe in. Once I told you, when it came time for you to leave, I would grant you any amount of money . . . ."

"Cormac!" I said sharply and with a growing dismay.

"I mean it. Even if you are right in what you say. Regardless of whether or not I am killed on the date it is supposed to happen, I think it's time for you to be paid so you can make your own way from now on."

"I wasn't ridiculing—"

"We've said enough. I won't insist you leave tomorrow or the next day. Take your time, but I shall see that a substantial sum is placed at your command in the morning."

"Before or after you attack Kerry Flynn?" I asked with a sigh of resignation.

"Now you're making fun of me again," he said angrily. "I'll not have it. I've put this to you in a kindly fashion, but if you must hear the truth, I can say that too."

"Say it, then, and be done with it," I said.

"Forget what I said before. It was said only to soften the blow of my death. I've not been in love with you. Not ever! You were a most desirable bed companion, and I took full advantage of that. With a clear conscience, after the first two times, when I paid you off in food."

"Oh, Cormac, let's not allow our tempers to govern us. I swear I meant only to try to convince you this legend has no basis in fact. Whatever I did or said was because of my love for you. I'm afraid you have taken the legend to your heart too strongly and that if you do fight Kerry Flynn a second time, you may do so under the assumption you cannot win that he is bound to kill you. And under those conditions, what kind of a fight will it be? If you believe in the legend, if you do fight Kerry Flynn, you will lose your life because you'll think you've lost it before the fight begins."

"In the morning," he said, unmoved by my plea, "I'll see to your payment. It will be in the bank when you wish to claim it."

"I don't want any of your money," I said bitterly.

"That is all I can offer you. Nothing more. I'm going to bed."

I sat there in the chill of the great hall. I heard his door close hard, as an angry man would close it. I'd gone too far. Perhaps, in his eyes, I'd taken the whole thing too lightly. I'd tried every method I could think of. From scolding to logic, to derision, and all had failed. I had failed. I'd infuriated him and was to be banished from the castle and his life. That hurt me, but not as deeply as the fact that Cormac would fight what he believed to be his last battle and lose it because he believed it was ordained that he die at this time, to be reborn nearly a century later, when the whole shabby business would start over again.

Yet I knew I'd not give up. Unless he forcibly ejected me from the castle, I would stay, because it was my belief that Cormac was not immortal up to the one hundredth year and that when he fought what was to be his final battle, he would not necessarily die. Far more likely, he'd win because of his skill and his enormous strength. If I could only convince him of that, he'd have a far better chance to defeat Kerry Flynn. I must find a way to convince him, so he'd not sacrifice his own life.

With that thought, I went to bed and slept, partly from weariness brought on by my futile pleas, but mostly because my mind was eased by my decision. I would not give up.

I awoke with a start, trying to figure out what it was I should do today. Then I recalled Cormac's intended battle with Kerry Flynn. I bathed and dressed hastily. It was still early, the servants had not yet arrived, but I cared little for breakfast. I looked for Cormac, but he was nowhere to be found.

I threw a shawl over my head and ran down to the stable area. Conan was seated outside Gavan's cabin, taking quick, nervous puffs on his pipe.

"Aye," he said, "I saddled a horse for him. He was going to the village to see about his banking. So he told me."

"Thank heaven. I thought he might have gone to meet Flynn and not returned."

"He'll be on his way to see Flynn after he finishes his bank business, Kate. What did you talk about last night?"

"I tried to convince him he was wrong, but I didn't do a very good job of it."

"He still believes he will die when he fights Flynn?"

"Not this time. He'll fight with the knowledge he can't lose, according to the legend. But when he fights him again on that hundredth-year day, then he'll die. I tell you, Conan, a man can talk his way into his own grave."

"There was no talk of marriage?"

"Oh, yes. He rejected it."

"Since he is convinced he will die, what purpose would there be in marriage?"

"Conan, you're growing old. You're forgetting what love is. I would rather be married to Cormac for one day than to another for a lifetime. Can you understand that?"

"Aye, too well," he said softly.

"I'm sorry," I said quickly. "I didn't mean to hurt you. I'm being selfish. It almost makes me wonder if it's only my own happiness I'm concerned for."

"No, Kate. It's your man you're fearful for. You're consumed with worry. Have you any new ideas in your head?"

"I'm not sure. Was there anything in that book of legends that you didn't tell me?"

"Why do you ask?" He was too quick with the question. I pretended not to notice him start, though I knew I had caught him off guard.

"Only because Cormac asked me if I knew everything in the book."

"You . . . know everything," Conan said. "You also know Cormac. If I were you, I'd take whatever settlement he has placed in the bank for you and go away from here. It will break your heart if you stay."

"No greater break than if I leave."

"It's a sad business, to be sure. Cormac told me last evening, soon after we brought him back, that he wanted me to take Gavan's place. That's why I'm here this morning. He also gave me an order which I must fulfill before the day is over."

"What are you trying not to tell me?" I said, tired of playing a game. "You're speaking as Gavan used to."

"This afternoon I am to meet the train from Dublin and

bring Ellen to the castle. He asked her to come before he left, after getting your urgent letter. He . . . is going to marry her, Kate."

"He is not!" I said loudly. "She is no woman for Cormac. I won't permit this to happen. I won't . . ." I bent my head, for all pride had drained out of me. I wept, not too silently, for my world had suddenly come to an end. If he had instructed Ellen to follow him, then it was clear he did not love me and preferred her. I'd not only failed in my attempt to convince him the fable was unworthy of belief, I'd lost him forever.

I raised my head and used the edge of the shawl to dry my eyes. "I would be grateful if you'd saddle a horse for me, Conan. I'm going to head him off before he reaches Kerry Flynn's castle."

"Kate, you can't stop him from that fight."

"I have no intention of doing so, but one never knows what will happen. Besides, it is not my wish that Kerry Flynn go unpunished. For what he did to poor Gavan, if not for what he did to me."

Conan went off to get the horse ready. I remained seated, trying to determine what I must do. There had to be something. I wasn't ready to turn my back and walk away from what was about to happen. Not after what I'd been through.

Cormac's sending for Ellen hurt more than Flynn's attack on me. It was too unexpected. It wasn't worthy of consideration, let alone belief, yet she was coming. Tonight she'd be here. No doubt they would sleep together and she would manipulate him into a quick marriage.

Conan brought the horse around, and I was given a boot up. I tapped the horse with my quirt and sent him galloping toward the road leading from Castle Lucane to that of Kerry Flynn.

When the smaller castle came into view, I looked carefully for any sign of Cormac's horse, and when I failed to see the animal, I felt certain he'd not yet arrived. So I pulled up and urged the horse behind a row of high bushes, where I waited.

Cormac came by ten minutes later, a look of black rage on his face. I rode out to fall in beside him, our horses moving neck to neck.

"Why are you here?" he asked roughly.

"I'm sure you recall what Kerry did to me, even if you're thinking more of his murder of Gavan. I came to see Kerry Flynn punished, for he is richly deserving of it."

"Is that the only reason?"

"No. I came to bind up your wounds if you are hurt."

"I shall not be. I swear it."

"Then perhaps I shall bind up Kerry Flynn's wounds."

"Do what you will."

"Conan told me Ellen is on her way."

"I asked her to come."

"Will you marry her, Cormac?"

"That is why I am bringing her here. On the hundredth-year anniversary I shall have her waiting in the castle, dressed in her wedding gown."

"You're recreating what happened to the first Cormac, aren't you? You are intent upon making the legend come true. Ellen will wait and wait, and finally she will be told that you are dead. You will have sought your own death because you think it is inevitable that you die on this day. You have already lost the battle."

"You won't be there to see it," he said.

"You're wrong there. I will not go away. If you order me out of the castle, I'll go back to my cottage and live there until this fight happens."

"Suit yourself. You've a sharper tongue than I thought you had."

"Now, to have this fight occur, according to the legend, Kerry Flynn will have to challenge you to a fight to the death. Is that true?"

"You know it is," he said.

"But what if you did not meet Kerry in combat today? What if he did not issue a challenge? Then would you still be compelled to fight him?"

"If I do not make it happen, the effects of that curse will see to it."

I dug my heels into the animal, and it broke into a run. I reached the slovenly castle before Cormac, and I was already dismounted as he rode up. Two huge dogs came bounding around the corner of the castle, proof that Flynn was here and, as usual, had seen us approach. Cormac had a way with dogs, and he had them under control before they could attack either of us.

The great door to the castle had already opened, and Kerry Flynn stood there regarding us with amusement.

"Be damned to your coming," he said, "and be damned to you, Cormac. Did your lovely whore tell you I took advantage of her favors?"

Cormac strode up to him, and without warning he brought up a blow that cracked against Kerry's chin and sent him reeling backward into the castle. Being propelled headlong backward, and dazed from the blow, Kerry tripped and fell heavily. Cormac wasted no time. He was upon the fallen man before Kerry was on his feet, but this time Kerry dodged the punch and Cormac was thrown off balance. Instantly Kerry arose and lashed out at Cormac, but the full force of the blow was reduced when Cormac rolled back with it.

Kerry backed away. I was watching closely. On a long table in the entrance hall a white cloth was covering some object, and I thought Kerry was trying to reach it.

The two men sparred now, looking for an opening, and Kerry kept on with his short backward steps, bringing him closer and closer to the table. I managed to circle the two and reach the table. Kerry's back was toward it. I lifted the white cloth and revealed a dagger and a rapier waiting there for Kerry to seize. Before Cormac could defend himself against such weapons, Kerry would surely use them effectively. I picked up the rapier with one hand, the dagger with the other, and quickly retreated farther down the entrance hall.

Kerry landed a hard blow against Cormac's chest, a punch that took the wind out of him for the moment. Kerry whirled about, snatched off the cloth, and began to reach for the weapons I held above my head. Cormac saw what had happened, and his fury increased. As Kerry turned back, disconcerted and suddenly fearful at the loss of his weapons, Cormac struck him alongside the head, then in the stomach, another to the side of the head, and Kerry was thrown forcibly against the wall.

He evaded Cormac for the moment and made a dive in my direction. I brought down the rapier, its point aimed at him. No words were spoken, for all the energy of the two went into the fight, which, I judged, was about to grow even more furious.

Kerry now knew he wouldn't have his weapons and must rely on his fists and his strength. Cormac, in a rage before he entered the castle, was now more angry than ever. The pair clashed, coming together with an impact that must have shaken both of them. Kerry, as a fighter, was perhaps a bit stronger and heavier than Cormac, but he lacked Cormac's finesse. His swings were mostly wild and not difficult for Cormac to block, whereas Cormac's punches were shorter, but more vicious, and each one found its mark somewhere in Kerry's abdomen or his chest. Less frequently, Kerry's head was rocked with a blow, and these were effective, for they were not the result of wild swings but of carefully aimed blows delivered with skill.

Kerry was beginning to weaken, and he looked desperately for a way out. Behind, I stood with rapier at the ready, and beyond me was the stairway. Kerry was going to make a run for it if he got the chance. Once on the stairs, he'd hold a certain advantage. Suddenly he spun about and made a mad dash, but Cormac had sensed exactly what he intended and caught up with him before he reached the bottom step. The two of them went past me faster than I could turn to follow them.

Cormac made a headlong dive, wrapped his arms around Kerry's legs, and brought him down. Cormac was back on his feet first, and when Kerry struggled desperately to get up, Cormac sent a short, fast punch straight into the center of Kerry's face. Blood spurted from lacerated lips and, no doubt, loosened teeth. Kerry fell back on his haunches and gently touched a hand to his face, to lower the hand and regard the blood as if he couldn't believe it.

Cormac said, "That's for what you did to Kate Moran. From here on, what you'll get is for the murder of Gavan. On your feet, you bastard. Defend yourself or I'll pound you to bits anyway."

"I'm going to kill you," Kerry mumbled. He was having difficulty with his speech now. "Kill you . . . cut you to pieces . . ."

"Will you, now? Get up and prove it."

"Not today," Kerry managed. "On the thirtieth I'll have you. And I'll kill you slowly, Cormac. I may take all day to do it, but you'll die."

All I could think of was the fact that Kerry had named the day when, according to the legend, Cormac was supposed to be killed. How did he know?

Cormac reached down, grabbed Kerry by his shirt, hauled him to his feet, and pushed him against the wall. He sank a hard right fist into Kerry's stomach, which brought a moan, and all Kerry's resistance ceased, because he'd been robbed of his last ounce of strength. Cormac now began to pound home lighter blows meant to inflict pain. He kept this up until Kerry's face was barely recognizable. Then Cormac drew back a fist, aimed it.

"With Gavan's curse upon you," he said.

The blow struck Kerry on the chin. It was accompanied by a crackling sound of bone splintering. Kerry's knees gave out, and with his back against the wall he slid down into an ignominious heap on the floor.

I walked up to Cormac and handed him the rapier. Cormac took it, waited until Kerry opened his right eye. His left was going to be closed for some time. Cormac set the point of the rapier against Kerry's throat and for one brief instant I thought he would run Kerry's neck through. Instead, with a swift movement Cormac broke the rapier on one knee and threw the two pieces as far away as he could. Then he walked out of the castle.

I followed him and caught up just before he mounted his horse.

"Why didn't you kill him?" I asked.

"It's not for me to kill that man."

"You believe he is the one who will kill you in a few days. Yet he gave you . . . I gave you . . . a chance to kill him now. But the legend must be served. A fairy tale started a thousand years ago must never be destroyed. You will die at the hands of Kerry Flynn and then you will be reborn in time to meet the next century, when the legend must once again bring you back to die all over again. If I didn't know you better, I'd believe you were simpleminded, Cormac."

"Kate, I realize you can't understand this, but it is true. The legend has not been false in all those centuries. If I had killed Kerry Flynn a few moments ago, someone else would come along."

"You don't know that," I protested, even while I recognized the folly of trying to convince him. "You only think you do."

"I want it to be Kerry. He may kill me, but he'll never be the same man again, and I can promise you one thing, Kate. He will never again rape a woman."

"You would sacrifice yourself for that! Damn you, Cormac! The legend will be your death, and there's no need for it. You could defeat Kerry Flynn with slingshots. He's no match for you. I've just seen that."

"Kate, I wish to heaven you'd leave the castle tomorrow. Today! For one thing, Ellen will be here, and I want no bickering between the two of you."

"You are going to ask her to marry you, set her up in a chapel or somewhere to wait for her bridegroom to come.

Then you will start out for the wedding, meet Kerry Flynn or whoever is going to kill you, and begin a fight that will end in your death and leave Ellen at the altar, not even a widow. Why? What sort of travesty is that?"

"I don't like her. She has been trying to get me to marry her for months, and she's annoyed me persistently. There has to be a bride waiting for me, and it might as well be Ellen. She'll get nothing out of it, and that will teach her a lesson, for she agreed to marry me strictly for my money and this castle. I cannot dispose of the castle. By tradition and law, it will go to Nial, but my estate . . . will go to you."

"Oh, Cormac." I moved up to him and threw my arms around him. "Why do you make me so damned angry and then make me weep for you? I don't want your estate. I want you."

"I know, Kate. I'm sorry."

"Now, should all this not come to pass, if you've lived a delusion, and even if Kerry Flynn fights you, is that a guarantee you'll lose? Suppose you don't lose? Then what? Will you go to Ellen and the wedding?"

"You worry about things that cannot happen."

"Suppose they did. I want to know."

"I . . . don't know, because I've never given it a thought."

I moved out of his arms. "All right, Cormac. There's no way I can change your mind. I would ask one thing. Gavan, before he died, urged me several times not to consider marrying you under any conditions. Conan, after he read that big book—after, mind you—said the same thing. I would be better off if I took your money for the work I did and go away. You yourself have hinted the same. What's behind this? What secret is in that big book that hasn't yet been revealed to me?"

"I know of no secret," he said. He walked to his horse and swung into the saddle. He was off at a full gallop before I even had my foot in the stirrup. I tried to catch him, but he rode like someone half-crazed with fear that I'd corner him again and insist on answers to my questions.

I felt frustrated and disheartened. Oh, Kerry Flynn had been punished, and well, but that was an insignificant thing compared to my failure at making Cormac give less credence to the fable of the Cormacs. The stage was now set, and Cormac wouldn't deviate from it. In a way, I couldn't blame him. He had grown up with this legend drilled into his poor head. There was the book, the family history, the busts of his ancestors as permanent reminders. He believed because he'd never been shown the fallacy of the fable. He thought he would die on the thirtieth, and die he would, because he was fated for it then.

Cormac went directly to his bedroom. If I followed him, I'd find the door bolted, so I didn't waste time there. I sought out Conan instead.

"He whipped Kerry Flynn like I haven't seen a man so beaten in my life," I reported to Conan.

"Good. That devil of a man had it coming."

"Aye, you'll get no disagreement on that from me. But Kerry Flynn, with hardly a breath left, told Cormac he would kill him on the thirtieth. Now, how could that man know the date? There's no chance he could have read the big book. No one else that I know of ever did, save Gavan, and certainly he wouldn't have told Flynn."

"It's a strange turn," Conan admitted. "I can't explain it."

"But I think you could explain why you, Gavan, and Cormac too were so against my marrying Cormac. He admitted to me he was bringing Ellen here because nothing would come of it anyway. He'd be dead before he was married. Now, why couldn't I take Ellen's place? Even under those circumstances?"

"That's another puzzle. I was for your leaving because I thought he was marrying Ellen because he preferred her to you."

"He doesn't like her at all. He said so. He knows she's after only his money and the castle. Cormac said there was no way she could get the castle because it goes to Nial. And Cormac has left everything else he owns to me."

"You'll be rich, Kate. There'll be none hereabouts who will have your wealth."

"I care not one fig for his money. I want him, and I'm not giving up. There are a few days left. I'm going to make use of them."

"I don't see how, Kate, but if I can help you . . ."

"Thank you. You're a dear friend. I'll talk to Nial when he gets here and then make up my mind what's to be done. Nial may not know much about this, but at least I may learn something about Cormac I didn't know before."

I'd not bargained on Ellen's attitude toward me. Conan drove to the depot to fetch her and Nial. When she entered the castle, she ignored me completely at first and rushed into Cormac's arms like a blushing bride. It sickened me to see the sham of this girl. Nial, on the other hand, was pleasant and warm in greeting me.

"For the life of me, I can't see what Cormac wants that silly girl for. My ears ache from listening to her boasting of what she is going to do as mistress of the castle."

"I know," I said. "And I'll wager she told you the first thing she'd do was get rid of me."

"Well, it was mentioned," Nial admitted with a smile.

"I want to talk to you about Cormac," I said. "Perhaps in the garden, where we can't be overheard. As soon as possible I'll go there."

"You," Ellen said loudly, pointing an imperious finger at me. "I'll want my bags unpacked, and be careful of the wedding gown. If you tear it, I'll have you beheaded."

"Yes, miss," I said dutifully.

"And I'll want your help in trying it on. In one hour. Make sure you are there."

"Of course, miss." I curtsied, ignoring Cormac's sheepish grin. Ellen saw nothing scornful about the gesture, which secretly amused me.

Cormac and Nial, arm in arm, went to the great hall, where I had a tray with brandy, wine, and glasses waiting. I served them while Conan carried Ellen's bags upstairs, with her following him and giving shrill instructions about picking out a riding horse for her.

Nial said, "How can you believe that foolish story about being reborn every hundred years? It's no more worthy of belief than the other ten thousand silly fables told all over Ireland. We're a nation of fables and legends. They made fine telling in the old days and good reading in modern times for those of us who are romantics, but they don't make any sense."

"You were brought up in this castle," Cormac defended himself. "You know for a fact that the big book has been in the family since the castle was built, and longer. You know how the busts were found, hidden away, covered by the dust of centuries. If there is no truth to the legend, why is it that the busts resemble me? Can you deny the one in black is not as perfect as if it was made by my sitting for a sculptor?"

"Yes, it is a perfect resemblance," Nial admitted, "but that doesn't mean it's one made of you hundreds of years before you were born. There are family resemblances, even going back in history, and if this bust—or even all of them—bear a close resemblance, there is nothing unusual about that."

"The white busts come close," Cormac said, "but the black one I think must be the last. The likeness of the Cormac who died a hundred years ago. Its resemblance to me is good proof that I did live then, and I died as that Cormac died."

Nial shook his head. "I've always tried to make you listen to reason and to believe that only chance made you the exact image of the bust, rather than the legend. You're going at this with the attitude of a man who not only can't win this battle, but is satisfied to lose it."

I couldn't help but break in on them. "Nial is right, Cormac. You're going to give up because you think you must. It's nonsense."

"No one asked you to interfere," Cormac said testily. "If I want your advice, I'll ask for it, but don't depend on the fact I will. To be truthful, your foolish exhortations have served only to irritate me. Now, go about your business and let Nial and me argue this out. If there is anything to argue."

"Aye," I said curtly. "You'll see no more of me this day."

I walked out, only to be hailed from the top of the stairway by Ellen. When I went up to see what she wanted, I was in a mood to take no guff from the likes of her.

"I want you to try on my wedding gown," she said. "Your figure is dumpier than mine, but you're still slender enough that it'll fit."

"I'm not as skinny as you, Ellen," I said, "and I'm glad of it. I'll try on your wedding gown. I suppose your mother also wore it. If you had a mother."

"I'll put up with no more of your sarcasm," she said. "Don't you forget, Kate, I'll be mistress of this castle in a few days, and you'd best behave yourself."

"In a few days I won't be here," I said. I removed my dress and held up Ellen's wedding gown. It was no heirloom. In fact, it held no appeal. The material was so cheap that the seams puckered.

"I said put it on, not examine it," she ordered.

When I made no reply, she said, "I'll be glad to have you out of here. Oh, I know what you've been to Cormac. You served your purpose, and there's no further place for you here anyway. And I'll see to it that Cormac doesn't overpay you. Now, get on with this fitting. As long as you're working here, I'll expect you to obey me."

I brought the skirt down over my head, settled it around my waist, then bent to pull the hem down. Ellen was exceptionally thin; the gown had been fitted to her, and it had little likelihood of fitting me. As I tried easing it over my hips, there was a resounding rip as a seam tore.

Ellen's shriek could be heard over the whole castle. Her outraged cries continued until both Cormac and Nial stormed into the room, probably expecting to find a scene of mayhem and wondering who had survived.

"She purposely tore my wedding dress, Cormac. She just tried to squeeze into it, and you can see she hasn't my slender figure. She did this on purpose because she hates me. She hates me because I'm going to marry you and you wouldn't have her."

Cormac looked at me, his features noncommittal. "I've asked you before to pack up and get out, Kate. This time it's an order. I want you out of here, bag and baggage, before the day is over. Do you understand?"

I took off the dress, and careful though I was, another seam ripped. Ellen renewed her screeching. I threw the gown on the bed.

"I insist you stay long enough to sew it up for me," Ellen shouted.

"Oh, mistress," I said in mock humility, "my ma never taught me to sew. I'm very sorry, mum, but the fine likes of you should have been well taught in the art."

Cormac gave a sigh of resignation. "That's enough, Kate. I don't want to see you again."

He stalked out of the room, followed by Nial, who favored me with a resigned shrug and a look of sympathy. I gathered up my own dress and slipped into it. Ellen had withdrawn to a corner of the room, which was wise of her. If she'd made one more comment, issued one more order, I would have started a fight to rival the one between Cormac and Kerry Flynn.

FIFTEEN

———◆◉◆———

I met Nial in the castle garden, where I had caused elaborate flowerbeds and lush green bushes to be planted. There were concrete benches and pools with goldfish swimming lazily about. It was a setting I loved and would hate to leave.

Nial said, "I'm afraid he means it this time, Kate. He truly wants you out of here."

"I never thought it would happen," I confessed. "I've been heedless of his threats before, but as you say, it's different this time, and all the worse for that, because the poor man has already set the date of his death."

"I can't but agree with you, Kate. You must realize that Cormac has always been like this. Ever since he was old enough to comprehend what it all meant, he believed he was the twelfth Cormac, of whom eleven had met their fate. The last ten because of the curse placed upon the first Cormac."

"When was the big book discovered? And the busts?" I asked.

"The book has always been in the family. So I've been given to understand. The busts were discovered by Cormac himself. He was about nineteen then, and when he came across them in one of the storage rooms, he took it for granted they were relics of the past. The uncanny resemblance of them to himself strengthened his belief in the legend."

"I take it you don't believe."

"I'm torn, Kate. The thing sounds absurd, especially to a man like me who has been trained in the law, but to others, people who have been brought up to believe in fairies and Little People by foolish elders, this legend would be real. Because it sounds as if it really did happen and the events over the centuries are perfectly plausible."

"I don't believe a word of it. Can you think of any way to prove the falseness of it?"

"I'm afraid not. Certainly not before Cormac is due to meet this man . . . What's his name?"

"Flynn. Kerry Flynn. He lives in another castle—the only other one for miles."

"Ah, yes, Flynn. They've been enemies for years. If there is any logic to the legend, Flynn is the man for Cormac to meet, for it has been said that each Cormac must meet an old and deadly enemy in the end."

"Do what you can for the poor man," I begged. "If he comes through this ordeal, see that he does not marry Ellen."

"That may be easy to do, because I know he's in love with you but for some reason won't make you his prospective bride."

"He doesn't want me widowed, I suppose. Or so he says."

"Well, that could be true. On the other hand, having asked you to leave and having placed Ellen as his bride, he may go through with it, because Cormac has more pride than sense."

"I'll tell you this, Nial, I won't have gone far before the battle takes place, and if Cormac survives the terms of the legend, I'll be back, whether he wants me or not."

"That's the attitude to take. I'll keep trying to talk him out of this day of doom that is coming up so soon. Maybe he'll throw me out too, but I'll take that chance. Good luck to you, Kate, and all my admiration goes with you."

I kissed his cheek and then went back into the castle, where I packed some of my things. Only that which could be easily carried. Conan, in anticipation of this, had brought around the sidecar. He helped me place my bags in the second seat and watched me drive away, no less sad than I.

But halfway to the village I pulled up and sat in deep thought for a few moments. I had suddenly come to the conclusion that I too was giving up, no less than Cormac had surrendered to the legend. Angered at my own thoughtlessness, I turned the cart around and drove back. I left the sidecar in front of the castle and went back inside. From my own room I procured a large suitcase. Making certain no one was about on this floor, I used my key to the room of the five statues. I was glad I'd not surrendered my keys. I unlocked the door, went in, and closed it behind me. Then I opened the big book, turning sheafs of pages until I came to the last one, which was apparently glued to the back cover. I couldn't peel it off, so I tried to tear the whole back of the book off, but that was beyond my strength. So I had to take more risks, and I managed to reach the kitchen without encountering anyone. There I helped myself to a sharp knife, returned to the secret room, and cut the back of the book free. I placed this in my suitcase and added the black bust and one of the white ones. This done, I added the knife to the contents of the suitcase, closed it, left the room, and was opposite the door of the room that had been mine when Ellen stepped out of her room. Her scornful gaze regarded me from head to toe. I felt as if I was being measured for a new gown.

"It's taken you long enough to clear out," she said. "Be on your way, and don't you dare come back."

"Yes, mistress," I agreed. I didn't want her to ask any questions or, perhaps, out of spite, ask to see what was in my suitcase.

I'd not stopped walking while this brief conversation went on, and I kept going. I was afraid I might bump into Cormac, but it didn't happen. If he knew what I was doing, his anger would reach heights I'd not seen before.

I placed the third suitcase on the sidecar and drove off, feeling much better. I knew precisely what I had to do, though the mechanics of doing it still escaped me.

That day and night I spent in my village cottage. Conan came by right after dark. He was seething with anger.

"I'm to meet the train in the morning, for this skinny wench has invited all of Cormac's old friends to come for the wedding. They'll mess up the castle as they did before, and turn this dreary day of battle into a worse one, whether Cormac lives or dies. I tell you, Kate, it'll be my last day there. I'm only staying to be of help if I can. For Cormac's sake alone."

"Will you stop by for me?" I asked.

"Aye, that I will, but you might tell me where you're going and what you're up to."

"I'm going to Dublin first. To London if I have to. I don't know exactly what I hope to learn there. But at least I'll be doing something."

"But what do you hope to gain by this? Cormac won't believe anything you may find out—if there is anything to find out. I'm coming to a point where I'm beginning to believe in the legend as much as Cormac does."

"Don't you dare, Conan. It's not true, and somehow I'm going to prove it."

"In what days there are left? There aren't many, Kate."

"That's why I want to leave in the morning."

"Aye, then I'll be here. We'll have to meet the train from

Dublin, and while all them backsliding hooligans from London and Dublin arrive, you'll have to wait for the afternoon train."

"I'll keep out of sight," I promised. "Don't let Cormac, or even Nial, know what I'm up to. If they ask, tell them I'm sitting in my cottage waiting for word from Cormac."

It did work out well, perhaps better than I deserved, for Conan got me to the depot, where I concealed myself while the boistering, already half-drunk friends of Ellen and Cormac got off the train, to the obvious relief of the conductor. I had hours to wait, and I spent them walking about the streets of this larger town. It boasted a small library, and I spent some time there studying what books there were on the era when the original Cormac lived and died. I could find no reference to the name anywhere, but then, it was not the best-equipped library in the world.

I did find a listing of sculptors in Dublin, and this I copied, along with the addresses of the two Dublin newspapers. Already armed with this information, I thought I would save considerable time after my arrival in Dublin.

During the boring, long, noisy, and sooty journey through the night, I began to formulate my plans, such as they were. I was concerned with the saving of as much time as possible, because I must be back at the castle in no more than seven days. The journey itself took up most of that time, so I was going to be hard-pressed. I'd taken a considerable sum of money with me in case there was the need of handing it out to obtain the information I wanted.

Upon arriving in Dublin, with the fervent hope I'd not have to extend the journey to London, I checked into a fine hotel. I took a much-needed bath, ate heartily, and rested for a few precious hours, for I was exhausted.

By early afternoon I felt better and eager to begin. The first place I went was to the biggest newspaper in Dublin. There I asked to see someone who handled their supply of paper, and I was led to a tiny office. A man in a leather apron greeted me in friendly-enough fashion.

I said, "I am in serious need of expert advice. If you will agree to help me, I'll pay for your services handsomely."

"I'm interested already," he told me with a grin. "Now, what is it that puzzles the heart of such a pretty colleen?"

"In my family is a great book said to have existed for a thousand years. . . ."

"That I would examine without charge, for the novelty of it, because I don't think a book could last that long."

"I'm comforted to hear that, because I would like to prove this book is a fraud." I opened the large envelope in which I carried the back cover of the book, and I placed it before this man. He examined it with considerable interest, to the point of loosening one corner of the glued page and tearing it free to hold it to the light. Next he examined the leather binding and whistled sharply, indicating he was surprised with that more than he'd been excited by the bit of paper. An indication he believed the binding to be genuinely very old. He next took out a magnifying lens and studied the handwriting.

"Now, before I give you my opinion, what's this all about?" he asked.

"It's become a question of inheritance, and I feel I am being cheated. To prove it, I must be able to say that this book is not a thousand years old, and I must be able to show about when the paper was made, when the entries were written. I understand there are ways to do this."

"The binding of the book is ancient. A thousand years? Possibly, though I doubt it. However, there could be more expert opinions than mine on the age of the leather. But not on the type of paper. A thousand years ago, a hundred years ago, paper of this type was not yet invented. And if the entries listed here are supposed to be authentic and to have been made a hundred years apart, I'm afraid that's not true. In the first place, the handwriting is by the same person."

"You're certain of this?" I asked hopefully.

"So sure I'll swear to it and give you a letter to that effect. Also, the ink used in making all of the entries is a recent nonfading type. Ink a hundred years old would have faded more than this by now. As for the entries made five hundred and more years ago, it's impossible they were."

I placed money on his desk, a great deal of it, but what he had told me was worth every penny. He cheerfully wrote out his opinion of the back binding's age, the similarity in all the entries, the quality and lasting effects of paper and ink. I had something, at least.

He also gave me the address of the most prominent artist-sculptor in Dublin, a man named Ahearn, and that became the subject of my next visit. It was some distance from the center, so I hired a carriage and ordered the driver to wait for me when we arrived. One other thing gave me hope. The name of the sculptor was Ahearn, and the base of the black statue bore the initial A.

We were well into the countryside, where the houses were those of people of means. My address was a stone cottage ten times the size of my own and built in the center of a fine garden.

A smiling white-haired woman came out and stood awaiting my approach. The stone-bordered path was long.

"Yes," she said in answer to my question, "my husband is Andrew Ahearn, an artist, and he is in his studio. Do you wish to make an appointment? I'm sure he'd be delighted to have you sit for him. You're a rosy-cheeked, very attractive girl with fine bone structure."

"I wish I could sit for him," I said, "but my business concerns something he may have done in the past. I understand he is also a sculptor, and in this box I carry are two busts that he may have made years ago. It's very important to me—and to someone I love—to verify that these busts were sculptured recently. By that I mean within twenty years, more or less. Probably much less."

"Come with me," she said, and I was led through a beautifully appointed house, so attractive that there was little need to ask if someone with the skill and eye of an artist was responsible.

She led me into a large studio at the rear of the house, facing the morning light. Standing before an easel was a slim, elderly man with a great mop of pure-white curly hair. He smoked a pipe as he wielded his brushes, but ceased work when we entered.

As I had explained to his wife, I told the artist about the busts, and I placed them on a bench for his inspection.

"The black one," I explained, "has a mark of some kind which may identify the sculptor. It's the letter A, which corresponds to your name."

Mr. Ahearn studied the black bust for a moment and then the white one. "They seem to be of the same man, though there is a difference between them."

"How old would you say the white one is, sir?"

"They're of plaster with a coating to simulate marble. That kind of work was done about twenty-five or thirty years ago, not before."

"Ah," I said with great satisfaction, "you've no idea how much that information means to me."

"I'm happy to have been of service," he said. "Now, as to the black one . . ."

"Perhaps you can tell me, by the mark on the underside, who made it."

"You mean the hallmark. I don't even have to look at the mark, my dear. This is a bust of Mack Cormac of Fion. I sculptured it. Now I must ask you to tell me why you require this information."

I sat down out of sheer relief at having completed my mission so quickly. I told the artist, in detail, omitting little. Stressing the fact that Cormac firmly believed this bust had been sculptured many years, even centuries, ago and that the white one, with the others in that locked room, was also aged.

"It's a weird story," Ahearn admitted, "but just weird enough to be true. We do fancy tales like that. Now I'll tell you how I came to do this work."

"But, sir, if you sculptured the bust, Cormac must have sat for it. Then he'd certainly have known it was recent."

"Cormac didn't know it was being done. He came to me to have his portrait painted. That required a number of sittings, and he was quite faithful. But every time he came, I did my work at the easel, and with his image fresh in my mind I worked on the bust after he left. If I made an error, I rectified it the next time he sat."

"Aye," I said with my breath held. "No doubt the bust was commissioned, then, by someone else?"

"It was. I was paid by a man who wished to surprise Cormac with the bust."

"Do you have his name, sir?"

"Yes. I recall the incident well, because it was unusual and . . . the man who commissioned it said he was Cormac's brother."

"Nial," I said softly.

"That's the name. He's a barrister in London, as I recall."

"Would you give me an affidavit to that effect, please?"

"After the circumstances you have described, I'll do more than that. I'll go with you and personally confront Cormac with the truth about this."

"It must be at once," I said. "There's not much time, sir."

"I'd like a little vacation, especially in your part of the country. A man has to refresh himself now and then."

"You've no idea how grateful I am. By chance, you may have saved the life of a good man."

"We could leave this evening," he suggested.

"I'll be here with a carriage at six," I told him. "I can at least promise you that Cormac's castle is worth seeing."

"It sounds like a conspiracy to me, Miss Moran. Certainly this half-brother of Cormac knew of the legend, but even so, this must have been started a long time ago. Possibly by Nial's father. And this man Kerry Flynn has to be aware of it and must be very confident in knowing that the legend says Cormac will die during the fight."

"Flynn would be no match for Cormac," I said, "unless he was sure he could win and if Cormac was beset by the idea he must lose and die."

Ahearn tapped his pipe empty and arose. "I'll tell my wife to pack enough for a week or so, and we'll be off on the night train. I would love to see this scheme stopped and this legend exposed as a fraud. I've never been a strong believer in legends anyway."

His wife packed a huge basket lunch for us to enjoy on the long train ride. To me the ride was pleasanter this time, for Mr. Ahearn and I spent a good deal of the time planning the moves by which we would not only destroy the legend but also bring the scheming of Nial and, possibly, Flynn into the open.

I'd made no agreement with Conan to meet us, so we hired a carriage for the ride to the castle. Everything had been well-planned, for the following day Cormac would meet Flynn to engage in his last battle, while Ellen waited in the castle for him to arrive and marry her. She, of course, had no idea there would be a fight before the ceremony. I felt strongly, and Mr. Ahearn agreed, that Ellen was likely too stupid to have been entrusted with any information about the scheme that would take Cormac's life.

"I have a friend named Conan," I said. "He knows what I'm up to, and he'll be no less delighted to hear the fine encouragement and help you have given me. I have been thinking how we might best approach Cormac so that he won't refuse to listen. Perhaps I should go to the castle alone while Conan keeps you company, and when there is need of you, I will have but to call you into the castle in the presence of Cormac. It would be best to confront Nial, listen to his cries of innocence, and then have you prove beyond any doubt that Cormac has been the victim of a hoax all these years."

"It would be best to handle it that way, Kate. You must remember that Cormac is a strong, intelligent man of fine breeding. If he'd not been brought up from a child with the legend confronting him every day, he'd be easier to convince. But let something like this, along with the proof—even if it's a fraud—that he will die as those supposed ancestors died, and he'll not wish to change that belief. And be just as sure it couldn't be changed. Even if the terms of the legend ensure his death."

"He's a trusting man," I said. "I know he hasn't any idea Nial is not the friendly, successful man he is supposed to be. Even while Cormac talks of the title to the castle going to Nial, never once has he ever suspected in the least that Nial might not care to wait until Cormac dies of old age before he can possess the castle."

"Then let Nial listen to your story and deny it in front of Cormac. Then, when I come in, Nial will be so shaken he'll quite likely show it. If Cormac can see this, he'll be better convinced."

"Perhaps," I said after considerable thought, "it might be best to wait until what's supposed to be his last day."

"He'd surely have less time to argue the matter," Ahearn said. "And he'll be so keyed up on the last day that he'd be easier to reach. Any man, even one who has believed most of his life that tomorrow is the day he is to die, will be looking for some scrap of evidence that will allow him to escape his fate. He must, by now, be like a man facing hanging in the morning."

"You may stay in my cottage if you don't mind," I said. "I'll go back to the castle and spend the night there."

"I thought he'd ordered you out forever."

"Aye, that he did, but at times my hearing is not too good. I can slip into that place and no one the wiser, it's that big. And beautiful. To think it would go into the hands of a man like Nial."

"Unless your Cormac is absolutely dedicated to dying because the legend says it will happen, I doubt Nial will ever lay eyes on the castle again. If he's able to see anything after Cormac gets through with him."

So it was arranged. I brought Mr. Ahearn to my humble cottage, which he swore he'd paint one day, then I drove to Conan's place and found him to be so nervous he was eating supper walking about the kitchen. He almost dropped his plate when I came to the door, and he was so overwhelmed with relief that he gathered me in his arms.

"I didn't think you'd get back in time," he said. "The man's beside himself. Did you find anything?"

"Enough to prove it's Nial behind the whole idea. The big book, or the page glued to the cover, is false, and so are the statues, the busts of Cormac. Oh, Conan, they were done by a man who is now staying at my cottage for the night so we can confront Cormac and Nial with him in the morning."

"By all the saints, I'm now a believer in prayer. There's no mistake? I couldn't stand this any longer than tomorrow."

"Tell me," I said as I sat down, for there was no hurry now. "How is Cormac getting along with Ellen, may I ask?"

"He's not bedded with her that I know of. He scarcely looks at her. The man spends most of his time in his bedroom alone. What he does there I don't know, except maybe he's doing some praying himself. Yet, so far as he knows, he has nothing to pray for. Not even heaven could interfere with the thousand-year-old curse that befell the first Cormac. Who, I would say, must have been as stubborn as this one."

"Ellen is prepared for the wedding?"

"She and her tribe. There are about ten of them drinking Cormac's brandy and whiskey and generally raising hell. Two of them were so drunk yesterday I refused to saddle horses for them. I was properly cursed and told I'd be fired, but so far Cormac hasn't come near me."

"You've little to concern yourself about getting fired," I assured him. "The only thing that gives me a few shivers is that Cormac won't believe anything we tell him or show him, and he'll fight Flynn anyway. He can be a stubborn man."

"You'll be spending the night in the castle?"

"Aye. It won't be hard to slip in, especially if all those wild friends of Ellen's are there. If they track up the place too much, I'm going to have Cormac make them clean it up. Now, that would be something, Conan."

"It would do my heart good, for not one of them lads has done a lick of work in his entire miserable life. I'll drive you to the castle when you wish."

"It's late enough now that I'll not be noticed. In the morning, go to my cottage and bring Mr. Ahearn. He has two of the busts and part of the big book with him. Be sure he brings them along. I would say it might be safe to get there early. Flynn may decide he can't wait to kill Cormac, and come in the morning."

"Aye, it will be as you say, Kate. You know, even now, I don't know if Cormac will weep, or swear, or yell in happiness when you tell him."

"He'll first curse me, and then he'll find joy in the entire business. After that, he'll get angry and perhaps tear something apart. I hope it's Nial."

Conan let me out of the carriage a quarter of a mile from the castle because this was one night I didn't want Ellen to see me and order me about, probably with the enthusiastic help of her friends. So I let myself in by first climbing that strange outside stairway, while I blessed the man who had it built.

Stealing along the wall, I easily reached my wing and went on in. Ellen had enough candles blazing in the corridor to light it up well. I commandeered two of them and went into my room. Nothing had been changed there. Once inside, with my bed turned down, I blew out the candles so there would be no light. Without undressing, I got into bed. I would fight sleep this night, for I must be awake before Cormac looked for his weapons and prepared for the last battle.

But it had been a long and wearying day. My eyes kept closing despite myself. I got out of bed and walked the floor in the dark, doing my best to avoid the furniture. Downstairs the sounds of revelry were dying out. Now I had something to stay awake for, even if my eyelids drooped. I heard the revelers coming up the stairs, then proceeding down the corridor to their respective rooms. Before long the castle had subsided into silence. Then I heard someone knocking on a door and calling out in whispers that could be heard from one end of the corridor to the other. I opened my door a crack, to see Ellen, in a clinging nightgown, her hair down, trying to arouse Cormac.

"Let me in," she begged ardently. "Cormac, it's Ellen! You haven't let me in since I got here. Cormac, please! Tomorrow I'll be your wife, but tonight I want to be with you. Cormac, I'll wither away waiting for you. How can you be so cruel?"

She kept it up for the better part of fifteen more minutes without drawing a single response, and I began to feel fine. At last Ellen gave up and returned to her room, to slam the door shut as noisily as possible. I went back to bed and curled up to dwell in the glory of Cormac's lack of interest in this woman.

Again I fought sleep, but it proved impossible, and I did sleep. Certainly my concern about not awakening before Cormac was off to fight his battle was foolishness on my part, because it was a wild, resounding shout from Cormac that awakened me. It was so loud I thought at first he must be standing at the foot of my bed. But he was all the way down

the corridor at the room of the five statues, for I saw him
emerge when I risked opening my door.

"Ellen!" he shouted. "Ellen . . . did you take those busts?
Ellen . . . and the rest of you . . . come out into the corridor. Someone has stolen the busts from this room. I want
them back, and no nonsense. They are of me. Open up, all of
you! Wake up, you good-for-nothing blathering idiots."

There was a flurry of doors opening and sleepy protests of
innocence. No one had seen the busts, or even knew what he
was talking about, for that room had always been locked and
held strictly private. Ellen too asked him what he was talking
about, and Cormac, with an oath, disappeared into his own
room. He had been in nightgown and a robe, so I assumed he
would now dress.

I put on my shoes, took time to pin up my hair as best I
could in the small amount of time I had to spend on it. It
was already well after daylight. Then I hurried downstairs to
seat myself in the big chair Cormac usually chose. I was
there when Ellen came down. I was expecting Cormac. I
must have shown my disappointment, for she looked at me
queerly.

"Ah," she said, eyeing me slyly, "now I know who the thief
is. Whatever Cormac has been looking for, you stole, you dis-
respectful, irresponsible whore."

"Sit down and be quiet," I said.

"Don't dare to give me orders. I'll fetch Cormac—"

"Please do. If you shout for him, I'll join in, but after that,
for heaven's sake, sit down and be quiet."

"Quiet, is it? I'm marrying Cormac at high noon. Who do
you think you are, coming back against his orders and turning into a thief as well."

"You're wasting time," I said.

"Do you deny that you did not take whatever Cormac is
missing?"

"I took them, and if you wish to call it stealing, you're welcome to, because I don't give a damn what you think, Ellen."

"Cormac!" she screamed. "Cormac, I have the thief. Cormac!"

I added my voice to hers with the last mention of his
name, and we did make quite a noise. Two of the guests
came running down, but they decided not to interfere. Then
Nial hurried into the room.

"What's going on? Kate . . . you're back."

"Aye, that I am. What's keeping Cormac?"

"He's been at prayer. You must not disturb him."

"Nial, will you go fetch the man before he goes out some other door and hunts down Flynn for the fight?"

"The fight will take place on the outside stairway," Nial said. "That's where all of them were held. Flynn is likely on his way by now."

"And a bad journey to him," I said. "If you don't shout Cormac down here, I will."

"I'll get him," Nial said. "But you'll not be able to stop him. Everything has gone too far. I've done my best, but he won't listen to me either. I'm sorry, Kate, but I don't think you should see him."

"I want her arrested because she's a thief," Ellen complained loudly.

"Don't be sillier than you are by nature," Nial said.

"She stole something out of that room Cormac keeps locked. She admitted she took something—busts or books, or something like that. Cormac was shouting about them."

I saw Nial's eyes narrow in suspicion. "Is that true, Kate?"

"Aye, it's true enough."

"You took the busts?"

"Only two of them," I said. "And I cut the back off the big book."

"Why? Tell me why, Kate. I want an answer. . . ."

"When Cormac comes down, you'll have it, Nial. I'll not spare a single word of what I know."

"Tell me! Now!" he said roughly.

Ellen, frightened by the intensity of his voice, began backing away as Nial approached me. I'd made a mistake. I'd talked too much, and Nial must realize that I'd learned something detrimental to him.

"Wait for Cormac," I said.

"Not a second will I wait. What have you found out with your prying and your lying? Tell me or, by heaven, I'll break your neck."

He was getting closer to me, and I didn't dare move for fear of provoking a sudden and swift attack that might be most unhealthy for me, because Nial was now in a rage.

"Nial!" Cormac's voice cut through the momentary silence as Nial came closer. He turned quickly, and the anger disappeared from his face.

"Kate's back, and I was ordering her to leave the castle. She's a stubborn girl with no respect for her betters."

"Why did you come back?" Cormac asked me.

"She stole something from one of the rooms upstairs," Ellen said.

Cormac pushed Nial aside and stood before me with his legs spread and a look of fury on his face.

"I never expected that of you, Kate. What have you done with my property?"

"It's not far away," I said. "And did you see how angry Nial was with me?"

"That's to be expected. He knows I don't want you here." He sighed, and his great shoulders hunched in a gesture of despair. "Oh, Kate, don't torture me this way. I've not the time for it. We've been in love, you and I. Remember that, and please bring the busts back. I don't care why you took them. . . ."

"As a souvenir, no doubt," Nial exclaimed sarcastically.

"I might have taken them for that purpose," I admitted, "but I had more important uses for two of the busts and the back of the big book. I'm sorry, Cormac, but I cut the back of the book away because I needed it."

Cormac sat down out of plain curiosity. "Now, what do you mean by that? What purpose could the back of that book serve?"

"I brought it to someone who knows about such matters," I explained. "This expert informed me that the book is old—"

"A thousand years old," Cormac interrupted me angrily.

"No, Cormac. Perhaps several hundred years old, that's possible. But you will remember there is a page listing the deaths of all the Cormacs before you, starting more than a thousand years ago. It was the page glued to the back binding."

"The book has been in my family for generations. If you've destroyed it . . ."

I couldn't deny it. I said, "But if you look closely, you may notice that the listing of the Cormacs who died is in similar handwriting. The expert who studied them for me said they were all written at the same time, by the same person, and the paper is of a quality nonexistent a hundred years ago."

"What are you trying to tell me?" Cormac demanded.

"She's trying to delay the fight, that's what she's up to," Nial said. "Flynn is on his way. You've not the time to listen to this nonsense."

"And the ink with which the words were written, Cormac," I went on, "is also of recent origin. So if the page is a register of the truth, then someone wrote the first entry more than a housand years ago, with ink not yet invented, on paper not known at that date. And the same man who did the writing repeated it every hundred years, so he must be a well-reserved gentleman, I would say."

"Flynn's here by now," Nial said. "You can't avoid him, Cormac."

Ellen, who had hurried from the room, now returned wearing her wedding gown. It wasn't on properly, and she was a pathetic sight in it, but she was hotheaded enough to show her anger.

"Look at me, Cormac. We are to be married in a few hours. Look at me!"

Cormac looked at her, at Nial, and at me, and his confusion was so apparent I began to feel sorry for him. Before he could express his doubts about the whole affair, I went on, preventing Nial from adding to Cormac's dilemma.

"There may be a legend," I said, "but that's all it is. There's no truth to it. Perhaps the first Cormac, a thousand years ago did die as the book relates, but none did after that, and there is no evidence that you are invincible to the day of your death and on that day you cannot win any battle. It's all in your mind, Cormac, put there by Nial and the kin on his side of the family. Nial wants the castle and the title. The only way he can get it is by your death, and he has schemed years for this day when you will die."

Nial had regained his composure and was able to put on a convincing show. "Now, Cormac, I don't want you killed. Perhaps you can be victorious over Flynn. You have to fight him, answer his challenge, but Flynn is not the greatest swordsman in the world, and you're better than he. Still, there is no way you can deny the legend."

"You can deny the legend by not fighting Flynn," I said.

"If not Flynn, there will be someone else." Cormac reiterated a phrase I'd heard him use before.

"She wants the castle, not you," Nial said. "She's been using you for months. Probably stealing from you all this time."

"I won't believe that," Cormac said, and my chilled heart warmed again. "Kate has never lied to me."

"She's not been honest with you. She proved it by stealing the busts and ruining that ancient book, which was invaluable up to now."

"Kate," Cormac said, "I have to meet Flynn in but a few more minutes. You accuse Nial of plotting all this, even nurturing my faith in the Cormac legend all these years. It's no easy to believe what you are saying."

"Do you want to believe in it?" I asked.

"Cormac," Nial broke in, "if she had any proof, she'd hav shown it to you by now."

"She's nothing but a cheap little whore," Ellen screamed i exasperation.

"Shut up!" Cormac told her.

I said, "Give me two minutes more and I'll prove what say. Even you won't be able to deny it, Cormac."

"She'll bring in proof that lies as much as she does," Nia warned.

"Still, I'll listen to it and make up my own mind. G ahead, Kate. Whatever you're keeping from me, bring it fortl now."

I went to the door and summoned Conan and Mr. Ahearn Cormac recognized the artist immediately. He arose an shook hands with him.

"What, in heaven's name, do you have to do with this?" Cormac asked.

Conan had placed the white bust and the black one on table and stood by as if to guard them. Cormac's confusio was now greater than ever.

"Mr. Ahearn, please explain," I prompted him. "Cormac you remember having your portrait painted by Mr. Ahearn."

"Aye, I remember it," Cormac said, still mystified.

Nial was slowly moving back, half a step at a time. Cor mac was not so confused he didn't notice. "Nial, stand wher you are until this is over."

Nial stopped, but his nervousness was increasing to a poin where I expected him to turn and make a run for it. Conar seemed to have adopted the same idea, for he moved to stand in the doorway and block any attempted abrupt departure by anyone.

Mr. Ahearn's explanation was brief, but it affected Corma deeply, for as Ahearn spoke, Cormac's face began to grow flushed.

"When you sat for me," Ahearn said, "I not only painted your portrait but also managed to create this black bust of you. It was done without your knowledge, sketched while you sat for the painting, and sculptured right after each of your visits. So you know how recently that bust was made. The white one is older, but not by much, and it is of a material

hat could not possibly have existed a thousand years ago, as
t seems you've been made to believe."

"Tell him who commissioned the bust," I said. There was
no keeping the triumph out of my voice, and I didn't even
try.

"Nial paid me," Ahearn explained. "He said it would be a
surprise gift to you and I must keep my work secret."

"Mr. Ahearn's hallmark is even on the base," I added.
"What more proof do you ask, Cormac? That's why I bor-
rowed the busts and the back binding of the book. I wanted
to prove they could not be connected with the legend, because I didn't believe there ever was a legend except the one
instilled in your mind over many years. Even to the wild theory about the outside stairs."

Ellen had endured enough. She still had no idea what we
were talking about. She pouted as prettily as she could. "Cormac, I'll wait in my room until you're ready to marry me.
But I won't wait too long. Mind that well. I won't wait."

Cormac didn't even answer her. He arose slowly and spoke
to Conan. "Have a look, Conan, and see if Flynn is here."

Conan returned in a few seconds. "Aye, he's riding up
now, and he's armed with a great sword."

"Nial," Cormac said, "you're coming to the outside stairs
with me."

Nial whirled and reached the doorway, where Conan
neatly tripped him. Cormac was upon the man before he
could arise. Seizing Nial by the collar, Cormac hoisted him to
his feet. With Nial struggling in this tight grip on his collar
and the seat of his pants, Cormac led the way. We followed
up the grand staircase and along the corridor to the door
leading onto the castle wall.

Conan and I were directly behind Cormac and Nial. Ellen
followed us, holding up the skirt of her wedding gown and
asking questions no one heeded. Behind her came the guests
she'd sent for, and they were as confused as she, but determined to enjoy whatever was about to happen.

Cormac looked back. "Conan, take hold of this scum and
make sure he won't get away. I'll be right back."

He walked briskly into the castle, thrusting aside Ellen's
friends, all of whom moved faster than Cormac when they
saw him coming. After a few moments I heard Flynn, somewhere along that flight of outside steps, calling his challenge.
Cormac returned with a great sword, a relic of the past, but

apparently the dueling weapon he had always intended t
use.

At the top of the stairs, Cormac looked down at Flynn
halfway up. I hurried to Cormac's side. That was where I be
longed now. Flynn was coming up the stairs confidently.

"Come down and meet me if you dare," he called out
"You're a coward, Cormac. If you're not, now is the time t
prove it."

"Before I do," Cormac called back, "I've a new weapon
Flynn. It's one you'll recognize quickly enough."

"Any weapon," Flynn shouted. "What's it matter to me
Before this day is out, you'll be a dead man, Cormac."

Cormac gestured to Conan, and Nial was pushed forward
Cormac shoved him to stand squarely at the head of th
stairs.

"You've often threatened to take this castle away from
me," Cormac said. "But in all your plotting with Nial, did h
ever tell you the castle would be his by inheritance at m
death?"

"I'll settle that with Nial after I settle with you." Flynn
continued his ascent.

Cormac pushed Nial aside, went down several steps, hold
ing the mighty sword in fighting position. "There is no legen
says I can't win this fight," Cormac said. "You're a damne
fool to believe it. You're not my equal in battle, Flynn, an
you know it."

"I don't scare that easily. Come down and fight."

I said, "Nial, tell him Cormac doesn't have to lose thi
fight. Tell him or, by heaven, I'll ask Cormac to kill you afte
he gets rid of Flynn."

Nial must have heard something in my voice that made
him think I meant what I said. "She's right," he called out
"The legend isn't true. Cormac will kill you."

Flynn lowered the blade he held. "You're a blathering foo
of a man, Cormac, but I don't think you're a liar. Send Nia
down the steps, and when I finish with him, I'll fight you any
way."

"For all of me, you can have Nial."

"No," Nial shouted. "Cormac, I'm your brother. He'll kil
me. I know he will. I'm your brother. We grew up to
gether. . . ."

"Let him go," I said. "I wouldn't want his death on any
one's conscience, not even Flynn's."

Nial didn't wait to hear any more. He pushed through th

tight crowd of onlookers, who were still confused. Nial vanished inside the castle. Before Flynn could go down the steps to reach him, he'd be gone. I didn't think we'd hear from him again.

"Come up," Cormac challenged Flynn. "I swear I will never again be a fighting man, but before I quit, I'll accommodate you, Flynn."

Flynn shook his head. "If Nial made a fool of me, I'm not going to make another of myself. I don't think you're my match, Cormac, but I'll admit you are if you'll call this off."

"It's off," Cormac said. "But I'm not forgetting what you did to Kate. Nor that you murdered poor Gavan. Stay out of my sight or I might forget my vow never to fight again."

Flynn fled down the steps as Cormac swung the great sword in his hand and sent it spiraling into the air, to fall somewhere at the base of the wall.

My voice chilled as I spoke. "If you intend to marry Ellen, I'll throw you off this wall myself. You'll not marry her, Cormac. I won't have it!"

"Who said I was going to marry Ellen? You take it upon yourself to believe whatever you wish to believe." He suddenly became aware of Ellen's friends, all of them smiling now that the suspense was over. "What are you loafers doing here? Get out! Every last one of you, and take Ellen with you. Conan, watch them, and count the silver before they ride off."

Cormac took my elbow. "I want no more of your sassy tongue, woman. Go get yourself ready to be married, and be quick about it. The priest is supposed to be here at noon."

"The banns . . ." I said.

"He'll have to take this wedding as it comes. The banns can be said later. Today is my wedding day, according to the legend. You wouldn't have me defy what was written a thousand years ago."

"No, Cormac," I said softly. "Not that part of the legend, but tell me, please, why did you bring Ellen here? Why did you torture me by arranging to marry her?"

"No Cormac ever married the girl who waited at the altar," he said. "It is written in the book, a part I never told you about and which Conan knew by reading the book. He never told you either. Even while I believed the legend and had to follow it to the wedding that would not take place, the woman who waited for me in her wedding laces . . . would kill herself, as the bride of the first Cormac did. According to the legend, so did all the other brides. Do you think I'd have wanted that?"

I walked into the castle with him. "I knew nothing of it, and it's a blessing I didn't. I forgive you, Cormac, for not telling me. But there is one other small thing which never puzzled me before because I'd not thought of it."

"There will be no more puzzles," he said. "What don't you understand now?"

"If each Cormac before you died before his wedding, and his bride then killed herself, how did it come about there was one generation after the other over all those years?"

Cormac and I walked side by side down the wide corridor. "Now, that never occurred to me either," he admitted. "But I can tell you one thing, we'll soon put a stop to that!"

"Aye, Cormac," I said happily.